THE BILLIONAIRE'S LAST-MINUTE MARRIAGE

AMANDA CINELLI

A DEAL FOR THE TYCOON'S DIAMONDS

EMMY GRAYSON

MILLS & BOON

THE BILLIONAIRE'S LAST-MINUTE MARRIAGE

AMANDA CINELLI

MILLS & BOON

To my editor, Charlotte,
who listened and guided me back to the true spirit
of this story when I was fully sure that I'd lost it.

And to The Wordmakers,
the fabulous band of quirky creatives who welcomed
me into the coven when my words had run dry.

This book was a labour of love
and a collaborative effort.

CHAPTER ONE

Xander Mytikas stood frozen on the steps of the Manhattan courthouse in his sleek black tuxedo and felt the rush of shocked anger simmer in his veins.

The crowd of distinguished guests and eager paparazzi seemed to meld into one around him, their expressions a mixture of sympathy and scandalised delight as they realised that they had just witnessed the stone-faced CEO of a global financial powerhouse get very publicly jilted by his socialite fiancée.

'I've never seen a bride run that fast.' A voice laughed, coming from somewhere in the ever-growing crowd of curious onlookers along the pavement.

'I'm sure he'll cry himself to sleep tonight in his piles of money,' another voice shouted, without an ounce of sympathy.

Considering some of the terrible accusations that had resurfaced since his tyrannical father's death two weeks previously, as the company's current acting CEO Xander had known he wasn't the most likeable face in the media right now. But this…he felt the sting of being reduced to an object of pure scorn and derision. This was simply theatre to the masses and he had given them front row seats to his own humiliation.

The previous moments seemed to replay in his mind

like a bad movie, Priya Davidson-Kahn standing frozen at the bottom of the steps in her giant white gown. His own concern and fruitless attempts to reach her through the crowd of paparazzi that had suddenly appeared… Then the look of apology on her face, right before she'd sprinted down the street in the rain.

In the handful of minutes since, he'd had his security team clear the perimeter and gather their guests back inside until the situation was contained. The details of the ceremony were supposed to have been kept strictly confidential, every attendee covered with a non-disclosure agreement and yet, judging by the seething mass of photographers being herded down the street, it appeared that someone had leaked their location to the press.

Was that why she had run?

His head of security appeared at his side, a beacon of calm amid the chaos. 'I sent a team in pursuit of Miss Davidson-Khan, but it appears that she had a car waiting for her. We confiscated this from one of the members of the press.'

The man held out a phone screen showing a brief video clip of what looked like his bride being carried by a man through the rain down an alleyway… The mystery man glanced back and Xander growled as he saw his face.

Eros.

Of course, his half-brother had been involved in disrupting his wedding. Since their father's death two weeks previously and the terms of his will had been revealed, Xander had been lying in wait for either one of Zeus Mytikas's other two by-blows to resurface. The first of the three brothers to marry and stay wed for one year took control of everything.

'*Christos,*' he cursed, resisting the urge to smash the image of Eros's smug face to the ground. Xander's arrangement with Priya had been strictly business, but seeing such undeniable evidence of her betrayal still hurt his pride.

'We already have a car in pursuit,' the guard assured him, taking the phone slowly from his hands as though he feared retribution for being the bearer of such bad news.

'No.' Xander exhaled, pinching the bridge of his nose where a dull ache was beginning to throb. 'The last thing I want is my security team involved in a car chase through the streets of Manhattan in broad daylight. The press are already having a field day.'

'You want us to just let her go?'

The noise around him was growing louder by the minute. The reporters down the street were hurling out their questions and the guests inside the doors of the courthouse too. Like sharks, they were all ravenous for the knowledge of what they had just witnessed. His usually unrivalled tactical mind tripped over such a senseless change to a seemingly perfect plan, fighting to make sense of it.

He had prepped his entire team to be on high alert today, to leave no stone unturned when it came to ensuring this quickie wedding remained a secret from both of his estranged half-brothers. His ruthless nature was infamous, as was his reputation for always getting what he wanted. But somehow, somewhere…he'd missed something. The scent of failure was enough to send him barrelling through the crowd, his guards rushing to clear the path through the gathering onlookers.

Xander slid into the nondescript black SUV and slammed the door, shutting out the din of their ravenous curiosity. It had been twenty years since he'd been thrust into this bloodthirsty world where pain was profitable and scandal was currency. No matter how much time his father had spent enforcing elocution lessons and private stylists, the same reporters who had hunted down his vulnerabilities as a naïve nineteen-year-old still found ways to make money from him. Such was the world.

'You lovebirds are done early.' A singsong voice sounded out in the dark interior as the privacy screen came down with a slow whir, revealing the smiling face and grey curls of his long-time driver, Mina. 'I finally get to meet your...'

Her expectant smile dropped, ebbing quickly into confusion when she saw that Xander sat alone and bride-less on the back seat. He felt his gut clench, his eyes landing on the freshly chilled bottle of champagne and two gold-tipped crystal flutes.

'Wedding's cancelled. The bride had other plans.' Xander undid his bow tie and popped the top button of his silk shirt open, fighting the urge to rip the garment off entirely. He needed a swim and a giant chocolate dessert, in that order. His muscles were wound so tight that a jolt of pain hit him in the solar plexus when a rogue reporter suddenly pressed their face up against the tinted glass of the car window, catching him completely by surprise.

Mina's familiar croaking curse was a welcome salve to his nerves as she revved the engine and honked her horn with such vehemence that the crowd fell away. As they finally pressed forward into the afternoon traffic, the privacy glass was raised back up but Xander could practically feel the pity coming off his trusted driver in waves. He didn't want her pity, or anyone else's for that matter. And yet, it was now inevitable, wasn't it? Gossip was one thing, but scandal...scandal would be the final nail in the coffin of his plans to take over Mytikas Holdings.

As the rain-soaked streets began to blur outside the tinted windows, Xander felt the throb in his brow turn into a full-blown migraine. He leaned back against the leather seats, feeling frustration and outrage battle against the soul-deep exhaustion that had plagued him for the past fortnight.

Christos…had it only been two weeks since his father's death? It seemed like a lifetime ago now, considering the gigantic organisational nightmare that had followed immediately afterwards.

After Zeus's death, it had been generally assumed that Xander would be the natural choice to succeed his father in the event of his passing. In fact, he had completed two decades of loyal service with that exact goal in mind. But apparently, the old man had had a last-minute change of heart. Somehow Xander hadn't been too surprised that Zeus had thrown a massive curveball his way as a parting gift.

He had long ago stopped trying to gain affection or approval from the man who'd ignored his existence for nineteen years. But what he hadn't expected was for Zeus to offer up the entire contents of his estate to the first of his children to marry and stay married for one year.

Xander growled under his breath, tapping the keys on his tablet to check his schedule. He would never demand his staff work on the weekend, but Sunday afternoons had become a regular occurrence in the past weeks considering their major planned expansion into Japan was imminent. The only reason he'd chosen to get married on a Sunday was because it would have the least impact on his schedule. Unlike his slovenly father, who seemed only to enjoy the status that came with his CEO title, Xander had always found solace in his work.

From a young age, he'd always noticed details that others missed and seen simple solutions for what most considered to be complex problems. As a young boy, growing up poor in Athens, he had been an enigma, a formidable opponent on both the chess team and on the football field. There was nothing he enjoyed more in life than learning how to play a game and winning.

But his talent had recently become more of a liability than a gift. His enemies accused him of underhanded dealings, comparing his success to that of his corrupt father.

The truth was, he just always paid attention. Couple that with his nerves of steel and, thus far, his gut had never steered him wrong. So, it came as no surprise that when faced with a seemingly iron-clad obstruction on his way to claiming his late father's estate, he had found a simple and easy solution.

Priya Davidson-Khan had needed a husband to access her own inheritance, so he had met with the heiress on a few occasions and instantly admired her professional, no-nonsense approach to their sham marriage. Plus, it came with the added bonus of having a bona fide upper-class socialite on his arm to help smooth his transition into the upper echelons of society. He had been ready for one year of socially staged wedded bliss, the exact amount of time listed in his father's will and not a minute more, before they planned to divorce. Neat and tidy, unlike most relationships he had witnessed in his lifetime.

He'd been just minutes away from victory. When he planned to achieve something, usually nothing got in his way.

But this was different, this wasn't just a snag in a contract he could tease out. This was a person. Human beings had pesky things like autonomy and free will and the right to change their minds about something as important as marriage at the drop of a hat.

His mind spun with the consequences that today's disastrous failure would have on his plans. So many things were at risk, so many chances for either one of his brothers to slide in and take everything he had worked so hard for the past two decades to achieve.

He'd changed everything about himself in order to fit into the mould Zeus had demanded of him. And now, even after almost twenty years of fighting tooth and nail against his humble beginnings to prove his worth…he still wasn't getting it without a fight.

He still wasn't good enough. He never had been.

When the car arrived at the gleaming tower on Lexington Avenue that housed their company headquarters, the rain had begun to slow somewhat. He stopped in the cavernous atrium and shook the last drops from his tuxedo jacket, then looked up, finding the towering portrait of his father looking down upon him. Cold determination filled his bones despite his exhaustion. He would not give up at the first hurdle, not when so much lay in the balance. Although now, thanks to Eros's actions, the outcome was suddenly a lot less certain than he normally preferred.

He took his own private elevator up to the top-floor suite, where he had a team of executive assistants that ran his day-to-day business. As expected, there were a few people still roaming the halls in between offices. Four months ago, he'd been summoned here from the European holdings to take the reins while Zeus recovered from his sudden illness. With shareholders and board members already seething after some of Zeus's very shady deals had come to light, the timing had felt rather serendipitous.

But even from his sickbed, Zeus's influence had still been in effect. His top-floor staff were the worst kind of pedants, enforcing archaic modus operandi and resisting all the changes Xander had tried to implement on the grounds that Zeus wouldn't like it. One assistant in particular had caused him more headaches than most.

Shaking off that familiar twang of annoyance, he

tapped the first button on his phone that was simply labelled 'Quinn' and waited for the inevitable Irish accent to answer.

He felt the pressure of the last two weeks circling him again, tightening its iron grip on his stomach with every shrill tone of the unanswered call. When it went to voicemail, he stared down at the screen in disbelief. Quinn never missed a call, even on the weekend.

When a second call also went unanswered, his jaw tightened, his mind cycling through the conversations they'd had in recent weeks. She'd seemed tense and distracted since Zeus's passing. He gritted his teeth and dialled again.

Only one person had been allowed to know all his plans for the wedding since Zeus's death—not that he'd had a choice in that matter. Pandora Quinn had been his father's executive assistant for a couple of months before the old man had fallen ill and he'd insisted on passing her on to Xander.

Zeus had never returned to his seat of power. His illness had been drawn out over the course of a few months but none of them had truly imagined that a man known for his almost superhuman ability to wield power in the corporate world would ever be extinguished by something so mundane as a cardiac arrest during a routine operation.

Xander had been thrust into the position of acting CEO, managing the biggest acquisition of their decades-long history, and with that power came the entire top-floor staff, including the much beloved Pandora. She was probably holding up traffic somewhere, doing something utterly ridiculous like performing mouth to mouth on an injured bird or hand-feeding a bumble bee. The image his mind created was one of pure chaos, truly no better descriptor for the woman herself. Speaking of which…

With a touch of a button, he called in the weekend receptionist, relieved when he immediately heard the sound of footsteps. At least *some* people were working today.

The woman entered slowly, with the nervousness of someone who had spent years under Zeus's tyrannical rule. Xander remained seated, his face a mask of polite serenity.

'I can't get through to Pandora Quinn. Has she been in this weekend?'

'Pandora…? She's already handed in her resignation,' the brunette answered, her voice sagging a little when Xander pinned her with a disbelieving glare. 'I… I assumed you knew.'

Years of working with Zeus had taught Xander how to conceal his own reactions. He had just been publicly humiliated by his supposed bride and he had barely even raised an eyebrow. But with this news…he felt his entire body tense, his iron grip on the edge of his desk turning his knuckles white.

'When did this happen?' Xander asked, tapping the screen of his phone to life. 'And why was I not informed?'

'Friday evening. I only found out because I was passing by the HR office on my way back to my desk,' she explained with a slight tremor to her voice. 'I think she waited until most of the office had left on purpose. I wouldn't expect anything less from that girl. There was always something a little off about her.'

'That will be all,' he snapped, pointedly cutting her off and striding past, out into the private space that housed the CEO's personal staff.

The walls in here were the same polished marble, with two large desk areas tucked into alcoves on either side. The desk on his right was home to his secretary, an older woman who manned the phones during the week with ruthless efficiency. Her desk space was tidy and nondescript. The opposite area, usually covered with coffee cups, written reminders and colourful knitting projects, was now utterly barren except for one lonely desk chair and a single red telephone. Everything that had ever suggested the nature of its occupant was gone.

Xander frowned at the empty space and felt a cold fury rise within him. What kind of professional executive assistant just resigned without a word of warning?

It was sudden and out of character, especially for a woman who had kept a schedule that rivalled his own in its predictability. Quinn had been the only one in charge of the short wedding-guest list and the non-disclosure agreements. He needed an immediate embargo to be issued to the press before anything damaging could be published. For that, he needed Pandora back and he was damned well going to tell her that.

He picked up the phone on his desk, dialling the direct line to his security team and filling them in on the situation with his usual efficiency.

'I need the location of Pandora Quinn. Now.'

Pandora Quinn had been in the late Zeus Mytikas's home office many times in the past six months of working at Mytikas Holdings, but not since his death. It seemed eerie now, walking along the echoing hallway of a dead man's home. But she had one last mission to complete before she could disappear. One last act of defiance.

She had never broken a law in her life, even when Zeus had forced her to act as his spy over the past four months. She had always done her best to keep her betrayal of Xander as minimal as possible, or at least so she'd reassured herself. But breaking into the Mytikas mansion…this was most certainly crossing a legal line she'd struggle to explain if she was caught.

One last thing to accomplish. Then she could finally go back home.

The polished marble stairs that led up to the private office wing of the mansion seemed to glitter ominously, like slippery ice. The walls were powder blue and ornamented with heavily accented columns that wouldn't look out of place in an ostentatious rococo palace. A vision of a similar pair of arctic-blue eyes came into her mind, tightening her stomach into a thick knot. She threw a quick glance over her shoulder to the foyer below, as though fearing she had somehow conjured Xander's magnifying presence through sheer force of thought.

She felt her balance shift on the steps, her stomach lurching painfully as she tilted a couple of centimetres backwards before finding her centre of gravity again. Her frequent trips and falls had become a bit of an in-joke around the office, along with her loud voice and quirky sense of humour. She'd laughed along with the others at first, but at a certain point it had felt a little less like harmless fun and more like…well, unkind judgement.

She probably could have explained that these traits were a permanent part of her neurology, but she just didn't fancy trying to describe the various nuances of the autism spectrum to people who barely even remembered her name most days. If they had wanted to know more about her, they would have asked.

Working for a corporation that dealt with almost every global financial market meant it wasn't unusual for her to be running errands on the weekend. But today wasn't just any normal Sunday. Today her boss, powerful Greek financier Xander Mytikas, was marrying one of the wealthiest socialites in New York.

Her *former* boss, she reminded herself sternly and couldn't resist the urge to take another quick glance at the sleek digital watch on her wrist. It was almost four in the afternoon. The wedding was probably long over by now, the happy couple most likely already on their way to the airport for their luxurious Asian honeymoon. Her stomach tightened uncomfortably.

She hadn't meant to reveal the details of Xander's top-secret wedding plans, or the connected business dealings. Especially not to Arista Theodorou, of all people. It was common knowledge within the company that Zeus's long-time mistress and Xander had been at war from the moment Zeus had fallen ill.

Guilt aside, she knew that this last step was necessary. She had already formally communicated her resignation to the HR department. Perhaps she had waited until the very last moment when she knew Xander would not see it until after he'd returned from his honeymoon, but she had done it nevertheless.

Swallowing past the lump in her throat, Pandora exhaled the breath she'd been holding in and began looking for the large safe that Arista had mentioned was in this office. She'd been surprised to find the house was completely deserted on her way in, so she didn't try to be quiet as she tapped and banged along the wall to find any hollow spots. A small cry of victory escaped when she finally heard the echo and opened up a hidden panel in the wall to reveal a large, reinforced steel door.

Her hands shook as she turned the dial and placed her ear next to the old-fashioned mechanism. Finally, a useful situation for her super-sensitive hearing. After a few unlucky attempts, she tried the short emergency combination from the private CEO elevator in the office, which she had never actually had the chance to use. To her surprise, she heard the pins click into place within the lock mechanism. The large heavy door swung open revealing an unlit, smallish rectangular room beyond.

The old house dated back to the prohibition era and was filled with hidden tunnels and exits, just perfect for a slippery, paranoid old man like Zeus.

Her skin grew clammy and everything within her clenched against the thought of going inside the enclosed space, but still she took that first step and then another. She couldn't find a light inside, so she used the torch on her phone to perform a quick scan of the shelves. All of Zeus's old files lined the walls and within them somewhere was the damning evidence of whatever it was Zeus had on her mother that Pandora had spent the past six months trying to retrieve.

Evidence that esteemed Irish senator Rosaline Quinn still refused to reveal the exact details of to her beloved daughter, other than to allude that it had the potential to end her long-running career. Which wasn't entirely unsurprising, Pandora thought with a frown, considering dear old Zeus had been best known for his shady deals and lascivious affairs.

Six months ago, her family had received an invitation to attend a gala in New York. It had seemed like such a glamorous opportunity at the time, and she'd been confused by her mother's reluctance to attend.

At the event with her family, dressed in all their finery, Pandora had overheard what was meant to be a private conversation between the Greek tycoon and her mother. Zeus had clearly been waiting to call in a favour from Rosaline. A favour that her mother had been unable to deliver. The old man had got an evil gleam in his eye, spotting Pandora and calling her to enter the room where they'd been arguing. She'd tried to play the hero for the first time in her life…and she had ended up indebted to the devil himself.

With that thought, she scanned the room and landed on another row of cases along the very back wall. The evidence had to be here, it just had to be. Her hands seemed to fly frantically, flipping through the files within.

The sound of her mobile phone ringing was a sudden shock to her system, making her jump and drop one of the black file boxes across the floor. But the name on the screen made her pause, frowning. Arista Theodorou. What on earth could she want now?

The woman's smug tone assaulted her ear and Pandora instinctively winced. 'Just saying thank you for the information, darling, and paying you back in kind. I'd get as far away from Xander as you can, if I were you. Being jilted certainly won't improve his temper and when he finds out you were involved, it won't end well for you.'

Jilted? What on earth did Arista mean? Her mind spinning, Pandora straightened her spine and stared down at the phone. 'I have no idea what you're talking about but I wasn't *involved* in the way you're implying. You were the one who tricked me into revealing confidential information. You got what you wanted when you found out about Xander's deal with his bride.'

She ended the call with a sharp press of her thumb, turning the screen black in her hand. For a long moment she simply stared down at the rectangle of metal and plastic, Arista's cryptic messages echoing in her ears. Guilt roiled in her stomach as she tried to ignore the word *jilted*…surely the older woman was lying. That kind of thing didn't happen in perfect society weddings, did it?

She returned to the safe, hefting a particularly large box out into the well-lit office. The lid lifted up on a hinge to reveal many smaller boxes embossed with the names of familiar luxury jewellery brands. Sure enough, one glimpse inside revealed an astonishingly expensive-looking diamond watch. She sat back on her heels, wondering if perhaps she should just give up. If she couldn't even find Zeus's evidence, who was to say that Xander would either? Maybe she was better off just cutting her losses and running back to Ireland. But if he came after her with legal action over the NDA for talking to Arista, she could bring further scandal to her mother's door...

She was so completely engrossed in her own anxious ruminations that it took a moment for her to register the faint sound of movement in the room behind her. Almost as though some part of her brain knew what she would find, she turned her head centimetre by centimetre, then felt the breath freeze in her lungs as she was pinned by a familiar ice-blue gaze.

'Hello, Quinn.'

Xander stood in the office doorway, his wide frame becoming very still as his eyes scanned the room, moving over her armful of treasures, and came to a stop upon the wide-open safe door. 'Am I interrupting something?'

Pandora became aware of three things at once. One, Xander Mytikas was absolutely devastating in a tuxedo. Two, he was staring at the mess of files behind her on the floor of the safe and was probably going to have her arrested for breaking and entering. And three, he should be on his honeymoon right now but he wasn't even wearing a wedding ring.

'Is this the reason you resigned?' Xander's voice was deceptively calm as he took one slow step into the room. 'Because you planned to hit the jackpot and run?'

Pandora shook her head, her mouth suddenly unable to form words as she took one equal step backwards, her eyes darting back towards the mess in the safe again before she could stop herself. Almost in slow motion, her eyes snagged on a particular label and she felt her jaw sag. There it was: her mother's maiden name in stark black lettering amid the chaos of a pile of blank brown folders. She froze, her body tightening like a coiled spring.

Xander's eyes followed her gaze towards the safe, his mouth twisting with anger.

'Don't. Move.'

His voice was a low warning, but she couldn't think of anything but retrieving that file. That had to be it, the evidence that Zeus had taunted her with for months. Giving her awful task after awful task to complete, forcing her to betray her own morals with lies and deceit, then still dangling it out of her reach like a carrot. She was done with being kept under someone else's control.

Six months of playing the part of the quiet, obedient executive assistant came crashing to the forefront of her limits and she knew she wouldn't obey Xander's command. She had come here to set herself and her mother free and she wasn't giving up without a fight. Before she could think about it, she bolted across the room.

Her smooth-soled shoes were slippery on the hard wood, setting her into a rather inelegant slide through the safe door, where she quickly launched herself on top of the files, grasping for the one she needed. She stood up and turned to run back out at the exact same time that two heavy hands gripped her shoulders.

Perhaps it was the darkness of the small space, or the painful adrenaline of the entire afternoon spiking her reflexes, but she felt something rise up within her, her body reacting to the uninvited touch in pure self-preservation. Time seemed to switch to slow motion as she watched her own small fist rise up in an elegant arc then fall, aiming a sucker punch directly at Xander Mytikas's handsome patrician nose.

His guttural grunt as he skilfully avoided the blow filled her ears, bringing instant shame that she'd even tried to hit him. And then they were both falling.

She heard herself squeak, sprawling backwards on the floor with the file underneath her back. She looked up and found herself pinned by that arctic-blue gaze once again. He loomed over her, his chest only inches from her own, and for a split second nothing existed but the twin sounds of their heartbeats thrumming in time. His breath fanned over her, his nostrils flared and pupils wide and dark with what had to be deep, incredulous anger.

Xander finally opened his mouth to speak, but was interrupted by the room suddenly getting darker. Pandora tensed, turning her face just as the last sliver of bright light from the office disappeared and the safe door slid shut with a bang.

CHAPTER TWO

XANDER'S BODY TENSED, pressing his weight down upon her for a split second before he was launching himself up and she could hear him rushing for the door. Her body felt a brief moment of loss at his departure before she stood up too, hands out grasping at the darkness to feel her way. She heard the harsh pounding of a fist against metal.

'Damn it,' he growled. 'Now look what you've done.'

'Me?' Pandora squeaked. 'You're the one who chased me in here.'

'Because you broke into my father's safe,' he hissed, sounding closer this time. The scraping of metal came next as he fumbled around, before he cursed softly.

'My phone is on the desk,' she said quietly. 'Have you got yours?'

'If I had my phone, do you think I would have spent the past five minutes trying to find an interior release mechanism?'

The darkness was absolute, the kind of dark that weighed in upon you, playing tricks on your senses. She sensed Xander move away from the door, his silk tuxedo trousers making a soft hissing sound as he continued to inspect the perimeter of their new prison cell. Suddenly, the small room was lit up by a dim artificial light. The one she'd failed to find earlier.

Xander stood a few steps away, his gaze one of barely restrained fury as he leaned back against the wall. 'It seems that we are stuck in here until my driver realises that I'm taking too long and calls Security. But I suppose I should be grateful for the privacy.'

Her mind tripped over his words, wondering why he'd be grateful for such a terrible accident. But then she noticed the dark intent in his gaze as he pulled out a chair from the side wall and slid it to the centre of the safe where the weak lighting was brightest.

'Take a seat, Quinn. We're not going anywhere for a while.'

She eyed the chair, but really the cold stone floor was a poor alternative, and they were going to have to have this conversation one way or another. She walked towards him, feeling his eyes inspect her in that intent way they always did. Only today, their icy blue depths were filled with mistrust and disappointment. Guilt threatened to choke her.

'I'll take this.' He gestured to the file she'd forgotten she'd tucked under one arm.

Before she had a moment to react, Xander reached out and grabbed it. She stared down in horror, trying and failing to conceal her reaction. She moved past him, her body seeming to act of its own volition and focused solely on self-preservation as she walked to the furthest end of the safe. Xander Mytikas was not a danger to her, she knew, not physically, anyway... But being under that laser focus was more dangerous than any of the other terrible things she had been forced to do over the past few months. She'd betrayed her own morality enough to last her a lifetime. And unwittingly, Xander had paid the price every time. But if he opened that file...

She couldn't lie to him, not again. But that didn't mean

she was prepared to look him in the eye when he realised the truth.

Xander didn't open it, instead simply placing it on the floor between them, dark promise in his eyes. His voice came from the shadows, low enough so that only she could hear his silky tone.

'You see, Quinn…technically you are no longer my employee, so you should have relinquished your security clearance the moment you left your resignation papers with HR. This puts us at a bit of an impasse. So when my guard gets here, he can take you to the police or…you can start telling me the truth about what you're doing here. The choice is yours.'

The possibility of being hauled off in a police car was only slightly less terrifying than the idea of revealing the truth to the man in front of her.

Pandora walked towards the back of the safe, feeling around in the shadows for rows of neatly packaged priceless art. When in fact she was simply trying to buy time. That felt like a pretty accurate way to sum up her life over the past couple of years, she thought morosely. It felt as if all she did was make mistakes and try to fix them, try to buy some time to unravel the tangle of the words she'd spoken or the impulsive choices she'd made. She closed her eyes, feeling the tension between her shoulder blades tighten like a vice.

She was so tired.

The effort of playing the organised and polite assistant by day had seemed simple, but it had turned out to be a Herculean task she never could have anticipated.

She was suddenly, painfully aware that they were alone together. Something that had only ever happened once before on the first day they'd met…but she did her best not to think of that time. No, that wouldn't help with her composure at all.

'Zeus promised to give me something,' she heard herself say as though from afar. 'And Arista knew about it, although she didn't know what it was. I'd thought she was being kind in telling me about the safe a few days ago, but I can see now she was really manipulating me into revealing the information she needed about your wedding.'

Xander's steps froze, even as he continued to speak in a tone that was almost casual. It was never a good sign when he became still.

'Did Arista tell you what she planned to do with the information?'

'She didn't say much at all,' Pandora murmured, her mind whirring through the facts that she had collected since that fateful mistake. She mentally sorted through relevant and irrelevant points, finally grasping the most pertinent one. 'But she booked a flight to Athens the following afternoon.'

'So she went to visit Eros personally. Well, he is her son…' Xander mused, the harsh laugh that escaped his throat in the darkness sounding even more ominous.

'Would Arista truly go to such lengths just to ruin your wedding day?' Pandora asked, needing to break the tense silence that had engulfed the space. The small echoing chamber with its flickering lights and dusty shelving was setting her entire body on edge.

Xander's sigh was part growl. 'Sadly, I have more than enough knowledge of what Arista is capable of. Her hatred of me has always defied all bounds and she'd want Eros to profit from my loss.' He turned away and began pacing the length of the safe in a way she had come to know very well.

Xander Mytikas was not just angry…he was furious.

'It seems my father was feeling extra charitable on his deathbed. What was it that he promised you from in here? Money? Jewels? Priceless art?'

Pandora stared back at him, feeling her insides tighten with the effort not to defend herself. She had no way of knowing for sure if Xander had also known about the blackmailing of her mother. And even if he didn't, she couldn't be certain that he wouldn't use the information against Rosaline just as his father had. It was too big a risk to confide in him, and so she remained silent, shrugging one shoulder and praying her act worked.

'You have to know that anything you took from this house, whether it was promised to you or not, would be theft.'

'I am not a criminal,' she said with conviction, feeling the force of those words burn her throat. He felt it too, judging by the widening of his eyes.

'Strong words for a woman who was just caught breaking and entering. Add that to breaking my non-disclosure agreement and helping Arista to make my bride run away, I'd say you're pretty far on the other side of the law right now.'

She closed her eyes, feeling the words catch in her throat even as she tried to find a way to explain. But there was no easy way to tell him that she had been blackmailed by Zeus for the past six months without revealing her mother's misdeeds. No way to get herself out of this mess without potentially throwing her mother's entire career into chaos.

She felt the world narrow around her, bringing the sound of her own breathing painfully into focus. Breathing that sounded far too shallow and far too rapid to be quite right. Warm palms settled upon both of her shoulders, pulling her back into the present with a jolt.

'Relax, Quinn. Breathe for me.'

Xander's face was a blur of shadows, but somehow she could sense his eyes on her. Without looking away, she obeyed. Air filled her lungs until the tight sensation in her chest fell away, leaving her shivering with reaction. It was the strangest feeling, because she'd been so sure she'd been about to lose control.

She shook off the swirling in her stomach, like swooping butterflies, and determinedly stared at a point across the dimly lit room, far away from Xander. She needed to avoid this ridiculous effect his touch seemed to have on her if she had any hope of speaking coherently and making him listen to her.

Pandora bit her lower lip, looking back into the dancing flames of his gaze. 'I swear, Xander, I had no idea that Arista planned to ruin the wedding.'

'What on earth did you think she would do with the information you gave her?'

'I don't usually know what people's intentions are until after the fact.'

To her surprise he didn't scoff at her words or disregard them, he simply stared at her in that discomfiting way of his, as though he could see right through to every thought in her head.

He folded his arms across his chest. 'The fact of the matter is, you did break a legal agreement. You betrayed my trust based on smooth lies from Arista Theodorou. And now…it seems it was all for nothing.'

The words hung in the air, laced with some tense emotion that deepened the furrow between his brows. Pandora nodded once finding her voice had failed her.

She didn't know what she had expected of this moment, if he'd ever found out an inkling of the truth. But seeing him turn away from her, tension in every muscle in his body, made the shame burn even deeper in her gut.

She had almost told Xander about Arista on Thursday night as they'd finished up a midnight conference meeting with their team in Osaka, who were out there struggling to close a crucial deal with the Tanaka Corporation. Her fluency in both Mandarin and Japanese had been Zeus's front for hiring her to become a part of his top-floor team. She had been his gift to Xander once he'd arrived from Europe, his very own Asian market specialist, privy to every call and email since he'd taken over operations in New York. Only she knew that she had been placed in such close proximity to Xander so she could act as Zeus's own personal spy on his oldest son while the old man was forced to convalesce in his big mansion.

'I can help you find Priya. I can explain,' she offered in what she hoped was a helpful tone. 'Perhaps it was just a simple case of the bridal jitters.'

Pandora could hardly believe the unravelling figure before her was actually the same perfectly polished automaton she'd strived to impress over the past few months. His dark hair was ruffled from agitated fingers and he had evidently pulled off the black tie at some point. Now the collar of his shirt lay wide open revealing a tanned, toned triangle of skin with just a hint of curling hair.

'You have no idea what all this means, do you?' His voice was a sudden ominous growl that seemed to scrape along her skin, agitating the burning guilt. She felt her own patience snap, her teeth gritting together painfully as she spoke.

'Perhaps I would know if you would damn well tell me.'

Xander paused mid-step, his mouth opening slightly. 'Did you just…curse at me?'

'Hardly a curse.' She stood tall, tilting her chin up.

'Xander, we could track her down and explain my part in it. Let me… I can fix this.'

'The damage has already been done. The information that you leaked contained changes to the prenup that Priya had not approved. She quite literally ran away the moment my brother informed her of the deception.'

Pandora felt her stomach drop at his words. Could it be true that Xander would have intentionally tried to deceive Priya like that? The marriage had been strangely sudden and devoid of any declarations of love or romance, but she had simply put that down to Xander's nature. He was an intensely private man for someone who was constantly in the public eye. They might have spent countless hours working together but she was under no illusion that she had come anywhere close to seeing what lay beneath his glacial surface.

'Nothing to say?' Xander bit out. 'No rushing to my defence?'

She bit her lower lip, trying to ignore the sensation of the walls of the safe closing in on her. 'I don't pretend to know where your morality compass lies, Xander. But I do know that you tend to prefer a more direct approach to getting your way rather than indulging in outright deceit.'

'That's almost a compliment, Quinn.' Xander paused, gathering his thoughts once more. 'No. I did not deliberately try to deceive Priya. The final part of the deal was done entirely through her uncle and I was told that she approved of the whole thing. But she clearly doesn't know that. Not that any of that matters now, considering she was last seen running from our wedding and into the waiting arms of my brother.'

'She really just walked away and left you standing there?' Pandora frowned.

'I told you, she ran. Quite fast for a woman in heels and haute couture.'

Pandora made a distressed sound.

'I never planned to ever get married and I highly resent being manipulated into the endeavour. That was actually something my bride and I had in common. It was a business agreement between us, really. A mutually beneficial one that I believed was foolproof.'

'Surely there is another way to achieve your publicity goals here, Xander. Other than getting married to a woman you barely know.'

'You think I entered into a whirlwind marriage just to get a line in the papers?' His stunned laugh was laced with a growl. '*Christos*, I wish it were that simple.'

'Then why did you do it?'

'It's common knowledge that my mother was Zeus's secretary in the Athens headquarters. He paid her handsomely to keep my existence a secret from the world. Until he found out he had become sterile and decided he needed to hunt down his illegitimate children to carry on his precious bloodline.' He paused, wondering why he was telling her this. But the words kept coming. 'I was nineteen when he found me, and my mother had long disappeared, so when he offered me a chance to make something of myself I took it. I joined the company and worked my way up from the bottom. I jumped through every hoop he asked of me until I reached the top of the pecking order and he accepted me as his right-hand man, running the European arm of the business. And then what does that bastard do, even after I fly over here and hold everything together while he's ill? He offers up the legacy that I rightfully earned, as a prize to be won.'

'This…the wedding…it's all because of Zeus?'

'He left a will. A very detailed one, in fact. The first

of his three illegitimate sons to marry and stay married for one year…takes everything.'

'And your brothers?' she asked. 'They know about this stipulation in the will?'

'Yes. Like me, Eros always vowed never to marry. He never cared about the fortune but if given the chance to exact revenge on me… Let's just say I need to find a re-placement bride fast or admit defeat.'

'I'll do it,' she said quickly, then froze, her mouth sag-ging open for a moment before she slapped a hand across the lower half of her face. 'I meant that I can help to find your replacement, not marry you myself.'

He pushed away the ridiculous sensation in his chest that felt far too close to disappointment. Sure, having her offer to take his bride's place would have made things a lot easier, but he could never have accepted. This was Quinn he was talking to here. Apart from the fact that he had just uncovered that she was completely untrustworthy, she was his employee, and employees were strictly off limits for romantic relationships in Xander Mytikas's book. Even fake relationships.

But…a small voice within him piped up, she had re-signed. Technically right now, she wasn't his assistant. She was the woman who had ruined his wedding and broken into his father's home for reasons he had yet to glean. She'd chosen to cease being his employee, hadn't she? He'd be lying if he said he hadn't chosen his previ-ous well-connected bride because she would ease his way to the top echelons of society, but that could all be pushed to the side for the moment. Right now, all he needed was a willing party. One that he could tolerate for the next twelve months.

He paused, taking in the woman before him and feeling the first flashes of his new strategy edge to the fore-front of his mind.

'You want to escape the consequences of your actions today, Quinn? Well, your redemption comes at a price, if you're willing to broker a deal with me.'

'You mean like a bargain for my soul or something?' she asked, eyes narrowed with suspicion.

'I'm not the villain here, Quinn. You're the one who ruined my wedding day, remember?'

She frowned, her fingers fidgeting fast by her side. 'What's the deal?'

'It's a new position, of sorts. A twelve-month contract. One that involves occasional travel and public appearances but, otherwise, is essentially just keeping a low profile.'

'This feels like a trick,' she mused, still looking wary. 'What's the catch?'

'In order to accept this offer, you would have to marry me.'

CHAPTER THREE

PANDORA FELT THE sound of laughter escape her throat, coming from a place filled half with dread, half hysteria. Like the kind of feeling she got when someone made a joke and everyone else laughed but she didn't quite get it. But Xander didn't make jokes, she reminded herself. It was part of the reason she had always found conversation with him to be so effortless. He was the kind of person who only spoke words that mattered and always with frank honesty. It was ludicrous for anyone to ever think he would have deceived Priya.

He was still looking at her, awaiting an answer to his ridiculous proposal, if she could even call it that.

'Quinn,' Xander gritted, 'I just asked you to marry me. Have you no response?'

'You didn't *ask*,' she pointed out. 'You demanded. There's a difference.'

It was utterly preposterous to even consider her as a last-minute replacement for his previous fiancée. She had only ever met Priya Davidson-Khan on one occasion, when the other woman had come to the office to sign some documents with her uncle. The entire office, including herself, had been a little transfixed at the woman's confident stride and effortless class. She wasn't just beautiful…she was the whole package. Intelligent, well bred and knowledgeable about the pitfalls of high-society circles that Xander needed to infiltrate. In short, she was the exact opposite of Pandora.

Men like Xander Mytikas did not choose the loud, quirky girls that didn't quite fit in.

She remembered one of the mornings during his first week at the office. He was impossible to miss really, him being all broad shoulders and piercing blue eyes. He'd noticed her with her earphones in chuckling to herself as she'd surveyed her latest cross-stitch project and stopped, staring down at the intricately crafted curse word decorated in pretty roses. She'd watched him for a long moment in her peripheral vision, puzzled at being the recipient of his infamous glare when she was pretty sure she'd done nothing wrong.

She'd tried to defuse the tension, asking if he needed anything. Only it had come out wrong, as happened sometimes when she was uncertain of somebody. Instead of a polite question, it had emerged as something harsh and accusatory.

There had been no mistaking the look on his face then. Irritation and impatience.

Over the next few weeks, she'd tried her best to avoid him but he'd seemed to be everywhere. In meetings where she'd acted as translator, she'd noticed he spoke in short, clipped sentences and he always said what he meant, no embellishing or pandering. In short, she was fascinated by him. Despite his clear disapproval of her, being around him seemed almost effortless. A rarity in her experience.

That was when she'd begun to feel that familiar pull, like when she'd first discovered a new language as a child and begun learning it, decoding and absorbing it into herself.

It was completely inappropriate and yet, she became

hyperaware of him. Dangerously so. After the years she'd spent being told by teachers and therapists to tone down the more intense facets of her autistic traits, she now tended to be rather pointed in letting her fixations have free rein. But she'd never felt the pull towards another human being before. At least, not a non-fictional one.

If her unwanted attraction to him meant working together had been almost unbearable…anything more would likely break her spirit entirely.

'You can't ask me to do this. I will help you find a replacement, someone more appropriate. Someone…' Someone who is not me. God, anyone but me.

He leaned his tall frame against the shelving. When he finally spoke, there was a calm to his voice that hadn't been there before. A cool determination that made her stomach twist.

'I've already thought through the probabilities of every other solution to this problem. Quinn, it has to be you.'

His words hit her squarely in the chest and for a moment she was floating, watching this surreal scene from above. Situations like this belonged on a cinema screen, not in real life. *It has to be you.* That was almost a declaration from a man who barely even muttered goodbye to her at the end of the day.

She caught herself at the ridiculous thought. It wasn't as if he'd said, 'Quinn, you're my only hope,' or begun chanting that her very existence completed him. This was a very serious real-life issue, not something she could dress up as a romantic movie moment.

But then, of course, like most of the vaguely nice things that Xander said to her, he went straight ahead and ruined it.

'You've already betrayed me once so at least I know where I stand with you. Better the devil I know, et cetera.'

'Just to be clear, I'm the devil in this situation?' she said dryly.

He folded his arms, surveying her with an air of impatient superiority that did nothing to soften the swirl of chaotic emotions inside her chest.

'I can't do this, Xander. Perhaps this is how situations are settled among high-society rich people but you're asking me to marry you as part of some kind of illicit bargain. It's highly improper. Probably illegal.'

'What was illegal was you breaking in here to steal from me. Not to mention breaking your NDA to talk to Arista.' He remained still…an ominous statue half bathed in shadows. 'This is an opportunity to redeem yourself. After the part you played in recent events, this is the only repayment I will accept.'

If his anger wasn't already evident in the taut set of his chiselled jawline, she heard it veiled under every syllable. An eye for an eye. A bride for a bride.

'You would become my wife in name only, so there would be very few demands other than signing your name beside mine on the legal documents, moving into my home and appearing in public occasionally to maintain the façade of a happy marriage.'

'Move in?' she squeaked, feeling uncomfortably hot all of a sudden. 'Xander, I can't…people would think that I was your…that we were…'

'That we were lovers?' His expression darkened suddenly. 'If this is going to be believable, that's the story we would tell. That our long nights in the office took an intimate turn and now that my business marriage to Priya is off, we're free to get married ourselves.'

Pandora felt her breathing quicken, remembering some of the more X-rated fantasies she'd entertained about her handsome boss while daydreaming at her desk. The desk, incidentally, had always played a starring role. He was watching her with cool interest, waiting for her to respond, she realised. She cleared her throat, praying he hadn't developed the ability to mind-read.

'But you're you, Xander. You're...' She gestured vaguely to his body, praying she wasn't blushing. It was much too warm in here. 'The last woman you dated was nominated for the most prestigious acting award, for goodness' sake.'

'You keep track of my dating life?'

'No,' she said quickly. 'What I mean is, you've never once dated anyone in the office. In fact, I was told when I started that you have strict rules about that sort of thing. So apart from the obvious reasons why I am entirely not your type, it's a thoroughly ridiculous plan that nobody will believe.'

'I'm thinking that perhaps all my rules were blown into the dust, with the power of our mutual attraction,' he mused, stroking a hand along his jaw. 'I only escorted that actress to one gala dinner, as a PR move. In general, I'm far too busy to date, Quinn, hence why I had to form a business plan in order to obtain a wife.'

'You're telling me that you don't realise there are a million women out there who would jump at the chance?'

'I'm a billionaire, of course there are. But an actual marriage would likely involve the kind of complex emotional entanglement that I'm not willing to give headspace to.'

'Not a romantic, then.' She fought the urge to smirk, finding this insight into her boss's cool, calculating exterior thoroughly fascinating.

He frowned at her words, running an agitated hand along his jaw. 'I need you to understand...at this very moment both of my brothers could be on their way to fulfil the terms of my father's will. Mytikas Holdings and every one of my employees could be on the verge of having their livelihoods snatched from under them. I am the only one of Zeus's heirs who cares about this company and the people who depend upon its existence.'

He looked tired, she realised. More tired than he'd ever let her see before. Perhaps it was that first glimpse of honesty that made her pause. As if sensing the shift in her, Xander moved closer. Just a step, but enough to bring him back into her line of vision.

'This would simply be a business agreement between two consenting adults.' He sat down in the chair in the centre of the safe, a reversal of the power move she had seen him make before in difficult negotiations.

'If this was a business agreement, then surely I would have some terms of my own.'

He straightened, surprise transforming his face for a split second before he nodded and crossed his arms, the picture of the polished businessman. 'Let's negotiate.'

'I have just one.' She inhaled, the air feeling hot in her lungs as she tried to calm her erratic heartbeat. 'You give me back that file and never ask of it again.'

He contemplated the slim folder for a second, darkness clouding his features. Then, to her surprise, he slid the folder across the floor, placing it at her feet.

'Just like that?' She breathed, narrowing her gaze upon him.

'I have CCTV footage of your actions tonight, that's enough collateral to satisfy me should you choose to cross me again.' He emphasised the last word with finality, standing up to his full height. 'I'm asking you for twelve months of marriage to be followed by a discreet divorce. Aside from the odd social function, we'd most likely live entirely separate lives.'

'You've really thought all this through.' Or was this the same deal he'd had this morning, with a different bride copied and pasted in? Sure, it hadn't been a love match with Priya, but the idea of trying to step into such a pivotal role in Xander's life that another woman had been set to play only a few hours ago still seemed wrong. This was so much more than mooning after her hot boss from across the office. They would be under the same roof. This would be personal.

She reflexively wrapped her arms around herself, tight enough to feel some of the deep pressure her body craved but as usual it wasn't enough. She couldn't even believe she was having these thoughts, because that meant that some tiny part of her was actually considering agreeing to his proposal…demand…threat? And that would be utter madness. Wouldn't it?

His jaw tightened. 'I would supply you with financial reimbursement to cover any losses incurred over the next twelve months.'

'You're suggesting that you would…pay me to quit working and marry you? That's hardly an ethical way to use your boss-employee privilege.'

She was not prepared for the sudden change that her words evoked. Xander froze, seeming to stiffen and coil up like a tiger who'd had his tail pulled. The mask of calm disappeared, leaving a harshness that made her take a half-step backwards. He took two steps towards her so that barely half a foot separated her chest from his and she could smell every individual scent in his cologne.

'I am not the kind of man to use my privilege in any manner. Unlike my father, I have very firm boundaries with my employees in that regard. You entered into a game that you had no business playing. I am offering you the opportunity to free yourself from the consequences of your own actions with the added bonus of keeping whatever is in that file.'

'I'll consider it,' she said, feeling the intensity of his gaze upon her like a flame. 'I'll think it over tonight and give you my answer in the morning.'

'And risk you disappearing without a trace?' He shook his head, stepping in her way. 'I've already had one potential bride disappear on me today.'

'Okay, then,' she said, with as much steel in her tone as she could muster.

'Okay?' he echoed, tilting his head to one side. 'Is that a yes?'

'Yes. I'll do it. I will marry you.'

Xander had expected the knot of tension in his stomach to ease once Mina had alerted his security team to come looking for him and they'd finally been let out of the safe. He'd decided to transport his assistant to his home immediately to complete the remainder of their bargain. His team of lawyers arrived swiftly, having drawn up the relevant documents with impressive speed. The three men now idled around the conference table of the penthouse apartment he kept at the top of the Mytikas building, watching the slim blonde who sat scanning over each word with quiet intensity.

Considering she regularly translated this kind of legal contract for her work, he shouldn't be surprised. But with every minute that passed with the pen untouched on the tabletop, he felt his impatience grow. When she finally declared the contracts satisfactory, he loomed over her, watching the smooth flourish of her signature with probably far more intensity than was necessary.

He insisted on escorting her home in his own car, the drive passing in the kind of peaceful silence that reminded him of evenings they had spent working together. She instructed him to pull up in front of a small nondescript brownstone with a bright purple door. She did not invite him inside, a fact that shouldn't have bothered him. And yet, the fact that he had worked alongside Quinn for months and never once had he considered where she lived bothered him, somehow.

He spent the rest of the evening arranging for the legal ceremony and necessary judge amendments to ensure their marriage was completed as soon as possible. He contemplated a phone call to deliver the news, but he knew she despised verbal communication, much preferring emails or texts. She really had been a poor fit for an executive assistant, he mused, wondering yet again why Zeus had hired her, while turning in his hands the small dark red booklet that held her travel documents.

It had been a harsh move, holding her passport as collateral, but a necessary one. He had seen the look in her eyes as she'd visibly considered her options. She had reminded him of a rabbit who had wandered too far from safety and found itself trapped in the path of a fox. He was under no illusion as to who played the part of the predator in this analogy.

But no matter how cruel she believed him to be, she had still agreed to his terms. She was prepared to sign her life over to him for the next twelve months and step into a role she had no preparation for whatsoever. Her words about societal expectations and reputation had not passed him by without impact.

Truthfully, he agreed with her. He'd never planned to marry at all because he had no desire to ever become romantically or emotionally vulnerable to anyone else by tying his life to theirs that closely. Bachelor life had suited him just fine for thirty-nine years. Using marriage as a bargaining tool to ensure he inherited the company he'd worked so hard for was Zeus's cruel way of taking Xander's beliefs and throwing them in his face.

He'd been nineteen on the day a shining black limousine had pulled up in front of his run-down Athens apartment block. For a young man, struggling financially thanks to his mother's extensive debts, the sight of Zeus in his sleek five-piece suit introducing himself as Papa had been every dream he'd ever dared to hope for. The offer of a world-class college tuition and a foothold into the world of wealthy elites had been too much to resist. He had promptly paid off his mother's debts and walked away from his past without a backward glance.

He'd learned that he had two brothers he had never met. Nysio Bacchetti was a descendant of Italian royalty with genius-level intelligence and Eros Theodorou, Arista's son, had been raised in the elite Greek social circles that were expected of a Mytikas heir. Xander might have been the oldest of Zeus's illegitimate sons but it hadn't taken long for him to find that he had not been his father's first choice to succeed him.

Nysio's powerful family had threatened death and ruin upon anyone who dared allude to their son's link to the Mytikas name, a fact that Xander had only learned of after his youngest brother had already been sent a copy of that damned will. With a paper document clearly listing him as an heir, Xander had been awaiting an imminent retaliation from the Italian. But instead, the attack had come from Eros. The brother he had actually known. They had begun working their way up the company ladder a few years apart and even worked side by side for a short time. Until Eros had left the company in a storm of scandal. A situation that his brother blamed him for, and rightly so. Guilt assailed him, but he pushed it down. Despite what

Zeus had thought of him, ultimately, Xander had been the only one to remain.

His thoughts intruded upon him even after he'd gone to bed and, as usual, sleep evaded him. His mind was far too preoccupied with the rapidly shifting pace of his plans to rest. As dawn broke over the city, he was back at his desk, looking down at the slim brown envelope that had been delivered via courier. Inside was the engagement ring he had given to Priya. Returned without any note or explanation, but, he supposed, the ring itself was explanation enough.

If that video was any indication, he already knew exactly where Priya had gone or, rather, to whom. Eros was a slippery opponent and one he knew would go to any lengths to get revenge on those who'd wronged him. Xander's actions fifteen years before had shaped their brotherhood into something cold and dangerous. But the news that Nysio Bacchetti had also been spotted in Manhattan had shocked him. Nysio had no need for Zeus's fortune; he was wealthy in his own right and had a reputation to uphold with his own family. But it wouldn't be a surprise if he'd seen the will as a broken promise, and in the circles the Italian frequented, such things were not taken lightly.

Xander sat back in his chair, pondering the fact that in Zeus's efforts to pit them against one another, he had inadvertently brought them all to the same city for possibly the first time ever. Surely that had to be an omen of sorts. He sat that way for a long time pondering what good could ever come from the meeting of three bastards born of scandal, each of them united only in their hatred for the man who'd sired them.

CHAPTER FOUR

IF SHE HADN'T known better, Pandora might have convinced herself that the previous night had been a dream. There was no outward evidence of the bargain she had made with her former boss as she strolled out of the elevator and onto the open-plan top floor of the executive offices. Xander's text for her to come into the office had been confusing seeing as she was no longer officially an employee, but the more she thought about it, the more she realised she had essentially left him in the lurch. It wasn't surprising that he wanted her to finish up with her commitments.

'Good morning,' she greeted the front desk receptionist brightly. Too brightly, judging by the way the man nodded once, then quickly scurried away.

She'd always seemed to only ever have two speeds: complete radio silence or a great impression of an over-excited chipmunk who forgot to breathe between words. She remembered the words spoken by a psychologist to her teenage self that had changed her thinking dramatically. 'You don't need to hide your differences, they're what make you who you are.'

The problem was, unless she pasted a thin veneer of false politeness over who she was, people noticed. If not immediately, they always noticed eventually. And not always in a positive way.

Everything seemed utterly normal for a Monday morning at Mytikas Holdings. She had seen no mention of their CEO's failed wedding in the papers, unsurprising considering the wealth and power of the Mytikas name meant it would be child's play for Xander to place a gag order on the media about what had occurred the day before.

Still, her heart ached just a little when she thought of him being put in the humiliating position of watching Priya fleeing from him as fast as her high heels could take her. Pandora got an odd little feeling, her fists tightening slightly, whenever she thought of Xander's beautiful first choice bride. A perfect society match, he had called her. That feeling... Knowing she herself was now essentially a consolation prize for someone who had hoped for much, much better...it was sadly not a new experience for her. Which meant she could easily switch off the uncomfortable swirl of thought and file it away with all the other pointless emotions she'd accumulated in her lifetime.

She'd made her decision, she only hoped it was the right one.

The next thing she was aware of was a shadow looming over her desk and a strange hush falling over the rest of the office.

'What are you doing?'

Pandora struggled for a moment to arrange her features into a polite mask. Her Executive Assistant face, she liked to call it. Xander stood dangerously close, his swarthy features carefully blank but his eyes blazing.

She frowned, lowering her voice to the merest murmur. 'You said to come into the office. I'm here.'

'I invited you here as my *fiancée*, Quinn, not to come to work.' He made a strange choking sound, running a hand through his hair. 'My office. Now.'

His own voice was a low whisper that made the skin on

her arms tighten and prickle with awareness. She watched him walk away, as did everyone else in their vicinity before their curious eyes slowly switched back to her. Someone whistled under their breath and the girl who sat at the desk next to her let out a rush of whispered questions.

She had long ago mastered the art of the shrug. It was one of her favourite weapons when language simply was not possible. Pursing her lips, Pandora rolled one shoulder and opened up the digital files on her tablet that she needed to get his signature on. Nerves made her extra uncoordinated, so she paid particular attention to her footing as she followed in Xander's wake.

At the very last moment, he took hold of her hand and pulled her in the rest of the way. She heard the audible gasp of her co-workers right before the door snapped shut, shielding them from view.

'What on earth are you thinking, doing that? Everybody was watching.' She spoke on a rush of breath as she yanked back her hand.

'Them watching us was the whole point. They will just assume that I have taken my fiancée somewhere private to wish her a good morning.'

'Why on earth would they…?' Her brow furrowed as his meaning dawned. 'You've already told them?'

'Have you completely forgotten the events of last night?'

'Of course not.'

'We've already signed a prenup, so it's best you haven't. I've just announced our engagement to the entire upper floor. Word had already got out about the whole runaway bride situation. They all think that now my convenient bride jilted me, I'm finally free to marry the woman I really love. Between you and me, the board are also happy that the scandal can be spun to our advantage.'

'I had a lot of things on my schedule for this week.' She heard the words leave her mouth almost as though she weren't speaking them.

'I have already arranged for your workload to be redistributed to a replacement temp.'

Her replacement. The word felt like a whip against her already flayed pride and she had to turn away. She had never set out to work behind a desk, but since she'd arrived in Manhattan, she'd fallen into an easy rhythm in the quiet top-floor office. The thought that she could be so easily replaced made her feel strange. As if perhaps she had inflated her own sense of importance.

She wondered if this was how Priya would feel upon finding out about Xander's lightning-fast acquisition of a new fiancée. She tried to push away the rapid-fire assault of her own thoughts, inhaling a deep calming breath before turning back to face him.

'This is all becoming very real.'

'I thought that I made it extremely clear to you; I need a marriage on paper. The moment you accepted my proposal, you became my fiancée, Pandora. Tonight, you will become my wife.'

'Tonight?' She felt her breathing falter slightly, her heart giving an odd little thump in her chest at the fact he'd just used her first name. She fought the urge to demand he take it back. That he call her Quinn as he always did, and she be allowed to continue to translate his meetings and sort his calendar and hide the fact that she'd agreed to act as his wife for the next year... But of course that was impossible. She felt the blood drain from her face as a tiny sound escaped her lips that was equal parts panic and disbelief. 'We're getting married tonight?'

'I believe I explained that this was a time-sensitive arrangement.'

She felt her stomach flip, knowing she had been on the verge of complete mental exhaustion as they'd finalised their agreement. He could have suggested they get married on the moon and she would have nodded along.

'This all seems very fast…' She turned away from him, frantically trying to gather her bearings in the small space, but of course Xander was everywhere. He was all broad shoulders and perfectly styled hair in his perfectly fitting suit and delicious cologne. This entire situation was utterly impossible.

New York law only needed twenty-four hours' notice for marriages, but she'd hardly thought he would try to pull together something so soon. It couldn't be that easy for him, could it?

Of course it was that easy. He was a Mytikas. He was the reigning monarch of an empire—if he wanted something done it would be done. She had known him long enough, for heaven's sake. Why had she thought that this would be any different?

She allowed herself to look at him then, to meet his eyes and stare. He stared right back. The sensation of being pinned by his gaze reminded her of the time she had spent locked in the safe with him the afternoon before. The time spent in the darkness trying to escape a situation she knew she had absolutely no way of avoiding.

She was going to become his wife.

'You're trembling,' he said, slowly reaching out for her left hand and holding it between his own. 'Already regretting your decision?'

There was a darkness in his tone, but what she saw on his face wasn't anger. He looked…vulnerable.

'I'm not going to jilt you like Priya did… If that's what you're asking.'

'Good, because my terms still stand,' he said silkily,

letting her hand go, having clearly taken a moment to compose himself. Whatever that flash of emotion had been, he had easily brushed past it and was dusting off the sleeves of his jacket with that arrogant air she was much more comfortable seeing.

This was the Xander she knew how to deal with. This was the Xander that she had spent the last four months infuriated by. She was already painfully attracted to that cold and ruthless version of him; if he were to start actually showing his humanity she would be a lost cause completely.

'What do you need me to do?' she asked, feeling too overwhelmed and too poorly dressed to be standing in Xander's office as his fiancée. Her plain black skirt and loose white blouse had been just fine when she'd simply been his executive assistant, but now her outfit felt like rags next to his perfectly tailored three-piece suit.

'You could start by looking a little less terrified of me,' he said dryly. 'I want people to believe that we're madly in love, not worry that I'm holding you hostage.'

'I'm not good with…intimacy.' Pandora forced the words from her lips, needing him to know the extent of her difficulties. 'I've only ever been in one adult relationship and let's just say…he had some criticisms.'

A dark look crossed Xander's features and for a moment she worried what he might say next, but he schooled the strange reaction quickly. 'I don't exactly have experience with fake relationships either, but I'm sure we can both figure out the basics.'

'Can you be more specific? Do you mean like giving each other compliments, holding hands, that kind of *lovey-dovey* stuff? Or do you mean…more than that?'

'I don't think *lovey-dovey* is quite my style.' He raised one brow, his Greek accent making the silly phrase sound needlessly erotic. 'I'm not planning to debauch you in public, Pandora, but it would be expected for us to at least touch one another on occasion.'

She glanced up to find herself pinned by eyes that seemed darker that their usual cerulean. As her pulse sped up, she swore she could feel his gaze travelling down below her chin in one long, slow sweep. Self-consciously, she raised a hand to her chest, feeling her skin heat from her toes right up to her cheeks.

'Okay.' She nodded, tapping her fingers on the door behind her in a sharp rhythm. 'I'll do my best to make it believable.'

'I think,' he said quietly, the deep baritone of his voice a low rumble, 'that the public will believe whatever we want them to…so long as we keep to the facts.'

'The facts?' She struggled to process his words, still slightly reeling at the effect the simple idea of his touch was having on her.

'We have worked in very close proximity together for months. Long days lead to long nights. We'll just let them put together the rest for themselves. I have always valued my privacy, and that won't change.'

'Privacy sounds good,' she breathed, hardly believing the rasp of her own voice.

'Once we are married and the inheritance matter is settled, everything will become much simpler. But right now I cannot give the board any more ammunition to use against me in this war. They already want to get rid of me. I need to take control of the narrative surrounding yesterday's disaster and this whirlwind romance is the best thing I can think of in so little time. We can't leave this room and have a single person question this union. The future of the entire company rests on it. Do you understand?'

He stepped closer, reaching down to take one of her

hands in his. He pulled a small black box from his coat pocket, opening it up to show a simple platinum-and-diamond solitaire ring.

Pandora froze, remembering another small box she had organised to be delivered to Priya only the week before. Dread churned in her stomach as she looked once then twice at the small silk interior of the box, assessing the contents.

She sighed in relief. It was a different ring. She wasn't sure why, but that small detail…mattered to her somehow.

'May I?' The request was surprisingly gentle, coming from a man from whom she had witnessed nothing but ruthless demands in the boardroom.

She nodded once but tensed as he went to slide the band slowly onto her finger.

Unable to tolerate the sensation his light touch provoked, she pulled her hand away quickly, then cursed herself as she saw his expression harden, his eyes narrowing on her briefly before he held out the ring for her to take and slide on herself.

The silence that followed was harsh and uncomfortable, tightening her already fraught nerves to what felt like snapping point. Unable to think of anything else to say, she simply stared at the beautiful glittering diamond and pondered the monumental shift in her reality that it represented. No more quiet evenings in her tiny apartment. No more morning coffee runs. No more predictable routine. Well, not for a year, anyway.

'Quinn, could you manage to look slightly less miserable?'

She snapped back to attention. 'Sorry.'

'I need you to act like you can't get enough of me. I'm going to have to touch you, maybe even kiss you on occasion. Can you handle that?'

Pandora inhaled, attractively choking on her own saliva for a split second before she recovered. God, if only he knew the terrible truth in his words. She had been entranced by Xander Mytikas before he had even spoken to her. It was just a surface attraction, of course; once she had realised how demanding he was to work for it had been a little easier to tone down her crush.

But kissing him… That was another matter entirely. Had she imagined kissing him? Sure, countless times. Had she ever intended to make that fantasy a reality? Goodness, no. She had barely survived her first attempts at kissing back in school, which had always been an utter disaster. She'd forced herself to kiss her ex-boyfriend because it was what was expected. But even Cormac had eventually agreed that she just wasn't very good at it.

She had grown comfortable in the quiet monotony of single life and now a Greek billionaire with luminous skin and perfect hair was calmly asking if he could touch her for the foreseeable future. They would play the part of man and wife and be forced to act as blissful newly-weds with all the physical displays of affection that entailed.

It was a recipe for disaster.

She was so used to living in this new life where no one knew who she was or what her life had once looked like back home in Ireland. Of the difficulties she'd grown up with, the difficulties she still managed now as an adult.

Here, she was just Pandora. But it was unfair to keep Xander in the dark, and there was no way she could keep that side of herself hidden away without sending herself into a spiral of exhaustion. It would be unfair to Xander but, mostly, it would be both unfair and self-destructive for her.

Biting her lower lip, she closed her eyes and took a deep fortifying breath.

'Xander, wait.' She waited a beat, until he was facing her, his deep blue eyes sincere and rapt with attention. He would hopefully be understanding, although not all people were, of course. But still, a little part of her shrank back and braced for impact.

'If we are going to do this, there are some things you should know. Things about me.'

'I don't mean to flinch at your touch… I'm just not used to interacting with you this way.' She spoke the words on a rush, her cheeks flushed and pink. She was…embarrassed, Xander realised. She was apologising. And of course, he was acting like a prize bastard.

'This is all just happening very fast,' she added, awkwardly studying the buttons at the top of his shirt rather than meeting his eyes.

'Neither of us were ready for this, Pandora. But we will have to be seen together eventually. We need to get a handle on this.'

She looked up quickly, surprise transforming her grey eyes to luminous silver.

'You used my first name again.' She grimaced. 'That just feels…weird coming from you.'

Had he been using her first name? He supposed he had. It wasn't something he'd begun doing intentionally, it had just kind of happened.

'*Quinn.*' He emphasised her surname purposefully. 'If this dislike of physical intimacy is going to continue, we're going to have a big problem on our hands.'

'I don't dislike it exactly. I just have some sensitivities. And I don't particularly enjoy kissing, but I could improve it with time and practice.'

Time being the one thing they didn't have much of, he thought with a slight frown. Practice, however… He cleared his throat, self-consciously readjusting his suit jacket. 'Would that make things easier for you? Practising?'

She thought for a moment, her lips pursing into a delicate bow shape. 'I suppose we could try it. Do you mean like, holding hands and posing for photographs? Or kissing…?' she added tentatively.

'Maybe just touching one another, for a start,' he suggested gruffly, feeling an unfamiliar tension tighten his abdomen. Call him egotistical but he'd never had to entice a woman to touch him before and yet this one seemed ready to run away screaming.

She frowned, running her tongue along her bottom lip. Her usually fair complexion had been graced with a rosy-pink blush high on her cheekbones and her lips taunted him with their fullness, slick and inviting. A scant few inches were all that separated him from claiming that perfect mouth, a gesture that would be solely for performance's sake, of course.

Still, he was reluctant to look away, as though they both stood frozen in time.

He lifted a hand and cupped her cheek and her eyelids with their ridiculously long lashes fluttered shut. Her perfect, usually creamy skin was hot and flushed under his hand and before he knew what he was doing, he touched his thumb against the sensitive flesh and she seemed to vibrate at the touch. He'd bet good money that underneath her eyelids, her pupils would be dilated with desire.

He hoped so. He wanted her to feel this too, even if they both knew nothing could come of it. He wanted to know that he wasn't alone in it. It was simply the veil of her control that had such a hold on him, the façade she portrayed. He wanted to know if it was real, or if deep down she was made of flesh and blood and lust just like him.

That would be enough, he told himself. It had to be.

But then, his shy little fiancée opened her eyes and what he saw there rocked him to his very core. Raw desire, pure and unbidden, burned in her gaze like molten silver. Xander felt his throat run dry, his palms flexing and tightening against her skin with the sheer effort of not pulling her closer to claim that fire for his own.

This wasn't real, he reminded himself. They had an audience to prepare for and an act to maintain but if this was all acting, then, good God, she was doing an award-worthy job.

'You're so good at this,' she whispered. 'Touching me.'

Xander fought against the roar of primitive desire that surged within him like a tidal wave. He had always been painfully selective in his dating life, preferring to wait for true attractions to take hold, which sadly for him were few and far between. He needed mental stimulation, not just physical, in order to feel drawn to a woman.

Four months of ignoring the pull towards this particular forbidden fruit weighed heavy upon him and he railed against the unfairness of chemistry. Why now, why this woman?

But as his mind fought against his own rapidly shredding control, he had missed the gradual softening of the woman in his arms. Without warning, Pandora made the choice for both of them, closing the remaining distance and pressing the sweet softness of her lips against his.

CHAPTER FIVE

OF ALL THE times that Pandora had wondered what kissing her boss would be like, she had never imagined herself being the one who initiated it. She had also not imagined it being so...right.

Because that was the only way that she could describe the feeling that came over her the moment their mouths connected. As though she had always kissed him. And that was just ridiculous, right? How on earth could she feel as if she had kissed someone before?

But even before her mind could continue to worry and overthink, in true Xander fashion he took control. His hands moved to her waist and tightened their hold, pulling her closer so that their chests didn't have an inch of space between them.

He angled his mouth against hers, deepening the intimate touch and sliding his tongue against the seam of her lips in a firm but gentle request for entrance.

She felt her body begin to tense, suddenly overwhelmed in the face of the complex sensory onslaught. As though he knew exactly what she needed, one of his hands moved to cup her jaw. The firm touch served as an anchor, holding her steady. The press of his skin against the sensitive area behind her ear was like being touched by a live wire, filling her with electric heat and urging her to take everything he offered.

The moment she opened her lips, Xander growled, a deep primal sound low enough that only she could hear. His fingertips pressed ever so slightly against her pulse point, and the action felt so possessive and raw that her entire body shivered in response.

The rhythm of his tongue was a smooth invasion, deepening and demanding more with each slow thrust. Heat pooled low in her abdomen and yet she didn't pull away. She didn't feel threatened or overwhelmed, in fact she gave as good as she got, reaching up to lace her hands around his neck. The impulse to run her fingers through the crop of salt-and-pepper hair at the base of his neck was strong but she hesitated, wondering if it might be too much.

She couldn't resist. She had always wondered how it would feel under her fingertips, if it would be hard and spiky, or bristly and rough, but no, it was silky soft like down. A shiver ran through her body again and she heard herself hum low in the back of her throat with approval, delighting in the various onslaught of sensory wonderment taking over her entire body.

He seemed to like that sound, his body moving against hers. Hardness against soft.

And he most certainly was hard, going by the taut ridge that she could feel against her thigh. Just as she began to wonder what it might be like to press against him, right there, he pulled back, and she almost growled herself.

Their eyes met for a split second, as they both simply stared at one another like opponents on a battlefield, breathing heavily. It dawned on her that it had always felt as if they had been in a battle of some sort, but perhaps she had misunderstood exactly what the context was.

She had always assumed he hated her. But could hatred produce this kind of heat?

He opened his mouth as though he planned to speak, then closed it just as quickly, his nostrils flaring and his breath still coming in hard gusts. Was it her imagination or were the tops of his cheeks slightly flushed? The idea that she could make the unflappable boardroom titan Xander Mytikas blush was a ridiculous one, and yet the evidence was rather shockingly stacked against him.

Who on earth was she? She had always detested kissing every time she had tried it as a teenager in her vain attempts to appear young and popular. Before she had given up on trying to fit in. It wasn't that she never felt romantic feelings or sexual desire, it was simply that every time she had tried to act on it, it had felt like struggling to understand an impossibly difficult language. She'd been called too intense or too cold. Never just right.

Never like this.

'That was better.' His voice was a rasp as he turned away from her, taking his phone out of his pocket and tapping a few keys as his chest continued to rise and fall swiftly. 'Of course, we will need to minimise that kind of…contact.'

'Why?' she asked impulsively, then cursed her fast mouth.

One dark brow rose, cutting her down further from the high of that kiss. 'Because this is purely a business arrangement, Quinn. It's not necessary or appropriate. Practice time is over.'

She felt herself deflate instantly. That kiss had been a revelation for her, it had been earth-shattering and made her rethink everything she'd always believed about herself. But the shift of tension in the room filled her with doubt. Had she done something wrong? Had she committed some sort of kissing faux pas?

And as Xander quickly launched into his plans for their quick legal ceremony later that evening, she quickly wondered if she had been mistaken in his blush, his heavy breathing. If he had even been affected by their kiss at all.

Xander resisted the urge to check his watch and tried to keep his gaze focused on the skyline of glittering buildings surrounding him. The rooftop terrace of Mytikas Holdings was hardly the most elite wedding destination, but when one was in a race against time to fulfil the terms of a will, needs must.

He had changed into a fresh suit at least, he thought with agitation.

What was she doing?

Quinn had outright refused his offer to have garments brought in from his Fifth Avenue stylist, insisting that she could dress herself just fine. He had felt the beginning of an argument rumbling within him but decided that he would choose his battles. Tonight's brief ceremony was essentially just signing their names on paper, a means to quickly ensure the legalities of their nuptials were taken care of. When it came to their actual society wedding, she would find that he could not be quite so lenient. He had an image to uphold and the kind of circles he moved in cared very much about the details, which he had found out very quickly upon entering the world of the wealthy as a poor teenager.

He would earn back their favour now after his failed first wedding, just as he had done then, with hard work and ruthless strategy. Mytikas Holdings belonged to him already, whether his brothers were prepared to accept it or not. He already owned forty per cent of the shares through his own tireless determination. The shadow corporation he had started up five years previously in Europe had originally been intended as an exit strategy if required. But then the opportunity had arisen for him to begin purchasing Mytikas shares legally and the plan had appeared in his mind fully formed. Titan Corp was on its way to becoming his own legacy, one that he would not allow to be taken from him.

Grinding his teeth at the thought, he wrenched his mind back to his upcoming wedding. Going to the jeweller's personally had not been a part of the plan, but sending his new fiancée to select her own wedding ring had seemed a step too far, even if this marriage wasn't real. He pulled the box out from his pocket, once more opening it to ensure the matching rings were still inside. Then he adjusted his collar for the fifth time.

It was just one year, he reminded himself. And it was likely to be the hardest year of his career, going by the malicious remarks made in this morning's board meeting.

The other shareholders had clearly been excited at the prospect of using the opportunity of his runaway bride creating an almighty scandal to push Xander out, and the only reason they were happy that he was marrying Pandora in such an apparently romantic, whirlwind fashion was that they thought the company would get a huge surge of public interest in the story. They hated and resented him for the progressive ideas that he had for the company's future because they were happy doing things the old way. The Zeus way. But that was just their tough luck, because Xander wasn't going anywhere.

The sound of the double glass doors of the atrium opening slowly caught his attention, he raised his gaze and found himself completely frozen on the spot.

His bride was wearing blue, a colour he didn't think

he'd ever seen her wear before. In the office, aside from bright lipsticks and jewellery she usually stuck to her black skirt and white blouse combo. The dress she was wearing was feminine and floaty and flared out from her slim waist in a way that reminded him of an old Audrey Hepburn movie he had watched many times with his grandmother. He half expected her to burst into song or twirl.

She was breathtakingly beautiful.

He didn't know if it was the moonlight that bathed the rooftop terrace or if her hair was simply glowing. He had never seen it unbound from its prisonlike bun. *Christos*, it was so long, like shining silk that tucked behind her ears and flowed down her back like molten silver. It was a crime to keep hair like that hidden away.

Just as much as it would be wrong for him to wonder what it would have been like to unravel it fist by fist over his hands.

He paused, shocked at the image in his mind's eye, inhaling sharply and feeling a shiver run through him as he exhaled a slow and steady gust of breath.

By the time she had crossed the few feet towards where he and the officiant stood, he had recovered from his momentary lapse and calmly extended his hand to her.

She smiled at him, a shy smile that didn't quite meet her eyes, and he resisted the urge to question her again, to make sure she truly wanted to go ahead with their bargain.

But then he thought of the possibility she might leave and he tightened his grip on her hand.

'I'm sorry I'm late.' Silver eyes flickered up to his, then slid away. 'I thought I had enough clothes to choose from…but it turns out there isn't exactly a dress code for a last-minute wedding ceremony.'

'Is the prospect of marriage to me so daunting?'

'Oh, no, of course not.' She paused. 'Oh, you're joking. Well, now, there's a first.'

Then she laughed, a deep belly laugh that was likely just nerves but still it did something strange to his insides. He felt his lips quirk, then quickly cleared his throat and introduced his driver, Mina, who would also be acting as their witness.

The officiant began to talk, laying out the rules of their arrangement and all the various legal jargon. As far as romantic elopements went, he realised that this was probably not every woman's dream. When he looked down, Pandora seemed tense but focused.

When they were told to join hands, he felt the weight of her palms warm and soft in his own and he found himself fighting the urge to demand that she look up, that she acknowledge him in this moment.

He wasn't quite sure what to make of that.

The rest of their vows were exchanged without a hitch. Not once in the entire ceremony did she speak other than to repeat her vows or nod her head in agreement. The entire thing had been a staid, solemn affair. Not unlike the eulogy that had been given at his father's funeral.

Before he knew it he had slid the small platinum band onto her finger and she had repeated the action with the second, larger ring in the box. He had already been sure to instruct the celebrant not to announce their union in the typical fashion of a kiss. The idea of claiming his bride in such a primal fashion had seemed unbearably wrong considering the nature of their agreement. He'd told himself that it had absolutely nothing to do with his own surprising reaction to her eager, unpractised kisses in his office earlier. He was not about to be undone by a woman fourteen years his junior with what he'd bet was infinitely less experience than he had.

But now, looking down at the matching bands on their fingers, he felt perhaps he had been hasty in removing the tradition. For the sake of appearances, perhaps he should have put more thought into this small formal affair, despite it being solely for legal purposes. Their much larger official wedding was already being planned for next month by his events team, as was expected for a man of his status.

They both knew that this marriage was a simple arrangement of convenience, but the urge was there for him to prove the validity of their union, wasn't it? Behind them, Mina stood, offering a rather staid applause.

He felt keenly aware of the curious eyes upon them, and perhaps that was why he stepped a little closer and encircled Pandora's wrists with his palms. Her breath hitched, and he felt the tremor of her response like a roaring victory within him. Her eyes flickered upwards for a split second, but that was all the time he needed to prove to himself that he was not alone in feeling this attraction.

He wasn't sure why that was so important to him in that moment, but it was. Good God it was.

He smiled with ease, leaning closer and feeling her stiffen when he pressed a single, chaste kiss against her cheek as he whispered softly into her ear. 'A little more enthusiasm would be great, *agape mou.*'

CHAPTER SIX

LATER THAT EVENING, Pandora was trying to concentrate on the words that Xander was speaking to the pilot and air hostess of his private jet, but she was far too focused on the weight of the smooth cold metal that now encircled her third finger.

Glasses of champagne had already been presented to them both, along with words of congratulation before they were seated for take-off. Once the jet was airborne on its way to Osaka for their supposed honeymoon, a lavish gourmet meal was served. But Pandora was too wound up, too tense to truly enjoy any of the delicious food spread out before them. Her flute of champagne was also still mostly full, Pandora having only been able to tolerate a small sip. She strongly suspected their 'honeymoon' would involve meeting delegates from the Tanaka Corporation, knowing how frustrated Xander was with the team who'd supposedly been near to closing the deal but who'd failed to persuade the Tanaka family to sign on the dotted line.

'This will all be over soon,' Xander said, interrupting her silent brooding. She froze, not entirely sure if he was referring to their meal or their marriage. The thought almost made her laugh aloud, inappropriate as it was. But upon seeing the small furrow between his brows, she had an inkling that he wouldn't find it quite so funny.

She remembered the darkness in his eyes as they'd stood in his office, when she'd casually promised not to jilt him as Priya had. And as she had walked down the makeshift aisle towards him earlier this evening, running slightly late, she had seen the tension in his jaw and the tightness around his eyes. She had noticed the small hiss of breath leave his lungs and his shoulders finally relax when the officiant had finally pronounced them man and wife. And when the woman had completely avoided any mention of kissing the bride...she had been disappointed. She had built herself up for that moment, for that repeat of their intimate contact. It wouldn't surprise her if he had specifically ordered the officiant to amend the usual ceremony.

Which was madness, because she absolutely hated kissing usually. Something about the sensation of having someone's face so close to her own, having their lips pressed against hers...it was always too much. It had only ever made her feel slightly nauseous.

But the way Xander had looked at her once they were man and wife... She had felt the strangest sensation tightening in her lower abdomen and flowing upwards throughout her body.

How he hadn't noticed when she was sure her pupils must have dilated to the size of saucers, and her breathing had sped up... She had been so sure everyone would have heard her erratic heartbeat, almost as if something inside her were throbbing along to its own frantic rhythm, each beat shouting, *Kiss me! Kiss me! Kiss me!*

Of course, she wasn't so foolish as to think he had been that eager to marry her, specifically. He had simply been eager to get married and fulfil the terms of the will before either of his brothers beat him to the punch. Any single woman would have done just as well.

She needed to remind herself that she was only a hasty replacement in his world. She had simply been the most convenient woman in his life at the time. The feeling of being tolerated by others was not unfamiliar, but it was one she had promised herself that she would never settle for in the relationships she chose for herself. But then again, she hadn't exactly chosen Xander either. She had been attracted to him from the moment they met, yes, but she had always disliked his ruthless, driven nature. He was a workaholic, that much was for sure. He never smiled, never engaged others unless it was about work.

This wasn't the same, she reminded herself, quickly straightening in her seat and turning her face towards her husband. 'I'm not quite sure how to behave now,' she said honestly. 'I've only ever been around people as a member of your team, and being congratulated by them now as though I'm…important is unsettling.'

He frowned, a strange darkness entering his eyes.

'When I first started working for my father,' he said quietly, his voice an intimate murmur, 'he refused to allow me to go to any of the social functions that he attended. His excuse was that my upbringing and deportment were not suitably satisfactory for a Mytikas. My younger brother Eros, on the other hand, had been raised in the bosom of high society and attended all the best schools.'

'How cruel of him,' Pandora breathed, a sudden surge of feeling clutching at her chest as she saw the flash of emotion in Xander's face. The memory hurt him, she realised. But just as quickly as he had shown his vulnerability he shut it down, lifting his glass of wine to his lips and looking away from her.

'Zeus was a cruel man. You should know this more than anyone.' He shrugged. 'I'm not trying to seek sympathy, Pandora. I'm just…'

He paused, his jaw ticcing. 'I'm trying to tell you I understand what this must feel like to you. That it can be strange, entering this world. I won't lie to you and say that it will all be smooth sailing. It can be an unforgiving place for those who were not born into it.'

'I have more than my fair share of experience of not fitting in,' she admitted, grateful for this moment of honesty between them. 'It would have been better for you to have a proper society bride in all this, but once I commit to something I follow it through, however challenging it turns out to be.' She meant the words, she realised with a little shock. Now that she was past the point of return on their bargain, she felt herself wanting not only to follow through but to do it well. To prove to herself that she *could* play this role, even if it was only for one year.

'I admire that.'

Their eyes met for a long moment, before she quickly glanced back down to her champagne glass. The moment was suddenly too intimate, too much for her to process.

She closed her eyes, inhaling a deep breath for five seconds and releasing it slowly with control. When she opened her eyes again Xander was right there, taking the glass from her hands and placing it gently on the table.

The jet's conditioned air was cool on her bare skin and she stood up, grabbing her wrap from where she'd abandoned it near the entry door. The space was sumptuous and sleek, decorated in white and silver with deep red marble-effect accents. It was one of the benefits of living in the clouds, she mused to herself as she took her time inspecting the fresh roses and hydrangeas that she'd picked in Xander's rooftop garden for her makeshift bouquet.

The rooftop garden of Xander's office where they'd been married was quite possibly the most beautiful place she had ever seen in New York. But that should not be a surprise as she knew that he seemed to gravitate towards rare and expensive items like his bespoke suits and the collector's edition sports car he drove. He was certainly an appreciator of perfection.

She wondered what she looked like through his eyes. Did he notice her autistic traits? She knew that there was no need to inform anyone about the fact that she was on the autism spectrum. But for some reason, she'd been ready to lay it all out for him that morning in his office… before she had got distracted by kissing him, of course.

Perhaps she had wanted to test him. Or maybe that small, scared part of her had hoped that if he knew, he might have called the whole thing off. Either way, they both knew that she was only a temporary fixture here. She would never truly fit into Xander Mytikas's perfect world on a permanent basis. She faltered a little at the thought, her steps scuffing slightly on the carpeted aisle between the jet's plush seats.

A firm hand cupped her elbow, fingers sliding around her skin like a band of steel. Holding her balance upright and preventing her from entering into an embarrassing tumble backwards as she sat down in her seat.

'I'm sorry, I get a little clumsier if I'm distracted.'

'That happens a lot around me, I've noticed.' He raised one brow, his lips quirking with wry amusement. 'Do I distract you?'

Pandora stiffened. Of course he couldn't know the impact that such a benign statement would have on her. But then again, he had no idea of the extent of her difficulties.

'I'm sure you've noticed many of my quirks by now.' She took a deep breath. 'It's because I'm autistic. If you have something you'd like to ask me about that, go ahead.' It was only once the words had left her mouth that she heard the hostility in them, and the defensiveness she was so used to holding at bay.

He raised a brow at her tone. 'If you're asking if I intend to interrogate you about the nuances of the autism spectrum, I thought I might save that for our wedding night.'

His words entered her mind on a jumble, and for a moment she couldn't focus on anything other than *wedding night* and the shockingly intimate picture that it evoked in her mind's eye. She coughed, realising he was probably being sarcastic, but she still needed to take a few hearty gulps of ice water in an effort to cool her deviant mind. It didn't work.

'Not that this is actually our wedding night in any real sense...' He tailed off, looking mildly concerned when she stood up again rather suddenly.

'You can, if you want. Interrogate me, I mean.' She moved away from him, inspecting some of the delightful desserts that had been laid out on a tray at the bar. A bar on a plane...this place was utterly ridiculous and she was pretty sure she'd never enjoy normal travel ever again.

'I wasn't actually planning to interrogate you,' he assured her with a frown. 'You haven't mentioned it to me before today, for your own good reasons, I'm sure, and despite my recent harsh demands...'

He stood up too, his powerful form only taking two strides before he was leaning against the counter beside her. She stiffened, inhaling the beguiling scent of him and feeling it stir up her senses ever more. Damn him. For a moment she almost wished he would say something inappropriate, like insist that she look at him, just so she could have an excuse to be as worked up as she currently felt.

'I do tend to respect people's boundaries, normally,' he said gently. 'These past twenty-four hours or so haven't exactly been business as usual for either of us.'

'I don't feel the need to disclose my diagnosis with everyone I meet, but that doesn't mean I avoid the topic either,' she explained stiltedly. 'As my husband, I assumed you might need to know, in case it ever came up.'

She felt a familiar tic in her jaw as she spoke, her body reacting to the uncomfortable conversation. She waited, counting her own breaths as Xander seemed to measure his own words before responding.

'Do I need to know all the details, if you'd rather keep them private?' he asked. 'I mean, do you need me to know them in order for me to understand you better?'

The air around them went too quiet, and she swore that she could feel a hum begin in her chest and move upwards into her throat. The surge of emotion choked her, somewhere between her chin and her collarbone. She swallowed hard, grateful that she was facing away from him so that he wouldn't see just how deeply his words had affected her.

No one had ever asked her that before…

She had always tried not to let her difference define her, but the truth was it did. It was a part of her identity, one that she had worked hard to understand and accept with love. The only problem was that other people didn't always see it that way. The idea that he was *asking* if she wanted him to understand her better…she had never even considered it.

'I didn't mean to sound flippant.' He moved closer, his face coming into view by her side. 'I simply mean that it's not a requirement that you tell me everything. This marriage will only work if we each maintain our personal boundaries.'

Pandora simply nodded and turned her back to continue making her tea, knowing that his words held a thinly veiled warning. The trouble was, she had always had difficulty with impulse control. And right now, Xander was a shiny red button, that read *do not press*.

So, of course, she immediately wanted to find out what would happen if she did, how far she could push him, even as the thought of it scared her to her core. It made no sense and yet it made her chest prickle with a kind of terrible excitement. The kind of excitement you only felt when you knew you were skirting the edge of danger. 'Chaos personified', he had once called her during a particularly frustrating meeting… He had no idea.

He moved past her, his suit trousers brushing against the voluminous skirt of her dress. Breath entered her lungs with such sharpness it almost hurt.

But as he paused, his eyes questioning hers silently before he moved back towards his seat, she realised with sudden clarity that she no longer just had a crush on her boss…this man was now her husband, and if she wasn't very, very careful she could easily find herself well out of her depth.

Xander lay back in the jet's recliner chair, sleep still evading him. The memory of that look on Pandora's face when he had moved in to kiss her cheek at their wedding… He definitely hadn't imagined the heat in those silver depths. But this was a woman he needed to keep at arm's length. He had known that from the very first moment he'd laid eyes on her and she'd smiled so warmly at him.

Of course, he'd soon understood that was pretty much how Pandora Quinn treated everybody that she worked with. Her sunny chaotic personality in the office was notorious. As was her seeming naivety, which he had seen in action a few times when he'd noticed people trying to take advantage of her kindness.

He'd put an end to that rather quickly, making his displeasure known to them.

Xander realised for the first time that he had not truly considered how a woman might feel at being a replacement bride. For there was no denying that was what she was.

He thought of the very first night that he'd seen Pandora Quinn, two months before he came to work in New York. That night she had simply been a nameless blonde who had caught his eye at the annual Mytikas Charity Gala, a pompous grand affair that Zeus had thrown every year under the guise of raising money for Greek orphans, when really it was simply another opportunity that he'd used to conduct his own nefarious dealings.

Her eyes had been what had drawn him first, filled with such tension. He had never been the kind of man attracted to a damsel in distress, but he had watched as she'd struggled to disengage from conversing with one of the wealthy businessmen in attendance, backing slowly towards one of the exit doors that led to the foyer. But the other man hadn't seemed to get the memo, and so after observing closely for a couple more minutes and feeling his own blood pressure rise, Xander had intervened.

He couldn't even remember what he had said, only that within a few moments he had extracted her from the situation and she had begged him to get her out of there. He had taken her outside, knowing the old library well considering he himself often ducked out of such events. Every year.

He'd led her to one of the smaller libraries, meaning to quickly deposit her there and head back to the party himself. But just as he had moved to leave he had felt her hand on his elbow and she had offered the words that had probably sealed their fate.

'You could always just hide here too.'

And he had. Before he'd realised it, an hour had passed and a single glance out at the corridor showed a crowd of guests had begun to disperse, some of them heading directly for them. His mystery blonde had excused herself to go to the bathroom and he had been commandeered by his father to break up a spat that had broken out between Arista and one of their board members.

When he had returned to find her, she had gone.

Disappeared as though she had never existed in the first place. And when he had asked his father if he knew the young blonde woman, Zeus had been strangely tight-lipped. Except for a malicious gleam, which Xander in retrospect should have been wary of.

Monday morning had dawned, and he had walked into his office to say goodbye before flying back to Europe, only to find his father waiting, his brand-new executive assistant, Pandora Quinn, in tow.

It had been wrong of him not to acknowledge in any way that they had already met, but rage and previous experience of people who'd tried to take advantage of knowing him had clouded his own judgement. Neither of them had ever once referenced that first night, not even when Zeus had announced his forced hiatus eight weeks later, recalling Xander from Europe, and they had been suddenly forced to work side by side.

He'd always wondered about the swiftness of her hiring. Now, after her attempts to retrieve something from the safe, something that Zeus had supposedly 'promised' her, he knew that something more had been going on behind her sudden employment with his father… He remembered her indignant claim that she was not a criminal, despite being caught red-handed—was it possible that Pandora had been just as much a victim of Zeus's machinations as he was?

And now, in the face of her questionable deceit, was it possible that he had decided to punish her in the same fashion as his father had always punished him? The thought made him absolutely sick to his stomach. His father had been cruel, he had played with people's emotions and used what they wanted against them in order to maintain control.

Xander never did that. But he had demanded that she become his wife, for goodness' sake. He had demanded she play the part of the temporary society bride, not even bothering to ask how that might impact her for the duration. In his mind, she had owed him the service. For him, she had got in the way of what he wanted and so she had to pay the price.

He was no better than Zeus. Perhaps, he was even worse. That thought was enough to keep him awake, stomach roiling and head pounding as the jet moved across the Pacific and into darkness once more.

Finally, having not had a wink of sleep, he got up to find her. He hovered outside the door of the main cabin, where she'd gone to rest, needing to clarify those points with her. To know if his suspicions about Zeus somehow manipulating her were true. But then, as though on cue, a bang sounded from the room within, granting him due cause to open the door and force his way inside, where the bed, though unmade, was completely empty.

Shock reverberated through him, filling him with adrenaline as he pushed his way further into the room, eyes scanning the perimeter. She had definitely come in here earlier. He had heard the door snap shut behind her.

He was just about to burst back into the main cabin and search every corner, when a small rustling sound caught his attention. The large double bed took up most of the cabin, but for small spaces on either side. The far side of the bed was where the noise had come from.

Xander climbed across the bed, peering down to where the Egyptian cotton duvet had apparently fallen to the floor. He lifted one corner and smelled the scent of roses.

Pandora lay in a foetal position, seemingly rolled up in the duvet like a delicate burrito of sorts.

Her eyes opened, her entire body snapping to attention with a speed that led him to believe that she hadn't been sleeping.

'What are you doing in here?' she asked. 'Have we landed?'

'I think a better question is what are you doing down there?' He resisted the urge to assist her as she pulled herself awkwardly upwards from the small space. 'This is a ten-thousand-dollar bed and you're sleeping on the floor.'

'I couldn't sleep.' She stared at the huge bed, clearly embarrassed. 'I move around a lot. It felt too open.'

He stared down at her, seeing the dark bruises under her eyes. There were still seven hours before they landed in Osaka, but at this rate they'd both be hallucinating from sleep deprivation. He helped her up from the small space, easing her shoulders back until she was sitting on the side of the bed.

'Okay, the way I see this we could both be stubborn and suffer, or we could just join forces here.' He gestured to the empty bed, then lifted a hand to silence her immediate interruption. 'Think about it, Quinn—I'll fill up the empty space and you will stop banging around my jet waking me up.'

'Xander, honestly, I'm used to finding new ways to cope.'

'You don't need to cope. You need to sleep.'

She blinked up at him, whatever words she'd been about

to say wiped out by a sudden gigantic yawn. He felt the urge to follow suit, his eyes feeling heavy almost as though he were drunk. Without thinking, he walked to the other side of the bed and sat down, removing his shoes and lying down to stretch out on the soft white sheets. As expected, the pillows were heaven and he let out a deep growl of appreciation.

'Lie down. Let's just try sleeping together.' He paused, inwardly cursing his own foolish choice of words. 'Sleep *beside* one another, I mean.'

She was already lowering herself to the pillow on the opposite side of the bed, her lips pursed as she stiffened. 'Sorry, I'm not good at accepting help.'

That simple admission cut through him, unravelling an anger within him towards whoever in her past had made her close up this way. 'Lie quietly with me for five minutes and if it doesn't work, we'll resort to alcohol.'

'Okay,' she breathed, eyes threatening to close even as she whispered, 'This probably won't work, Xander.'

'Why is that?' he whispered back, simultaneously amused and curious.

'You're too good-looking,' she mumbled, sighing. 'And you kissed me.'

He stilled, suddenly realising his own mistake as she relaxed fully into sleep and lazily slid one of her legs outwards, anchoring it under his. The sigh she let out was glorious torture as she drifted into what was most certainly a sound sleep. And he knew he was definitely not going to be getting any rest himself.

CHAPTER SEVEN

PANDORA AWOKE GROGGY and disorientated after what had possibly been the most peaceful few hours' sleep of her life, only to find herself alone in a strange bedroom with Xander's scent all over her skin. A quick peek through the doorway showed him reclined and sleeping peacefully on one of the large seats in the main cabin.

She had practically used him as a teddy bear, she thought with a grimace. A six-foot-four solidly muscled teddy bear who emanated a mind-fogging cloud of pure sex.

She exited the bedroom to her own chair in the cabin and readjusted herself in her seat, feeling a familiar discomfort creep over her body. Her clothes felt too tight, her shoes pinched and every tiny sound in the plane seemed to build together, forming an orchestra of minute micro irritations.

Her sensory system was overloaded and every sound and movement around her had all the impact of a pane of glass shattering against her skin.

New places and exciting experiences were something she absolutely adored but still had to work extra hard to participate in. That kind of mental exertion usually took a huge toll on her energy levels, even if she'd managed a full night's sleep. This was something that she had figured out quite quickly as a child when she'd spent most of her time shouldering the burden of her parents' busy travel and events schedules. She had unconsciously developed ways of hiding her own discomfort, coping silently through the pain so as not to be an extra burden.

But this wasn't the same, she reminded herself. Here with Xander, she was consciously stepping into the temporary role of the billionaire's bride with her eyes wide open. She wasn't denying herself or breaking that silent vow she'd made with herself all those months ago. This was just business.

Xander awoke just as the pilot announced their descent just before midnight in Osaka.

The interior of the sleek car that came to pick them up on the tarmac bore the Tanaka emblem, confirming Pandora's suspicions, but she nevertheless relished the opportunity to talk briefly to the chauffeur in his own language. Japanese had been the fourth language she'd learned but it was one of her favourites. Still, the effort of focusing on the flow of conversation was far more difficult than usual and when they finally slid into the passenger area, she almost groaned with relief. The modern car was dark and soothing and smelled of expensive leather. But most of all, it was incredibly quiet thanks to the modern engine, and for once she was immensely grateful for her husband's stony silence as he tapped away on the screen on his lap.

She watched as the city lights came into view and Xander asked the driver to take the scenic route, though his eyes didn't venture up to take it in himself. Pandora drank in the luminescent skyscrapers and impossibly bright displays that made up the modern city at night. Go-karts with colourful cartoon characters whizzed past them as they made their way along, tourists and locals lining the streets. Midnight in Osaka was evidently prime time for fun. She took in the chic mannequins lining the shopfronts in the fashion district, noting with interest that this seemed like a city of style. She looked down at her own simple black jeans and teal T-shirt combination and cringed.

Her eyes growing tired again, she turned in her seat slightly, allowing herself a fleeting glance upwards, and was rewarded with the sleek profile of Xander's patrician nose and razor-sharp jawline. His long, lean frame took up most of his side of the car, a scant few inches separating their thighs from touching. He was distracted, catching up on whatever email correspondence he'd missed out on during his sleep. As his EA, her job would normally have been to prioritise those emails for him. Running a corporation with multiple global time zones was no joke, as she'd found out pretty quickly.

It wasn't that she was lamenting the loss of working with Xander himself, but she had genuinely enjoyed her job. It had been the longest position she'd held, other than working with her mother, and she had just started to feel as if she was settling in. She'd had a reputation as a problem solver, despite her truly terrible organisational skills. She had felt a sense of purpose in her work. She had even begun to feel as if she was good at it, well, good at the translation side of things anyway.

But Xander had told her he'd already hired her replacement, so evidently she wasn't as necessary or valuable to Mytikas Holdings as she might have liked to imagine. What exactly was she expected to do while they were here, if Xander was going to work?

Of course, he chose that moment to look up, capturing her with his icy gaze.

'Problem?' he asked normally enough, but in his deep baritone the word jolted her sensitive nerves and she tensed a little, frozen like a deer in the headlights.

'No, no problem,' she said quickly, lowering her gaze as she fidgeted in her seat.

She had hoped her obvious rebuttal would be enough to close down the interaction and take them back to the pleasant silence that had engulfed them before, but in her peripheral vision she'd seen him place his screen face down on the seat, his gaze still pointedly in her direction.

'You seemed deep in thought.'

'I'm always deep in thought.' She looked up at him briefly, forcing a tight smile to her lips and hoping he didn't see through it. Of course, Xander Mytikas saw everything, a fact she should well know by now.

The silence was back again, only this was not the comfortable one that usually lay between them. This one was filled with a strange tension. When the car finally came to a stop in the wealthy upscale district of Umeda, he exited the car first and offered her his hand, escorting her out into the warm midnight air. Even for early October, the city was still far from the frigid New York autumnal air they had left. But Pandora shivered and stared up at the giant skyscraper where Xander had explained he owned a number of luxury apartments. The interior of the building was rather cold and disappointing, nothing at all like the traditional Japanese décor she'd been expecting.

A doorman escorted them up to the fortieth floor, where Pandora found her bags had already been delivered and unpacked. A light meal sat waiting for them in a modern dining area that boasted a spectacular view of the city lights. The sea of sparkling colours was mesmerising, demanding her full attention. So much so that she didn't hear Xander leave the room until she heard the unmistakeable sound of the shower running.

She was still painfully jet-lagged and disorientated but feeling a mad urge to go and explore the wild urban jungle.

This was what she'd promised herself, wasn't it? When she'd accepted Zeus's deal and moved to Manhattan, she'd promised herself more adventures. Surely a billionaire's convenient wife would still be allowed to have fun? Tomorrow, she'd begin her bravery, she assured herself.

The sound of running water came from the larger of the two bedrooms in the sprawling luxury unit, each wall more sleek and polished than the next. She entered the smaller bedroom, frowning to find her things weren't put away in the closets there. They must be in the other room. The water was still running but no way was she risking traipsing into Xander's room to retrieve her things. She had already practically wrapped herself around him on the plane, the last thing she needed was for him to have more reasons to be suspicious of her.

Kicking off her shoes and jeans, Pandora flopped back in the centre of the large four-poster bed in just her T-shirt and underwear and wondered why on earth she had agreed to any of this. It was one thing to find herself married to her boss in twenty-four hours, but it was entirely another to have found herself sharing a bed with him in the sky. Was that something to do with the mile-high club?

The sound of the shower running elicited all kinds of visions in her mind of expensive soap being lathered upon toned muscles and the scent of lemon verbena in the air. There would be steam, she imagined. So much steam and heat and a teasing expanse of slick, freshly scrubbed olive-toned skin…

A door in her own room opened suddenly, making her jump. There must be connecting doorways between the bathroom and both bedrooms, and he'd opened the wrong one. Xander strode out on a cloud of steam, his broad shoulders seeming to fill the doorway.

The towel he had wrapped around his hips was slung

so low she gulped. She knew what his workout regimen was like; she had often commented on the predictability of his schedule after all. And yet seeing the deliciously sculpted results of that daily routine was another matter entirely. The definition of his pectorals and the lean dips in his hips, the bulging muscles of his thighs, well, the part of his thighs that she could see. It was too much and yet somehow not enough. She licked her lower lip, feeling suddenly parched.

Good grief, he was staring at her and she suddenly remembered that she was sprawled out on her bed in her underwear. Letting out a very unladylike squeak of dismay, she pulled a pillow down into her lap, not that he would be interested much, she told herself. Perhaps he would simply ignore her entirely and pretend she didn't exist. That, she could deal with.

She inhaled a deep breath, letting it hiss out slowly between her teeth as she forced herself to look him in the eye.

Xander Mytikas was trying his very best not to laugh at her.

Good God, she was an absolute train wreck. And instead of answering with some clever quip that made her seem sophisticated or, better yet, made him completely doubt his sexual prowess, Pandora did the worst possible thing.

She threw the pillow at him.

She didn't know why she did it, she only knew that she needed to defuse the awful tension threatening to burn her abdominal muscles to cinders. It seemed to arc across the bedroom in slow motion in a direct line for his smirking face. He caught it before it even came close to hitting him, his still-wet muscles glistening as he flexed.

Of course, the infuriating man had the reflexes of a cat as well as the body of a god.

'Sorry.' She sat up against the headboard. 'I didn't mean to...'

'You didn't mean to pick up a pillow and deliberately aim it at my face?' One dark brow was raised in her direction. 'You know, if we were still in the office, this *could* be classed as bullying.'

'You were mocking my discomfort. I acted in self-defence.' She sniffed, pressing a hand against her stomach to tamp down that annoying heat once again.

'Tell me, Pandora...what exactly was making you so uncomfortable?'

His question was seemingly innocent, but...was she imagining it or had his voice lowered slightly? He still stood a few feet from the bed, patiently waiting for her answer.

'You know what you look like, Xander. I'm not going to inflate your monstrous male ego any further.'

'Monstrous.' That damned smirk was widening. 'That's a very unattractive word to use. I'm wounded. And yet... my looks have never made you act this way in the past. What changed, I wonder?'

'This, obviously.' She gestured vaguely in the direction of his naked chest where the red pillow was fast devolving into a soggy mess. Goodness, she knew the feeling.

'Which part, exactly?' He made a show of looking confused, glancing downwards. 'Just so I know what to keep out of your sight for future reference.'

Against her will, her eyes followed, raking over his perfect pectorals and downwards to where a treasure trail of trimmed hair led to... She inhaled sharply, looking up to find his eyes on her, watching her without a single trace of the humour that was there before. In fact, he looked almost…angry. Which was utterly ridiculous, because he was the one who'd started this whole thing, not her.

After a moment he cleared his throat. 'You're in the wrong bed.' And with that he strode from the room, leaving all the connecting doors open behind him.

She lay still, listening to the sounds of him moving around his bedroom, no doubt trying to find something to cover up his nudity so that his awkward little bride would stop ogling him like some kind of sex-starved nymphomaniac.

Fighting the urge to groan her sheer mortification into her pillow, she lay back and stared at the silky ivory canopy above the bed.

Perhaps if they had been a true married couple this would be the kind of thing that they would laugh about. But they were not truly married, he was not truly her husband and he most definitely was not hers to stare at like a piece of cake in a shop window.

She felt the bed dip and suddenly she was no longer alone under the canopy.

'What are you doing?' She sat up bolt straight.

'I'm a man of my word,' he said simply, lying back on the pillows. 'If you won't come into the other room, I'll sleep with you in here.'

It was a ridiculously large bed, big enough for them to both spread out and still be in no danger of touching. And yet, she swore the entire room heated up by a few degrees, as though her skin could sense him nearby.

'Are you comfortable?' he asked, his voice floating across the bed. 'Do you need me to move closer so you can sleep?'

She made a prim noise of assent as she continued to ensure that her body remained still and out of accidental touching range. The bed moved as she felt a large weight dip to her left. She didn't dare to look.

'That's enough, thanks.' She practically breathed the words. Praying he didn't choose this time to ask any more questions.

She didn't know how long she lay stiff, her mind racing. It was like this sometimes, during times of change. As if she had drunk a vat of caffeine and seven different streams of consciousness were battling for prime position in the forefront of her mind's eye. Couple that with sharing a close space with Xander's delicious scent and, well... She closed her eyes in frustration rather than hope, knowing she would not get any more sleep that night.

She could sense it, the moment his breathing deepened and sleep claimed him. A quick glance over her shoulder confirmed it, as his long eyelashes lay completely still at the top of his cheeks. It seemed there was nothing unattractive about him, as was evidenced by his strong patrician profile in the moonlight as Pandora tried and failed to drift off to sleep. She hadn't meant to stare at him, while she was tossing and turning, but she could only ever fall asleep on her left side, so therefore the only thing in her vision was his face.

He had such a touchable face.

She closed her eyes at the thought, feeling the urge rise within her to follow through on it, to reach out and touch his strong jaw, his sharply jutting cheekbones. This had always been a problem for her, going right back to her childhood. Much to the horror of her parents, their unruly daughter had once insisted on touching every single dish at a celebration buffet just to see what they all felt like.

Impulsivity, her father would check off on his mental list. Father seemed to be the only one who noticed all her quirks and kept a log of her progress over the years.

Mother was so busy with her career that she'd had no choice but to delegate the management of the daughter who'd needed so much extra time to her husband.

But when her brother had come along, with his inability to speak at all and his very obvious physical stimming and his wild mood swings… Well, no one had been able to ignore that. She had been twelve the first time she'd heard the word *autism* spoken, but it had not been in relation to herself. Her brother, Odin, had been three then, just started in preschool. Her own diagnosis had come more than a year later, and pretty soon family life had devolved into a series of appointments and progress charts.

Now, the only tracking of her own progress she did was trying to shave down her time on the treadmill. Running centred her mind and helped with her coordination. It was the only part of the intense therapies she'd endured that she elected to continue as an adult.

Regular movement was essential to her well-being, as was nurturing her other innate needs, even if they weren't exactly considered to be normal.

Whatever *normal* was supposed to be.

As her thoughts wandered, she became aware of a heavy weight sliding over her thigh. But rather than feeling threatened, she felt grounded and leaned into his touch, glorying when he covered her leg with his own completely.

She opened one eye, her breathing slow and deliberate and her heartbeat thundering in her ears. His face was still completely relaxed in sleep. But as she watched him, he moved again, a low moan escaping his lips. Pandora inhaled a deep breath, scandalised by the erotic noise and her own body's instant response to it. She should turn around, she told herself firmly and began to inch backwards, carefully trying to dislodge the heavy weight of his thigh.

Her progress was stopped by a firm male arm sliding around her waist.

'Stop moving, Quinn.'

The low rumble of his voice murmured against her hair, startling her. He was clearly still asleep, but Pandora instantly obeyed the command. She focused on steadying her own erratic breathing, inhaling the delicious scent of his lemon verbena soap. To her surprise, every muscle in her body began to relax, almost as though she were melting. She fought the urge not to groan in sheer delight.

She highly doubted that her convenient husband would be pleased to wake up and find himself wound around her so closely. She would just wait another couple of minutes until she was sure he was asleep, and then she would move him.

That was the last thought she had before sleep claimed her.

The morning was already well advanced outside the bedroom window when Xander felt his body snap to attention. Someone had been…moaning? He stilled, listening to the sound of heavy breathing for a long moment before he realised that the sound had come from his own chest.

He had been dreaming. He never dreamed. It had been so detailed, so intense… A fine sheen of sweat beaded his brow and his chest barrelled out with his still-fast breaths. He felt as if he'd just finished completing the erotic acts that had played out in his subconscious mind. He had taken Pandora gently at first, and then much harder until they were both loud and frantic with pleasure. The memory of it was enough to have all the blood in his body immediately rushing south.

Soft curves nestled firmly against his front from sternum to knee.

But worse, his erection was now pressed between the indentation of his new wife's deliciously toned buttocks.

He supposed waking up nestled into a soft, vanilla-scented female body without any chance of release would do that to a man. Even a female he didn't fully trust. Or did he?

Even if he was still suspicious of her behaviour in the safe, he was not so arrogant as to believe that she would deliberately engineer a situation that had them sharing a bed. He had seen her on the plane; she'd been vulnerable. And no matter how out of control his libido seemed to be around her soft curves, he would not be taking advantage of his new wife by seducing her.

He carefully backed away, managing to get off the bed and into the bathroom without waking her.

But even after showering vigorously, he still swore he could feel the heat of her against him.

She didn't wear the usual heavy exotic brands of perfume of the women he'd dated in the past. Her scent was lighter, almost like a breeze in a summer garden. He remembered her face as she had watched him emerge from the bathroom. If he had any doubts as to her level of sexual experience before, her stunned reaction had spoken volumes.

Pandora Quinn was not often in the presence of semi-nude men, he would bet his life on it.

Not that he had any business ruminating over her relationship history. But she was his wife for the next year, so didn't he deserve to know that he would not be made to look a fool in public from any romantic skeletons in her closet?

His own inability to remember whether or not he'd mentioned these terms to her suddenly seemed vitally important and took up much of his attention on the short drive to the Osaka headquarters of the Tanaka Corporation for his lunchtime meeting. The building had an older feel to it than the others on the streets of the upscale financial district, which was fitting considering the Tanaka family had been among the first families to set up their investment firms in Japan.

The Tanaka Corporation owned the entire building including an impressive top-floor jungle made of glass and wood, filled with exotic plants and solar lighting; it truly was the jewel of the city. He felt the familiar pull of longing, the urge to obtain it. This particular building was the main draw for him in buying them out. He had grand plans for what he would do with it, but first, he needed to clinch the final part of this deal in person.

The investors were already seated at the long table when he entered, and he felt the awareness of dozens of curious eyes upon him as he strode into the room. Ran Tanaka, oldest daughter of the family and a powerful businesswoman in her own right, had been their key contact over the past weeks as they'd tried to broker the extremely time-sensitive and urgent acquisition. Tanaka Corporation was sinking and needed a silent buyout fast in order to keep their historic image intact. It was a deal that Xander urgently needed to make if he wanted to be able to take a foothold in Japan, after decades of bad press and disrespectful moves by Zeus had previously shut them out.

He had expected a difficult summit meeting as both sides finalised the last of their demands, but what he hadn't expected was the atmosphere of sheer disdain when he arrived at the meeting alone, without his highly regarded EA in tow. It seemed that Pandora was a firm favourite, especially with Ran. The other woman's face noticeably dropped when Xander revealed their hasty nuptials and Pandora's sudden resignation from the office.

'She's far too talented to be cooped up in the tea rooms all day like a tourist, Xander. She was at the very heart of this deal and you've left her out.' The other woman sighed, then sat up straight as there was a hubbub out in the hallway.

A man burst into the room, his face wrinkled and worn, showing his ancient years. Hari Tanaka, the family's patriarch and former CEO, burst into the room, his gaze immediately landing on Xander, before launching into a speech that Xander was clueless to interpret. Maybe he should have swallowed his pride and his doubts, and brought Pandora with him regardless of what she'd been doing in Zeus's safe?

'He wants to know why you fired Pandora,' Ran said softly under her breath. 'He hears everything. Good grief, Xander, you do realise that girl was pretty much the only thing keeping this deal afloat.'

'Tell him that as the acting CEO of Mytikas Holdings, I am here to finalise the deal personally.' He pasted on a serene smile, only dropping it when everyone at the table remained stubbornly silent as Hari kept talking.

'He says that he cannot trust a man who loses his employees so easily and treats his wife so disrespectfully by leaving her alone on her honeymoon instead of bringing her.' Ran sat back in her chair, pinching the bridge of her nose. 'Especially considering the crimes we already hold your father accountable for. He too was well known for his disregard of honour and tradition.'

Xander stood up, feeling the tension within him soar. 'I am not my father.'

'That remains to be seen.' The old man stood up, switching into perfect English. A bad sign. 'We have received two other offers, lower than yours but from more reputable companies. Either of those would be preferable to doing business with you. We're done here.'

When Xander finally returned to the apartment after walking the streets for several hours deep in thought, Pandora was out on the balcony with her back to him, the evening light turning her hair into a halo around her shoulders. He made sure to clear his throat before sliding the door open, feeling a strange little twist in his abdomen when she turned. But she didn't smile at him in her usual sunny way; in fact, one look at the downset of her mouth and he knew that something was very wrong.

'How did the meeting go?' she asked flatly.

'Terribly, but why do I have a feeling you already know that?'

She grimaced, looking down at the phone in her hand. 'I just got off the phone with Ran Tanaka.'

Xander felt his blood pressure rise.

'Why is she calling you?'

She ignored his question, opening up her tablet to what looked like a presentation. He narrowed his gaze. 'Why do you have a copy of today's files? They're highly con-fidential.'

'Ran sent them over to me after you stormed out of their building in a rage.'

Xander scowled. 'Miss Tanaka should be directing any changes to me, not my wife, who she knows damn well is no longer working for my company.'

CHAPTER EIGHT

'XANDER, I'VE BEEN working on this deal alongside you for months now,' Pandora urged, walking to the opposite side of the balcony. The normally unflappable businessman she knew Xander to be was gone and she hardly recognised the man in his place. 'What was said to make you react this way?'

'Does it matter?' he growled. 'The Tanaka family are doing this on purpose to make me walk away from the deal. They've either got a better offer or they're trying to up the bidding.'

'Ran is opposed to her father's position. She still believes in your vision for the merger and called me to ask for my help in…handling you.'

She swore if Xander's brows flew up any further they'd go into orbit.

'*Handling* me? I am the acting CEO of this company.'

'And right now you are acting like a spoilt child.' Pandora placed her hands on her hips. 'Your previous approach in the boardroom will not work here, so if you don't want to lose this deal then you will need to change. Adapt.'

'I cannot believe this! The old man was supposed to have stepped down and left Ran in charge. That was the entire reason for my confidence in this whole—'

'Listen. You can sit here and throw a handsome-billionaire fit over the unfairness of it all, or you can listen to my plan.'

Xander scowled, leaning against the railing of the balcony, said handsome-billionaire jaw gleaming with the impressive beginnings of a silver five o'clock shadow. Pandora gulped, resisting the urge to move closer and run her fingers over that jawline; it looked razor sharp but she'd bet it was still soft to the touch. Realising her thoughts were wandering, she cleared her throat loudly and opened up the files Ran had already talked her through.

'Mr Tanaka has his heart set on the business remaining family-owned, even after the buyout. He's concerned for his employees and his children's futures. Ran believes that if you show him that you are not the lone wolf he has heard about, he will withdraw his objections.'

'He won't care what my family values are. I'm Zeus Mytikas's son and that's all he can see. He's already made up his mind about me.'

'You may share his bloodline, but you and I both know the similarities end there.' She frowned at how quickly he brushed off her words, at how determined he was to keep himself inside this box of his own making. Quaking a little, she stepped in front of the balcony doors, blocking him from retreating. 'Xander, most people see the world through their own selfish lens but you're different. I noticed it from the first moment we met. You have this aloof, self-possessed air and yet you care about every single person who works for you. You can try to deny it but… I've watched you.' She pressed her lips together, continuing when he didn't interrupt.

'You make people feel seen. You made me feel seen. You're on this mission to change all the bad things your father has done but you seem so determined not to look at the good that is already there. We need to show him that we are a team and that Mytikas Holdings also has strong family values. That we value tradition and honour, despite the bad blood that Zeus has stirred up over the last couple of decades.'

'How exactly am I supposed to do that?'

'By using your secret weapon, of course.' Pandora smiled, taking a theatrical curtsy. 'Ran has arranged for us to attend a grand reopening ceremony in Kyoto. It's the Tanaka family's home city and a very traditional event.'

He frowned. 'Appearing at an event won't turn the tables in our favour.'

'Of course not,' she agreed. 'But in the meantime, I'd like to temporarily resume working with you until the deal is done. Together, I think we can do this.'

She waited, holding her breath and worrying she'd overplayed her hand until, shockingly, Xander nodded in agreement. 'We could do with your eyes on it, I agree. I'll have you hired as a freelance translator.'

Freelance. The words rang in her mind all evening like a revelation as they ate take-out sushi side by side in the apartment's dining area and she got up to speed on what she'd missed from the meeting. Happiness filled her up, her mind whirring with the relief of having a problem to unpick once more. She was determined to show the Tanakas the true Xander Mytikas, the one he didn't even seem to know himself.

The following days were a blur of public appearances around Osaka to show their front of perfect coupledom. Late nights were spent hunched over market research and contracts while Xander crunched the numbers. The moment Ran heard that Pandora was now freelancing, she insisted on giving her a temporary office on the top floor of the Tanaka Corporation skyscraper, one that overlooked the city with fabulous views.

Apart from chatting during the select few appearances they made in public, she and Xander didn't speak much to one another, but every night he kept his promise and slept in her bed. Every night she struggled not to reach out and touch him, breaking their fragile truce. And every morning she woke up tangled in his arms for a brief few seconds of bliss before he rolled away.

If he was uncomfortable with their quiet working relationship or intimate nightly routine, he didn't show it. If anything, he seemed to seek her out more and more, arranging a quick private lunch for them in the ground-floor restaurant or asking her to grab some fresh air on one of the airy top-floor terrace areas. As far as the first week of a marriage went, she was pretty sure that theirs was rather unusual. But she felt…happy. Her mind was fulfilled and her nights were peaceful… If only she could get a handle on the rapidly growing feelings she was developing for her husband, everything would be rather perfect.

More than once Ran approached her quietly about hiring her skills for future projects, but Pandora always tactfully steered the conversation away. Xander might have labelled her as a freelance specialist, but she wasn't silly enough to believe that was true. He was just bolstering her ego to make her feel less useless, giving her a title so that his wife wasn't his official employee, but a loophole still existed to allow her to help him close this deal. Yet she discovered she didn't completely want to refuse Ran's tentative job offers and found herself pondering them more than once. But above all there was the small matter of her temporary billionaire husband and the intimidating shadow of the grand society wedding that she was set to return to. Followed by a year of playing the role of his wife…

Ran had assured her that if she wanted to work for the Tanaka Corporation, she could simply make a call. She was fast considering the other woman to be a kind of… friend. Friends had always been few and far between for her, with her childhood filled with travel and her adulthood tucked close under her family's anxiously caring influence. Perhaps a little too caring, she realised, now that she'd had time away from them all. Still, she made sure to send her dad regular photo updates and videos, pointedly leaving out the fact that she was in Japan with her husband.

There was no point in telling them of her hasty marriage just yet, she had already decided. She couldn't lie to the people she loved, yet she wasn't able to tell the truth without revealing all of it…so she'd decided to simply wait it out. She'd have to tell them before the big wedding, otherwise they'd probably see it in the world's media anyway, but she wouldn't expect them to travel so they could attend and, truthfully, she really didn't want them there. Family were for real weddings, not PR stunts, she reminded herself. If she had her father walk her down the aisle, her foolish mind might start actually believing that her fairy-tale wedding was true.

On their final day of new and improved negotiations, they broke new ground and she felt a buzz of excitement building in their small team. It was late in the evening when a large meeting was held on the top floor between Xander and the board of directors. Pandora wasn't allowed in and so she'd gone back to the apartment to wait, passing the time by sitting on the sofa in the living area with one of the small cross-stitching projects she'd brought with her. She was terrible at it, but it kept her hands busy.

Two whole hours had passed by the time Xander strode in, a huge smile on his face.

'We did it,' he announced, looking exhausted and elated and devastatingly handsome. Pandora stood from where she'd been anxiously awaiting the news, relief making her limbs heavy. She wasn't quite sure what the appropriate response was in this case, uncertainty pinning her feet in place as Xander continued to cross the room towards her. Without warning, he lifted her up against his chest and pressed his mouth to hers.

His kiss was hard and hot and filled with so much passion it quite literally took her breath away. But he pulled back almost as quickly as he'd started, a look of complete surprise on his face. 'I didn't mean for that to happen.'

'It's fine,' she said breathlessly, pursing her lips as Xander took a few steps away from her, leaving her body feeling cold.

'*Christos.* I just wanted to thank you.' He attempted to straighten his tie, then lost his patience and pulled it off completely. 'Just when I think I've pulled us back from dangerous territory...'

'It's only a kiss,' she said quietly, leaning against the arm of the sofa.

'We both know it's not. Do you regularly go around kissing people?'

'For me, dating and kissing are unavoidably connected.' She shrugged. 'I don't enjoy one, therefore I don't particularly engage in either.'

'You seemed to enjoy it with me.' Xander frowned, then froze. 'Pandora, are you telling me that I was...forcing myself on you?'

His last words came out slightly strangled and she moved forward quickly, placing a hand in the centre of his chest. 'Absolutely not! I enjoy your kisses, Xander. Probably more than I should.'

His gaze darkened. 'Good.'

'Is it?' she whispered. 'It doesn't feel good. It feels like…torture most of the time. I don't understand why all of a sudden I'm craving something that I've never particularly enjoyed before. Why it would suddenly become appealing with the one person who has made it very clear that he doesn't feel the same.'

She took a step back, feeling vulnerable and unsure of herself. This conversation felt strange, foreign to all their others. But, she supposed, they hadn't been sharing a bed before. As if she had just realised how thoroughly far apart this was from their sensible business arrangement.

'But then again, you're you,' she added, forcing a light laugh from her cold lips. 'We've come to know one another better, so maybe that's the difference. It makes sense that kissing you would feel safe.'

'Safe,' he repeated, the expression on his face dark and unreadable.

'What I mean is…' She scrambled for words. 'We have an agreement between us. There's no emotion involved, no feelings to hurt. It's simple.'

'Simple and safe.' He raised one brow. 'A man wouldn't want to have an ego to uphold around here.'

Xander prowled towards her so that a mere foot lay between them. 'There is nothing simple or safe about the way I feel right now, let me make that clear. If you could see the fantasies I've concocted in my mind…'

The air around them turned thick and heated and she was suddenly thankful for the privacy of their apartment.

'Tell me,' she breathed.

'I want to do more than tell you.' He leaned forward, his hand cupping the underside of her jaw.

Pandora felt the needy heat within her flare to boiling point just from that small contact. This was scandalous, what they were doing. It was wrong. Her eyes were glued to his lips, as though she were transfixed by him. Nothing new there then, she reminded herself. She had felt the inexorable pull towards this man from the moment they'd first met.

But when he was her boss, the line between wrong and right had been very black and white back then, so keeping him at arm's length had been an easy decision.

Xander Mytikas would never have done something so wrong as kiss his plain little assistant. He had been her boss. She had been off-limits.

But that line had been erased and the one that separated them now seemed faded and broken and easily stepped over.

She met his eyes, their cerulean blue filling her with fizzy warmth, and she almost felt the urge to run. But then he slid an arm around her and held her, her chest pressed so deliciously against his. She took her time staring at the perfect square angles of his jaw and how it met the curve of his ear surrounded by jet-black close-cropped hair liberally speckled with grey, which made him even sexier in her eyes.

All week, she had resisted the urge to run her fingers through his hair. She had despised herself for the impulse that constantly nagged at her awareness whenever he leaned closer over the boardroom table and ran his hand through it as he thought over a particularly difficult point of the negotiation.

She had promised herself that she was strong enough to withstand this pull she felt towards him. She had not banked on the fact that he might feel it towards her too.

Feeling bold, she reached up to the nape of his neck and

splayed her fingers through his hair, centimetre by delicious centimetre. It was cool to the touch but smooth as silk, just as she remembered from the last time she'd had her fingers in it. She knew exactly what Xander smelled like. She had been unable to remove the memory of him and his delicious scent from her mind.

And yet it felt right somehow. As if she had always known how it would feel to touch him so intimately. He didn't move to stop her when her other hand moved up the side of his neck to glide along the stubble on his jaw.

'You're stroking me.' He growled huskily, leaning into her touch.

Even though they were alone with no possible reason to be playing their parts, she was plagued with uncertainty. She didn't want that darkness in his eyes to be fake. She wanted that darkness to be hers alone, a result of his powerful attraction to her. An attraction that they both felt.

Feeling foolish, she slowly slid her hands back to rest on his shoulders.

'I wasn't asking you to stop.' Xander took her hands in his and laced her fingers under his own at the back of his neck. He leaned down and pressed his lips against the side of her neck and all thoughts exited her mind.

He murmured something to himself under his breath. His eyes closing as if on a prayer. *'Months.'*

She heard the last word clearly, considering it was growled against her skin like a curse. She felt the vibration of it, of him, as though she'd absorbed it into her. He stilled, breathing heavily, and she could feel the hesitation in him. But he didn't move to back away, if anything he leaned further into the delicious embrace of their bodies.

Pandora felt vulnerable and powerful all at once with the way Xander's hooded gaze roved over every inch of her body. The top two buttons of her white shirt were undone, her lacy bra peeking out.

'I wanted you from the first moment I laid eyes on you. I'm no better than Zeus.'

She reached up, cupping both hands around his face and feeling the heat of his skin under her fingertips. 'I wanted you too. You're nothing like him, Xander. I'm not your employee any more. I'm your wife.'

The word seemed to light a fire in him and before she could think, he was spreading her legs wide and stepping into the space between them, all the better to undress her...

Xander looked at the dazed expression on Pandora's face and fought the urge to kiss her again, hard and fast. Thinking she might not be ready for that just yet, he settled for bending down and laying a series of hot wet kisses along her naked midriff, tracing a slow path upwards until once again they were on an even eye level.

She was shy without her clothes, not quite meeting his eyes and, *Christos*, if it didn't drive him even more wild. He shrugged off his suit jacket and pulled at the shirt on his back, hearing the pop of a few buttons and the ping as they hit the floor. He didn't care, only pausing long enough to pull it off the rest of the way.

Pandora looked up at him and her eyes traced over his naked chest with slow intensity, her mouth opening to form a little O shape.

'You're so perfect,' she whispered.

Xander paused, looking down to find her eyes filled with such raw desire he thought he might come on the spot. When she touched the rippling muscles on his abdomen, he felt himself shudder. What was she doing to him?

Breathing heavily, he grasped her wandering hand and

took it captive, holding it above her head while he finally leaned down to claim her mouth. She gave back as good as she got, holding onto his grip with her other hand and digging her nails in ever so slightly. That hint of pain was enough to tip him over the edge of his control.

His heart pounded in his ears like a war cry, his body demanding the satisfaction of conquering this beautiful, lush bounty. Something pushed against the walls of his subconscious, warning him to hold back, to take a moment, but then her hands moved to grip his waist, pulling him to her, and his body reacted instantly, pulsing forward against her soft core.

Christos.

Too much fabric, his mind roared, and he reached down for the zip of his trousers, fighting the urge to rip them off completely. She joined the frenzy, both of them pulling at his clothing until finally his skin was just as bare as hers. Then he was on her once more, pressing her back onto the sofa and coming over her to lie chest to chest, skin against skin. She opened her mouth to speak but he was already kissing her again, already sinking his free hand into her hair and laying claim to her as their bodies moved against one another with building urgency.

He communicated with each writhing thrust against her thighs that there was no time for words, no time for anything but the primal force beating between them, demanding more. There was no time for anything but this. He had to have her, right here, right now.

He pulled back from the kiss, reaching down to grip the hard, hot length that sat heavy and aching. Biting his lip, he touched his thumb against her molten core, feeling the heat of her coating his skin. Pandora was looking at his erection and, again, the expression of wonder and sheer lust on her face damn near undid him.

'Don't look at me like that. I want this to last.'

'Wait,' she said softly. 'Do you have protection?'

The air seemed to leave his lungs on a single, punishing exhalation and Xander felt his entire world shudder to a grounding stop at that simple question. His mind came crashing back online with stunning focus, taking stock of what they had just been about to do. What Xander had been about to do.

'Xander?'

He heard her voice but he was unable to speak, to look up, for fear of his own reaction. He felt her gentle hands on his chest in a silent question and it was too much, it was all too much right then. He stood up, feeling the cool air hit the raging inferno of his body, and it took all his strength not to just lie back down and continue. With every step he took away from her, his body roared with outrage, his heartbeat pounding in his ears.

The bathroom light felt like a white-hot laser, piercing the haze of lust. He slammed the door behind him, not trusting himself if she decided to follow him.

He felt wild and depraved, holding onto his sanity by the barest thread, and that realisation made his heart race even more. This never happened to him, never. He never lost sight of this part of him, this deep-rooted need he had to be in control all the time. Furious, he slammed his hand down on the marble countertop, feeling pain shoot upwards into his wrist. Ignoring the pain, he slammed it down once more, as though daring his own body to defy him any more than it just had.

He had been ready to plunge himself into her without protection, without any care for the consequences. This arrangement, this marriage…it had got so far under his skin he felt as if someone had reached into his soul and stirred wildly so that every deep, dark part of him had risen to the surface.

It wasn't her fault. And yet, inexplicably, he resented her for it, for being the catalyst that made him feel this way. For a split second he felt the urge to demand that she leave, that he remove the problem at its source, the temptation that was Pandora Quinn. But as he looked at himself in the mirror, imagining the look on her face as he sent her away, he felt himself resist and he knew with absolute certainty that the problem would not disappear just because his wife was no longer within arm's reach.

He wanted to roar his frustration at all of it, every damn thing that bound him and tightened the constraints of being Zeus Mytikas's son. But instead he ran cold water over his sore fist for a few minutes, and then walked back out into the living area.

Pandora sat on the sofa, her body mostly shielded by a red silk throw blanket, but still he ached for her. He pushed the feeling away, pushed everything down until all he felt was cool, hard focus as he reached for his trousers and pulled them on. Pain lanced through his knuckles but he ignored it, his only care focused upon the silent woman studiously avoiding his gaze.

'That can't happen again, Pandora.' He spoke with a remoteness that stunned even him. He saw her flinch ever so slightly and hated himself for it. But instead of responding she simply stood up and grappled silently with the throw, trying not to show any more naked skin than she had to. She walked past him without another look, her chin held high, not stopping until she reached the door of her bedroom. He saw the rise and fall of her shoulders in the moonlight as she inhaled a deep breath, blonde hair shimmering as she shook her head ever so slowly.

'I was wrong.' She looked back over her shoulder. 'You

are the furthest thing from safe for me. And there is nothing simple about this attraction between us. I'll try harder to remember that.'

He took a step towards her, needing to explain to her why this was the only option for him. Why this attraction between them could only spell disaster for them both... but Pandora raised her hand to stop him, warning him without words to stay away.

So he did.

Xander didn't come to their bed that night, and she told herself she was relieved.

Pandora sat for a long time, staring out at the bright lights of the cityscape until dawn broke, her thoughts an unbearable vortex of confusion. Confusion over how they had allowed things to go so far so quickly. How she had been so close to making love with a man she had vowed to remain professional with. How she had adored every single minute of it and felt a kind of comfort and connection she had never thought she'd ever feel. And pleasure... so much pleasure.

She felt the uncomfortable clench of chaos whirling within her. There was no work to occupy her mind now. For all the euphoria they'd felt yesterday in winning the contract, she hadn't really processed the fact that, in doing so, she had now completed her temporary freelance contract with Xander. They would travel to Kyoto this evening for the reopening ceremony that the Tanaka family had invited them to, and then tomorrow their 'business trip slash honeymoon' would be over and they would return to New York... Return to whatever came next in this charade of a marriage.

She decided that she would forgo her usual morning run on the treadmill in the building's world-class gym if it meant she could avoid seeing her husband and having to face the fallout of the disaster that was the night before. She needed to get out of this apartment right now. If he woke up and wanted to talk…she knew she would just crumble. Anger fuelled her once more, stiffening her movements as she pulled on her favourite skinny jeans and T-shirt, her feet stumbling slightly in her haste as she stepped into her boots.

He made absolutely no sense. One minute he was hot and heavy, ready to plunge into her, and the next he had practically run from the room. Yes, they had almost forgotten to use protection, but she had remembered in time. There was no risk, no danger. And yet he'd behaved so harshly, returning to the room as though nothing had happened between them, and calmly informed her that there would be no repeat performance.

She closed her eyes, wondering how on earth she was supposed to survive twelve more months of playing Xander's dutiful wife when this first week already had her at the limits of her control.

CHAPTER NINE

If Xander had been slightly worried at Pandora's ability to perform in light of last night's events, all his concerns had been eased within the first five minutes of their entry into the beautiful gardens where the reopening ceremony was being held.

He looked down at the woman by his side, her delicate porcelain features serene and polite as she conversed easily in Japanese with one of the senior board members of the Tanaka Corporation. His own Japanese was basic and reduced simply to greetings and culturally appropriate words of congratulations or commiserations as he needed in the boardroom. Switching between his native Greek and English was usually enough to stretch his tolerance.

Pandora looked up at him, a slight frown marring her brow when she leaned in ever so slightly, increasing the pressure of her fingers where they rested on his forearm. The movement sent a jolt of electricity through him.

She really needed to stop touching him.

All these small gestures, guiding him, whispering the names of various contacts just before they stood in front of them, offering to get him a drink. She was no more acting like his wife than he was acting like her husband.

The need to confirm to this entire gathering that Pandora was his, in the most primitive sense of the word, consumed him. But he was not the same out-of-control brute he had been the night before so he resisted it. Their marriage was not a tool that he could use to his advantage in the current situation. So why then did he feel such an urge to claim her here, to wipe away the polite façade that she had presented in her perfectly pressed black dress and her tight sensible chignon? Why did anything about her professional conduct all day bother him so badly?

Wasn't it exactly what he had asked for?

It wasn't long before the Tanaka family arrived, finally gracing them with their presence with their usual lack of fanfare, and he was swept into conversation after conversation about the deal they had just made.

'My congratulations again on your excellent choice of bride,' Ran said quietly, drawing him to one side as they watched the festivities. 'I truly believed that you would never find another woman to live up to me.'

'Our time together never leaves my thoughts.' Xander smiled at his own joke, enjoying Ran's sly reference to their single, solitary date a couple of years previously. 'If you ever need my assistance again in that regard, you have my number.'

'You're a married man, behave yourself.' She laughed, smacking at his arm.

A small shuffle sounded from behind them, derailing their conversation while a waiter cleared up someone's spilled drink. Xander took the opportunity to scan the area, finally finding his wife on the path ahead, Hari Tanaka chatting away happily by her side.

'You're happy with her.' Ran smiled. 'I suppose it was a good thing that your brother stole your first bride.'

His gaze snapped up. 'You know about that, then?'

'Everyone knows about that. Their marriage is public knowledge, is it not?'

Xander froze. Eros and Priya had got married? It hadn't been public knowledge last time he'd checked in with his team in New York, but with the time difference, perhaps he'd been off his game. Ran moved away to chat with other guests but Xander stayed put, brooding.

Being made a fool of was the one certain way to strike through his infamous glacial control. And even now, surrounded by the elite of Japanese society, he felt his boyhood temper flare, the old talk of sibling rivalry drawing him down into the primal core of himself that he had fought for years to suppress.

Pandora's stomach clenched, cold seeping into her bones as she moved quickly away from the private conversation between Xander and Ran that she'd accidentally overheard. She swept through the gardens, her polite smile in place as she inspected the exterior of the shrine, finally coming to a stop on a beautiful red bridge surrounded by tall maple trees. It was quieter here, with most guests mingling nearer to where a fire show was being set up for the evening's entertainment.

Her thoughts swirled darkly as she thought of Xander with the beautiful Tanaka heiress, imagining them together. Why hadn't he told her that they had been an item? Why hadn't Ran told her?

A dark echo of some painful emotion bobbed to the surface within her as she wondered…had they agreed to keep her in the dark together? An uncomfortable emotion made her insides prick up in a strange way, one that in all the months they had known one another she had never felt before. Xander had hurt her.

And for all the giddy excitement she had felt being in this beautiful place, surrounded by such affluence and history, she suddenly felt like the small child at the playground who had absolutely no idea what was going on but was fairly sure that she was the butt of the joke.

It wasn't long before she heard footsteps intruding on her solitude; she turned and found Xander looking painfully handsome.

She tensed, immediately moving a scant few inches away from him. She couldn't think with him touching her. She couldn't breathe.

Suddenly, she felt utterly ridiculous.

'You and Ran seem to be hitting it off nicely,' she said evenly, hoping that her voice held none of the tight emotion that had begun to creep into her chest. They might not have discussed dating other people as part of their marriage agreement, but she was under no illusion that a man like Xander wouldn't be flooded with attention from potential suitors.

Plus, she liked Ran.

'Is that a problem?' He was assessing her face curiously, tension tightening the hand now curved around her elbow.

'Of course not,' she blurted. 'You're a very popular, handsome man in your prime.'

'And you deem that relevant to our current situation, how?'

'Xander, I would simply rather know when you would prefer me to slip away. For appearances' sake, perhaps a higher level of discretion may be needed, but we can always arrange for separate rooms if you're…entertaining someone.'

His eyes widened, a sudden flaring of his nostrils that startled her. Again, his fingers flexed against her bare skin, and her treacherous body responded with an equally sudden shiver of pleasure at the firm contact and she pulled away. She really needed to stop doing that.

Someone touched her elbow unexpectedly and she turned to see Ran smiling by her side. Reflexively she took a step back, her balance shifting unexpectedly. For a long moment, the swathe of beautiful red and orange maples surrounding them seemed to tip and she felt herself falling.

Strong arms caught her and she looked up into Xander's serious gaze. How on earth had he moved so quickly?

Ran's worried voice came from nearby. 'Are you okay?'

Great, Pandora thought wryly, if she hadn't already been the object of their pity before she certainly was now. She could feel the familiar sensation of her social battery beginning to crash, and like Cinderella she suddenly needed to run away, she needed to get out of here before her internal clock struck midnight and she made an even bigger fool of herself than she already had.

But just as she was poised to make some dull excuse and leave her husband to enjoy the rest of the event without her, she felt a familiar warmth settle around her waist. Almost like a dream, she heard Xander make a polite excuse to Ran that they would be leaving early and, just like that, he began propelling her towards the exit.

Pandora followed in a daze until they stood at the bottom of the steep stairs and Xander dipped his head towards her.

'Where is the driver?' He scowled with obvious annoyance. He altered their course, pulling her slowly in his wake. Slowly...he was walking so slowly and carefully, holding her tight as though she might break.

'Stop.' She tripped a little as she removed her arm from his gentle clutches. 'I don't expect you to...mind me. I'm not a child.'

'No, you're not. You're my wife and you're clearly exhausted. Forgive me if I don't want to see you endure a full evening of discomfort when we can easily leave early.'

'But you were enjoying yourself with Ran,' she said, feeling more and more like a petulant child.

Realisation seemed to dawn on him, his lips pressing together. Their driver arrived and Xander herded her into the car, his large body sliding onto the seat beside her. He waited a few moments before he spoke. 'So you overheard my conversation with Ran Tanaka and immediately jumped to the conclusion that I was arranging a… romantic interlude with her.'

'I don't know what you were arranging. It doesn't matter, does it? While I'm quite annoyed with both of you for keeping your personal history a secret, I understand that it's not quite my business.'

Xander turned towards her, one arm sliding along the seat behind her head. 'You are my wife. I'd argue that it's exactly your business.'

Fear and excitement mingled in her blood, making her lose track of her words. Why did he have to affect her like this?

'I helped Ran out, a couple of years back. She needed a handsome date on her arm to make someone else jealous. She's only ever been a friend.' He emphasised the last word softly.

Pandora processed his words slowly, feeling relief and embarrassment war within her chest. 'I've made a mess of tonight, Xander, I'm sorry. Just, please go back and enjoy the rest of the event. I can go back to Osaka alone.'

'You're tired and we are newly-weds, so it's hardly suspicious for us to duck out of an event early.' He sat back in his seat, staring out at the passing lights. 'We're not going back to Osaka. I've arranged for accommodations here.'

Pandora paused, puzzling over the sudden change in plans. 'Why?'

His jaw tightened and he looked strangely self-conscious for a moment. 'Our flight back to New York isn't until tomorrow afternoon and I have no further meetings planned. You said you'd never seen Kyoto. I didn't want you to come all this way and miss out.'

The honest kindness in his words made her throat clench and she barely managed to utter a thank you before her words left her entirely. Why did he have to keep acting so perfectly? The car moved through the ancient city quietly, no more words passing between them. Their driver expertly navigated them through a set of tall wrought-iron gates and wove them uphill, through an avenue of tall maples.

Dusk had fallen, the lights of Kyoto shining in the distance now as they rounded a bend and a beautiful house came into view. It was breathtaking, a mixture of traditional Japanese design and stark modern lines. It was silent and serene as they made their way up the stone steps, the sound of running water coming faintly from nearby.

But once they were inside, alone, Xander turned to her.

'I've been honest with you tonight. I've trusted you with this deal and yet it seems you're determined not to trust me. In my experience, those who seek out lies are usually the ones hiding something themselves. I think it's time you told me the truth, don't you?'

She felt her anxiety begin to rise and swell once more. He had been honest with her about Ran, even when she'd thought the worst of him. And yet she continued to keep a secret from him that she knew he deserved to know. She trusted him enough to know that he wouldn't punish her in the way that she'd once feared. And yet, she'd still resisted, not wanting to see the look in his eyes when he found out her true deception.

'I know about Titan Corp,' she said on a rush of breath.

CHAPTER TEN

XANDER FROZE, HIS eyes narrowing to slits. 'Explain.'

'I know that you're planning to stage a hostile takeover of Mytikas Holdings once you've accumulated enough shares. I know this because... Zeus told me. He used me... to spy on you and report back.'

'How long?' he gritted out.

'From the moment you arrived in New York he told me that I would be used to get secrets from you. But I promise, I only ever told him the bare minimum I could get away with. He was blackmailing me to work for him.'

'What? How?' Xander looked appalled.

'The first night we met, I was at that gala as a guest with my mother. I had no idea who you were, or who Zeus was to you. You and I never exchanged second names. I'd just had an argument with my mother, I'd overheard her arguing with Zeus and realised that she'd lied about the true nature of our trip to the States. Zeus was holding something over her and was trying to call in a favour, but...she couldn't do whatever he wanted.'

She forced the words past her lips in a rush, knowing that if she stopped, if she so much as looked at him, she would lose her nerve. But still, she could feel his eyes on her.

'Zeus said he had evidence of whatever she'd done, so

to get it back, I agreed to work for him. Initially because I had the language skills he urgently needed, and then, after he became ill, he instructed me to spy on you for him. The evidence he had against my mother was what I was looking for in the safe that day of your and Priya's wedding. It was supposed to have been in the file I bargained with you for.'

'Supposed to be? So it wasn't inside?'

Pandora felt her bottom lip quiver, remembering that night when she'd got home and pulled open the file only to find it empty. Not a single scandalous picture or damning email to be found. She'd contemplated calling her mother, but then she would have had to reveal her own bargain with Xander.

'It must have been truly important information, for your mother to sacrifice you into a bargain with a man like Zeus.' His tone was filled with anger. She looked up and was shocked to see barely constrained rage in his eyes.

'My mother refused to allow me to do it, actually. She has always been overprotective of me, my father too. Maybe that was why I defied her orders and insisted that I could handle it.' She could still see the older man towering above her mother, hear him threaten her. 'That night set something off within me, it spurred a need I'd long ignored to take control and prove myself. To show that I was capable of protecting her too.

'You helped me to see that, you know,' she said softly. 'In the midst of it all, before Zeus sought me out once more and made his bargain… I met you. I realised that I wanted more from my life than what I had living in Ireland. You made me realise that I wanted more. I should have known then. It's not normal to have such thoughts about a complete stranger.'

'What kind of thoughts?' he rasped, stepping closer.

'Because they couldn't be any more scandalous than the ones that I've harboured.'

'You…you have?'

'Months,' he whispered. 'Months of remembering that night and wondering what might have happened if we hadn't been interrupted. Months of resisting you and despising him for placing you in front of me. I'm sorry that he used you against me this way. I'm sorry that he deceived you and your mother. Zeus…he knew exactly what he was doing.' The last sentence was a growl, wrought from him.

'Why were you so cold towards me these last four months? Did you believe that I sought you out at the gala deliberately?'

'I was furious with myself. It's no secret that I am the product of my own father's lack of control around his employees. I'd never had a whiff of scandal with anyone who was even remotely subordinate to me. And then there you were, the biggest walking temptation that I'd ever encountered.'

She swallowed the knot of emotion forming in her throat and tried to focus past the pool of longing building within her. With sudden clarity, she knew that if they gave in to the madness again, this time, there would be no stopping either of them.

She wanted to make love with him more than she wanted to breathe. Her body hurt from trying to hold herself together, from trying to deny the raw primal need that filled her every time his body was close. But it was more than just wanting a warm male body against her own; she wanted him. She wanted Xander. And for that reason she took a deep breath and spoke, knowing he might walk away but needing to take that risk.

'I can't pretend that I'm not affected by you, Xander,'

she said, pushing herself to get the words out. 'It's just not the way I'm wired.'

He'd warned her not to expect anything from this marriage. Especially not love. So she needed to keep guarding her heart for all she was worth if she wanted to survive the next twelve months.

'You think that I'm not affected by you?' he asked.

'I have no idea what you think or feel, you are the most infuriating puzzle I have ever encountered and yet… I just keep wanting to push you. To try to unravel that iron-clad control of yours…to see what's underneath that mask you wear for the world. To show what is underneath my own.'

'Is this what you wished I would do?' He pulled her closer. 'You wanted me to take control, to be the demanding boss of your fantasies?'

'Yes,' she breathed, not even caring how crazed she sounded.

'*Christos*… I can barely look at you without wanting to pull you away to the nearest hard surface whether it's a bed or a floor…or a wall.'

'Or a desk?' she suggested.

He groaned, his hands on her face and in her hair, and his mouth sought out hers. She was instinctively sinking into the kiss before she had the sense to pull back.

'This can't be normal, feeling this way. I'm going to combust,' she heard herself say.

'I'm in control here, remember. And, Pandora, this is not normal for me either.'

She felt the hard, hot evidence of his arousal pressing below her belly button, branding her with molten heat. His lips sought the soft flesh beneath her ear, his tongue tracing a slow path along the sensitive lobe that made her shiver. She felt that pull, that delicious fire threatening to burn again and swallow her whole…but she resisted. She needed to get her thoughts out of her head before they took this any further past the invisible line they had already drawn in the sand. Because sexual arousal faded and she had agreed to stay married to him, to stand by his side as his wife for the next year.

Suddenly, what they were doing seemed utterly ridiculous.

She pulled back in the circle of his arms but he kept his hold on her hips, flexing his fingers slightly and sending little bites of sensation through her.

'There's a reason why I don't just sleep with every woman who catches my attention, Pandora.' His voice was like gravel, his eyes dark with intensity. 'I've never even come close to breaking my own rules. Until you…'

She closed her eyes at his words, resisting the warm sensation they evoked deep in her core. A sensation that felt perilously close to hope. That was the one emotion that she had promised herself she would not unleash on their arrangement, no matter what happened between them.

'I've spent four months controlling myself for every moment that I was in your presence.' Xander frowned, running one finger down the centre of her chest, making her shiver. The wide muscular span of his hands came to rest under her ribcage and she felt deliciously caged in, held together by the firm pressure.

'I need to know that you won't regret this in the morning. That if we take this one night for ourselves, we can live with it,' she said. One night would have to be enough. Risking more was to risk a shattered heart.

'One night?' he teased, pulling her closer, fisting one hand through her hair with a touch that managed to be both sensual and deliciously firm all at once. 'Do you deliberately set these limitations, knowing that I am a man who always wants more?'

'I'm serious.' She met his eyes with every ounce of steel she could muster, considering his touch had turned her entire body into a writhing mess. 'It's important to me.'

'One night,' he repeated, his voice as dark as molasses, taunting her resolve and screaming at her to take back the terms. To take as much as she could get of him and his dominant sensuality. To give herself up to him and be damned to the consequences.

But she knew herself too well. She knew how deeply her feelings could run and how quickly that could get a girl like her in trouble. She was too soft for a man like him, she was too trusting. If he gave her an inch of his affection, she would be powerless not to hold out hope for more…and more…

She deserved more than that. Maybe some day she would get it, although she wasn't holding out any hope it would be Xander who gave it to her. But until then, one night with Xander was her own gift to herself. One night of making the bad choice for once in her life, of being selfish and taking what she wanted and dealing with the consequences later. One night…before reality came crashing back down and she remembered all the reasons why this was a terrible idea.

She ran her tongue along her bottom lip and watched as his gaze locked on the movement. She loved how he looked at her, how his gaze tracked her and seemed to home in on every slight shift in her mood. And whatever he saw in her right now seemed to affect him instantly.

Taking her by the hand, he led her up to one of the beautiful master bedrooms, where, sure enough, their luggage had been delivered and put away. She was so busy admiring the view of Kyoto from the terrace windows, she hardly noticed Xander's arms snaking around her waist until he had lifted her and deposited her in the centre of the giant bed. He crawled over her, keeping most of his weight on his forearms, but still she felt the weight of him pressing her down into the soft silk sheets.

But when he gently trailed a finger down her face, she stiffened, her body flinching against the unpleasant sensation.

He paused, and her heart melted a little at the flash of concern in silent question in the furrow between his brows. But how on earth was she supposed to tell him that she needed a firmer touch without it sounding vaguely kinky? She shook her head, determined to just let the moment pass and focus on the delicious sensation of his mouth moving ever closer to the hyper-sensitive skin at the tips of her breasts. But she was forgetting that this wasn't just any man kissing her, this was Xander.

He touched her jaw, again too softly, but there was a hint of steel in his voice that made her shiver. 'If I'm doing something you don't like, tell me.'

She felt the breath whoosh from her lungs at that simple command. And it most definitely was a command.

'I prefer a firm touch,' she admitted.

'Like this?' he asked, his eyes following the path of his fingers as he applied a little more pressure.

Her answer was a low moan and he smiled, his lips filled with pure masculine satisfaction. 'I'm a perfectionist,' he murmured. 'And that trait applies both in and outside the boardroom. I'm going to figure out exactly what you like in bed, Pandora. And then I want to do it over and over again until you can't think any more...just feel.'

'I like...your hand here,' she murmured, shocking herself by placing her own hand on top of his. She closed her eyes, fighting the urge to groan at the pleasure of being touched by him this way. Just his touch… God, she was in so much trouble.

She drowned in the onslaught of pure sensation as Xander kept one hand on her neck and kissed a slow path down into the valley between her breasts. He didn't kiss her breasts so much as he devoured them, slow and steady and with devastating precision. He held her in place as he licked and sucked each throbbing pink tip in turn and she found she was utterly powerless to look away. She felt herself grow even more aroused, imagining watching him do that somewhere else on her needy body. Imagining taking hold of his thick hair and guiding him to where she needed his mouth even more urgently.

She felt herself throb, her body begging for more. Begging for him. But still, she held back. A part of her not fully giving over to the pleasure she was feeling, a part of her still staying on alert just in case she did something wrong.

The thought made her close her eyes suddenly. She would not second-guess herself now. But her body insisted and she was powerless against the urge to switch off.

Xander murmured soothing words against her skin, but the sensations dimmed and her heartbeat slowed a little, as though her subconscious had flipped a dimmer switch. She felt him pause, heard him say her name twice before she remembered to react.

'You with me?' His words were part concern, part rough demand and something about the intensity in his gaze seemed to pull her back from the brink, reminding her that she was not with anyone else. She was with him. Xander.

Almost as though he'd heard her inner struggle, he moved up over her, caging her in with his big muscular body, anchoring her down to the earth once more. She felt her body relax and finally she looked up, her gaze immediately pinned by twin flames of electric blue.

'Just...kiss me,' she whispered and she was relieved when he immediately claimed her mouth, hard and fast.

She breathed into the kiss, into the glorious sensation of having Xander's body on hers, pushing her down. She felt her own body awaken once more, her thighs clamping tightly around his hips so that she could move against him. The taste of him on her tongue like honey, so sweet she couldn't get enough. She wanted to devour him.

He pulled away slowly and to her own embarrassment she let out a little growl, her body rising up to follow him, protesting against the loss of heat.

'There you are.' His smile was pure sin, his eyes dark mirrors of the wild desire she felt thrumming within her own chest. When he began undoing the zip of her dress, she helped him, their fingers a messy tangle of urgency. She laughed out loud when he gave up on decency and pulled it open the rest of the way with his teeth. He laughed too.

She marvelled at the fact that she was able to find humour in such an intimate moment and wondered if that was usual for a one-night deal. Maybe it was. She had always imagined a one-night stand to be something fast and thoughtless but this...this felt so right. The urge to ponder that pulled at her but she pushed it away, focusing her attention down to the fine point of contact between her abdomen and his hands. She watched him, watched his dark head lower as he peeled open the edges of her dress slowly, his big hands spreading over every inch of bare skin. She writhed, pleasure drugging her as his lips continued their slow descent along each part of her body he exposed.

'This dress has tortured me all evening. I can't count

the times I have imagined doing this, unwrapping you like a mouth-watering delicacy.'

'You make me sound like candy,' she murmured, her breath catching as he paused just above the centre of her, shoving the skirt of her dress up above where her body pulsated and begged the most.

His eyes met hers for a split second, his pupils dark with desire as he drew her silk panties down her legs and his lips touched her core with the barest featherlight kiss. Then another. When his tongue joined in, she thought she might actually pass out from the pleasure. But he kept his hands firmly on hers, pressing down into her hips as he continued to devour her with relentless precision.

She felt the pressure building within her like an earthquake, small ripples followed by larger ones until she could feel her spine draw tight as a bowstring. It was too much and yet not quite enough, and the anticipation was such a beautiful torture she feared she might actually faint. Xander paused, looking up at her like a dark angel with his lips parted and glistening.

'Show me what you need, Pandora.'

To her own shock she felt herself reach down one trembling hand to touch his jaw, moving him just the tiniest fraction to one side where the pleasure was deeper and more intense.

'Yes.' He murmured approvingly against her. 'Show me, *agape mou*. Let me get you there.'

She felt her release build again, this time with an intensity that had her body rising like a wave. He held her tight, keeping her steady as she finally cried out and shook with each blissful tremor and aftershock. When she finally stilled, he lifted his head, a look of victory on his face that shouted primal male satisfaction.

'The condoms are in my bag,' he purred, nibbling at her earlobe, sending shivers of excitement down her spine.

'Oh…' she murmured. *'Oh…'* Realisation dawning, she blushed. She'd almost forgotten again. The shoulders of her dress had already been pulled down, leaving her breasts exposed. With one quick pull, it finally landed in a pool of silk on the floor next to the bed.

She lay there completely naked, and his gaze drank her in. His face showed appreciation as only a man could. It made her blush but she made no attempt to hide herself. What was the point when he'd already had his mouth all over her?

Xander could hardly contain his need. Gone was the shy, reserved Pandora he once knew, leaving in her place this vixen who seemed determined to drive him utterly wild.

Her eyes were a mirror of his own, blazing with fire and need.

'Now.' Her whisper was urgent, said between shallow gasps for breath.

He needed no further encouragement. Pressing her down onto the bed with his body, he quickly removed the rest of his clothing before reaching down into his bag on the floor for protection.

He moved himself inside her in one slow thrust. They both moaned with relief from the final joining of their two bodies. He stayed still for a moment, afraid to break the sensation of pure pleasure coursing through him.

Her hips moved against him, her thighs spreading further apart, and he sank into her more deeply, beginning a rhythm of pleasure that was driving him higher and higher. Her body was all around him, suffocating him with need. Moving his head down, he sucked one hard nipple into his mouth. She gasped, a mixture of pleasure and pain, pulling him deeper inside her, wanting more.

His breath was laboured now, he couldn't hold on much longer. He could feel his stomach clenching. His balls tightening, ready to explode.

'Come for me...' she whispered throatily.

That was all it took, suddenly he was over the edge, exploding in a pleasure so delicious he could feel it in the tips of his toes. His body convulsed with the efforts of his orgasm and she ground her hips underneath him, drawing out his pleasure as she reached her own. He fell down beside her, drawing her into his arms, out of breath and elated from his release.

Pandora sat in the Kyoto house looking out of the window the following morning. Silence enveloped her and she instinctively wrapped her arms around her knees. They were flying back home from Osaka later today, once Xander returned from wherever he'd gone while she was still asleep. She looked at her watch. They were going to miss their flight slot if he didn't come back soon.

The morning outside was grey, a light drizzle making the mountains look as if they were gradually disappearing into the clouds. She wasn't sure how long she stayed in that position, staring out into nothing.

What would things look like once they were back in New York? Would he even speak to her unless it was for an event? The thought of their wedding looming, the ever-growing guest list she'd seen him scrolling through... Her stomach lurched. She felt shaky and off balance and she knew exactly who was to blame. Xander Mytikas had done nothing but unsettle her delicate equilibrium from the moment they'd met and she didn't just mean in the physical sense.

She'd never had a one-night stand in her entire life, the very idea of it went against everything she'd always thought she'd require in order to enjoy sex. But with Xander, it hadn't felt like a one-night stand at all. It had felt like finally walking through the right door after months of wandering around completely lost in the wilderness. It had felt like coming home.

She shook off that dangerous thought, knowing nothing good could come of it. In the end, she had simply taken what he'd been willing to give and they both knew it was the smartest choice. But a tiny part of her wished she had resisted, wished she didn't know what it felt like to have his lips on hers and his body stretching her own to its limits. She wished she were still wondering, unknowing, because she now knew that knowledge wasn't always power. She had never felt so utterly powerless in her life. She glanced at her watch again. It looked as if she might be flying back solo. She'd better get ready to leave.

But when she walked down the steps of the house with her suitcase, it was to see Xander's powerful form striding towards her.

'I had a few loose ends to tidy up with Ran Tanaka.' Xander frowned down at her suitcase. 'Where are you going? I was hoping you'd still be sleeping.'

'You weren't there when I woke up,' Pandora heard herself say, her voice flat as she continued to stare past his left shoulder. 'I thought perhaps you had decided on a clean break. No hard feelings. So I decided to head back to Osaka to catch the flight.'

'You thought I'd spent the night making love to you more times than either of us can remember and then just leave you to return to New York by yourself?' His eyes turned grave and serious as he reached for her hand.

Pandora took a step back, knowing if he touched her...

especially if he touched her with the same kindness she could see in his eyes…she would be lost. She wanted to walk away from this impulsive, reckless mistake with her dignity intact, a feat that would be entirely impossible to achieve if she gave in to the wild impulse she had to simply throw herself into his arms.

But it seemed she didn't need to do that, because before she'd had a moment to react he had closed the space between them. His chest was almost flush against hers, his eyes bearing down upon her in a way that strangely reminded her of his angry office death glare. Was he planning to fire her as his wife already? Had he decided that winning his inheritance wasn't enough of a reason to endure her presence for the next twelve months?

'I never planned for us to sleep together in the first place and we both know it's probably a terrible idea to keep tempting fate, but clearly we are both completely unable to exhibit any self-control,' he said.

'Speak for yourself. I could totally stop any time I wanted to,' she retorted, lying for all she was worth.

His gaze turned gentle. 'I thought we might stay in Japan a little longer.'

Stay. The word was like a war cry within her, lighting up all the darkness that had begun to encroach. It seemed too good to be true, him asking her to stay and it meaning exactly what she wanted it to mean. 'For how long?'

'I don't actually need to be back in New York until next week for a board meeting. They can do without me until then. I haven't taken a vacation from the company in three years.'

'That's it, you just want a break?'

'I think we both deserve it, don't you? Consider it a celebration of our expansion. We can pass it off as wanting to extend our honeymoon. We are supposed to be madly in love, after all.'

Pass it off. Of course, they were still playing a part, weren't they? He was still thinking of how this would look to his board. How he could use it, spin it to his best advantage. His simple words hit her hard, making her almost accidentally reveal all her messy feelings in one terrible tide of truth. He wanted her, at least for now. And, God…she wanted him too. But still she held back, needing to protect herself.

'It has to be just for this week. Promise me, Xander.' Her body practically hummed like a tuning fork, struck boneless with desire for this impossible magnetic force of a man. But she needed to know exactly where the boundary was here, or her mind would ruminate endlessly over the possibilities. She'd lose herself in this, in him, unless she had a clear idea of what they were doing.

'I promise. I'm not looking for anything more,' he murmured softly against her earlobe, biting down to seal their deal.

He was her drug, there was absolutely no doubt about that. And she knew with absolute certainty that she would take whatever she could get of him while she could, and to hell with the consequences. She would deal with them later.

CHAPTER ELEVEN

THE ADVENTURE THAT Xander had planned turned out to begin with a full day exploring the wonders of Kyoto, followed by their arrival at a private train, which was to be their home for the next five nights. The car was the height of luxury, usually only available to eight individual guest parties with a minimum of a two-year waiting list for the privilege. Of course, Xander had managed to buy out the entire train for their own private use for the week with hardly any notice at all.

They had a private chef and a small staff, each of whom were an absolute delight in creating the most perfect authentic Japanese experience while they travelled along the famous Seto Inland Sea, taking in the most beautiful sights. Their bedroom had a wall of one-way glass that expanded almost across the ceiling and Xander had made quick time in getting them alone so that he could make love to her while the countryside passed by.

On their penultimate day, they stopped at Miyajima Itsukushima, a mountainous island covered in the most glorious shades of red and orange maple trees that were renowned across the country. It was a little like travelling back in time, Pandora mused as she watched a group of children walk ahead of them in school uniforms. No traffic lights guided the roads, only patience and courtesy.

Even with the tourists there, it was still quiet enough to hear the breeze rustle the leaves and the birds chirping above. It was also home to a great many deer, which they found out when one almost trampled Pandora as she became too distracted looking up at the trees.

Xander simply tightened his hold on her, not admonishing her for her carelessness, which she appreciated. It still confused her how his caring touch and attentive gestures didn't feel like being minded. Of course, that was exactly what he was doing, minding her. But it didn't feel bad. It felt different, somehow.

Like how he had draped a blanket over her the night before when she'd fallen asleep while reading. Or when he had taken her by the hand and led her to the viewing deck for a romantic dessert date while the sun began to set. Or when he had made sure to leave her an extra vegetable gyoza at lunch today, because he instinctively knew that they were her favourite. Not to mention his selflessness and impeccable instincts in the bedroom…

Shaking off heated thoughts of the previous night, she focused on finding her footing on the uneven path and tried to recentre her sex-addled brain. But admitting the definite increase in the number of times that her husband had begun to feature in her thoughts and dreams didn't change the fact that Xander was still Xander.

He had made his position on their relationship quite clear right from the start, and she had been perfectly happy to take one week of mindless pleasure. She was fully prepared to return to New York afterwards and play the role she'd originally been assigned to.

They walked in silence along the path, wind rustling the trees all around them. Until finally they reached steep steps, rising above them like a mountain. By the time they reached the famous temple, a fine sheen of sweat had broken out all over her body but she felt strangely exhilarated. Knowing Xander was beside her had made her feel confident enough to simply push her own limits. Not once had she panicked or felt the urge to retreat.

But knowing that his strength had such an effect on her made that prickle of emotion in her heart burn all the more and she found she couldn't quite look at him without feeling the urge to throw herself into his arms.

Thankfully, Xander distracted her from such messy inappropriate impulses by launching into his knowledge of the shrine's history. In true Xander form, he had collated some research at some point before they'd left that morning, most likely while she'd been sleeping. They were such opposites in so many ways and yet when he eagerly explained the basics of the Shinto faith and the emperor who had chosen Miyajima as a sacred place, she couldn't help but be fascinated too.

His thirst for knowledge made him the perfect tour guide, but she liked to think that she took some of the edge off his controlling ways with her slightly silly questions and requests for off-path explorations. Where she was a little chaotic and distracted, Xander was observant and organised, and she had absolute faith that they would not get lost so long as he was in command. It was strange, trusting someone so blindly.

Even as a teenager travelling with her parents, she had always felt a level of anxiety that urged her to remain behind, to not relax too much. With Xander, she felt free. She felt as if she could let her mind wander and allow herself to truly embrace the scenery, knowing that he would be right there by her side to nudge her if she missed a step.

Now that she had experienced travelling with him by her side this way, she had no idea what life would be like without him. She imagined all her grand plans, travelling the world and being spontaneous… And it all just seemed so colourless.

Once their year was up, they would probably never see one another again. The thought hit her with such jarring force her footing wavered and she stumbled slightly. Xander caught her, of course. He had an uncanny talent for saving her from falling flat on her face. But suddenly, his touch on her elbow was too much. She found herself lagging behind as they explored, keeping a little more distance between them.

Just because they had decided to take this week to explore the sexual connection between them, didn't mean that he had suddenly changed his outlook on relationships, and she seriously needed to remind herself of that.

She was a grown woman, she reassured herself with a steely determination. She was not so weak that she would fall to pieces over a short fling with her temporary husband, right?

As they walked back down to the small sandy beach near the harbour, Pandora ignored the puzzled looks that Xander threw her way. She knew she was being too quiet. She could feel his curious gaze on her and see the puzzled look on his handsome face. But how could she even begin to explain why words were too much? Why she suddenly felt so sensitive and vulnerable?

She had got too comfortable, she realised. She had begun to sink into his strength like a balm, and that was something she simply could not afford to get used to. Fear of the unknown had always been a huge trigger for her, but, strangely, knowing exactly when this entanglement would end was far more of a torture.

She wasn't supposed to become attached. She had promised him that this short fling was exactly what she wanted. Maybe in the beginning, she had believed it herself too. But now, there was no denying the fact that it was going to destroy her when he gave her what she'd asked for. She hadn't even been in love with her first boyfriend when he'd broken up with her and she'd still struggled for a couple of weeks. Forming successful intimate relationships was a complex and intense process for her and so, naturally, the ending of such attachments was equally hard.

But she had survived being dumped by that weasel Cormac Nally, hadn't she? She'd picked up her pieces and moved to New York City, for goodness' sake, even if it had taken being blackmailed by Zeus to get her there. Maybe once this year was up and their divorce was finalised, she could move back to Japan for a while. She had become a rather seasoned traveller...almost. Okay, so she might still need a chaperone to avoid being trampled by the occasional sacred deer.

But she'd be fine.

She paused at a low wall, staring out at the calm sea as the evening began to darken. The light breeze soothed her skin and cooled her heated cheeks as she tried to calm herself. Her heart was beating a little too fast, her breath hurting a little as she exhaled on one long gust of breath.

Almost as though he sensed the emotional distance she was busy building between them, Xander moved closer. Strong arms enveloped her with warmth as the wind blew her hair around her face.

A confusing cocktail of emotions began to swirl in her chest, taking her completely by surprise. The term *heartache* had always seemed so ridiculous to her, and yet if it had been possible to feel actual pain in that vital organ she'd bet that this was what it would have felt like. Her chest squeezed with pressure, her throat dry and aching as she hid her face in the front of his sweater.

She breathed in, inhaling the scent of his cologne and skin as though she could use it to cement this memory in her mind for ever. Because she knew with sudden clarity that eventually memories would be all that she had left of their time together.

'You've gone quiet on me,' he murmured, his lips pressed against the side of her temple.

When she didn't immediately respond, he moved back a couple of inches, gently tipping her chin up to search her face. 'Hi.'

'Hello,' she responded, forcing an easy smile to her lips.

'Everything okay?'

'I'm feeling a little...off balance,' she said, shocking herself with the truth of her words. Surprised that she hadn't felt the need to lie to placate his feelings. Even more evidence that this relationship was more than anything she had ever thought a connection with another person could be. But, she supposed, she hadn't actually voiced that development to Xander. So she inhaled a deep breath and braced for the inevitable set-down.

'The past few days, it's been like living in a romantic comedy movie montage. The food and the laughter. It's been amazing, but I know that once we go back to New York... Once this truce is over, we go back to reality and I'm worried we'll go back to being...what we were.'

'You mean, you wonder if I'll go back to the way I was?' he asked perceptively, his hands still on her, not breaking contact. 'The cold, aloof, removed bastard of a boss.'

'I've never seen you as cold.'

'I was a bit of a bastard, though?' He raised one brow.

Pandora felt a rush of laughter bubble up into her throat, despite the seriousness of the feelings swirling within her.

'Perhaps just a bit.' She smiled, biting down on her

lower lip as he leaned forward and nipped her jaw playfully with his teeth. She turned her face away, feeling a little whiplash from his swift change from intimacy to humour.

For a long time, no words were spoken and yet his hands remained on hers as the sunlight began to wane and the ferry moved smoothly across the water. She felt the tiredness creep into her bones as they journeyed in silence through the twilight back to the railway station.

The staff greeted them with warm smiles and hot tea upon arrival. Their private carriage had been freshly cleaned and candles had been lit in preparation for another beautiful starlight supper. A light array of snacks had also been laid out on the dining table, including fresh fruits and sweet cakes. But Pandora had no appetite at all. Suddenly she felt the weight of her decision to enter into this brief affair with Xander descending upon her, with all the impossible consequences that she hadn't foreseen. She had thought she could be spontaneous and carefree, although she should have known better.

When Xander excused himself to take a call, she jumped at the chance to escape to the bathroom, splashing some cool water on her wrists and face. She didn't know how long she stood there, staring at her own reflection and trying to calm her erratic heartbeat but when she exited into the bedroom, Xander sat on the end of the bed, waiting for her.

'I just needed to get changed,' she said quickly, brushing her hair behind her ears and hoping that he didn't see the evidence of the tears she'd shed. But one look into his eyes and she knew that he'd seen.

'There's more to it than that,' Xander murmured. '*Agape mou*…talk to me.'

She closed her eyes at the endearment, knowing just

enough Greek now to know what it meant. But she was not his love. She would never be his love.

She felt the final wall crumble within her and she met his gaze, her voice a breathy shiver.

'Maybe I'm just inexperienced, but I have no idea how people can share a bed for a week and then go back to normal. This kind of wild sexual abandon isn't normal for me.'

'This isn't normal for me either.' He paused, an uncharacteristic hesitation and hitch in his breath, and when he looked up at her she caught a glimpse of vulnerability in his expression that shocked her to her core. 'I knew that there was chemistry between us, but it's becoming quite the addiction.'

He stood quickly, reaching her in quick strides, and she felt his large hands cupping her cheeks. The single, solemn *'Quinn'* that he murmured against her temple was almost more than she could bear.

'Could you stop being so wonderful?' She swallowed past the lump in her throat and placed a playful punch on his biceps. 'Otherwise, when we get back to New York, I don't know how I'm going to be in a room with you and not want to climb you like a tree.'

A dark look entered his eyes for a split second, then it was gone and he was stepping closer and pulling her against him. He growled her name against the tender skin of her neck, lifting her tighter against him. Their bodies melted into one another like twin flames, and for a moment Pandora felt a little frightened by the intensity of it. The intensity of the passion that seemed to consume her every time he was near. It somehow managed to feel like too much and not enough, never enough.

She would never be free of him.

She closed her eyes and felt a single tear escape her lid,

trailing down to fall into his silky salt and pepper hair. He didn't notice, he was too far gone as he licked and laved a trail down between her breasts. He lowered to his knees on the floor before her, his large hands a dark contrast against her pale hips as he pressed her back against the door of the cabin.

'Let me help?' He quirked one dark brow, his expression one of pure sin as he leaned in to press a single kiss against her lower abdomen.

Pandora shivered, her body melting into his caress. His hands were firm as he held her in place, taking one of her knees and hooking it carefully over his shoulder. The train was moving fast now, the world spinning past them in a blur. She closed her eyes as his mouth found its target and began to work, spiralling scorching hot pleasure along her limbs.

Even with her thoughts racing, her release came with shocking speed; the only thing stopping her from falling to the ground was Xander's strong arms holding her up. When she risked a glance downwards, he was watching her, his expression one she had never seen before. She felt the urge to cover herself or move away from that look, from the vulnerable and shaky feeling it evoked within her.

Time and time again this man had intimated that he was incapable of caring for others or falling in love, just like his father. But the way he cared for her, the way he made love to her... The way he was looking at her right now as he lifted her into his arms and carried her across the room to place her carefully on the bed... He murmured something unintelligible in Greek, pressing his face to her hair and inhaling deeply. The action seemed shockingly intimate, even in light of the many other, more scandalous things they had done together in the past week. She suddenly wished she had put more effort into learning his native language.

Of course, her first experience of falling in love would be with a man determined to keep her at arm's length. She closed her eyes in despair. She'd tried to protect herself, but it was far too late for that now. What had happened in Japan was going to have to stay in Japan. It was what she'd insisted on, after all.

'What's wrong?' Xander asked as he drew back and looked at her face.

'I've broken your rule,' she said simply.

Xander stilled, almost afraid to take another breath until she clarified that point.

'Broken my rule, how?' he heard himself say, his body still and unmoving on the large bed. Pandora stood up, folding her arms over her chest and walking over to the window. The world whizzed by in a blur of red leaves and blue skies but Xander's gaze was glued to Pandora's face and the whirlwind of emotions passing through it one by one until she finally closed her eyes.

Not liking being blocked out, he stood up before he could even remind himself of all the reasons why he didn't really want to push her for an answer. Why he should leave her to compose herself and they could brush over her misstep and pretend it hadn't happened.

'I'm not just addicted to this, Xander. I'm...' She shook her head, swallowing hard before she turned back to face him. 'I'm in love with you.'

'No, you're *not*,' he responded, the reflexive answer escaping his lips before he had a chance to catch himself. He'd seen her wince at his words, seen the pain on her face even as she closed her eyes against it.

'Is it really so impossible to believe?' she asked. She

shook her head, her eyes meeting his for the briefest seconds, before sliding away. 'I've…never said that to anyone before.'

His thoughts were consumed by the need to pull her back to him, to demand that they moved past this conversation and all the jagged edges it unleashed within him. Moments ago, they had been wrapped in one another—how had it come to this?

'I don't understand you,' she said. 'You have let Zeus take so much from you. He is dead, Xander, and yet you still use your fear of being like him to keep everyone at arm's length. I believe that your actions with Eros were not done out of selfishness, but of love. You don't have to keep shutting everyone out, Xander.'

He shook his head, words failing him as he reached for her. He would just kiss her, he decided. He would kiss away these doubts and remind her of what was good between them, what could still be good…

'No.' She pushed his hand away. Steel laced that single word, her shoulders squaring, shutting him out further.

Xander froze, his arm slowly dropping back to his side.

'I can't keep doing this. I will play my part when we return to New York,' she continued as he remained silent. 'But what has happened here in Japan between us… will stay here.'

'Is that what you want?' he finally gritted out. 'That we leave it like this?'

'I'm still technically your wife for the next year. Did you expect me to just keep sleeping with you indefinitely?' She swallowed, her lower lip trembling. 'This is how it needs to end. I'm ending it.'

He looked up at the ceiling, rage threatening to consume him. He wasn't capable of returning her feelings, whatever she said. He'd never been cut out for relationships, he was too selfish, too cold and focused on growing his empire. He had seen what loving his father had done to his own mother, to most of the women Zeus had ever been with. To take Pandora's love would be to doom her to a life of heartbreak. She deserved somebody more worthy of her love than him, maybe someone closer to her own age.

Of course, she was right that this should end now, but he wasn't ready to do without the pleasure they'd found in each other's arms just yet. If that made him totally selfish, then so be it. He'd had nearly a week of making love to her, of waking up to her face each morning. This...infatuation should have begun to feel less intense by now.

He'd never had much willpower when it came to the things he enjoyed most and Pandora Quinn had become the most delectable dessert to his starved, sugar-crazed palate. But truthfully, he knew that if the choice was his... he wouldn't end it until they were both in ruins and she hated him for not being enough for her, for being unable to love her back the way she deserved.

So in the end, he simply nodded once, his own pride forcing him to walk away, even as hurt crossed her beautiful face.

CHAPTER TWELVE

PANDORA WINCED, STRUGGLING for the third time to comprehend what the handsome make-up artist was saying to her. The younger man frowned, looking over at his assistant with a thinly veiled exasperation. But just when she thought she was about to receive another snarky comment, the younger man directed his gaze at the woman who was blow-drying her hair to within an inch of its life. He made a small gesture towards the hairstylist and all at once the incessant noise in the room seemed to dip and Pandora let out a heaving sigh of relief.

Her thoughts had been a swirling vortex of anxiety all day. All contact with her husband over the past week since their return to New York had been limited to a few wedding-related email updates. He'd left every morning before she woke and not returned home until well after midnight. She should be glad that dealing with his brothers and the inheritance was taking up his time and giving them space in the aftermath of her mortifying declaration of unrequited love. She should be busying herself with her own plans to accept Ran's job offer once the wedding was over. But she couldn't stop herself from growing steadily more annoyed with Xander's ice-man demeanour, wanting to poke at him like a child at an anthill. If she'd thought he'd been difficult before, when he had simply been her boss…that was nothing compared to the intense way she caught him staring at her every time they had the misfortune of being together in the same room.

On one such occasion, she'd got into the elevator to attend her final dress fitting only to have him step in at the last moment. The tension on the long ride down to the ground floor from his penthouse had been almost unbearable. He'd asked her how she was doing with the wedding preparations and she'd responded honestly that she was feeling quite overwhelmed. He'd nodded, but said nothing more.

He had looked tired, and she'd longed to reach out and brush the hair from his brow. But she'd remained still and calm, both of them silent for the rest of the journey out to their separate chauffeur-driven cars.

The next day, she'd been assigned a virtual assistant to filter out the remaining calls and tasks that she could read through and confirm or amend via email. Other than today's final hair and make-up trial, she had nothing left to do other than show up on the day. There were no social events or dinners, no reason for her to stand by Xander's side and play the part of his adoring wife. She should be relieved he'd taken the pressure off, she realised. In a way, it felt strangely close to being cared for, though she knew that wasn't his intention. He was likely just trying to ensure there were no more embarrassing moments or public arguments to put the illusion of his perfect marriage in jeopardy.

Her thoughts were so busy, she almost didn't hear the huddled conversation going on between the make-up artist and hairstylist in the background.

'We can't both work on her at the same time, it will be too much for her,' the woman said, then winced. 'Poor girl is probably already uncomfortable.'

Pandora stiffened, no stranger to that particular tone of pity in the woman's voice and the answering dismissal in the other. They were discussing her as if she weren't here...as if she were a subject to pity and handle. That was it, she was being handled.

After experiencing the easy acceptance of her autism from people like Xander and Ran, the contrast was so glaringly obvious it made her grit her teeth, fuelling her determination as she turned in her swivel chair to pin the two beautiful people with her iciest glare. She smiled, of course, the kind of polite smile she'd seen Xander use in the past. He'd been the one to teach her that the strongest weapon she held was her integrity, after all.

And so she set them straight, grateful when they apologised and actually listened when she explained why it was inappropriate to assume things about her abilities or sensitivities.

'I'm so sorry.' The blonde looked embarrassed. 'My little nephew is autistic too, so I just presumed...'

'It's fine.'

It wasn't, really, but the woman looked so uncomfortable that Pandora just wanted to end the awkward moment. She almost didn't notice the most troubling part of the entire interaction was that the stylist had been acting this way from the moment she'd arrived, long before she might have noticed anything that might have tipped her off. She'd already known Pandora was autistic. How?

Frowning, she turned back and asked the question aloud, seeing the other woman's face tighten with discomfort.

'Oh. It was mentioned in the article that was posted the other day.'

'What article?' Pandora felt something sink and tighten

within her, like that moment when a plane lost turbulence and you dropped a couple of metres mid-air.

The two stylists looked at each other, and one of them picked up her slim tablet, tapping the screen a few times with her sharp red-tipped nails. Click, click, click. Pandora felt her teeth grinding against one another in the back of her jaw as she waited, her body filling with tension with each passing moment.

The tablet was placed on her lap and she looked down at a perfectly polished image of her own face smiling eagerly up into Xander's. She remembered that day at the gala, remembered her own nerves at being so close to him for the first time. She remembered how short and clipped he had been and wondered if he'd felt it too, even then. Of course, he'd admitted as much, hadn't he? He'd said he'd struggled to control his own reaction to her ever since that first night. But, of course, he'd also admitted that to her while they'd been in Japan. And all confidences of that nature had to be left behind there, as per their agreement…

Shaking her head, she refocused, scrolling down past the cover photo to the large headline that simply said *Heir of Zeus*. The article wasn't from a respectable business publication, but another magazine entirely and began with a heavy focus on Xander's handling of Mytikas Holdings in the face of his father's illness and passing. They mentioned Zeus as a powerful man but spoke nothing of his shady dealings, instead painting Xander as a rags-to-riches opportunist who had landed on his feet thanks purely to his gold-digging mother.

She lifted her hand to the lump of emotion that had formed in her throat, knowing the truth behind Xander's parentage and how it had affected him. She hated this article, hated whoever had written such thinly veiled words of jealousy and hate.

But then her eyes caught on her own name in the next paragraph and as she scrolled down another picture emerged. A picture of herself sitting at the formal dance held during her final year in university.

She told herself not to read any more, but still her finger pushed the text up, revealing a final paragraph containing details that were apparently sourced from 'someone close to the bride'.

...daughter of Irish senator Rosaline Quinn...gifted with languages...troubled teenage years...quirky and scatterbrained...autism spectrum disorder...

The final line of the paragraph questioned if Miss Quinn was built for the life of a society bride, and if Xander Mytikas was taking advantage of his meek, delicate secretary just as his own father had allegedly done numerous times with his own subordinates. Pandora closed the tab, feeling nausea swirl in her stomach and a slight rushing sound in her ears.

She was still sitting in the living room an hour later, in the exact same spot, when Xander returned from work. The penthouse apartment was silent and dark, and it took him a moment before he saw her. When he did, he rushed over, kneeling down on the carpet beside her where she'd been staring at her own picture in the terrible article.

'I was hoping you hadn't seen it yet.' He sighed, then seemed to debate for a moment before wrapping his arms around her. It was the first time they'd touched in several days, ever since they'd returned from Japan, and yet it felt like weeks.

As she relaxed against him, feeling the familiar heat of his lips tracing a path from her neck to her shoulder, she felt a surge of emotion catch her by surprise, tightening her throat.

When exactly had she begun to feel as if the world wasn't quite right if he wasn't nearby? It was a dangerous way to think, considering he would most definitely not be a permanent fixture in her life.

Her thoughts closed in on the sensual moment like a dark cloud on a rainy day, tightening a coil of anxiety within her that Xander proceeded to kiss away with his usual deftness. His eyes locked on hers for a split second and her breath caught with the intensity of feeling just looking at him stirred within her. She wanted to reach up and pull his face down to hers and kiss him until neither of them could breathe.

She wanted to kiss and lick every inch of his glorious body and memorise every line like her own personal map. As if she were a magnet and he had somehow become her true north. Fighting off the surge of anxiety over her whirling thoughts, she turned in the circle of his arms and sought his mouth, revelling in the deep groan that rumbled in his chest as their lips finally made contact.

Her kiss was not gentle. She felt his surprise as he gripped her waist, attempting to hold her to him and guide her rhythm but she refused. She needed to be the one in control right now. If they had nothing else, they at least had this wild sensual connection and she wanted a taste of being the one in the driver's seat of that runaway train for once.

As they flung off their clothes, she told herself she wanted to use him, to just take what she wanted like all the other modern, independent women. But even as she slid down upon his hard length and felt her body open to accept him, she knew she was only fooling herself. She still wanted so much more. The realisation only served to spur her on further, as if she might drive away the pain of her thoughts by riding him faster.

Xander reached up, holding her face in his hands, tethering her to him as he took control. His pace turned slower and deeper and as he thrust upwards he told her in a hoarse voice how beautiful she was. How wild she made him feel. How he could make love to her for hours. Words and phrases that made her foolish heart throb with longing.

She pushed the emotions down and focused on driving them both towards the peak. Xander's guttural moan of his impending climax was like a flip switch, shutting off all coherent thought. Her own orgasm was a full body quake that seemed to shatter her from the inside out. If she'd thought the lump in her throat had been hard to fight back, the sensation in her chest at that moment was almost more than she could bear.

Pandora awoke a while later to find Xander sitting up on the side of the bed, where they'd moved for a second round of passionate sex, his head in his hands, the picture of a man tortured. The sight of him made her sit up, covering herself reflexively.

'I wasn't going to apologise,' he growled. 'But I'm not a complete bastard, despite my previous actions. I've treated you badly, and you deserve better.'

'Yes, I do,' she agreed, satisfied when his eyes dropped to the ground. Let him feel some tiny bit of the pain he was causing her, causing both of them, by being completely closed off to what was so obvious to her. He might believe himself incapable of love and he might have very good reasons for believing that, but it was only fear holding him back. And if he wanted to badly enough, he could overcome that.

'I can't be what you need, Quinn.'

The use of her old nickname jarred her, poking a little hole in her fragile heart. Quinn again. She opened her mouth to reply, but the sky above them chose that exact moment to let out a rumble of thunder followed by a sharp flash that lit up his face.

Apparently he remembered how much she hated storms like this because he instantly reached out and took hold of her elbow, anchoring her. The gesture was so small and yet it touched her fragile heart, reminding her of all the other micro acts of care he seemed to perform reflexively. Damn, even when she was determined to hate this man he made it utterly impossible.

'You were apologising,' she breathed, cradling her own arms around herself and moving backwards on the bed to avoid her own impulse to lean into his touch. Or worse, to hug him. She wasn't sure how that would feel more intimate than the things they'd shared with one another already, but hugs had always seemed like the height of intimacy to her. Hugs were for family, close friends or lovers, none of which qualified as anything close to whatever she and Xander were to one another now.

'You made it clear that we were done when we left Japan. But when I walked in and saw you hurting like that...' He ran a hand over his unshaven jawline. 'I should have had more control.'

'I was a willing participant, Xander. Don't worry about it.'

Before she could fully break down, she strode into the en suite bathroom, locking the door behind her. She took more time than usual in the shower, refusing to cry as she washed her hair. When she eventually emerged into the bedroom, fully dressed once more, he was gone.

Not quite a professional relationship but a far cry from a true marriage—they seemed to have become stuck somewhere in between. She'd always hated grey areas, but that seemed the only logical way to categorise it. They were frozen, halfway between darkness and light. But no matter what way she looked at it, everything had changed between them most irrevocably.

Suddenly the idea of staying in this apartment for the next week, just waiting for her grand wedding, was like a slowly tightening noose. She should have accepted the job offer from Ran. If she had, maybe now she'd feel a bit more purpose and a bit less alone. The loneliness of being Xander's wife was suddenly more than she could bear. They were only a few weeks into their marriage— could she really survive an entire year feeling this way?

Allowing her impulse free rein, she clicked open her phone and started a video call, feeling butterflies swoop and flutter in her stomach. She closed her eyes, twirling the bracelets on her left wrist as the call connected and Ran's perfectly made-up face appeared on screen.

'I want to take the job,' Pandora said quickly, knowing she needed to get the words out and stay in control of the storm about to break inside her. 'If it's still on offer.'

'Of course it's still on offer. I always get what I want.' Ran smiled, triumphant.

Pandora tried to smile, but felt it go wrong. Her face seemed to crumble, her lips wobbling and her eyes filling with embarrassing tears. It was humiliating that Ran wanted her more than Xander did right now.

Ran frowned, peering closer at the screen. 'What happened?'

'I'm fine.' She shook her head and gasped, feeling her chest shudder. 'I'll be fine… I just needed to call you. You said if I changed my mind, I could take the job. I was thinking I could start working remotely. I just need… something.'

'I can do better than just something.' Ran sat up straight. 'The Tanaka jet's in New York. I'll have them wait for you and you can fly out first thing tomorrow.'

It was only once the arrangements had been made and she was left alone in the silence once again that she crumbled and felt herself break.

CHAPTER THIRTEEN

XANDER BARKED ONE final order at his chief operating officer and pressed the button for the privacy glass that surrounded his office. The replacement translator had made a couple of crucial mistakes on the final contracts for the Tanaka deal and it had created a twenty-four-hour panic to rectify before it was officially announced to the press yesterday.

After a morning of media interviews where he'd dodged question after question about his wife and her whereabouts, he was once again feeling the urge to hit the gym and punch things. A full week of arguments and subtle attempts at sabotage by the mutinous board over his actions in Japan had exhausted him, but, no matter how tired he was from eighteen-hour days, the minute he lay down, his thoughts always returned to Pandora.

He hadn't spoken to her since she had walked away from him that night in his penthouse. She'd sent him an email early the next morning informing him of her plans to leave for the job in Japan, but by the time he'd got out of the emergency board meeting, Ran Tanaka's jet had already been flying high above the clouds. Not that he would have stopped her, of course. Besides the fact that she had no personal commitments in New York, she had

every right to want her space from him. He had been nothing but distant from her since Japan.

Her decision to end their liaison had been logical, of
course, but tell that to the dark part of him who didn't give
a damn if their agreement was jeopardised. Her confession of love had scorched him to his bones, making him
tighten his hold on her as though he could reshape her feelings into something less dangerous through sheer force
of will. But in not responding in kind, he'd hurt her even
more deeply than he'd realised.

He leaned back in his chair, closing his eyes at the infuriating reminder that this distance between them was
not only necessary but essential. He'd just had his own
things moved to Zeus's town house, where he would stay
for the remainder of their marriage. It was only eleven
more months…after which point she would be free to go.
Free to move on and find someone more in touch with
their humanity. Someone who wasn't a workaholic with
a grouchy temper and an inability to fall in love.

The image of his wife with another man suddenly had
him standing up on his feet and contemplating heading up
to the office gym to assault a punching bag. He inhaled
deeply, pacing to the windows on stiff legs, and stared out
at the dark clouds gathering above the city.

He had spent the past week rushing through his days at
the office, unfocused and irritable with his new assistant
as he'd counted down the days to today when she would
return for their rehearsal dinner. Tonight, they would hold
a small dinner and then tomorrow was the larger event.
But now, knowing that she was only an hour away at
their Hamptons venue waiting for him…he felt nothing
but unease.

He'd seen glimpses of her exploring Tokyo through pe-
riodic checks of Ran Tanaka's very popular public social

media feed. She looked happy and bright, far from appearing to be experiencing the same dark irritability he'd been subjecting his own staff to in her absence. Seeing her clear bond with her new friend, he was jealous. The guilt assailed him when he thought of his initial reaction to her job offer and how he had wanted to convince her to turn it down. He hadn't outright demanded that she return to New York to be by his side, but he'd wanted to. He'd wanted to convince her to stay with him, in his bed, wrapped around him.

And so he had stalked the corridors of his office like a coward, knowing that if he didn't keep himself busy, he'd do something stupid. Such as follow her to Japan and beg her to come home. He'd learnt long ago that it was always better to maintain control of such situations and avoid weakness. Pandora Quinn was most definitely a weakness to him, no matter how much something inside him railed against the thought.

He growled under his breath, twirling his wedding ring around on his finger. This break apart was exactly what they had both needed. Things had got too intense in Japan, too…domestic. He had become entirely too comfortable waking up alongside her every morning, working together, exploring together. Was it any wonder that things had gone as far as they had?

With his workaholic tendencies and impatient nature, he had long ago decided that he had no interest in a family of his own. A choice that had only cemented in his mind as he learned of the devastation his father had wrought on the women in his life. Pandora's words haunted him, her perceptive comment that he used his father's evil misdeeds to reinforce the wall he had built around himself and push people away. But she was wrong about his reasons for doing so; he wasn't protecting himself, he was protecting her. He was giving her a chance to truly find happiness with someone who truly deserved her love.

With distance would come clarity for them both…and sanity.

But today was the day she had returned, tonight would be their wedding rehearsal and tomorrow he would stand in front of a crowd of people he barely knew and cement his position as one of them. Their wedding guest list included politicians, actors, even a couple of well-known rock stars. It was the kind of PR power move that he had long dreamed of.

The elite events team he'd hired had planned the weddings of royalty but still Xander had ensured certain accommodations were made for his bride. The team had been discreet and thorough, even arranging for a full run-through of the ceremony before the event itself.

Pandora had assured him that she was prepared for the pressures of such a large event and despite his own reservations he knew she would be. So why then did he suddenly wish they had planned something smaller? Something more intimate? Something…real.

The thought jarred him, making him rock back on his feet for a split second. He knew the terms of their marriage. He had set them, after all. They both knew what this was and what it could not be. Why then did he have the sneaking feeling that he had decided, in his usual way, that she somehow had become his?

He knew that was ridiculous, Pandora was not an object to be possessed, but whenever he thought of their deadline divorce date looming in the not-too-distant future…

But before he could finish up his working day and head off to the Hamptons, he had to deal with one minor annoyance in the form of his brother's arrival in his office. He made Eros wait, his usual move when he wanted to maintain control of a meeting. Eros might be his brother but, as far as he was concerned, this was not a house call. There would only be one reason for Eros to come here when Xander had already had word that he'd been spotted in the Caribbean on honeymoon with his new wife.

As he stalked into the room to face Eros, he waited for any hint of resentment or anger at the fact that his brother had married his ex-fiancée, but nothing came. His and Priya's match had been short-lived and strictly professional, after all. To his own surprise, he bit back the urge to congratulate his brother on his nuptials, but then remembered that they were still technically rivals in this race.

'You look…tanned,' he said simply.

'You look like death warmed up. Clearly marriage has affected us in very different ways, brother.' Eros quirked one brow, leaning back in his chair in a way that made Xander's teeth grit hard.

Though there were only six years between them, Xander had always envied his younger brother's youthful energy. He remembered the first day they met, and Eros had introduced himself loudly as the other bastard, much to their father's horror. They hadn't always been rivals. In fact, he would go so far as to say they had been friends once. Until Xander had been forced to make a choice that still haunted him to this very day.

'I hear you've neglected to invite me to yet another one of your weddings?'

'If you came here to ask for an invite, you could have just emailed.'

'Don't worry, your wife already ensured we were sent an invite. Priya has been video-calling her about renting office space when she returns to the city.'

Xander stilled. His wife and the woman who'd jilted him were working together? But strangely, it felt…nice.

He imagined a future where he and Eros ran in the same circles once more, perhaps even had a friendly dinner party with their wives. Would it be strange?

He shook off the thought, knowing it was far too early to entertain such thoughts. He didn't even know why Eros was here. He crossed his arms, staring out at the view he had coveted for most of his adult life, the view that was now his so long as he maintained control of the board. Eros had already informed him he'd forfeited his right to the inheritance; Nysio was still unmarried and determined to remain unconnected to the Mytikas name.

'I have a wedding rehearsal to attend shortly,' Xander said stiffly.

'Well, then, allow me to get straight to the point.' Eros stood up. Placing his tablet on the conference table, he tapped the screen a few times, then extended it for Xander to take a look.

Xander peered down, taking a moment to make sense of the charts and projections in his brother's trademark chaotic organisation. But then he realised exactly what he was looking at…and his blood turned cold.

'Arcum…' he gritted. 'You mean to tell me that the shadow corporation that's been buying up Mytikas shares all over this city—that was you?'

'That is correct. And you are Titan Corp.' Eros's face was devoid of humour for once, his expression one of utmost seriousness that reminded Xander of…himself.

'How did you come by this information?'

'For the past ten years, I've made it my business to know everything that my enemies have done.'

Taking a deep breath, Xander scanned the charts again. 'If you are here to leverage me or try to buy me out…'

'Let me clarify. Things are not the same now as they were fifteen years ago. Zeus is dead and through my relationship with Priya I've come to realise a great many things. She made me realise, rather.' He smiled ruefully, then straightened. 'I'm not here as your enemy, Xander. I'm here as your brother. I've contacted the Italian too. I have a plan to propose that I think may just change everything for all of us.'

And so Xander found himself seated side by side with his brother for the first time in more than a decade as Eros outlined the details of his proposal to conspire with his brothers in a coup that would shock the business world for evermore. Together they controlled the majority shares of Mytikas Holdings.

It was scandalous, it was aggressive…it was brilliant.

Zeus had always made it clear that his youngest son would have been his first choice to carry on the Mytikas name. Though technically Xander had been given the powerful name at birth by his socially reaching mother, he hadn't truly felt as if it was his until Eros had left. With no one else there to challenge him, his victory had felt hollow.

His resentment for Zeus had only grown, fuelling him to investigate the accusations of corruption himself. Unlike Eros, Xander had the patience and foresight to play the long game. On the surface, he had been the dutiful son, Zeus's right-hand man. But beneath all his blind faith he had been laying the foundations for this very moment. He had trapped the beast that was Mytikas Holdings in a snare of its own corruption and, in doing so, he had aimed to make himself their only possible saviour. But taking the glory for himself had never been the plan. He hadn't been the only person that Zeus had hurt and therefore he wasn't the only one who deserved a chance at retribution. His brothers did too.

'What you are proposing is unheard of.' Xander finally spoke after a long silence.

'I don't expect you to trust me,' Eros said, his features hardening. 'But considering our history, I didn't need to bring this to you at all.'

There it was. Xander let out a slow breath at the reminder of his actions. The reminder of the bitter rivalry that had cut short their tentative bond of brotherhood years before.

'When I ran you out of New York, it was because Zeus had already found out what you'd uncovered. He planned to make an example of you. To teach you a lesson by implicating you in a corruption case that would have possibly cost you years of freedom. I chose your freedom over brotherhood. I knew that you would never forgive me or believe me if I tried to tell you the truth.'

'You're telling me that you weren't trying to get me out of the way?'

'Maybe it started that way—I am a selfish bastard in many ways. But I realise now that I made the wrong choice. I'm sorry, I should have told you and then let you fight your own battle.'

'Did you just…apologise to me?' Eros raised an incredulous brow. 'Marriage must have really done a number on you.'

It had, Xander realised. Pandora had been the one to sow the seeds of all this openness and communication and forgiveness. He knew now that if Eros hadn't come to him, he would have sought him out anyway to make this same apology. Because he meant every word.

He looked at the man he'd spent so long hating and memories of their short-lived brotherhood returned. He'd played it cool back then but his time working with his brother had been the happiest in his memory. They'd been a seamless working machine, both driven by the desire to improve things at their father's company. He wondered how their relationship might have grown and developed if he hadn't been so focused on proving himself to be more than just a consolation prize as a son.

Eros was silent, the only sound the dull tick of the grandfather clock in the hall. Then he stood and began striding towards him. Xander exhaled in shock as he was enveloped in a brief brotherly embrace.

'You know what this means, don't you?' Eros said.

'Yes, that with our combined shares we have control over Mytikas Holdings regardless of the rest of the board.'

'So you can let your wife go.'

'What?' Xander exclaimed in shock.

Eros looked taken aback. 'I'm sorry, I just assumed that your marriage to Pandora was the same arrangement as the one you had with Priya, one of convenience just to win the inheritance.'

'I have an arrangement with Pandora, yes.' He spoke the words, hating the sound of them as they came out of his mouth. Hating how wrong they felt. But it was the truth.

'Really? You don't sound convinced,' Eros mused. 'If that's the case, I'm sure she will be happy to be let off the hook and get her pay-off early.'

'Pandora is not just some gold-digger and I won't have her thought of that way,' Xander warned darkly, walking away and pinching the bridge of his nose. 'I wasn't prepared for any of this, but you're right about the combined shares—it makes perfect sense. I'd be a fool not to join forces with you. I just… I need a moment to think over all the angles.'

'Why do I get the feeling that you're not just thinking about the company right now?' Eros surveyed him with shrewd interest. 'Will this impact your fancy nuptials tomorrow?'

'She deserves to be released from our contract, yes. It's the best solution for everyone involved.'

'Ah.' Eros nodded once. 'Spoken like a man in love.'

Xander froze, his stomach tensing uncomfortably. 'Don't be ridiculous.'

'It sneaks up on the best of us.' Eros clapped him on the back. 'Do me a favour, go and talk to your wife before you take any action on this. Trust me, I learned my mistake the hard way on that one.'

Xander nodded, his mind moving quickly over all the details and changes, trying to navigate it all. He hardly noticed himself saying goodbye to his brother, who promised to see him at the wedding. He hardly noticed anything at all, other than the increasingly uncomfortable sense of dread filling his chest with every minute that passed.

The feeling persisted as he travelled to the helipad on the roof of Mytikas Holdings. Clearly, he was not as okay with this new development as he'd thought.

As had been made clear in countless meetings this week, this society wedding was a pivotal moment for Mytikas Holdings and his plans for the future as their CEO.

But now, in light of his conversation with Eros…all of that had changed. He could take over everything on his own terms. As far as moments went, this was huge, the culmination of a decade of strategising. But strangely, he felt no urge to celebrate.

Pandora had been in Japan for the best part of a week, not that he'd counted, of course. He simply kept track of such things. But even as he tried to convince himself of that truth, he felt the impatience and need to see her growing within him. He'd been like this all week, distracted and irritable, his thoughts consumed by soft porcelain skin and her stunning silver eyes. But it wasn't just her body he'd missed. It was everything about her. She'd unknowingly become the brightest part of his day from the moment they'd begun working together. He'd savoured their arguments and her set-downs and he'd valued her opinions and sharp mind.

What on earth had happened to his plans for a cold marriage of convenience?

Even trying to minimise what they had shared during that week in Japan was useless; his mind knew the reality. It was never just about sex or physical attraction with Pandora. What they had was so much more, it practically consumed him.

It was madness. It was dangerous. But he couldn't seem to make himself stop wanting her with him. Not just for one more night or one more week or even one more year… but as a permanent fixture. He couldn't imagine his life without her in it, but when had that happened? When had she become something so intrinsic to his happiness?

Eros's words seemed to float through his mind, taunting him. *Spoken like a man in love.* He stiffened at the thought, reflexively pushing it away. In his world, love had only ever meant weakness and vulnerability. It was the arrow you gave to another person to slice through your heart on a whim. It was weakness.

But the look on Pandora's face when she'd spoken those words to him on the train in Japan…she hadn't looked weak. She had been glorious. Her silver eyes incandescent and aglow with the terrible truth of her heart, even when he'd tried to extinguish that flame. His fists tightened on his knees as he leaned forward, his forehead pressing hard against the cold window of the helicopter as the city lights began to blur in the distance below.

This was madness, thinking that a man like him had any right to her heart. He had broken her enough already

and for once he would do the right thing. If she was no longer bound to him through their deal, she would be set free.

He needed to set her free.

Pandora rose from her chair, taking in her appearance
with swift efficiency and calmly telling the stylist that
she would finish dressing alone.

If they had any complaints, they didn't voice them. The
kind-eyed make-up artist took charge in shooing them out
and made sure to ask her if she needed anything before
he left himself. Then she was alone, in blissful silence.

She felt a coldness settle over her as she focused on
removing some of the heavier make-up and curling her
hair around her face. Simple pink pearl earrings adorned
her ears and a matching necklace sat just above her collarbone. The dress she'd chosen for the rehearsal was a
blush pink shift that teamed beautifully with flat golden
pumps that sparkled in the light as she turned from side
to side before finally leaving the confines of her room.

Show time.

She was infinitely glad that she hadn't been pressured
to wear heels as the steps already felt unsteady beneath
her feet as she descended. Her heart thumped hard in her
chest as she spied Xander waiting for her in the foyer of
the venue, his back turned as he studied the glass in his
hands. Whiskey, she realised with disappointment. Was
he dreading the spectacle of pledging himself to her in
front of his precious society? Was he worried she would
embarrass him and his image?

For a moment, she briefly contemplated running back
to her room to compose herself, but then he looked up and
their eyes locked and she felt something within her melt.

She had seen Xander in a suit a thousand times since
the day they'd first met, but the look on his face was what

caught her breath. There was a level of heat there that seemed to burn through the fabric of her dress, touching her very heart. It should be a crime for a man to look the way he did in this moment.

She reached the bottom step and he was right there, taking her hand in his but not pulling her any closer. The foyer was just filled with a handful of staff members, readying the place for the rehearsal dinner. There was no need to put on a show. Yet she ached to reach up and touch his jaw, to kiss his lips and get carried away in that electric heat of desire that always seemed to end with them in a tangle of limbs in a bed, on a desk or even on the floor on occasion.

But something was different today. For someone who had always struggled to read people's meaning in their words, she had always been extra sensitive to their moods. But with Xander, it sometimes felt as if he had become an extension of her, as if she could feel his energy simply by being in the same room as him. In Japan, that feeling had only intensified, making her lose focus and fuelling her anxiety whenever he'd behaved in a way she hadn't expected. Like right now.

'You look beautiful,' he said, guiding her along the hall that led to the outdoor ceremony area. He paused just before they exited the double doors, where their celebrant waited along with the events team. Xander had made sure to send Pandora detailed reports of every decision that was made, ensuring that she knew what to expect. Slowly she had begun to understand the enormity of what she had agreed to. This was to be a finely executed event. But it would be okay, she told herself.

Xander would be by her side. She was simply playing a different role, just like the ones she had played all her life. The roles that smoothed out her edges and made her more palatable to others, the masks she wore to stop herself from standing out or being an embarrassment to the people she cared about. And she did care about Xander, probably far more than was sensible for a woman who had entered into a marriage with a one-year expiry date.

One year.

During her time alone in Japan she had stopped thinking about the fact that they had set a limit on their arrangement. But clearly he'd never forgotten.

She had never dreamed of more for herself than her studies and visiting her family, challenging herself to move to new countries and adapt. She had been content before meeting Xander, before he had shown her just what it meant to feel connected with someone in such a primal way. She felt as if before their first kiss, she had just been existing. From the moment his lips had touched hers, he had unleashed something inside her. He had opened up some hidden box within her soul and now there was no way to put it all back again. But still, a foolish hope stubbornly bloomed within her, growing and moving towards him like a flower seeking the sun.

It wasn't fair to him, putting him in such a position. He had never offered to be her sun or her moon. He hadn't even offered to be her husband, in truth. They had gone from a fraught working relationship to the tentative alliance of their temporary marriage then somehow had become lovers before either of them had had the chance to catch their breath.

They walked out into the evening light and she was stunned to see the ceremony had been completely set up in the few hours she'd been holed away upstairs with the styling team. The long lawn now boasted satin-covered chairs and flower stands spilling over with yellow roses. Her breath caught. Had he done that? The idea that he would request her favourite flower on purpose was a reach, the more likely situation was that an event planner had chosen them in pure coincidence. But the lawn was spilling with them, fragrant arrangements filling every corner.

Love for him filled her chest and she fought the urge to claim him once again, to demand that they give up on this foolish charade made up of restraint and rules that she knew neither of them wanted.

Xander might care about the propriety of their arrangement, but she didn't. Call her impulsive, but if this was a terrible decision, she wanted to dive in head first.

What if this connection between them was meant to be more, what if this marriage was meant to be real? The moment she felt the question take shape in her mind, she felt it fill up and expand. She couldn't marry him like this, she couldn't give up on the chance that they might actually be something to one another outside this deal.

She felt the pressure of reality weighing her down with every step, crushing her with expectation and responsibility.

Suddenly her feet refused to move.

She heard Xander ask if she was okay as though he were on the opposite side of a wall, while her thoughts swirled and caved in upon her with raucous vengeance.

The event planner smiled brightly, explaining that the usual series of vows would follow. The woman's shrill excited voice was impossible to keep up with, along with the banging from the chairs still being arranged on the lawn. So many chairs. So many strangers, watching her, wondering how on earth someone like her had wound up married to a handsome Greek billionaire.

Quirky and scatterbrained...autistic spectrum disorder...

'I'll get you to stand right here.' The woman nudged Pandora lightly on her shoulder, placing her at an angle to Xander's left. Pandora felt her mind grow foggy with the effort of withstanding her own panic. Still, the event planner continued to chatter mindlessly while Xander nodded, his hands stuffed into the pockets of his designer trousers. She focused on the watch upon his wrist, noting how dull the metal looked. How out of place it seemed. Was this how people would always see her? She had thought she was immune to the pain of being an object of public speculation. But that was before...

Before she'd realised that it wasn't just her that was affected by public opinion of their marriage. By the public opinion of her. Before she'd cared about Xander's happiness so much, a happiness that was directly affected by his social reputation.

The thought came with blinding clarity, like a sudden beam of torchlight. Painful and impossible to ignore. She knitted her hands together, wondering how on earth she had ever thought she could maintain the façade of a perfect wife for him. It would be laughable, really, if it weren't so impossibly sad.

'...and then I will ask you, Pandora, if you're ready to take this man as your husband, and you, of course, say—'

'No.'

She looked up from the anxious twist of her fingers and realised, by the number of eyes on them, that she had said it out loud.

She poised to apologise, to retract that tiny damning syllable. She didn't want to let him down. Didn't want to hurt him...or his reputation more than she already had.

But the words she knew she needed to say to smooth the moment over wouldn't come and, with every passing second of awkward silence, she felt the tension tighten, suffocating her.

CHAPTER FOURTEEN

XANDER TOOK ONE look at Pandora's face and knew he couldn't hold off on this conversation until after dinner, it needed to happen now.

She looked exhausted, he realised. A few loud bangs sounded out as a couple of waiters moved a table and he saw her wince. He fought the urge to growl at the men to leave, at everyone to leave. But he held back, politely asking the coordinator to empty out the marquee and give them some time to talk. It took a few torturous minutes to send away the team and waitstaff in the vicinity, a few minutes of watching Pandora shut down more and more with each second that passed.

Then suddenly, for what felt like the first time in weeks but was only a matter of days…they were alone.

Xander inhaled a deep breath, his mind wrangling the thoughts and feelings within him and pondering which combination of words might achieve the best result. Which magic phrase would allow him to let her go, to undo all the tangled wires of deceit and demands that had criss-crossed between them and at least have them parting on good terms.

But it was Pandora who spoke first.

'I'm sorry, Xander. I thought I was fine.' She half laughed sadly, a sound he found he didn't like at all. Her voice was barely more than a whisper. 'But then I saw my own face spread across a newspaper article.'

'I didn't approve any of the research performed on your family or you.'

'I know, you would never do that.' She met his eyes. 'It's not even about that... It's just being in Japan alone, without you... I had a lot of time to think. I had some things I wanted to ask you, but we had no time alone and now all this is happening. It's overwhelming.'

He'd seen it in her face, in the tense line of her shoulders. Even hearing her dismiss that cursed article as not being his fault made him angry. Of course it was his fault. Everything about her current situation had been caused by him or his family name, all of it.

He circled her wrist with his thumb and forefinger, the warmth of her skin sending a jolt of fire through him, but he let her go abruptly. He knew what he needed to do, knew that he couldn't keep her trapped in this life when it wasn't going to make her happy.

'I had a meeting with Eros today.'

Her eyes met his, surprise and a tiny hint of fear glimmering in their grey depths.

'There was no bloodshed. It was quite civil, actually. I...missed him.'

'Xander, that's wonderful,' she breathed, emotion glimmering.

'I realised how difficult I've been in the past, in refusing to change my opinions on certain things. Apparently, I can be quite stubborn.' He raised one brow and saw her expression soften with amusement. Still, he felt as if he stood on the edge of one of those circus ladders, high above the ground. He needed to do this, needed to tell her the full truth of her options. She'd said she loved him once and he'd pushed it away like a fool. What he'd give to hear it again from her right now. But he couldn't be selfish, he couldn't hold her tight like a spoilt child; she was not an object for him to possess. She was not his wife in truth; she had been forced into the position. Now it was time to give her the choice she deserved.

'Eros owns the company that we have been investigating for a while. Arcum. Apparently I wasn't the only one gathering shares using a shadow company. If we were to join forces, with the considerable percentage of shares we hold between us, we can stage a complete takeover of Mytikas Holdings. We could take everything.'

'And in doing so, you could bypass the terms of the will,' she said softly, her eyes not quite meeting his as she chewed at her bottom lip.

'I never had an interest in the rest of Zeus's estate anyway. Just the company.'

'Can you trust Eros?'

'Yes... I think I can. After all these years, it's become clear that Zeus deliberately kept us at each other's throats.'

Pandora was silent as she nodded, and he allowed her a moment to process the words before he proceeded.

'I suppose what I'm trying to say is that I know you don't want all this, Pandora. The big society wedding, the newspaper articles, the circus that is my life. I know that I have been asking a lot of you from the beginning...' He paused and ran a hand through his hair. 'These past few days, I realised some things and I...'

'You wanted to find a way out of all this,' she finished for him.

'Yes,' he said, then frowned. 'Not out of this entirely, just out of the part where I demanded that you be my wife for twelve months. Pandora... I think back to that night and I am so deeply ashamed at myself. At how heavy-handed I was, how I judged you and blamed you for everything. You deserved better from me and I can only hope you'll come to forgive me. That's why I'm setting you free from our deal. I will have divorce papers drawn up as soon as possible and you will still receive the financial settlement we agreed upon.'

Pandora made a tiny, strangled sound and when he looked down at her he could see she was shaking her head, the strangest expression on her face.

'Are you laughing? I'm making a very serious speech here and you're somehow amused by all this?'

'The exact opposite. I'm frankly amazed at the fact that I was just about to…' She shook her head, the tiniest hitch in her breath the only outward sign that she was not amused at all. 'You never contacted me, the entire time I was in Japan with Ran, apart from sending over information about the wedding. It's like you weren't even affected by anything that happened between us. And now you've decided on all this without even asking me what I want. So yes, I'm entitled to be upset.'

She was…upset? Hope bloomed in his chest like a weed, careening up the stony walls around his heart and finally crumbling them to dust. She had already told him that she loved him once…was he a fool to think that her love hadn't completely died when he'd behaved so badly? He'd acted out of fear before, he had practically pushed her to leave. But now…he felt the significance of the moment stretch out before him like a murky precipice. There was no guarantee that she wouldn't still walk away, but he had to try. He had to take that leap of faith and trust it wouldn't destroy him.

Quickly, he stepped in front of her, blocking her from walking away from the raised podium they stood upon.

He looked around them at the rose-covered archway and the candles flickering in the light twilight breeze.

Pandora felt the last tiny ember of hope she'd clung to that he'd missed her while she was gone over the past week fade, giving way to a torrent of white-hot anger. How *dared* he? He had the gall to insist on this preposterous marriage deal in the first place, and now, barely a month later, when she was no longer useful to him, he was abandoning her as quickly as he could?

It had felt as though his words had come at her like arrows, hitting her squarely in the chest.

She shouldn't feel so hurt by his offer of a divorce. It had always been going to happen in less than a year's time. But hearing him say it so cavalierly, so soon, surrounded by this ridiculous wedding tent and what felt like a million of her favourite roses...she felt the last final piece of her heart shatter.

Unable to look up at him, she let the cold numbness that had threatened her all day finally take hold, steeling her features to blankness. Protecting her from falling down into a huddled pile of pain at his feet. But suddenly, the realisation of the ridiculousness of their situation dawned on her and she felt a semi-hysterical bubble of laughter escape her lips.

She covered her face with embarrassment, wishing she could simply click her fingers and return to the solitude of her room to have what was probably going to be a spectacular breakdown of sorts. She felt Xander move forward, the heat of him pressing along her bare arm making her jump with surprise.

'Pandora...please, don't cry. God, I'm messing all this up.' He touched her hands, concern lacing his voice for a split second. 'Wait, you're...laughing?'

'Sorry, I'm just…this is completely ridiculous.' She shook off his hand as another bubble of laughter escaped her chest, sending a tear down her cheek. 'We're starring in our very own soap opera here. You do know that, don't you? The jilted groom, jilting his replacement bride at the altar.'

He frowned at her words, looking almost hurt, which made absolutely no sense considering he was the one ending things between them. She felt unhinged and exhausted and, God, why was he still looking at her that way?

'Jilting?' he echoed. 'Do you honestly think I would do that to you?'

She paused, something about his tone making her stand very still. He stood under the archway, looking like every fantasy bridegroom in her wildest dreams. But it was the look in his eyes that made her swallow hard. In all the months they'd worked together, she had never once seen Xander Mytikas admit fault or apologise the way he'd apologised to her tonight.

He'd practically begged for her forgiveness. And now, looking at him, steadfast under the arch where they'd been set to pledge their vows… She wondered if perhaps she'd got it all wrong. Still, she couldn't quite bring herself to ask him. That small, shaky part of her had already taken a catastrophic bruising. So she did the next best thing and uncrossed her arms, letting them lie flat at her sides. She took one step towards him, then another, until finally they were only slightly more than arm's width apart.

'I don't think you would hurt me like that on purpose, Xander,' she said softly. 'But the truth of the matter is, there is no reason for us to remain married now. I don't even work for you any more.'

'Without the deals and obligations…you can't think of one reason why we should?' he asked hoarsely.

He reached out and took her left hand in his, his thumb rubbing over the polished platinum rings on her third finger. 'You want to know why I've been quiet? Why I have barely been able to trust myself to be around you without an audience? It's because I've been wracking my brain to try to find a way to keep you. I just didn't think I deserved you.'

'Oh.' The single syllable left her on a rush of breath and she felt the world slow right down to a fine point. Everything else fell away and suddenly all she could see was Xander. For the first time since she'd walked down the steps, she looked at him, really looked at him.

There were fine lines of pressure around his mouth and a tiny unshaven patch of hair just under his ear, he had dark circles under his eyes and he looked thinner, as if he'd been exercising too much and forgetting to eat. Goodness…he looked just as terrible as she felt. How had she not noticed that?

All this time she'd been operating under the impression that she had been the fool who had fallen face first into love, but now as she looked into his eyes… That tiny spark of hope winked back to life within her chest once again.

'Knowing you were across the world in Japan this past week has been the most tortured I've felt in a long time. I know why you left. You are immensely talented and passionate and you shouldn't have been sitting around waiting to be wheeled out as my society bride. I was selfish to not continue to use your tremendous talents. I'm so sorry. Your replacement is utterly useless, if that's any consolation.'

She opened her mouth to respond but felt his index finger press gently against her lips, his left hand reaching for hers, his thumb smoothing over the rings that she had yet to remove.

'Pandora... I woke every morning this past week alone and surrounded by your scent. At first it made me angry, knowing you had left me. But as I calmed and your scent began to fade with every day...' He looked up, his eyes dark and earnest. 'I think it was while I burrowed my face into that damned pillow, trying to get one more breath of you... I think that was when I knew.'

'You knew that you wanted more?' she whispered, needing to clarify, needing to know exactly what he meant.

'So much more.' He lifted her hand to his lips, inhaling softly against her skin, breathing her in. 'I don't just want you in my bed for a week, *agape mou*. I was stupid to ever think that was all we could be. You are worth more to me than I could ever confine to one night, one week, or even one year.'

'Are you saying that you...?' She breathed in, feeling her heartbeat thrum so hard in her throat she felt a little dizzy. 'Xander... I need you to be clear before I...'

His eyes darkened. 'Before you what, Quinn?'

'Before I do something utterly ridiculous like jump your bones right here on this altar. It might not be a church but I'm pretty sure it would still be illegal.'

'Maybe I'll draw this speech out a little longer, then,' he mused.

Pandora fought the urge to playfully punch him like she wanted to, and took the final step, bringing them chest to chest so that she could look up into his eyes.

'I want to hear you say it again a few more times,' she said simply, fighting a smile so strong it made her cheeks ache with the sweetest pain. 'Then maybe I'll put you out of your misery.'

'If you want to divorce me right now, Pandora, I'll accept that, and I will throw every ounce of myself into wooing you for real. Because you are not just a name on a certificate to me, you're my everything. You're all that matters any more because I love you so much.'

She almost melted right then. Only she couldn't help teasing him a little more... 'You sure you don't want to keep that prenup?'

He winced, as if the memory of that day, of the words he'd thrown at her, caused him actual physical pain. 'I'd hoped to forget my behaviour.'

'Well, I don't.' She shook her head, noting the remorseful look in his eyes. 'You can't get to a happy ever after without a few moments of conflict along the way.'

He raised an eyebrow. 'Is that what we're calling the time I demanded that you marry me or I would have you carted off to jail?'

Pandora laughed and, after a moment of fighting it, her stern, serious husband laughed too. Then he scooped her up against his chest and kissed the last bubbles of mirth from her lips until she was boneless and sighing.

Emotion was hot and pulsing in her throat as she met his gaze, one hand reaching up to cup his jaw as she spoke those three beautiful words, cementing their vows all over again.

'I love you,' she whispered. 'I don't want a divorce. I don't care about any of the legal mumbo jumbo anyway. But I suppose we can't really tell our kids the story of our awful first wedding, can we?'

'Our kids?' He choked a little. 'You're thinking about that already, are you?'

'Oh, not for a while yet. I have a five-year business plan to execute first, of course.' She smiled, a little laugh escaping her lips.

Xander laughed too, as if he too could hardly believe how things could feel this wonderful. It was fast, it was intense, and it was so completely, perfectly right.

'I have one last thing I'd like to do,' she whispered.

'Anything,' he breathed, holding her even tighter.

The first item on her list was to get her husband alone for a proper reunion, which turned out to be in the office of the grand house. Once the door had been locked, Xander proceeded to show her just how much he had missed her by spreading her out on top of the desk and promising to fulfil every fantasy about her sexy boss that she'd ever had. But in reality, neither of them had enough patience for that kind of lovemaking. Their union was simply frantic and raw, filled with whispers of love and the promise of a much slower exploration later.

Then, still naked and slightly sweaty from their efforts, she stepped away from him, taking his hand and sliding the platinum band off his finger and clutching it in her fist. She did the same to her own and placed it in the centre of his palm. Meeting his eyes, she cleared her throat, praying she could get through this without dissolving into a sobbing pile of tears.

'Xander, I take you as my husband, I promise to love you and explore the world with you and remind you to relax when you're becoming a little too highly strung. For ever and always.' She placed the ring on his finger, surprised when she felt his hand shake a little.

He cleared his throat, taking a deep breath as he prepared to do the same. 'Pandora, I promise to love you and worship you and devotedly organise the itinerary for whatever far-flung corner of the world you decide to drag me to.'

Pandora tried to laugh, but the tears had already begun and all she managed was a little strangled sigh. He slid the ring onto her finger slowly, his eyes not leaving hers.

'Gia pánta kai pánta i agápi mou.' He repeated her words reverently in both of their languages. 'For ever and always.'

EPILOGUE

Four years later

PANDORA FELT SWEAT trickle down the centre of her back as she focused very hard on lowering herself into a nearby chair in the busy banquet area. The tiny baby she was holding wriggled quite a bit more than she'd anticipated and her upper arms had begun to ache.

'I'll only be gone for ten minutes at the most,' her sister-in-law Priya had said cheerfully as she brushed a lock of hair back on her daughter's jet-black curls. That had been twenty minutes ago and there was still no sign of her return from picking up her husband at the nearby dock.

Nor had there been a sign of her own husband during that time. She frowned, averting her gaze up for a moment to scan the open-air terrace of the large Greek villa. Other guests at the charity event milled around, sipping afternoon tea and networking. Xander had probably struck up a conversation with one of the countless European monarchs or global tycoons in attendance, she thought with a smile. He'd return triumphant, probably after negotiating a handful of deals.

But when she finally spotted him, he was quite alone, seated at a nearby table and unmistakeably focused on the very spot where she sat. Frowning, she did a small queen's wave, swaying her new niece gently in one arm. He nodded once and raised a glass of champagne in her direction, before rising and stalking purposefully towards her. His expression was strange, his eyes seeming to drink her in as he came closer before he stopped and reached out to touch his niece's chubby cheek.

The baby let out an instant gurgle of appreciation, grabbing onto her uncle's finger as if to stop him from leaving.

'If you tell me that this suits me, be prepared for me to roll my eyes,' Pandora said with a teasing smile.

'Okay, it doesn't suit you. You are the most unattractive sight I've ever seen, and I just sat at that table for the past five minutes staring at you…in sheer repulsion.' He leaned in to kiss her once, then twice for good measure before pulling back to stare once more.

He whispered something into the baby's ear conspiratorially, his eyes darting back up to meet hers dramatically. 'What's that, little one? You want to meet your baby cousin right now?'

She made an urgent shushing sound, looking around them. 'Xander, it's far too early to be talking about it in public.'

He ignored her, his eyes now apparently only for his little niece alone. 'I think it's a boy too. But it's okay. I'll keep going until we get you a girl cousin.'

'Oh, you will, will you?' Pandora couldn't help but grin as her husband's hand moved to splay across the still-flat expanse of her stomach. She had only just had a positive test days before.

'You're sure you don't want to tell anyone yet?' he asked, far too innocently. 'I know they say it's bad luck, but…'

'You are like a child, begging to unwrap his Christmas gift early. But no, I don't think I'm ready to share our news just yet.' She laughed, covering his hand with her own and feeling a brief intense burst of love for him and the tiny life growing steadily beneath their joint palms.

'I don't think I've ever even held a baby before today.' She frowned down at the little girl in her arms. Amara Theodorou blew a bubble and laughed, patting at the beads on Pandora's dress. 'I'm feeling a little out of my depth already.'

'I could tell by the stack of pregnancy books you packed in your overnight bag.'

Pandora looked away, feeling the ripples of uncertainty rise a little higher. She'd made no secret of her compulsion to study and prepare for every possibility of what lay ahead of her. But something about entering into this particular new phase of her life made her wish she were a more easy-going type. Perhaps if she could go with the flow, letting go of control of her body and life as she knew it wouldn't feel quite so terrifying.

'Hey, I wasn't making fun of your books.' Xander's palms touched her cheeks, applying gentle pressure and filling her with warmth. 'Once I saw them I actually downloaded some audio versions onto my phone. I've been learning all about the trimesters and stages on my morning runs.'

She paused, looking up into his face and taking a moment to gauge whether or not he was making fun of her. 'You've been studying too?'

'You're not the only one who likes to be prepared, *agape mou*. I have grand plans,' he murmured against her cheek.

'You can't win at fatherhood, Xander.' She smiled, feeling the tension ease within her ever so slightly. Trust her husband to turn parenthood into a competition with his brother.

She inhaled deeply, leaning forward to touch her forehead gently against his in silent communication of thanks. They had developed these small gestures over the years, tiny movements and touches that needed no words. She'd never dreamed of having such an easy connection with someone.

After a long moment, she looked up into his impossibly blue eyes and smiled, knowing he understood her worries and accepted them just as he accepted everything else about her. In their four years of marriage he'd kept his promise every single day, showing her that love didn't have to be something you earned or performed for. His love was unconditional and constant, and if there was one thing she could count on it was that Xander would throw himself into fatherhood with that same fierce strength and loyalty.

Warm lips touched hers and she smiled against his mouth, feeling a tentative spark of excitement bloom within her at the idea of them as parents. She'd never dreamed of this life for herself.

'We're in this together, remember?' Xander cupped her neck, kissing her once more. 'We can always ask my brother if we can take this little one again for practice.'

'Practice for what?' A familiar female voice spoke from behind Xander's shoulder. Priya appeared, her shrewd eyes homing in on their hushed conversation and lowering to where Xander's hand still rested. Pandora felt her facial muscles freeze a little as her brain struggled to formulate an excuse.

'Where is she?' Eros Theodorou appeared, his eyes scanning them all, and for a moment Pandora thought he was referring to her. But then his eyes lit up as they landed on his daughter and Amara was promptly scooped up into her father's arms.

Xander quickly worked his magic, distracting his brother and sister-in-law with some good-natured ribbing about their extended absence and obviously flushed cheeks but still Priya's eyes moved speculatively over her more than once.

As the conversation came to a momentary silence, Pandora felt the urge to share their news bubbling upwards until she couldn't hold it in any longer.

'I'm pregnant,' she blurted, much louder than she'd intended, instantly slamming a hand over her mouth. Priya's stunned smile was instantaneous, her hands clapping together with glee while Eros simply raised one brow in his brother's direction.

For a moment, the look of surprise on her husband's face made Pandora pause. She was poised to apologise for her own impulsive move but quickly felt the shudders of Xander's body crumpling into laughter beside her.

'And she was worried that I would let the news out.' His eyes creased as he was engulfed in a hug by Priya and then his younger brother, their embrace a thoroughly masculine movement of back-thumping and grunts but still a hug nonetheless.

Seeing Xander's relationship with his brother improve to this point had been something she'd never dreamed of, along with so many other wonderful developments that had happened in their family. Their unexpected joining of forces to take over the company had been an instant power pairing, with Eros's creativity and intuition coupling rather perfectly with Xander's intensity and ruthless precision in the boardroom. Together, they had cut out the rot left by their father and created something brand new that they could both be proud of.

Despite his refusal to enter into their deal, Nysio Bacchetti had eventually approached his two half-brothers with an offer that none of them could have predicted. But that was a story for another time.

'I think our secret won't be a secret for long.' She laughed as Xander continued to pull her away from the party towards where their helicopter lay in wait, whispering all the things he planned to do to help her relax.

'That does not sound very restful, husband dearest. In fact, it sounds quite the opposite.' She raised one brow as they paused under an archway of gloriously vibrant bougainvillea. 'I think we should plant some of these at the house… I wonder how long they take to grow…'

Xander barely flinched at her rapid change in topic. 'I'll order an acre of them.'

'And as for my credentials, I'll cite four years of studious observation and active research in ensuring the happiness of the woman I love.' He pulled her close so that their bodies met from chest to knee. 'I've come to the scientific conclusion that you are at your most relaxed when your mind and body are engaged and captivated…so I plan to spend the next eight months working very hard to achieve both.'

'You know me so well.' She smiled as he began kissing up her neck, holding her close in a tight embrace. This was all she needed, she realised with a throbbing lump in her throat. This man, this wonderful man and the life that lay nestled within her.

She no longer worried about where they would live if his work took them away, she simply focused on her own work and handed the reins to Xander, trusting him completely to take care of the details.

Xander's love had shored up all the holes in her own self-confidence, showing her how wonderful it could be to be accepted and loved, just as she was. That kind of unconditional love had run through her like a river until it wasn't just coming from him, it was from within too.

This newfound sense of strength seemed to interrupt every negative thought or moment of uncertainty she had, clearing her mind and helping her find better solutions. It was him. It was his love and unwavering belief that made her feel as if she could do anything. It was a heady feeling, being loved so much by such a force of a man.

As the helicopter lifted up into the air, she felt her husband's hand cover her own and their eyes met, an unspoken thrill of wonder and excitement passing between them. She smiled, realising they had always had this seamless connection, as though they were reading from the exact same page.

They might not have begun in the traditional fairy-tale fashion, but then again how many love stories ever did? This was her own perfectly imperfect storybook, and she had a feeling they had only just got started on building their happily-ever-after together.

* * * * *

A DEAL FOR THE TYCOON'S DIAMONDS

EMMY GRAYSON

MILLS & BOON

To the people who provided me with love, support, and the most epic lakeside game of *Cards Against Humanity* this summer. Thank you.

CHAPTER ONE

Rome, Italy

LIGHTS FLASHED AS techno music pulsed through Anna Vega's veins. She stopped on the catwalk, bestowed a shaky Mona Lisa smile to the nearest camera and then cursed inwardly. Hadn't someone told her *not* to smile, to look mysterious and aloof?

Too late now. Besides, she needed to concentrate on walking. One foot in front of the other on sky-high heels that were a feat of engineering. The shoes, a silver creation covered in sapphires, clicked on the glass walkway. The crystal-clear waters of the courtyard fountain bubbled behind her as she stopped for one last look before she disappeared behind the drapes and headed toward the room off the hotel courtyard that housed the rest of the models and their entourages.

Before she could suck in a breath, she walked through the double glass doors and into the waiting arms of half a dozen stylists.

"Brush out Anna's hair!"

"No, no, the petal for her lips, not vixen!"

"Final dress is the tulle and organza!"

Anna closed her eyes, not letting the crowd pulsing around her witness her conflicting feelings of pride and pain. The final dress she would wear tonight, a gown with a full skirt and a deep neckline, was in honor of her mother. The skirt, a nod to the first formal dress her mother had bought her for family Christmas photos when she was four years old. The top, a nod to the countless times her mother had mentioned that one day she would get the confidence to wear something "just a little more daring." A day that had never come thanks to a reckless driver on a Louisiana bayou backroad.

Yet her mother would be proud, too. The first design she'd created that was truly her own. No replicating, no playing it safe. No, this one was *hers*.

Although, Anna contended as she opened her eyes, she wouldn't have made the plunge neckline quite so deep if she'd known she would be the one to wear it. But when Kess had called her up and told her that she needed Anna and would she please fly to Rome immediately with a suitcase of her designs, she'd put the dress and a few of her old passable works into a case and gone.

Except now she'd been catapulted from slow to light speed. What had started off as filling in some holes in Kess's first fashion show after a designer had pulled out had turned into her debut as a model when one of the girls had come down with food poisoning.

In classic Kess style, aside from a slight tightening of her lips, she hadn't shown how much each blow had stressed her out. No, she'd just sighed and plowed forward, determined to make her first show a success. When she'd approached Anna with the modeling request, it had terrified her. But Kess had always been there for her. It had been time for Anna to step up.

The gold of her dress shimmered beneath the lights backstage. A departure from the pastels she normally favored. She used to love the airiness, the crisp feeling, when she slid on something white. But after that damned article, all she saw was bland. Boring.

Virginal.

Even now she cringed at the picture of her that had been selected, the sensationalized text beneath. Although, she acknowledged with a slight smile, that article had at least done some good. In a moment of blazing *I'll show them* anger, she'd ordered the fabric that had turned into this dress.

"You okay?"

Anna opened her eyes to see Kess standing in front of her. Violet silk clung to the newest producer of Hampton Events's statuesque frame, stopping just short of her ankles. A seductive drape gave the audience a glimpse of the sparkles a makeup artist had dusted across Kess's ebony chest. She looked stunning.

Anna tried to give her friend a confident smile as someone tugged the fluffy layers of the skirt down over her legs. "A little different than T-shirts and sweatpants for late-night studying?"

Kess smiled as the concern disappeared. "A little. We're definitely not in Granada anymore."

"Kess!"

The stage manager's bellow cut through the cacophony of voices, hair dryers and music blaring over the crowd. Kess squeezed Anna's hand and hurried away. Two seconds later, the manager yelled for Anna to get in place.

She tapped the toe of her matching gold heel on the ground as butterflies danced in her chest.

One last walk. One last walk and then you're done and you never have to do this again.

Getting outside of her comfort zone was one thing. Being the center of attention was something else entirely.

"Last walk," she muttered to herself. "You can do it, you can do it."

The assistant in charge of the curtain glanced at her and then looked away, a small smile on his face. Compared to the legions of models he'd most likely seen over his career, she probably seemed ridiculous. Inexperienced.

Imposter syndrome reared its vicious head. What was she doing here? She wasn't a model. She was a barely there fashion designer who had only recently gotten noticed because of a magazine article that had focused more on her personal choices than her art. Even then, the interest had been fleeting, the majority of the requests related to her very loose relationship with one of the wealthiest families in Europe. The couple of inquiries on her actual work hadn't gone past portfolio requests.

She bit down on her lower lip. A nervous habit she'd developed as a child, one she'd mostly overcome. But moments like these brought it back; when she felt out of her depth and was thrust into the body of a frightened little girl who'd just lost her parents and heard over and over again that she would be protected, shielded from the cruelties of the world. Who, every time she had tried to venture out on her own, was faced with more restrictions, more rules, more questions about whether she was capable of doing this or that on her own. Over time, hearing how much her aunt and uncle didn't think she was strong had sunk into her bones. Her parents' deaths had changed her, zapped so much of who'd she been and left her hollowed out by grief, that she'd accepted their overbearing coddling, allowed herself to eventually believe that she was weak and needed others to depend on.

Except for one. She shook her head. No, he'd always encouraged her, told her she could do anything, be anyone.

Just not his lover.

She scrunched her eyes shut against the memory. Now was not the time to be thinking of one of her biggest failures.

"Go!"

The assistant's voice banished the last bits of the past. She opened her eyes, squared her shoulders and walked forward. A quick turn to the right after the drapery ended and she was back on the catwalk. Even though the blaring music made it impossible to hear almost anything else, the incessant click of cameras echoed as flashes went off around her.

Then it happened. The heel of the right shoe snapped. Thrown off balance, she stumbled once, twice, then pitched to the side and off the catwalk. In that moment, she heard the collective gasp of the crowd, the frantic clicking of the cameras, her own heartbeat thundering as the wisps of her skirt flew up into her face and thankfully blinded her to her most humiliating moment.

She landed in someone's lap. She couldn't see who, but she could feel him. *Most definitely a him*, she thought as strong arms wrapped around her and steadied her. Despite the severity of the moment, her body registered the muscular chest she was clasped against, the spicy amber scent rolling off her rescuer that simultaneously teased her with its familiarity and comforted her.

"I'm so sorry, I…" Her words trailed off as she pushed the material down and met the glittering brown eyes of the man she'd once loved.

Antonio Cabrera.

The world returned in a rush as the flashes intensified. Her first instinct was to hide her face in her hands, to try to slink off into the crowd and hope the paparazzi wouldn't follow.

Coward.

She swallowed hard. No matter how tempting, running away wouldn't solve anything. Plus, it would detract from Kess's show. And it would prove what Antonio had said all those years ago.

You're just a child, Anna.

She inhaled deeply and then looked Antonio straight in the eye.

"Could I request your assistance? Please," she added softly.

His lips quirked. "Other than rescuing a damsel in distress?"

It had been ten years since they'd last spoken. She thought she'd remembered his voice, but memories were nothing compared to the deep velvet that slid over her skin.

Steady. Now was not the time to be indulging in any kind of fantasy. Especially when she had a job to do.

"I need to get these heels off. Could you help me stand?"

Before she could stop him, he fisted his hand in the folds of her skirt and tugged up. Just to the middle of her calves, but the gesture froze her breath in her lungs. Her heart kicked into overdrive as his tan fingers slid over her ankles, undid the strap of the offending shoe with skilled dexterity, and slid it off. He repeated the same process with the other as she sat there like a child, barely keeping her mouth closed even as she wanted to release a sigh at how wonderful the brief grazes of his fingertips felt on her skin.

She should be embarrassed. Humiliated. Petrified as the cameras clicked on and the hum of audience gossip built like bees buzzing furiously.

But she didn't. All she felt, all she saw, was tied up in that moment.

"Thank you."

His eyes met hers and, for one second, she saw a mahogany fire flash within the depths.

Then it disappeared just as quickly as it had come. Whatever emotion she'd hoped she'd seen was probably nothing more than a reflection of the cameras capturing her literal fall from grace.

"Anna!"

She turned to see Kess approaching them.

"I'm getting back up." She shot her friend something that she hoped resembled a smile, aware that the world was watching every moment of her little drama. She started to shift on Antonio's lap and stand. A grunt escaped his lips.

"Oh! I'm sorry, did I hurt—"

He stood in one smooth motion, an arm wrapped around

her back, the other holding her legs as he strode forward and set her on the catwalk.

"You can do this," Kess whispered from behind her as Anna stood. Anna glanced down at her friend then silently chastised herself as her eyes inadvertently drifted to Antonio. He stared at her for one long moment, his gaze opaque, before giving her a nod of silent encouragement.

Anna swallowed hard and turned to face the audience. Thunderous applause rose up, echoing through the plaza as people cheered. She forced a smile onto her face to acknowledge the support of the crowd, inclined her head and then started forward, holding up the skirt so she didn't have a repeat performance.

Despite the warm reception to her tumble, her eyes grew hot. For one blissful moment she'd been distracted by Antonio. But now, standing alone on stage with all eyes fixed on her, it was a struggle to finish her walk without giving in to the embarrassment that tightened her throat or the worry in the back of her mind that she'd sunk Kess's show.

And then there was the knowledge that as she reached the end of the runway and posed, Antonio was watching her.

You can do this.

Kess's words added fuel to the fire that started to burn low in her belly. She could do this. She raised her chin, aimed one last watery smile right at the cameras, then turned and walked back down the runway.

She saw him out of the corner of her eye, could feel his gaze pinned on her. But she stayed focused, looking neither right nor left, as she neared the end.

Antonio had helped her tonight; that much was true. She would have to send him a thank-you card or something to the Cabrera family home in Spain. But his one moment of kindness didn't change that he had taken her offered heart and cruelly shattered it. That he'd never once reached out in all the time they'd been apart. At one time, he had been her friend, her strength, her first love.

But that time had come and gone.

She passed by him, proud of herself for not giving in to the temptation to look at him. This time, she was the one who would get to walk away.

CHAPTER TWO

An hour later, Anna sat facing the Trevi Fountain, arms crossed over her stomach as she stared up at the illuminated statues guarding the bubbling waters of the most famous fountain in the world. At nearly eleven o'clock at night, most of the crowds that had congregated to watch water flow from the historic landmark had disappeared, leaving her with a pleasant sensation of having the small plaza almost completely to herself.

After the show, Kess's firm had hosted a cocktail party. Anna had somehow made it through the hour-long event, her feet encased in flat sandals beneath the folds of her skirt. Judging by the praise she'd overheard Kess's boss bestowing on her, the fall hadn't negatively affected the show. If anything, it sounded like it was going to bring more attention to Kess, the featured designer, and Hampton Events.

After changing and wiping the layers of makeup off her face, Kess, who had turned the after-party over to her assistant, had invited her to walk to the Trevi Fountain. Kess's mom had called from Nigeria, so now she stood off to the side chatting about how her first show had gone, giving Anna time to just sit and breathe.

At first it had been blissful; the music of the water, the heat of the day giving way to the gentle warmth of an Italian summer evening. But the initial magic had dissipated, a fresh wave of embarrassment suffusing her limbs. Embarrassment and irritation that Antonio of all people had been the one to rescue her. What were the odds that she would not only fall at a fashion show, but fall into the arms of the man who'd rejected her so many years ago?

Her stomach rolled and she focused on the statue of Oceanus's nearly naked figure standing guard over the fountain. She was in *Rome*. Why ruminate on the past when she was in one of the most incredible cities on the planet? When just eight months ago she'd barely ventured out of Granada, let alone Spain? And now she was in front of one of the most iconic fountains known to man, letting her mind wander yet again to the city that had once seemed like her saving grace, only to turn into a prison.

Crossing her arms over her chest, she gazed out over the centuries-old architecture. The bearded, muscular statue of Oceanus presided over the masterpiece. Horses leapt out of stone on either side. Two nude male figures led the beasts, one trying to tame the wilder of the horses, the other raising a conch shell to his lips. Water splashed from beneath Oceanus's feet and tumbled down over three ledges before cascading into the massive pool filled with coins.

One coin tossed with your back to the fountain and you'll return to Rome.

She smiled. Kess had told her the legend on their walk to the fountain.

Two coins and you'll fall in love.

Antonio's face as she'd last seen it, youthful and yet so mature and serious at the tender age of nineteen, appeared in her mind.

Three coins and you'll be married soon.

Not a chance. She'd once dreamed of love, marriage, children. One day she'd circle back to that. But ever since she'd been let go from her job as a fashion buyer for a clothing retailer, she'd decided to finally stop existing and start living. The firing should have felt like a failure. But it had felt like a new beginning. Moving away from Granada, financing her own apartment in Paris for a year through a combination of her savings and a small inheritance, and finally picking back up the fashion design career she'd dreamed of in college. Granted, the portfolios she'd sent out the first half of the year had garnered almost no interest.

As angry as she was at Leo White, the fashion columnist, and how he'd used her, she did owe him one favor. He'd forced her to confront why her work wasn't getting any attention. The anger at how he'd used her had also uncovered confidence she hadn't even realized she possessed. Without his interference, the gold gown wouldn't exist and she would have never set foot on that catwalk.

Another glance at Kess confirmed she was still conversing with her mom.

The exhaustion spread, dragging Anna's shoulders down as she yawned. She'd flown into Rome last night, caught a few hours of sleep and dragged herself out of bed just after dawn. The thought of crawling into her cozy bed with its crisp sheets made her head droop.

But she wouldn't leave Kess. Not after everything she'd done for her. She'd been the first person since Antonio to push her, tell her she could achieve something on her own like switching her degree from generic business to the passion her mother had instilled in her with trips to thrift stores and dressing up at home. She hadn't recognized it at the time, but changing her degree against her aunt and uncle's strongly worded advice had been her first step toward moving away from their heavy influence.

Not that her uncle Diego or any of the others back at Casa de Cabrera had meant to be so controlling or to hurt her. Her uncle, especially. He'd gained a child while losing his beloved baby sister in that car accident. She knew that, as she'd grown, it had pained him to look at her sometimes.

When she glanced in the mirror, she saw her mother, just as he did.

A light breeze whispered across her skin. She looked up

again, taking in the exquisitely carved detail of the statues, lit up by the warm glow of spotlights. The lullaby of dancing water soothed the tension brought on by her hectic day.

Her eyes dropped once more to the coins winking at her from the fountain floor.

"Legend says if you toss a coin into the fountain, you'll return to Rome one day."

Her body tensed. Time had deepened his voice into a richer timbre that resonated through every nerve ending in her body and rooted her to the stones beneath her feet. The chaos of earlier had dimmed the effect. But now she felt it, every intonation seeping deep into her bones with an intoxicating, delicious warmth.

A hand appeared in front of her, palm up, a coin resting on long fingers.

How many times had she held that hand as a child, clasping those fingers as he'd led the way up a mountain path or under the winding vines of the vineyard, offering her a respite from the suffocating confines of her adopted home?

Or the last time she'd seen him, when he'd pulled his hand back and walked away from her?

"Rome is beautiful," she replied, inwardly wincing at the breathiness in her voice. "But why go back to what you've already seen when the world has so much more to offer?"

For a moment, he said nothing. Then, with a casual flip of his fingers, the coin arced up into the night air before dropping into the water.

You can do this.

Steeling herself, she faced Antonio Cabrera for the second time that evening.

The butterflies returned with a vengeance, madly fluttering in her chest as her heartbeat raced. When he'd walked away from her, he'd been just shy of twenty, with a smile so sweet it had made her ache. But now...

Sexy. That was the best word to describe the tall, brooding man standing just a couple of feet away. A black suit,

Armani label, judging by the cut and the glimpse she got of the unadorned silk lining. The material clung to his broad shoulders, customized for his muscular body. Even though he'd been shorter than his brothers, he still loomed over her. She should have kept her heels on. Then she wouldn't have to tilt her head back to meet his gaze.

His mahogany-brown gaze that ignited a spark deep inside her. One that burned brighter as her eyes slid over him, taking in both the familiar and the new. The familiar square jaw and sharp cheekbones, now dusted with dark stubble that should have looked scruffy but on him radiated roguish masculinity. The familiar chestnut hair, now trimmed on the sides and thick and wavy on top.

And his mouth. Familiar, but no longer gentle as it curved up into a smile. A sensual, brooding smile that fanned the flames burning inside her.

"Hello, Anna."

CHAPTER THREE

¡Dios mío!

Desire reared in his head, unbidden, unwanted, and dark with intensity as Antonio Cabrera watched Anna. *Anna Vega*, he reminded himself, an *A* and a *V* intertwined on the labels of her designs. He'd honed his skills over the past few years as head of Cabrera Properties, specifically their three luxury hotels. Negotiations, sales, the occasional ferreting out of an unsavory business partner. His reputation as tough but fair, an overall good man, had been hard fought.

What would his associates say if they could read his mind now? He'd thought his nineteen-year-old dream of Anna and him in bed had been bad; a dream that had been seceded days later by the fracturing of their friendship. But his adolescent fantasy was nothing compared to the want that had bolted through him when Anna had first stepped onto that runway in a gold gown with a skirt that shimmered like stars as she'd walked. Although the skirt had only held his attention for a second before his gaze had been drawn to the plunging neckline that almost reached her trim waist. Two panels of gauze had covered her breasts but left an enticing expanse of bare skin. The hint of a shy smile on her lips, painted a dusky pink, paired with a strength he'd never seen in the thrust of her shoulders and the tip of her chin, had upped the heat simmering in his veins.

The heat that had nearly spiraled out of control into a white-hot inferno when she'd landed in his lap.

He breathed in through his nose.

Off-limits. Old friend. Broke her heart. Virgin.

The reminders fell flat as he subtly flicked his eyes down her incredibly long legs. Anna Vega had grown into a stunning woman. Still slender but no longer the willow-thin wisp she'd been as a girl. No, he'd most definitely felt the curve of her hips, the nip of her waist when he'd briefly clasped her in his arms. Brown-black hair had grown down to her waist. The wide, rosy lips and those hypnotic eyes, one the rich color of amber, the other a pale blue.

Stunning. A sexiness he could have written off as mere attraction to a woman based on physical interest had she not gotten back up on the catwalk and finished her walk. He couldn't picture the old Anna facing the world after an embarrassing incident, let alone get up there in the first place. But this new Anna, the one who wore eye-popping gowns and modeled, was an entirely different and very enticing woman.

Diego had said nothing of modeling, he thought testily. Only that Anna's friend had talked her into showcasing her designs at a fashion show in Rome.

"I'm worried about her," Diego had said two days ago when he'd come into Antonio's office and asked for a favor. The wrinkles carved into his weathered face had deepened with his frown. "First, she lost her job. Then she ran off to Paris. And that magazine article that shared all her personal details…" His voice had trailed off, he'd inhaled deeply then pinned Antonio in place with a desperate gaze. "You said you'd be in Italy for a while. Would you check in on her? Make sure she's okay?"

Not his first choice of activities given how he and Anna had parted. He also didn't like that the butler apparently still treated Anna like a child. Diego's protective measures for Anna had rivaled that of Javier Cabrera and the restrictions he'd placed on his middle son, Alejandro.

But Diego had made a compelling argument. And it was the first thing the old butler had asked for in his thirty-plus years of service to the Cabrera family.

So he'd found out where Anna's friend's show was being held and secured a ticket. The company, Hampton Events, had checked out. So had Anna's friend, Kess. Still, he'd decided to watch the show, attend the after-party, confirm with his own eyes that Anna was okay before slipping away. She didn't even have to know he was there.

But then Anna had walked out on stage in that dress and he'd barely kept his mouth from dropping open. Each creation she'd worn, ones he'd read in the program had been designed by Anna herself, had shown just how much she'd grown into her woman's body. The first few had looked good on her, although they'd seemed fairly mundane.

But the gold gown…he hadn't been able to look away.

He'd convinced himself as he'd waited for her after the show that it was an anomaly, months of abstinence combined with the shock of seeing the "new" Anna. After the intensity of his reaction when she'd fallen into his arms, he'd been even more determined to see her; not just for old times' sake, but to see her in ordinary clothes, face scrubbed free of makeup, so his brain could let a certain part of his anatomy know she wasn't that stunning.

Bad idea.

Very bad, because Anna was even more beautiful without the dressings of couture. A lean face with sharp angles softened by wide lips and her gentle multicolored gaze presented an alluring contrast.

The last time he'd seen her, she'd been growing into the gangly limbs that had propelled her and her wild imagination through the vineyards year after year as he'd tried to keep up. Back then, she'd had to tilt her head back to meet his eyes. Now she stood just a few inches shorter than his own six-foot-two. The black jacket over a white T-shirt and slim jeans she wore should have looked casual. But the damned clothes drew his eye to the curves of her breasts and her long, long legs.

"I'm well."

Her abrupt answer snapped him out of his inappropriate perusal.

"Quite a different environment than Granada." He nodded toward the sparkling waters of the fountain.

"I bet you're used to glamorous destinations like this."

He frowned. She'd surprised him by not taking the coin he'd offered. The old Anna would have clutched it to her chest, closed her eyes, murmured a wish and tossed it into the fountain with glee. The rejection, small as it was, unsettled him.

Now you know what it feels like.

The nasty whisper inside his head deepened his frown. He had no reason to feel guilty about what had transpired between him and Anna the last time they'd spoken. None.

"I do travel a lot, yes. But apparently you have, too. Diego mentioned you've been living in Paris?"

Her lips softened a fraction. "It's been fun."

The distance in her voice was very un-Anna-like. He also didn't like that she didn't take the bait, acknowledge that she'd been at Adrian and Everleigh's party. He'd seen her from the balcony, felt a prickle of awareness and looked up just in time to see her run away. Surprisingly, it had hurt. Growing up, and especially after Alejandro had been banished to England, Anna had been his best friend.

"Sorry I landed on your lap."

He waved the apology aside. "Not a planned event, I'm sure."

"No. What are you doing here?" she asked as she crossed her arms over her chest.

"One of my hotels is just a few blocks over. I know the owner of the Hotel dell'Orchidea. He offered me a ticket to tonight's event." The lie rolled off his tongue. "I wasn't expecting to see you on the runway."

She huffed. "I wasn't, either. My friend Kess is the producer of the show. A model got sick this afternoon, and I wanted Kess's first show to be a success." She glanced down at her feet, one hand drifting up to tuck a wisp of hair behind her ear. "I don't know if you've talked to my uncle recently, but I was let go from my job in Granada earlier this year."

"He mentioned it."

She bit down on her lower lip. "Yeah. Embarrassing for the girl who wanted to make a career in fashion."

He frowned. "From what your uncle said, the company was bought out and downsized your office. Nothing about your talent."

"I guess." She looked up but not at him. Her gaze drifted back to the fountain, her expression one of defeat. "I know that, logically. Stupid that it still kicked my pride."

Her dejected tone negated her agreement and thrust him back to the little girl who had appeared in the grand foyer of Casa de Cabrera seventeen years ago, newly orphaned, eyes downcast, and a pink suitcase clutched in her tiny hand like a lifeline.

He followed her line of sight to the fountain.

"Tell me what you see."

She glanced at him, a little V forming between her brows. "What?"

"I'm curious what you're seeing as a first-time visitor. Whenever I'm in Rome, I pass by the Trevi Fountain multiple times a day." He turned and pointed to the sandstone-colored towers of the Hotel de Cabrera standing proudly against the sky just beyond the plaza. "After a while, you get used to it." He stepped toward her. Satisfaction wound its way through him as he noted the flare in her gaze, the quick intake of breath.

What kind of a bastard did that make him? To reject

her years ago, yet still thrill at the confirmation that she wasn't immune to him, at least physically? After the horrific night that had almost resulted in death, he'd tried to make amends and resume the mantle of the good son he'd worn so well during his teenage years, even if his parents didn't know what had happened.

His brothers did. They knew every sordid detail, which was why, after that night, he'd kept them at arm's length. He loved his brothers, respected them, appreciated their discretion and, when he'd needed it most, their support. But their knowing what he'd done, taking care of his mistakes and making sure that nothing was leaked by the hospital or the police, had made him withdraw.

In a way, his reverting to being "the good son" and making up for the effects their behavior had had on their parents in the ensuing years felt like repaying a debt. Adrian's distant coolness had hurt their mother, while Alejandro's misadventures had infuriated their father. Antonio's warm relationship with his mother and his respectable reputation had eased his parents' pain and taken the burden off his brothers. It had also felt justly like punishment. Why should he get to enjoy life when he'd nearly taken someone else's?

But apparently his body was tired of being the good son because right now the faint floral scent emanating from Anna's lush hair had him imagining her sprawled across the silk sheet of the Presidential Suite, her dark tendrils spread across a pillow as he slid the gold gown off her body.

"Tell me," he said again, managing to keep his voice even, "what do you see? What's it like to see the most famous fountain in the world for the first time?"

She watched him for a moment, eyes narrowed. Suspicion rolled off her in thick, palpable waves. He stared right back. He'd faced down furious hotel owners, greedy executives and, earlier in the summer, a very angry supermodel who couldn't understand why going through his phone would result in him sending her away from the Caribbean resort he'd whisked her to. He could most certainly face down his former best friend and, hopefully, yank her out of her melancholy state. It was the least he could do.

Although, the longer she stared at him, those colorful eyes glittering in the evening light, the more he wondered if he'd made a mistake. Anna had always seen what others hadn't. The hurt of Alejandro's absence. His anger at his father for taking away his brother. The helplessness at being unable to solve his mother's pain over Adrian's coldness.

What did she see now?

Finally, she turned away and faced the fountain. As the water splashed and the lights illuminated the centuries-old architecture, her shoulders relaxed.

"It's incredible."

She uttered the words in a breathy, sensuous voice. *Damn it.* But he'd started this game, goaded her into spinning a story just like she had when they'd traipsed around the Granada estate. A leaf carried on the wind had become a vessel carrying fairies to the nearby woods. A scuff mark in the dirt had been the result of a goblin being spooked from napping in the vineyards. Anna had lived in a world of make-believe. As a child, he'd found it enchanting. As a young man, it had been one of the many reasons that had convinced him that Anna was off-limits. She'd been so young, so sweet in her dreamy-eyed innocence.

"I can imagine all the people who have come here over the years," she continued, her eyes wide as she visually feasted on the sight before her. "Lovers in the eighteenth century stealing out at night to toss a coin in the fountain and share a kiss. A mother praying her son would come home from a war. An old man paying homage to his late wife." Her lips turned up into the first true smile he'd seen. "Remember all the fairy tales I read as a child? Perhaps at night the statues come to life and the horses gallop across the water." Her laugh electrified him, as bubbly as the water cascading down into the pool. "If I close my eyes, I can hear them." She turned to look at him and, upon meeting his stare, froze. Pink tinted her cheeks and she lowered her eyes, as if embarrassed. "Sorry. Probably not what a travel connoisseur like yourself would put in a guidebook."

He'd wanted to hear the old Anna. Be reminded of some of the happiest times of his life while also being reminded that this was *Anna*. Fashion designer, model, or whatever she'd become, she was an old friend, not a woman to be lusted after.

Unfortunately, as she'd spoken, he'd realized that while the old Anna who found magic in a sunset still existed, she'd grown up. Grown up and mixed that intoxicating magic with confidence that wove a spell so tight he could barely take a breath.

"You'd be surprised," he found himself saying. "Not what I'd put in a guidebook," he added with the slightest hint of a smile, "but an Instagram post or a review to share with our guests? Absolutely."

Her face lit up with joy once more as she grinned.

"Maybe I can translate telling tall tales into a career if my designs don't take off." She nodded in the direction of the hotel. "Kess's first time producing and the first time my designs have been on a runway."

"Is that what you've been doing since you moved to Paris? Designing?"

She nodded. "Not much success. Yet."

The desire to ask about the magazine article lingered on the tip of his tongue. When he'd read Leo White's description of Anna—*The niece of the Cabreras' long-time butler, an aspiring fashion designer with a love of fairy tales who's saving herself for her Prince Charming*—he'd been livid at such a private detail being aired to the world and…shocked. Intrigued. A tendril of lust he'd squelched as quickly as it had appeared.

"Who is Kess?" he asked. A much safer topic of conversation.

Anna gestured toward the far side of the fountain, where a tall black woman in a blue sundress stood chatting on the phone, although her gaze was trained on him and Anna. Even at this distance, he recognized the photos his private investigator had delivered in a thick folder, part of the dossier he'd put together.

"Kess Abiola?"

"Yes. We went to school together in Granada. Kind of cool knowing someone who actually made it in the industry and got hired by a big firm like Hampton. This is her first show, but she'll be booking big names within the year."

Antonio bit back a smile. Anna had always been a loyal friend. The pride for Kess rang strong in her voice.

"Although," she added, the brief sparkle of her expression dimming, "I guess you're probably used to rubbing elbows with the rich and famous."

"Alejandro, as you know, was much more drawn to supermodels and actresses and heiresses than I was."

"I saw he's engaged." Anna shuddered. "Hard to imagine the boy who put peanut butter in my sneakers and a fake spider in my coat pocket having a wife."

"Would you believe he's marrying a woman who's a straitlaced rule follower?"

Anna laughed, a sound that was as cheerful as it was deep and rich.

"I think I met her, actually, at Adrian and Everleigh's engagement party. She was very kind to me. And Adrian is married now, and expecting." Anna smiled. "Your mother must be thrilled."

"She is." Although the last time he'd seen his mother, just before journeying to Rome, she'd been unusually pensive for a woman who had gained two daughters-in-law who seemed to adore her.

"I saw you. At the engagement party."

Anna's eyes darted down.

"Did you? I didn't see you."

"Didn't you?" She looked up, startled, and he held her gaze. "I could have sworn when I looked out from the balcony you saw me and turned away."

She sighed.

"I didn't feel like having the first time we saw each other after…" Her voice trailed off and she waved a hand in the air. "The *incident* be at your brother's engagement party."

The Incident. She sounded almost disdainful when she said the words. He narrowed his eyes. She was physically attracted to him. And when she'd fallen into his arms, he could have sworn he'd seen the same emotion on her face that he'd seen when she'd told him she loved him.

Now…now he couldn't tell. Her blue-amber gaze was shuttered, her face still as if it had been carved from the same marble as the statues behind her.

"Anna."

Kess approached them, the sundress molded to her tall frame. So tall, in fact, that her dark green eyes were level with his.

"I didn't realize you had friends in Rome."

She stopped next to Anna, her eyes razor-sharp, her look of warning clear in its meaning. Anna was someone she cared about and if Antonio did anything to hurt her, she'd make him sorry.

He gave her a slight nod.

"This is Antonio. He's an old friend."

The producer extended her hand. "Kess."

"I know." He smiled as he accepted her hand, acknowledging her place in Anna's life and her subtle threat.

Kess stared at him a moment longer. Whatever she saw must have passed her test because she returned his smile.

"Ready to go back to the hotel?" Kess asked Anna.

Dismay settled heavily in his chest. He'd only planned on stopping by to see the show and say hello, make sure she was handling the newfound publicity all right and then leave. But the evening had gone by in a flash, each moment whirring by so quickly, time had been like water in his hands.

That he wanted just a few more minutes in her company was indicator enough it was time for him to bid farewell and put as much distance between Anna and him as possible. He'd hurt her once in his quest to do the right thing. He wouldn't risk hurting her again.

That and, despite his brothers' obvious happiness, a long-term relationship wasn't in the cards for him. Most definitely not now, perhaps not ever. His career took him all over the world. With the addition of his collaboration with Alejandro on the floating hotel *La Reina* in Marseille, and future projects in the works, he had no time for a girlfriend, let alone a wife or children. Anna had spoken often of wanting to be a mother. As much as the thought of another man being with her—*touching her*—bothered him, someone else would have to give her the gifts of commitment and motherhood.

Even if he'd been interested in marriage, even if they'd both be able to get past the pain of their last encounter, he would never be able to trust himself to take a risk again.

And Anna was most definitely a risk.

"I don't know," Anna replied to Kess's question, drawing him out of his thoughts. "I'd thought about going to see the Spanish Steps."

"It can be crowded at night," Antonio interrupted.

"Is there a good time to go?"

"Dawn."

Anna scrunched up her nose. "Not my first choice of time. But I'll try."

"I hope you enjoy it." He glanced at his watch. "I have to get back to my hotel. Duty calls." An excuse, but a tried-and-true one. He nodded to Kess and then to Anna. "It was good to see you. I assume I'll see you at Alejandro's wedding in a couple of weeks."

She stared at him for a long moment, those eyes gleaming with something he couldn't quite decipher.

"Sorry again about earlier. Good to see you, too, Antonio."

He paused. He didn't like leaving things this way.

But you have to. He'd built his identity on his principles, on doing the right thing. Seducing his virginal childhood best friend whose heart he'd already broken once was most definitely the wrong thing. He would withdraw, take an ice-cold shower, and regroup in the morning. He'd fulfilled his promise to Diego, made sure Anna was all right. Now he needed to leave and let Anna live her life.

With that thought resonating in his mind, he walked away, leaving Anna and all the temptation she presented behind him.

CHAPTER FOUR

PINK RAYS OF early morning sun nudged the remaining shadows of night aside and bathed the ancient buildings of Rome in a rosy glow.

Beautiful. Anna wrapped her arms around her middle and breathed in. All her life she'd dreamed of traveling to places like this. Especially in the last five years as her friends from university had left Granada for bigger and better things while she'd returned night after night to the same yellow bedroom with its white chintz curtains and twin bed. Still stuck in the past. Stuck in the confines of her uncle's fears. Stuck in her own.

But no more.

She passed by a bakery, the doors thrown open, golden light falling on the stones outside the shop and freshly baked rosemary bread scenting the air. One of the few businesses open before sunrise. A bird flitted past. Violet flowers spilled from an urn. The only signs of life on the otherwise empty cobblestone streets.

Amazing, she thought with a little thrill, that she was in one of the most visited places in the world and yet felt like she had the entire city to herself.

She turned a corner and stopped in her tracks. Some of her joy dissipated as she read the black lettering emblazoned over the glass doors of a tall building sprawled across the entire front of the plaza she'd just walked into.

Hotel de Cabrera.

"Of course," she muttered.

Italian flags framed the doors on either side. Perfectly arranged sconce lights created intricate diamond patterns on the cream-colored stones. Most of the arched windows were covered by burgundy curtains. Although, as she looked up to the top floor, one curtain twitched then was drawn aside. A woman in black lingerie stood in the window, framed like a seductive painting as she gazed confidently out over the plaza. A man appeared behind her, pressed a lingering kiss to her neck as she smiled and then the curtain fell back over the window.

What would it be like to have that kind of confidence? To look out over the world with such assurance?

Granted, she'd surprised herself with her own strength the last few months. Although, she acknowledged irritably, yesterday's bravado when faced with her first love had not come effortlessly. She'd had to make multiple mental trips into the past, summoning up the hot flush of shame that had swept over her when Antonio had stared at her like she'd grown an extra head and not just confessed her love at the tender age of seventeen. Or the freezing sting of rejection that had rooted her in place when he'd walked away.

Amazing how fresh the hurt felt after all these years. But it had done its job yesterday; helped her keep her distance even though her heart had been pounding so hard the beat had echoed in her ears.

He is attractive, she reminded herself as she resumed her trek across the plaza. *Perfectly reasonable reaction.*

Well, not just attractive. More like sexy as hell. She'd been in such a rush to hide at Adrian and Everleigh's engagement party that she'd only caught a glimpse of his dark handsomeness. And when she'd fallen yesterday, her flustered mind had latched onto two details: the deep, dark brown of his eyes and his rich, woodsy scent that had momentarily stolen her voice.

But when they'd talked by the Trevi Fountain, she'd had the opportunity to see him, truly see him, for the first time since their parting at the vineyards in Granada. His strong jaw, fierce lines still evident beneath his dark beard. The boyish smile she'd remembered so fondly replaced by a brooding smirk that had chased away her girlhood dreams and replaced them with dark, sensual fantasies. Fantasies that included Antonio's masculine arms wrapped around her as he lowered his mouth to hers...

As if her naughty musings had summoned him, there he was, striding out of the doors of the hotel. Dressed in tan slacks and a forest-green polo that fit his muscular chest to perfection, he looked far too awake and professional for such an early hour as he scrolled through his phone.

The confidence that had empowered her last night took one look at Antonio in all his handsome glory, turned and fled, leaving her in the middle of the plaza with nothing but her old insecurities and self-doubt. His attention was fixed on his phone. If she quickened her pace and kept her head down, she could reach the other side before he—

"Anna?"

Too late.

She forced herself to stop and smile casually at him, even though the closer he drew, the faster the butterfly wings in her stomach beat until she felt like her entire body fluttered.

"*Buongiorno*, Antonio."

He arched a brow as he stopped a few feet away. She remembered his older brother, Adrian, doing that when he'd found them in the vineyards stuffing themselves with grapes. On him, it had looked arrogant and stuffy. On Antonio, it looked masculine and sensual.

"You're up early."

"You said the best viewing of the Steps was at dawn." She nodded toward the burgeoning glow above the rooftops. "It's almost here."

He glanced over his shoulder then back at her, chocolate eyes dark and unreadable.

"That's the only reason you're here?"

She frowned. "Why else would I be?"

He stared at her a moment longer before flashing her the tiniest smile.

"I'm going with you."

For a moment, she just gazed at him, the words not making sense.

"Go with me?" she repeated.

"To the Spanish Steps."

Her pulse kicked into overdrive as she blinked at him like a deer caught in the glare of headlights. Conflict raged inside her chest. More time spent in his company was risky given the roller coaster of emotions she'd been riding since last night. Not to mention all the opportunities it created for her to stick her foot in her mouth. Her rational mind listed off these reasons even as temptation whispered for her to seize what Antonio offered.

Say no. Say no.

"Why?"

A frown clouded his face. Most women probably said yes to anything he asked without a second thought. She hadn't sought out information about him but that hadn't stopped pictures gracing the covers of magazines, or popping up on Instagram from time to time, of Antonio occasionally in front of one of his resorts or at some high-profile meeting, and once in a while with his arm securely around the waist of a gorgeous actress or heiress to such-and-such a business empire.

Each picture had been a stab to her heart. Over time, those stabs had become less painful, more of a quick, dull ache. Except now the images paraded through her mind, ripping the Band-Aids off her wounds and flooding her with fresh pain.

She must be a glutton for punishment to even consider

spending time with him when all he'd brought her the last ten years was hurt.

"I haven't seen the Spanish Steps in a long time. I haven't seen you in even longer."

"You saw me last night."

"For five minutes."

"And then you left," she retorted, unexpected irritation hardening her voice. She didn't get angry. Anger hadn't been a part of her idyllic childhood before the car accident that had claimed her parents' lives. After she'd been sent from the sultry wet heat of Louisiana's bayous to the dry, arid slopes of the Sierra Nevada mountains to live with her uncle Diego and aunt Lonita, she'd quickly learned that anything other than a demure smile sent her new family into a tailspin. Tears led to more restrictions to keep her safe from sadness. Ire led to caution about the dangers of going too far down the path of anger...followed by more restrictions.

Safety had become synonymous with repression. Diego's fear of losing his sister's daughter had colored his decisions on everything from the friends she spent time with outside of school to where she went to university. He had always stepped in, taking care of things for her, encouraging her to ask for help, ask for help, always ask for help, never feel like she had to do anything alone.

Sometimes she asked for help because she knew if she attempted something on her own, it would frighten him. Other times, even when she thought herself capable, a fear had sprouted up inside her, a fear that the reason everyone was always offering to help her, to watch out for her, was that she really couldn't do it on her own. She still felt that fear, felt that pervasive intrusion at the worst possible moments.

Perhaps it was the absence of fear that had allowed her frustration at Antonio's sudden about-face to come through. Because there was nothing to fear, she realized. Yes, she'd had an adolescent crush at him at one point. A part of her would always care for him. At one point, he'd been her best friend, the only person in her life who'd believed her capable of more.

But the worst had already happened. He'd rejected her. She'd dealt with the pain. She'd gotten a degree in fashion, made friends, moved to Paris.

And now… She raised her chin. She was going after her dream. Whether she and Antonio parted ways now or spent an hour in each other's company, it wouldn't change all she'd accomplished on her own.

Or that, after today, aside from Alejandro and Calandra's wedding, she probably wouldn't see Antonio again.

The ache pulsing in her chest dimmed a little as elation spread through her. She *could* do this. She could act like a mature adult, sightsee with an old friend and then say goodbye. And if his departure hurt a little, she'd been through worse and survived.

"All right."

"Don't sound too excited," he replied dryly.

A small smile tugged at her lips. "I am excited to see the Steps."

His low chuckle stirred a warmth in her belly. He stepped forward, took her hand in his and tucked it into the crook of his arm.

Relax. Enjoy the moment.

With that mantra playing on Repeat in her head, she flashed a smile up at Antonio and moved forward. The sun was rising, she was in one of the oldest cities in the world, and a very handsome and very famous billionaire was escorting her through the streets.

Antonio played the perfect tour guide, pointing out the history of a random building here or a random statue there. At first, she enjoyed it; the deepness of his voice, the heat of his arm beneath her hand, the magic of Rome.

But every now and then something about his tone unsettled her. Commanding, self-assured in his knowledge, yet distant. An occasional glance confirmed that his face was smooth, almost devoid of expression. The teasing glint she'd glimpsed last night when she'd fallen off the stage, the whimsical offer of a coin to toss in the fountain, were absent, replaced by a mysterious man she didn't know.

The thought dimmed some of her excitement. He reminded her of his older brother, Adrian. A little more personable but restrained, in control. Granted, he was in charge of two European luxury hotels, a hotel in the Caribbean and a real estate firm with properties around the world. Being intimidating was probably a billionaire requirement.

It didn't take away some of the nostalgic sadness for the boy with a kind smile and a deep soul who had been her friend, her protector and eventually her love. Come to think of it, she'd noticed that distance in him before yesterday. The one and only other time she'd seen him in the last ten years, at the party in Paris. She'd remembered him being happy, carefree, almost worshipping of his brothers back in Granada. But that day, even though she'd seen him congratulating Adrian on the balcony, there had been something reserved in his manner.

Whatever had happened to Antonio had affected more than just their friendship. Curiosity and sadness trickled through her.

"Everything all right?"

She looked up into his handsome face. Eyes the color of molten dark chocolate, thick brows drawn into a slight frown. She'd once been able to tell him everything. She'd taken a leap last night when she'd gotten back up on the catwalk. What if she took another leap now? Asked what had happened, what had changed him?

"Anna?"

"Fine," she responded brightly. What was the point in pushing? She didn't know the man escorting her through

Rome. She knew who he used to be. But what would it accomplish to ask an intimate question when in an hour or two he'd once again be out of her life?

His lips parted, probably to pursue. He'd been the one person Uncle Diego had trusted her with. Would Diego have allowed the friendship had he known that Antonio pushed her, encouraged her? The adventures he'd planned, from wandering the streets of Granada after school to exploring the mountain slopes, had reinvigorated her joy for life after her parents' deaths. He'd drawn her out of the armor everyone else had built to keep her safe, dismantling it piece by piece, then done the unthinkable; handed her the reins to fix whatever obstacle she'd been facing, from bullies at school to what she wanted to do after graduation. It had been empowering. Strengthening.

It had made her fall in love with him.

She looked away, searching for something, anything, to distract him.

"Oh!"

The exclamation that burst from her lips was authentic. A stone boat sat in the middle of the street, partially sunk below the cobblestones. The boat lay in a small pool, water trailing over the sides and out the bow and stern. A smaller fountain stood in the middle of the boat, shedding water into its belly.

"I didn't even know this existed," she breathed as they drew closer. "I can't believe it's just sitting in the middle of the road."

"It's suffered damage here and there."

"I'd never have guessed with how perfect it looks. What's it called?"

"Fontana della Barcaccia. Fountain of the Leaky Boat."

She laughed. "Descriptive."

The corner of his mouth quirked. "Legend has it that when the city flooded in 1598, a boat was left in this exact spot when the waters receded."

"What a lovely piece of lore." Her eyes moved past him and settled on the Spanish Steps climbing up to the Trinità dei Monti, the crosses of the church's two towers standing tall against the backdrop of a few puffy clouds drifting lazily across the sky. Terra-cotta pots overflowing with bright pink flowers were artfully placed all over the staircase.

"I don't know which is more beautiful," Anna said with another laugh as she darted around the fountain and started for the stairs. She bounced up the first flight, giddiness and anticipation filling her with every step. She stopped at the first landing and spun around, her smile so wide it almost hurt, but she couldn't stop it even if she'd wanted to as she breathed Rome in. The gentle fragrance of the flowers surrounding her, the soft hum of conversation as more people moved into the plaza and ascended the Steps, the warmth of the sun on her back as it climbed higher into the sky. Somewhere, a musician started to play an accordion, the rich, reedy melody adding the perfect festive touch to an already perfect scene.

And Antonio. Against all odds, she was sharing this incredible moment with someone who had been a dear friend, her fellow adventurer. She smiled down at him…

For a moment she thought a cloud had moved over the sun as the plaza dimmed. Goose bumps pebbled on her skin. Antonio was staring at her, standing on the bottom step, eyes narrowed, jaw tight and expression almost cold. A look she'd seen once before, an expression of disdain.

She crossed her arms over her stomach. She knew what would come next…unless she left before he could reject her again.

Had she truly thought she could handle the pain she'd known was waiting at the end? She should have told him no outside the hotel, walked away with her head held high instead of setting herself up for this.

She swallowed hard and hurried back along the steps.

"Sorry, got caught up in the moment. It's starting to get

busy." Her lips began to ache they were stretched so tight
into an overly bright smile "It was nice to see you, Antonio.
I have to get back, we're supposed to leave by—"

"Anna." He stepped in front of her and blocked her path.

She inhaled deeply to steady herself, but all it did was
fill her with the scent of him.

You can do this.

She'd faced down a runway full of professional models,
a crowd of the crème de la crème of European society, and
an ex-best friend. She'd gotten back up after she'd fallen,
both figuratively and literally.

She squared her shoulders and raised her eyes to meet
his.

His gaze hardened. She took a step back as uncertainty
whispered through her. He took her arm and she gasped as
his fingers circled her wrist, firm and warm, like they had
been last night when he'd so deftly removed her heels. Gone
were her teenage fantasies of a chaste kiss on the lips. Instead, her innocent dreams had been replaced by the deep,
dark desire to feel his hard, muscular body against hers.

"Anna," he repeated, and she jolted, her cheeks heating.
"Yes?"

"We need to talk."

CHAPTER FIVE

ANNA'S EYES WIDENED. Judging by how he'd tried to rush off, she'd probably been expecting some form of rejection. Not that Antonio could blame her. When she'd spun around on the Steps, he'd been captivated. He hadn't been able to discern which shone brighter, the sunlight that backlit her body or the smile on her face. It had sparked a cascade of memories, of how much Anna had enjoyed anything and everything with a joy he'd experienced just by being around her and seeing the world through her eyes.

He knew as soon as he'd seen her in the plaza this morning that he should have said hello and continued on. Dealt with the other matter by email or a phone call. Something where they weren't in close physical proximity.

But, his conscience had argued, that was the coward's way out. This needed to be dealt with in person. So he'd placed himself in his own private hell as he'd escorted her, her hand tucked into the crook of his arm making heat simmer in his blood. The initial touch had burned like hot silk gliding over his skin. He'd managed to quell his subsequent lust by recalling the article Alejandro had gleefully texted him at two in the morning.

He'd wondered when he'd seen her outside the hotel if she'd seen it, had been waiting for him to talk or even seek out the comfort of an old friend. He never would have thought he'd be playing her knight in shining armor once more, but here they were, twice in less than twenty-four hours, at the mercy of the gossip-hungry media.

Unease rippled through him. Would they dig up what had happened? What he'd spent the past ten years trying to atone for? The one night he'd slipped, tried to indulge in a bit of illicit fun, for which his best friend had nearly paid the ultimate price. It had confirmed that taking personal risks wasn't something he could afford to do. Especially when he had the guilt of William's brush with death and the humiliation of both his brothers having to come to his recue constantly lurking in the background of everything he did.

He'd put everyone at arm's length since that night. William. His brothers. Anna. He'd always been the "good son" growing up, but after the accident, he'd sought out, and achieved, perfection. The perfect son, the perfect student, the perfect CEO. His mother's sadness over her lack of a relationship with her oldest son had been assuaged by her youngest's achievements. His own aspirations of translating his enjoyment of travel had been transformed into a career when his father had handed him control of Cabrera Properties and the opening of the French Riviera hotel because of his stellar academics and internship with the family's hotels in London, his successes mollifying the effects of Alejandro's antics on their sire. He was generous to those who demonstrated loyalty and definitive in cutting those who weren't out of his life and his business. And now his holdings, especially his three hotels, were thriving because of his leadership, with a fourth hotel in the works. A unique property that, when successful, would be another notch in his professional portfolio.

He enjoyed women, too. Not as much of a monk as Adrian, but not as much of a libertine as Alejandro. Conversation, companionship, and good sex coupled with discretion made for the best relationships. If any one of those factors were missing, he ended it, swiftly and usually generously.

A well-ordered life. Predictable, more luxurious than he deserved, yet controlled. One that had been upset with the media's suddenly obsessive attention on the older Cabrera brothers both getting engaged so quickly. The mania surrounding his family had reached new heights as reporters had turned their eye on him, wondering who would catch "the last Cabrera bachelor." It had reached a fever pitch in the weeks following Adrian and Everleigh's wedding in New York. Reporters camped out on the sidewalk across from his hotels, trying to get a photo of whomever he might be escorting home after a date. The last time someone had been bold enough to approach him directly, he'd brushed them off with a bland, "Who I'm seeing is none of your concern." That reporter had run with a story that Antonio *was* dating someone, leading to a new feeding frenzy of discovering who had captured the youngest Cabrera's heart.

This article, no doubt one of many in the pipeline after Anna's landing in his lap, was only going to make it worse. Not only were the papers gleefully declaring that they had uncovered his secret girlfriend, but he hadn't been able to get her out of his mind since last night. Usually, nightmares plagued his evenings. Waking up drenched in sweat to the echoes of glass breaking and metal screeching was not unusual.

But last night… No, last night when he'd woken, it had been to blood pounding through his veins and vivid images of Anna splayed across his bed. That was why, when she'd spun around, eyes full of dreams and her thousand-watt smile aimed right at him, he'd been furious with himself. He'd told himself he'd escorted her so they could talk about the article. But it had been selfish motivation that had made him offer to walk her, not a desire to help. He'd wanted more time in her company, to bask in the happiness she created and savor time with the beautiful, confident young woman she'd grown into.

A flash cut him off before he could speak. He turned in time to see a wiry young man with sunglasses and a baseball cap pulled down low streak across the plaza, a camera clutched in his hand.

"Maldito."

The oath escaped as the wind caught the photographer's hat and lifted it off his head. The man slowed, glanced back... And quickened his pace into a sprint when he realized he was in the crosshairs of Antonio's furious gaze.

Antonio crossed the plaza in several quick strides, his legs eating up the distance. He plucked the ball cap off the cobblestones and made a mental note of the logo emblazoned on the front before throwing it in a nearby trashcan.

"We need to get out of sight," he said as he crossed back to Anna. He reached out, grabbed her hand and dragged her along the stairs.

"Antonio, what—"

"Now, Anna."

For a moment, she hesitated. Then she fell silent and allowed him to pull her down the Steps, across the stones and into a narrow alley. Greenery-filled terra-cotta pots lined the street as vines twisted their way up walls. Aside from the waiter sleepily draping white cloths over tables outside a café, the neighborhood was empty.

"Where are we?"

"The Via Margutta. An artistic quarter."

"This is from *Roman Holiday*!"

He tempered his fury as Anna pulled away and walked a few steps down the alley. She obviously hadn't seen the article, didn't understand the implications of a photographer following them and snapping their photo this early in the morning. Let her have a few more moments of bliss before he yanked the rug out from under her.

He gritted his teeth. He'd grown up with the media scrutinizing his every move. He knew the importance in addressing potentially harmful news. Since she'd arrived in Spain, Anna had grown up in a bubble. As much as he respected Diego, he hadn't understood the obsession with keeping Anna locked down so tightly. Anyone could have seen how miserable she was at being so restrained.

And yet, as he watched her look around the alley in wide-eyed wonder, he felt a moment of kinship with the family's butler. In that moment he wanted to keep her safe, bundle her back to Granada before a reporter climbed up the drainpipe outside her hotel to sneak a picture of her getting out of the shower or stalked her all over town.

Determination settled in his bones. By showing up last night, he'd done more harm than good. He was responsible for this, so it was up to him to fix it.

"Gregory Peck's character lived on this street. A reporter," she said as she looked up, eyes fixed on the windows above them. "Started out scummy, but ended very sweetly."

"Unfortunately, most reporters don't undergo such a dramatic character revision," Antonio replied dryly. "I have evidence of that."

"So do I." She frowned, a frustrated huff escaping her lips. "Did you see the magazine article?"

He paused then answered truthfully. "Yes."

She closed her eyes for a moment, then opened them, pinning him with that arresting amber-blue gaze.

"He spoke to me at Alejandro and Everleigh's party." She huffed again and tucked a strand of loose hair behind her ear. "At first I was…flattered. He asked about the dress I was wearing, one I designed."

"How did he find out…" He let his voice trail off, one eyebrow going up suggestively. Cool, collected. Even though he was anything but on the inside.

She grimaced. "Because I'm an idiot. He made a raunchy joke, I replied I wouldn't know because I'd barely even been kissed. He lasered in on my comment like a sniper. Asked if I was waiting for Prince Charming. I got flustered and said 'Something like that.'"

More hair fell out of the loose bun on top of her head. A messy style that should have looked frazzled, but on her looked carefree an, like she'd just rolled out of bed. She probably had, he realized, an image of her in bed in nothing but a negligee flaring in his mind.

She sighed, brushed the hair behind her ears again in a gesture that reawakened a memory of her scampering up a hillside, perching atop a boulder and smiling down at him, cheeky and barefoot and innocent.

Innocent.

The word burst through his illicit daydreams.

"You would think," she said, continuing on with no clue as to what debauchery his mind had just entertained, "that a mention in a top fashion magazine would be everything an aspiring designer could want. But the inquiries I've gotten haven't been about my work. Well, hardly," she amended as she started fiddling with her bun, tugging and pulling loose strands up through the band. "Most have been about your family, inside information on Adrian and Alejandro. Do I know who you're dating…blah-blah-blah." She yanked so hard on one strand of hair, he nearly winced on her behalf. "Leo White made me sound like a naïve goof. No respectable brand is taking me seriously—they just remember that I'm 'the aspiring virgin designer.'"

Her head snapped up at the sound of his snort.

"What?"

"Did someone actually say that to you?"

"Yes. And don't you laugh," she retorted with a fire that intrigued him. The old Anna had never stood up for herself. "The couple of portfolio requests haven't gone past a 'thanks for sending this.'" She shook her head, the strands she'd just put in place falling once more to form a halo of dark brown around her face. "Although that's my own fault."

"How so?"

Another shake, dislodging more hair. "Long story. A problem for me to fix."

Her words caught his attention. At the age of ten, she'd been more than happy to let him take the reins, rely on him. With the void of Alejandro's company, he'd welcomed the role of not only friend but protector.

But the resolve he'd glimpsed last night was apparently not a fleeting thing.

"Besides," she continued, "most of the people who contacted me are just trying to use me to get to your family."

She shuddered, wrapping her arms around herself as if trying to ward off some unseen enemy. The result of the sudden shove headfirst into the world of the rich and famous.

That meant that what he had to show her next wasn't going to make things any better.

She suddenly gave him a sweet smile tinged with embarrassment. "Sorry. All this time and I'm still using you as a sounding board for my problems." She closed the distance between them and, before he could guess what she was about, went up on tiptoe and kissed his cheek. The simple gesture tugged at his heart. "It was nice catching up, Antonio. Thanks for showing me the fountain and the Steps."

Get it over with.

He pulled his phone out of his pocket, clicked on the link Alejandro had texted him, and handed it to her. She accepted the phone with a quizzical look. Then her eyes focused on the glaring headline and her lips parted.

For several long moments, the only sounds were the scrape of table legs as the waiter continued to set up the café and the soft coos of a couple of pigeons dancing around his feet in hope of scraps. He gazed around the street even as he kept Anna's face in his peripheral vision. Her expression was surprisingly hard to read. He'd expected trembling lips, perhaps even a few tears or a full-on collapse into crying. But she surprised him, her face unexpectedly smooth except for a tiny little V between her brows as she read.

Although, he reminded himself, Anna had truly changed since he'd seen her last. The Anna of his childhood would have turned crimson and run off after falling off the catwalk. She had blushed last night, but she'd gotten back up, and done so without a single tear. He admired her for that.

Finally, she looked up. She didn't say anything, just stared at him with wide eyes.

"*Sí*, Anna. We have a problem."

Anna looked back at the phone then slowly read out loud. "*'The Virgin and the Billionaire?'*"

The headline burst off the screen, splayed across the page in large block letters. But even worse was the picture beneath—a photo of Anna splayed across Antonio's lap, the gold gauze of her skirt hiked up past her knees to showcase her bare legs. Her eyes were locked on Antonio's face, lips parted, arms wrapped around his neck. His gaze was fixed on her, one arm curled possessively around her back as the audience around them stared in openmouthed glee at the drama unfolding just feet away.

Alejandro had thought it was hilarious. Adrian had yet to reach out. Neither had his parents or Diego.

A small sigh escaped Anna's lips. "I don't see how this is newsworthy."

Her irritated tone made him suppress a grin. He was enjoying the feisty version of Anna far too much.

"Apparently, a slow news day."

"And what kind of title is that?" She looked up, her eyes sparking with a fire that made him grit his teeth at the desire it reignited. "It sounds like a lurid romance novel."

He nodded at the picture. "It does look like the covers of the books you see for sale at the airport."

She looked back down. Her cheeks pinked. "Yes, well…"

His lips quirked. "You read them, don't you?"

She paused a moment then raised her chin and shot him a smile. "I do." She handed the phone back to him. "I'm sorry, Antonio. Truly." She looked at her feet, the gesture more reminiscent of the Anna he'd known. "I can't believe that one stupid shoe has caused all this trouble."

He cleared his throat. "Yes, well, the damage is done. Now we just have to decide what to do about it."

CHAPTER SIX

ANNA BIT BACK a groan. The image of her body inelegantly splayed across Antonio's lap with that horrible title, written all in caps, would forever be burned into her brain. She looked ridiculous. Like one of those perpetually stunned heroines on the covers of a gothic romance running across a cliff in her frilly nightgown toward a dark castle. Antonio, on the other hand, oozed confidence and sexuality, as if a woman hadn't just landed in his lap.

"Maybe it'll go away in a day or two?" she finally managed to say.

"I'd hoped for the same when Alejandro texted me." He pulled up something else and handed it back to her. Her stomach dropped. Tweet after tweet accosted her, along with her name and the photo underneath Twitter's "What's Happening" column.

She'd been turned into an international joke in less than twelve hours.

"I'm sorry," she repeated, her eyes sweeping over the cobblestones, the planter on the stoop just to her right, her own feet. Anything but him.

"It's fine, Anna."

He didn't sound fine. He sounded tense, frustrated. That was understandable. From what Uncle Diego had said when he and Aunt Lonita had visited her in Paris last month—a visit where Diego had spent part of the time installing new locks on the doors and windows while Lonita had piled food into her cupboards and asked not so subtle questions about the crime rate in the surrounding neighborhood—Antonio had become notoriously secretive about his personal life. He was respected and admired in both his professional and social circles. Landing on the cover of a global tabloid was most likely at the bottom of the list of what he considered respectable media coverage.

He shifted in front of her, drawing her eyes from her own feet to his polished leather shoes. She frowned. There had been a time when he'd run wild across the slopes of the Sierra Nevada with her, his feet bare and covered in mud as they'd climbed trees and scaled boulders.

What had happened to that carefree, adventurous soul? She'd loved that about him; the tap of a pebble at her window or a note slipped under her door, inviting her on an afternoon of adventure. The times she'd felt free, felt like she was truly herself, had been those afternoons spent barreling through fields of wildflowers or splashing in a nearby creek. The girl who disappeared into grief and fear that she wasn't capable, wasn't strong enough, was truly too fragile to accomplish anything on her own, had morphed into someone strong, someone daring and exciting, with Antonio. It was one of the reasons she'd fallen for him.

But from what she could see, if there was any trace of that adventure left, Antonio had buried it very, very deep.

"Not exactly the coverage either of us needed," she finally croaked.

Not to mention the humiliation of Antonio knowing she was still a virgin. She didn't really care if anyone else knew. But Antonio knowing…she bit back a sigh.

"Walk me through the last few months of your life."

Antonio's command surprised her. "What?"

"If we're going to make a decision on how best to handle this, I need more information."

"Since when do you ask for more information? I remember you diving headfirst into everything."

His jaw tightened as his eyes glittered. She suppressed a shiver. Something had happened to Antonio, something dark, to make him look so forbidding.

"I know you lost your job. Start there."

The bald statement made her flinch. If he noticed, he didn't care. *Fine*, she thought with not a small degree of anger. The harsher he was, the easier it was to push away her physical attraction to him.

"After I graduated, I landed a job with a clothing retail chain based out of Granada. They were bought up earlier this year by some American company and downsized our office." She frowned. "It wasn't my dream job. I suspected they used factories that weren't employing the best labor practices."

"A common theme in fashion."

"It shouldn't be," she shot back. "If I ever get a chance to sell my designs, I'll make sure the manufacturers are sustainable and ethical."

He tilted his head to the side. "A noble goal. Then Paris?"

"Yes. Kess challenged me to take a year off, put together a few portfolios and see what I could accomplish. I moved to Paris in the spring, before Adrian and Everleigh's engagement party. A short-term rental on a flat." A flat with curling wallpaper, a leaky faucet that only seemed to drip once she was in bed, and a wrought-iron balcony that sagged away from the brick exterior. But it was cheap. No point in running through her inheritance and her savings just in case she needed it later. Plus, the top floor boasted the most incredible floor-to-ceiling windows that lit up the room she'd claimed as her studio. She swam in swathes of fabric and scribbled designs, sipping on coffee in the morning and red wine at night.

It was the first time she had truly been happy in years.

"You said almost no requests on your work since the article?"

She shrugged. "Some. None that went anywhere. The

companies I submitted to on my own…" Her face flamed as she remembered the video chat with a sour-faced woman whose lips had pinched together as she'd rapidly clicked through Anna's submission on her laptop and referred to Anna as the "virgin designer." "They're not taking me seriously after the way Leo made me sound. It's going to take work to get past that."

As much as she wanted to blame Leo for all her misfortunes, the hard truth was, all of her work up until the gold gown had been inspired by other people's ideas. Even in college, she'd recreated the gowns of her favorite princesses and heroines. Not once had she made something original.

It was going to take work. But it was time to take the risk and get out of her own damn way.

Amazing how at the beginning of the year moving to Paris had seemed like a mountain in itself with what she was facing now.

"What about the show?"

"I might get some inquiries about the gold gown. But I need to create a stronger portfolio, and soon," she added with a wrinkle of her nose. "Strike soon while this show is still fresh in people's minds."

Antonio stepped forward, his shoes drawing closer to her flip-flops. He placed a finger under her chin. Her breath caught as he slowly raised her face. She wanted to pull away, but that would show her hand, how much his touch affected her physically.

Or did he already know what effect he caused? The desire to slip her hand into his like she used to when they were kids, to feel his palm against hers? But now, as an adult, to imagine his hands sliding down her body, settling on her waist with the same possessive touch he'd shown when he'd pulled her down the Steps and into the Via Margutta?

"Why did I have to pry all of that out of you?" His voice came out low and warm. "You once used to confide in me."

"As did you to me. Guess that makes us even."

The words had tumbled out before she could stop them. She blinked in surprise at her own audacity. When was the last time she had challenged Antonio? Never, if memory served. She had talked his ear off as a child, as if all the words she'd kept to herself in her uncle's house bubbled up at once and flowed forth. But as the years had passed and Antonio had grown from gangly youth into a strapping young man with dark hair that tumbled down to his rock-hewn jaw, she'd talked less. She hadn't wanted to tax him, to risk driving him away, when he had so many other things to occupy his time, more interesting people to see. Like his other friend William and all the girls at school who had fawned over him.

Now she just didn't care. In fact, driving him away was sounding better and better. If it wasn't his know-it-all attitude driving her nuts, it was how damned handsome he looked in that polo.

He ran away last time. Just say the L-word again and watch how fast he runs.

She stepped back and, thankfully, his hand fell to his side.

"I didn't mean to drag you into this. It's my problem to deal with."

He arched a brow and held up the phone, the sight of the picture making her wince. "You didn't really drag me in. You fell on me."

She rolled her eyes. "Thanks for the reminder."

"It's a problem for both of us. Although, if anyone is to blame here, aside from the press, it's whoever manufactured that shoe."

The comment startled a laugh out of her. "Fair." She rubbed at the bridge of her nose as a headache started to build. "Look, I'm headed back to Paris for the rest of the year. I'll be far away from you—" *thank God* "—so no more paparazzi photos. We won't be together. This whole mess will die down." She sucked in a breath. "Even if the designing doesn't go the way I want it to and the press bug me for a bit, it'll die down once they realize they made a mistake."

"Or we could pretend to date."

CHAPTER SEVEN

ANNA STARED AT him as if he'd just announced his decision to give away his fortune and go live in a hut on the beach. Given their history, she had every right to question his sanity. But his solution was a viable one. Being seen on his arm would catapult Anna from magazine footnote to international star. Brands would be clamoring for her portfolios. And he would get the damned picture-snapping fools off his back.

"What… I don't even know how to respond to that."

Jazz music filtered out of the café speakers as the waiter placed a chalkboard sign on the street advertising their menu.

"Let's grab a coffee and I'll explain."

Anna stared at him for a moment longer before tentatively following him to the café. The waiter seated them and, after taking their order, disappeared inside.

"You need to get the attention on you refocused."

"Need is a strong word. I'd like to, but—"

"You just said you didn't like the direction your career was heading. As much as I despise articles and photos like this, it's giving you an opportunity to change that direction."

She frowned. "Doesn't pretending to be your girlfriend keep the attention on who I know?"

"At first, yes. And the first week we give them exactly

what they want. Photos of us holding hands, going on dates. Brands are either not focusing on your work at all or won't take you seriously."

"Yes, but my work could be better. I—"

He took his phone out of his pocket, pulled the article up and slid the phone across the table. Anna put her hand over the screen.

"Seeing it once was more than enough."

"What better way to get rid of the naïve label than by dating one of the world's richest men?" He motioned to the text beneath the photo. "The story has written itself. We act it out and change the way people see you. Wear some of your designs when we're seen together. Your work starts getting international attention."

She bit down on her lower lip. "So we pretend to be a couple for a few weeks and then…what? Fake breakup?"

"Yes."

Her teeth dug deeper into her lip. It dawned on him that his offer could be perceived as cruel. She'd poured out her heart to him once, imagining herself in love with her best friend, only to have him rip away the blinders of innocence and cut off contact.

Now here he was, offering to pretend and give her a shadow of what she had wanted all those years ago.

Not the same. They were both adults now. She hadn't given any indication that she still harbored feelings for him. A thought that should be a relief but instead bothered him, a persistent scratch on his skin he couldn't quite shake.

The waiter came out and set two steaming cups and cannoli on the table, the ricotta cheese cream spilling out from either end of the fried pastries. Anna swiped a bit of filling and slid a finger into her mouth.

"Mmm. That's really good."

He looked away and focused on the wrought-iron balcony two stories up on the other side of the street. "It is."

"What do you get out of this?"

Thankfully, by the time he turned back, she was holding her cup.

"A couple of things. One, we would start off the charade in Positano, which is the site of my newest hotel. The media will follow, especially after that incident this morning in front of the Steps. They'll take photos of you with your new boyfriend, and at some point someone will casually mention my newest hotel or even get a photo of us there together."

"Free advertising."

"Yes."

She nodded once, her eyes fixed on the foamy top of her cappuccino. Did she think him a bastard for taking such a mercenary approach to the arrangement? If she did, it was probably a good thing. Better for her to think of him as cold than to entertain any possibility of something real happening between them.

"And the second thing?"

"I'm grateful for the happiness my brothers have found." Even if he did experience the odd occasional pang of envy. "But marriage is not in my future. The tabloids haven't stopped following me around since Alejandro and Calandra's wedding this summer. They aren't focusing on Cabrera Properties or the new hotel, just who I'm dating."

"Is something wrong between you and your brothers?"

"No. Why?"

She took another sip of her cappuccino. "You seemed... distant at the engagement party."

Warning whispered across the back of his neck. Not once in ten years had anyone commented on the change in his relationship with his brothers. HWas this wise, being around someone who had once known him almost better than he'd known himself? Who still picked up on details no one else did?

Bile rose in his throat, thick and bitter. What if she found out what he'd done? What he was capable of?

Before he could explore that thought, a figure paused at the end of the alley. Even from this distance, he could see the camera in their hands. Irritation and resolve wiped away his concerns. He needed to get the media off his back.

"It was a busy day, that's all. Back to my proposal. We'll start today, and I'll make the arrangements up through Alejandro's wedding."

Anna frowned. "I haven't said yes yet."

But you will. He smiled at her. A slow, sensual smile he'd used on women who'd captured his interest over the years.

"What can I say to persuade you?"

She didn't even bat an eye. Instead of swooning, her frown deepened. "You said you want to get the media off your back about who you're dating. But isn't that what this whole arrangement will do? Put the focus on who you're seeing and not your new property?"

Her lack of response rankled him. But he maintained a neutral expression as he dove into the negotiation.

"Initially, yes. But it will refocus the narrative from who I might be dating to who I am supposedly dating. Every time I go out with a woman, the media splashes photos everywhere, publishes everything they can find on my companion." Irritation stirred in his gut. "Not the best way to conduct business with flashbulbs going off every time you meet with someone of the opposite sex. Their husbands and lovers aren't fans of seeing their names tied to mine along with the words 'rumored affair.'" One such article had severely threatened a business relationship he'd cultivated for years. "And as an added insult, the coverage of my new hotel has been spotty at best. At any rate, it'll lessen the scrutiny I've been under."

"This just seems a little farfetched."

Antonio shrugged. "Unusual, yes, but it's not implausible. Even if we published a statement saying we're not dating, they won't listen. If we take control of the narrative now, we can influence the outcome."

"Do we tell your family what's really going on? Mine?"

Maldito, he hadn't thought of Diego. The butler liked him. How would he feel about this sudden change from checking in on his niece to supposedly dating her? "I won't tell my family the real reason, no. Your uncle, though—"

"He's always liked you. Even said once he thought we would…" She shook her head. "As long as we don't rec-reate some of Alejandro's more sensational public acts, I don't think he'll be breathing down my neck about who I'm dating."

His hands curled around his cup. He didn't like the thought of her dating anyone.

"So that's a yes?"

She sighed. "I don't know."

He leaned in. "You could take back your life, Anna. You'll be staying in a luxury hotel with time to build your portfolio. Once this is over, you'll have designs to send out and the reputation to get a contract."

Devious? Yes. But how could she not see that this was the solution she needed? Yes, he would get the benefit of finally doing something for her instead of hurting her. Re-directing the media attention was another bonus.

As long as he kept his hands and fantasies to himself, it was perfect.

She stared at him for a long moment.

Then sighed. "All right."

Her resigned tone crawled across his skin. "All right?"

"Let's do it."

"Don't sound so excited."

"I'm not sure it's going to work. And you have to admit, it's weird that we went from best friends to…" Her voice trailed off for a moment and she focused her attention back on her coffee. "To not, followed by years of no contact, and then in twelve hours we make international headlines and dive into a fake relationship so the media gets off your back and I can try to get my career on track. Doesn't that all sound a little crazy to you?"

A smile tugged at his lips as excitement tingled in his chest. "It does. But I haven't done crazy in a long time."

CHAPTER EIGHT

"This is a bad idea," Anna repeated for the seventh time as wrought-iron gates parted to reveal a stone-paved drive.

"You mentioned that." She could hear Kess's grin through the phone. "I think it's exactly what you need."

"Yeah, sure."

The car started forward. The driveway sloped upward, the stones glowing beneath the lanterns that marched up to the imposing mansion in the distance.

Le Porto. The Haven. Antonio's boutique hotel for the wealthiest people in the world. The one that their little charade would place in the spotlight. It had stung, hearing that he had no problem pretending to be in love, or at least in lust, with her to get free publicity.

But, as he'd pointed out several times, she was getting something out of it, too. So why didn't she feel more excited, hopeful?

She leaned her head against the cool glass of the window and stared out over the darkening ocean to her right. Probably because it still didn't sit well with her that she was doing exactly what some of those fame-hungry brands had tried to do—use the Cabrera name to advance themselves.

After she'd signed her soul over to the devil himself, Antonio had insisted on escorting her back to her hotel. She'd let him, walking in a daze as he'd rattled off a list of details. His car would pick her up at the airport. He'd meet her in Positano, where they would discuss a strategy for the upcoming week.

By the time he'd deposited her on the steps of her hotel, the sun had climbed into the sky and crowds of tourists were swelling in the streets. Kess had found her fumbling with her key out in the hall, taken one look at her face and followed her inside, where she'd gently but firmly demanded an explanation for Anna's shell-shocked expression.

Perhaps it had been the roller coaster of emotions she'd been riding since last night. Or maybe she'd been too tired to put up a fight. Whatever the reason, she'd let Kess guide her out to the balcony overlooking a quiet garden and press another cup of coffee into her hands. Kess had barely sat down before the whole story had come pouring out.

Kess, bless her, had just sat and listened. Nearly fifteen minutes later, Anna had finally run out of steam and drooped in her chair. She'd covered it all. The young boy who had befriended an orphaned girl newly arrived in a strange country. How free she had felt with her best friend when everyone else around her had suppressed her, creating a foundation of emotion that had evolved, as she'd grown older, into affection and then her first love. How she'd finally mustered up the courage to tell him how she felt his first summer back from college, only to have him tell her he'd never be able to see her as more than a little sister.

And how she had now done the most foolish thing of her life and agreed to be in a fake relationship with the man who'd broken her teenage heart.

Unfortunately, Kess hadn't uttered words of caution or talked her out of it. No, she'd been *thrilled,* encouraged the charade. Then she'd hugged Anna, said all the things a best friend would, and made Anna promise to text daily updates. Ten minutes after Kess had left, the front desk had rung to say that her limo had arrived. She'd almost laughed. *Her* limo? She hadn't missed the photographers clustered on the sidewalk opposite the hotel.

When she'd arrived at the airport, it had been to find that Antonio had stepped in once more and swapped out the ticket she'd managed to snag on her favorite airline for one of his family's private jets for the short flight to Naples, where yet another limo had awaited. She'd called Kess as soon as the limo pulled onto the winding road that led to Positano.

To her fake boyfriend.

"You know what you have to do, right?"

"Um…call and tell him I changed my mind?"

"No. Seduce him."

"Kess, he has no interest in me like that, even now," she protested, even though her heart flip-flopped at the word *seduce.* The woman in the hotel window materialized in her mind. She hadn't needed to see the details of her face to know she was the kind of woman men lusted after. Even if she wasn't a classic beauty or a femme fatale, her poise alone attracted men like moths to a flame.

A passing lantern threw her reflection onto the window of the limo. Plain brown hair pulled into a ponytail. Freckles on her nose. A swipe of mascara, a dash of tinted lip balm and she looked…the same. She wasn't unattractive, but she wasn't the kind of beauty men like Antonio and his brothers escorted. Everleigh Cabrera was a jaw-dropping blonde who sparkled. Calandra, whom Anna had only met once at the party in Paris, had had a bewitching dark vibe, aloof and mysterious yet surprisingly kind.

Her stomach dropped. Who on earth would believe that a Cabrera would date someone like her?

"The way he was looking at you last night by the fountain—"

"I appreciate the support, but you're wrong," Anna said firmly. "This is just business."

She said goodbye to Kess and watched the mansion grow closer.

You're getting a leg up in your career, she reminded herself, even if the thought of getting her big break because of her "romantic" connections and not her talent tied her up in knots. *You get to stay here. In a seaside Italian mansion.*

The intermittent changes of her travels had helped keep her mind off what was waiting for her at the end of her journey. Until now, that is, as the magnificent three-story mansion came into sharper view. The exterior was painted a seashell pink, so soft it was almost white, yet it glowed like a jewel as the last rays of the setting sun bathed it with an ethereal light. Balconies dotted the top two floors, and it looked like the right side of the mansion boasted a much larger balcony overlooking the sea. Columns covered in ivy provided privacy.

Pride surged past her trepidation. Antonio had shared how he wanted to make a career out of traveling. As much as she'd missed him when he'd traveled with his mom and brothers, she knew those had been some of the happiest times of his life.

The car pulled around the circular drive and stopped. On one side stood a three-tiered stone fountain, bone-dry and surrounded by an empty garden bed. Not what she had expected to see, but based on the articles Kess had texted her, the hotel was scheduled to open next month. On the other side, stone steps rose up to a double set of glass doors.

Scrolling through the stories had also confirmed what Antonio had said. The four articles Kess had sent gossiped about Adrian's recent wedding, Alejandro's upcoming nuptials, or speculated on Antonio's mystery girlfriend. The few snippets about the actual hotel quickly deviated to rumors like where Alejandro and Calandra would spend their honeymoon.

She swallowed hard. She had never once envied the scrutiny the Cabrera family lived under. Now, entering into this arrangement with Antonio, she was inviting the same kind of examination into her own life.

Despite her complicated relationship with her aunt and uncle, she'd texted them. Told them the lie of how she'd reconnected with Antonio unexpectedly in Rome and they were going to spend a couple weeks together catching up. As overbearing as they'd been, she still loved them. They deserved to hear at least something from her instead of seeing it in the news.

Their response had been surprisingly mundane. Her aunt had wished her a good time. Her uncle had simply said he liked Antonio and was glad they had reconnected. No third degree. No background checks like the poor boy she'd gone on two dates with in college who had angrily broken things off with her in the hallway of their dormitory when he'd learned a private detective had been calling around asking questions about him.

Was it possible they were finally letting go? Trusting her to make her own decisions? The thought of having finally earned their trust, overcoming their fears with her own smart decision-making, had been cathartic.

The limo stopped and the driver got out, moving around to open the door for her like she was a queen. Her courage evaporated. The tightness in her chest returned and twisted even further as she sucked in a shuddering breath. This was supposed to be fun, a harmless pretense and brief sojourn into luxury.

Instead, as the driver helped her out of the back seat, the sound of the limo door closing echoed in her mind with the clanging of a prison gate slamming shut. Before she could crawl back into the limo, the doors of the hotel swung open to reveal Antonio.

He walked down the steps, confidence rolling off his broad shoulders that had somehow been stuffed into a deceptively simple white T-shirt that probably cost the same as one of the evening gowns she'd put together last week.

His fingers closed over hers and she bit back a sigh at how wonderful his skin felt on hers, warm and firm. She looked up at him, prepared to say hello…and nearly yelped when he wrapped his arms around her waist and pulled her against him.

"Welcome, *tesoro*," he said as he kissed her temple.

Oh, no…oh, no…oh, no. What had she done? How could she possibly have agreed to this?

"Tesoro?" she managed to croak.

"It means 'darling'in Italian."

Luckily, she had put her arms around his torso in response to being hauled against him because her knees went weak at hearing his words.

"Good thing Kess isn't here."

He frowned. "Why?"

"She'd make something out of our deal. Kess was convinced you were attracted to me when we were talking by the fountain. Which is ridiculous," she babbled. "I know you weren't, but she's a die-hard romantic and wants to believe that everyone is going to find love—"

Antonio put a finger to her lips. "Anna. It's going to be okay."

The urge to nip the pad of his finger pressed to her mouth was too tempting. She turned her head away. Between the naughty images that had run through her mind last night and her sexy dreams, she had a darker side that craved much more than a kiss on the forehead from Antonio Cabrera.

Deep breath. Okay, she was insanely attracted to him. But she wasn't going to do what Kess had suggested. Business. This was a business arrangement.

"I appreciate everything you're doing, Antonio."

"You just don't think it's going to work?"

"Um…"

Antonio leaned down, his beard scraping gently against

her cheek. She closed her eyes and inhaled. A mistake, as the intoxicatingly masculine scent of his cologne filled her.

"On the beach below is a photographer with a long-range lens. He's been hiding down there for nearly an hour and, I'm guessing, right now is busy clicking away."

Anna started to rear back, but Antonio kept her locked against his body.

"It's already working." He pulled away, a smug smile on his handsome face.

"But how did they know…" Her voice trailed off. "You called the media."

His grin turned even cockier. "I didn't. But some strategic phone calls from my secretary in Rome may have hinted at a possible change in plans for the beautiful woman who landed in my lap last night."

She couldn't help it; she laughed.

He winked. The small gesture twisted her heart, reminding her of the boy who had been such an incredible friend in her darkest hour. Was he still there, behind this cool façade?

"Once we get inside, we can further discuss our plans."

"Yes, sir," she responded with a salute. "Do you have maps? Intel on the reporters?"

He cast a suspicious glance her way as he led her inside. "Were you always this feisty and I just missed it?"

"No. I think I…"

Anna's mouth dropped open as they walked into the hotel. She took in the marble floor made up of swirling whites and creams, the pale colors and soft peach-colored walls glowing beneath the stunning chandelier hanging from the two-story ceiling. A white desk dominated the back wall, framed between two pots overflowing with bougainvillea. A magnificent staircase on either side of the room led up to a balcony overlooking the foyer.

"Antonio," she breathed, "this is magnificent."

"Signor Cabrera?"

Anna looked up as a tall, tanned man with an elaborately stylized moustache, wearing khaki slacks and a white polo, appeared on the balcony.

"Yes, Paul?"

"Shall I escort Signorina Vega to the room?"

"No, thank you. I'll show her myself."

Excitement danced up her spine. If the lobby alone was this fantastic, she could only imagine what the rooms looked like.

"Which room will I be staying in?"

Antonio looked at her, his face smoothing out until it was the unreadable mask he'd sported last night.

"Mine."

CHAPTER NINE

ANTONIO WATCHED AS Anna drifted to the edge of the balcony, her hands settling on the railing as she gazed out over the sea. She looked toward the reddish glow on the horizon, her profile in stark relief against the deep blue waves turning black.

He was a masochist to torture himself like this. When he'd suggested the idea of a fake relationship, it had seemed like a brilliant solution to both their problems. And when he'd spied the photographer on the beach, he'd seized the opportunity to kick off their charade. What better way to start the articles rolling than to be spied welcoming his paramour to his private hotel?

Yet when he'd pulled Anna into his arms, the alarm bells that had been dinging softly in his mind trilled into a full-blown cacophony. His blood had roared as his arms had closed around her tall, slender frame.

His hands fisted. He thought through everything with razor precision. His first property, a stunning resort in the French Riviera, had been on the verge of collapse when his father had tasked him with saving it. Visits to his competitors, frank conversations with numerous luxury travelers he'd wined and dined in the finest restaurants across Europe and, finally, a cohesive plan that addressed everything from room renovations to grounds-keeping to marketing, had led to profits in the first year that had impressed even his Javier. His subsequent successes had followed the same pattern, from burgeoning commercial real estate sales that he'd turned over to trusted parties last year to his ultimate pride. His hotels.

When he followed the rules, he achieved success.

But with Anna, he'd thrown all those rules out the window. He'd made a split-second decision that morning. Had he thought it through, he would have put more guidelines in place for how they would conduct their farce. Or he would have carried out a more accurate analysis of his physical response to Anna and realized the payoff wasn't worth it.

She moved closer to one of the pillars and tilted her head up and closed her eyes as she breathed in the scent of wisteria clinging to the column before walking back to the doorway that led into his chambers. Her gaze roamed over the room.

"It's not what I would expect for a billionaire businessman," she finally said.

"Oh?"

She walked deeper into the room. His chest tightened as she neared the bed.

"It's…cozier." She sat on the chaise longue in front of the bed and nodded in the direction of the fireplace. The architect had replicated Antonio's vision perfectly, mounting it in stone that stood proudly from floor to ceiling, while the glass provided a window into the sitting room beyond.

"This hotel is different than my others. With only having twenty rooms, including this penthouse, it provides more intimacy and exclusivity for my guests."

"And why am I sharing this room with you when there are nineteen empty ones?"

"To keep up the pretense."

She frowned. "For who?"

"The construction workers. The employees with the interior design firm. Anyone other than Paul."

The frown deepened. "I don't remember you being so suspicious."

"In my line of work, I have to be. A freckle-faced waitress could turn out to be a corporate spy from another hospitality chain. Or a vendor who schedules a meeting with me could be trying to get the layout of my office so they can break in and try to access my computer. Both have happened, by the way," he added with a nonchalance he didn't quite feel.

It had been unnerving to be thrust out of the bubble of security he'd enjoyed in Granada to the cutthroat world of reality when he'd entered the halls of Cambridge. He didn't keep friends, partially because of the past, but also because the people he came across in the outside world seemed to care more about his money than him. He dated casually but selectively. When the relationship moved further into intimacy, he'd taken Adrian's recommendation of having background checks performed or only dating women who moved in the same social circles as he did. It had kept his reputation intact, a professional necessity. As much as he might look back on his freer past in Granada with nostalgic longing, his current method was safer, logical.

If he occasionally felt the urge to resist the confines he'd set in place for himself, too bad. What right did he have to enjoy life when he'd nearly taken it from someone else?

"People can be cruel," Anna said as she stood up and moved to the fireplace. She ran a hand along the nearly black wood of the mantel. "Although they can be kind. Alejandro's wife was very kind to me at the party in Paris."

"She's a special kind of woman to be able to put up with Alejandro," Antonio replied dryly. "But then again, so is Everleigh to put up with Adrian's musty old soul."

Anna's lips twitched. "An apt description." She continued to walk around, her footsteps muffled by the thick rug between the fireplace and the chaise longue. "There are good people in the world."

"There are. There are also bad people. You trusted Leo White. Look what happened. The real world is a far nastier place than the vineyards back home."

Her shoulders slumped. "That's true." A self-derisive laugh escaped. "I was so naïve thinking that I could break into designing on my work alone. Like you said, it's who you know."

He suddenly found himself wishing the world was a gentler place, a place that didn't gobble up people like Anna and leave them hardened.

"You mentioned a long story about why your designs aren't being picked up?"

"Yeah."

She drifted away from him, walked into the sitting room. He followed at a distance, hands in his pockets. She sat on the low-slung leather couch, resting her chin in one hand as she gazed at the empty grate.

"You saw the article."

He leaned against the wall, nodded once.

"At first I was embarrassed that I had been duped and shared something so personal. I sounded like a five-year-old wanting to play dress-up." She sat back and scrubbed her hands over her face. "He didn't want to talk about my work. Just wanted dirt on people for his puff piece on the 'engagement party of the summer.'"

The face she made and the snobby accent she affected as she quoted Leo's article made him press his lips together to repress his laughter.

"But then…" The room grew so quiet, he could hear the slight whisper of her breathing as she inhaled. "I looked at what I was wearing."

He frowned. "What you were wearing?"

"At the party."

In his mind's eyes, he recalled the picture that had been posted next to Anna's biography.

"Pale blue dress, right?"

She nodded, her face sad. The urge to cross to her, pull her into his arms and soothe away the pain made him lean harder against the wall. He'd comforted her once before as a friend. But his role had changed drastically. He didn't trust himself not to take things too far in the confines of his private suite.

One hand moved back and forth over the buttery leather, her fingertips tapping out a nervous beat.

"When I saw the dress, it hit me. I used to think I was inspired by the fairy-tale movies my mother and I used to watch together. But I wasn't designing anything new." She flopped back against the cushions, the drooping of her limbs speaking to her personal sense of defeat. "Plain. Uninspired. Been done before. Nothing that was me."

The admission sounded torn from some deep dark place.

"You're being hard on yourself."

"Those aren't my words. Those are some of the comments on the portfolios I submitted before the engagement party."

Anger burned low in his stomach. He'd said similar things, and much harsher sentiments, in his career. Yet to hear that Anna had been subjugated to such bald and unforgiving commentary made him livid.

"Anna—"

She held up a hand. "Don't make excuses. When I saw that dress, saw how similar it was to another design, it hit me. After I moved to Granada, I was so sheltered, so repressed, I could barely breathe sometimes. And yet… I let my aunt and uncle take care of me."

"You were ten and you'd just lost your parents. Of course you should have let your family take care of you."

"But I didn't even fight it!" Frustration suffused her tone as she stood and started to pace. "I just let them treat me like a little girl for years. I'm twenty-seven now, and I just moved out on my own for the first time eight months ago. I didn't do anything on my own, including my designs."

Maldito, he could no longer take it, seeing her beat herself up like this. He crossed the room and stopped a few feet away, far enough to not touch her, but close enough to make his point.

"What about the gold dress?"

Her lips quirked. "The one I was wearing when I fell on you?"

"Sí."

Pride brought her mouth up into a tentative smile. "It's actually the first dress I did after the party. I reworked and reworked it so many times, afraid each draft was just another replica, but…"

"It was beautiful, Anna."

She nodded, happiness brightening her eyes. "Thank you. It was, wasn't it?"

Amazing, the strength in this woman who had been through so much and, when confronted with the publication of intimate details that would have made women of his acquaintance run for the hills, had instead reflected on how she could improve and seized the opportunity with both hands.

Her body was sexy. But her confidence, her determination…that was alluring in an entirely different and very dangerous way.

Before he could pursue the topic further, she shook her head.

"Sorry. How did I even start talking about that?" She plowed ahead before he could get a word in. "What's the plan with this whole charade?"

He stepped back, putting both physical and emotional space between them. He wanted to know more, dig deeper. A sure sign that he needed to accept the chance to refocus on the business aspect of their arrangement.

"A few sojourns into town. Chances to be seen, photographed. A lunch here, a dinner there. Two weeks that will culminate in us being seen as an official couple at Alejandro and Calandra's wedding in Marseille. I was thinking we could start off light tomorrow with a lunch at a seaside bistro."

Something about their conversation had made her nervous. It was evident in her fingers tapping against her thighs, the tension in her neck.

"Something wrong?"

"What happened outside, the way you hugged me...is that going to be a regular thing?"

"Couples who are dating tend to hug and hold hands, yes."

"You kissed me on the forehead," she said almost accusingly.

The temptation to tease her proved too much to resist. "Would you have rather I kissed you somewhere else?"

She flushed and looked away, giving him a delicious view of her neck, the slightly gaping V of her dress that hinted at the curves of her breasts, barely visible in the dim light.

"I'm just wondering how much physical demonstration is going to be required."

"Some, Anna, but I'm not going to force you."

"I know that." Her gaze swung back around, narrowed and almost irritated. "I would never think that of you, Antonio." She blew out a breath. "It's probably just me, then. Our parting was an embarrassing experience for me. I feel like it's lingering on the edge of my interactions with you."

He shrugged. "You were seventeen, Anna. You were young and you had a crush."

He waited for her to correct him. Rationally knew that when she didn't correct his use of the word *had*, he should be relieved.

Except he wasn't. The sting of knowing she no longer cared about him was poetic justice for the pain he'd inflicted on her. It would make it easier for him to carry out the pretense of being in a relationship.

"So we'll leave tomorrow. We'll have lunch. Then… two weeks?"

"Yes." Two weeks was good. Two weeks was enough time to sell the idea of a couple escaping to a romantic hideaway, followed by a few weeks of them disappearing off the media radar following the wedding. Gradually, the interest would die down. Anna and he would part ways, he without a bull's-eye on his back from the media and she with newfound attention on her designs.

Neat, planned-out and detailed. Just the way it should be.

She nodded once. "Two weeks. Got it." She glanced around. "Are there sheets or something for the couch?"

"You're not sleeping on the couch."

"I'm not taking your bed."

He leaned forward. "It's not a request. I will take the couch, and if you try to take it, I'll dump you on the floor."

Her mouth dropped open. "That sounds like the exact opposite of the chivalrous act of offering me your bed to sleep in."

"Take it or leave it. I shoved you into the pool how many times? Rolling you onto the floor is nothing."

The reminder of their old camaraderie made her smile despite her best efforts to keep glowering at him.

"Fine. Tonight. But we'll rotate. I'm not going to have you pretend to be my boyfriend and give up your bed the whole time we're doing this."

She stood and walked past him toward the balcony, leaving that damned floral scent in her wake. He sat back in his chair and scrubbed a hand over his face. It was going to be a very long two weeks.

CHAPTER TEN

ANTONIO GLANCED AT the form reclining on the balcony for about the sixth time since she'd walked outside and lowered her incredible body onto the chaise longue. Knowing that she had no comprehension of how sensual she looked, dark hair spread over the pillow and the skirt of that damned sundress riding up to expose a hint of her thighs, made it even more erotic.

He refocused on his laptop, his fingers tapping out a rhythm across the keys. The latest reports on two of his three properties were positive. The third, his resort in the Caribbean, was in need of a new manager after his last had made the unfortunate decision to sleep with the wife of a powerful guest. The first and last time he had trusted someone other than himself to make a critical hiring decision. Fortunately, the guest was also a longtime friend and had agreed to keep the matter quiet, especially in light of how his divorce had become a public spectacle.

Yet another example of why marriage had never been on his radar. As a youth, his parents' union had been unappealing at best, no matter how much Isabella had tried to portray their marriage as a love match. The few times their father, Javier, had mentioned heirs to inherit the Cabrera business empire, Alejandro had reminded Antonio that that lovely duty fell to the oldest.

Antonio smirked. Funny how his wayward brother had

fallen victim to the trap of matrimony and parenthood. The way he talked about his new bride, as if she were God's gift to womanhood, was in stark contrast to this time last year when he'd been running through girlfriends faster than Antonio could blink.

Although, both he and Adrian had seemed very happy the last time he'd seen them at Fox Vineyards in New York following Adrian's wedding to Everleigh. Even though he hadn't been emotionally close with his brothers in years, ever since he'd graduated from college and taken hold of Cabrera Properties, he'd formed a bond with Adrian and Alejandro built on respect and their shared successes. But instead of discussing strategies, Adrian and Alejandro had talked of pregnancy symptoms, first-anniversary gift plans and the years-long wait for an exclusive preschool.

His brothers had both been averse to marriage. What had changed their minds so drastically?

Anna shifted onto her side, propping her body up on one elbow as she thumbed through a book. The new position made the bodice of her top gape.

He punched out a sentence on his computer, focusing on the clicking of the keys and not the delectable body of the woman just a few dozen feet away. His phone dinged. A screenshot from Adrian of the news story and a single-character text message: ?

Trust Adrian to keep his communication abrupt and to the point.

He scrubbed a hand over his face. It wasn't just the temptation Anna presented that had him questioning what he'd set in motion. In his mind, he'd estimated entertaining this fake relationship for no more than two weeks. Long enough to give the illusion that he was seeing someone exclusively, followed by a few months of him lying low, and the media would go after someone else.

Yet what would happen when Adrian's and Alejandro's

wives gave birth? When the media realized that he and Anna were no longer an "item"?

He pinched the bridge of his nose. He hadn't thought this through. Not beyond the initial idea of getting the media off his back *now* and giving Anna's career a boost. Although he could admit the latter reason had formed more out of guilt than a desire to help. Guilt had been a powerful motivator for him these last ten years. It had kept him in line, kept his education and then his business on the fast track to success.

But this time guilt had propelled him into making a hasty decision.

Too late for another option. Yes, it was. Even if it didn't solve his long-term problem, at least he would get a break for a few months and repay Anna for the heartbreak he'd caused her.

Although she was certainly paying him back in her own way. That she didn't know it, made it even worse. Even as he watched out of the corner of his eye, she ran a hand through those long, silken tresses, strands of dark hair falling forward to caress the column of her neck.

"Antonio?"

The sound of his name tumbling off her lips yanked his mind out of the gutter. He blinked and focused on her.

"Yes?"

Anna had sat up and was now watching him with a concerned look on her face. "Are you all right?"

"Yes. Why?"

"You look angry."

He smoothed his expression. "Apologies. Just thinking."

She stood and walked toward the door, leaning casually against the doorframe with her arms wrapped around her middle. In the blue-and-white-striped shorts and loose white tank she'd changed into for a moonlit walk on the beach where they'd held hands and pretended not to notice the photographers further down, she looked like any other woman he might have spied around Positano.

Except she wasn't just any other woman. She was his former best friend, the person he'd trusted more than anyone else still . And now little Anna was gone, replaced by Anna Vega, stunningly beautiful and yet still sweet and innocent, it made him feel like a first-rate bastard even thinking about her the way he did.

"Thinking about what?"

"Business," he replied shortly as he turned back to his computer.

"I don't believe you."

His gaze snapped up. Anna's eyes were pinned on him, roaming over his face like a hot caress that could see past all the defenses he'd built up.

"Why not?"

"Because I know you." She cocked her head to one side. "Something's bugging you."

"If I feel the need to share, I will."

His words came out colder than he'd intended, but they elicited the desired effect. Anna reared back as if she'd been slapped, stared at him for one long moment then turned and walked back onto the balcony. She grabbed her book off the chaise and disappeared around the corner.

Good. When she was in view, she was too much distraction. While everything seemed to be lining up for the grand opening, his attention needed to be focused on that.

Except it wasn't. It was on that damned scent—*her* scent—lurking on the air. The feistiness in her voice, the vulnerability she'd shared with him. The vivid image of her amber-blue eyes widening in pain before she'd walked away. Not with the flamboyant flair of drama his Caribbean lover had exhibited. Not with tears pouring down her cheeks like the opera singer he'd seen last summer. No, she'd walked away with quiet dignity and grace.

Damn it.

He stood and stalked to the balcony door. A glance to the right confirmed that Anna had sought refuge at the far end. But instead of sitting on the bench built into the wall or cozying up in one of the plush chairs he'd had brought in from Paris, she'd chosen to perch on the edge of the balcony railing, one bare foot resting on the tile and the other on the railing. His body tightened as he stalked toward her.

"That's a long drop down."

She didn't even look at him, just kept her back to him as she gazed out over the sea, the sky appearing starless behind the bright white of the moon. "Yes. Good thing there's a railing here."

"Railings are fallible."

For a moment, there was nothing other than the faint roar of the ocean. Then, so quiet he barely heard it, a dejected sigh.

"I remember a time when you played, Antonio. Barefoot. In the rain."

He remembered the last time he'd done that. He remembered that day all too well. It was the day he'd no longer seen Anna as a friend and little sister. The summer after his first year at university, just a week away from flying back to England, Anna had insisted on taking him out for a picnic she'd packed. A picnic decimated by an unexpected rainstorm. Instead of running for shelter, Anna had kicked off her shoes and jumped in the fast-forming puddles. Antonio had joined her, indulging in one last bit of childhood.

Until she'd spun around, wet hair clinging to her face, a stunning smile on her lips, and white shirt molded to the growing curves of her breasts. The sight of her, followed by the unexpected hard jolt of desire, had turned his world upside down.

His guilt over his sudden lascivious turn of thoughts had set him on the road to destruction, prompted him to borrow Javier's Bugatti and take the curves of the winding mountain roads too fast on the way to a party he had initially turned down an invite to.

With his other best friend in the passenger seat. A friend who hadn't even wanted to get out that night.

"I grew up, Anna. It happens to most of us."

Her shoulders tensed. He swore again. Why was he so on edge with her? What had happened to him, to William, wasn't her fault. A large part of his goal in offering this arrangement had been to rectify the hurt he'd caused her, not add to it.

"Perhaps you're right."

Her soft voice reminded him of a day he'd discovered her talking with her uncle, Diego, who still served the Cabrera family as the butler at their Granada estate. She'd spoken quietly, almost meekly. Usually, when they'd spent time together, it had been just the two of them. He'd started to pay attention more after that, seen how Diego constantly warned her to be careful, set rules even stricter than Javier's guidelines for Alejandro.

The one person Diego had seemed to trust with Anna had been Antonio. Whether it was because he was the good child or because Isabella had initially encouraged the friendship, who could say. Back then, he'd taken the time Diego had given them and created as much fun as he could for the girl who, at first, had been a curiosity and a reprieve from loneliness. But over time, her sweetness, her growing confidence as she'd not only risen to but taken the reins on their adventures, her acceptance of him without expecting anything in return, had created a friend he hadn't been able to picture his life without.

And now he was decrying one of the things he'd loved most about spending time with her; her innocent joy.

An apology rose to his lips. His comment had been out of line. He wanted to keep distance between them, yes, but not like this.

But before he could say sorry, she turned slightly and

raised her chin. "Although I'd rather still believe in magic and fairy tales than become a stiff shirt who doesn't know how to have fun."

He stood frozen to the spot. No one talked to him like that. He took a few more steps until he was standing in front of her, an arm's reach away.

"Stiff shirt?"

She pinpointed him with gleaming eyes. "Shirt is the appropriate version of what first came to mind. I may be a dreamer, Antonio, but that doesn't make me stupid."

He ran a hand through his hair as he let out a frustrated sigh. "I never said you were stupid, Anna."

"You treating me like a child and making remarks like the one you just did implies enough. If you don't think that much of me, then why would you propose an idea that required spending time together?"

"I do like you," he ground out. "You were my best friend for years."

"Emphasis on 'were,'" she retorted. Where had this fire come from? Her spirit back then, strong as it was, had been energetic, bright, not this fierceness that blazed forth.

"We haven't been friends for some time, that's true." He stepped forward It was time to take charge of a situation that had spiraled wildly out of control. Another failure in his normally well-planned-out existence. "But we were friends. We can be again, or at least get along while we ride out this arrangement."

Ride was the wrong word to use. Because as he took another step closer, smelled the faintt scent of daisies, an image of Anna straddling his hips, her body rising up and down as she took him inside her, nearly knocked him off his feet.

"I don't know if I want to be friends with someone as priggish as you."

That stopped him short. "Adrian is priggish. I'm not."

She watched him for a long moment. With a huff, she

started to swing her other leg up onto the railing. His heart jumped into his throat and he surged forward, one arm wrapping around her waist and snatching her back.

"Antonio!"

"That was foolish," he growled as he spun her away from the edge.

"How?" she cried as she placed both her hands on his chest to steady herself. "I was perfectly balanced, that railing is over a foot wide and there's a roof right below the railing."

"A roof that slants down and leads to a drop down a cliff side into the ocean," he snapped.

Fire snapped in her eyes. "You're just like my *tío*. Controlling, overbearing, and suspicious of everyone."

The comparison ignited his anger. "So I'm like the man who kept you under lock and key? Me, the one who pulled you out of your grief and told you time and time again that you were capable of so much more than you gave yourself credit for?"

"That man is gone." Her chin tilted up. "The man I knew told me everything. The one in front of me is distant, bosses me around—" she leaned in "—and is hiding something."

Maldito. He started to pull back, but her fingers fisted in his shirt, refusing to let him go. The electricity charging through the night air crackled, changed from angry to sensual in the span of a heartbeat. Her beautiful gaze widened, her eyes drifting down to his lips then back up, searching for answers he didn't have.

Her fingers fisted in his shirt, the slight scrape of her nails through the fabric making him suppress a groan of need. He needed to let go of her, needed to put distance between them.

"Antonio…"

Her voice nearly undid him. Husky, filled with naked desire. When she'd confessed her feelings on the slopes of the mountains where they'd spent so many hours running wild,

it had been shyly, sweetly. Now her voice filled him, electrified every vein. His hands tightened on her waist as his
gaze fell on her lips, slightly parted, ready to be kissed…

No!

He stepped back so quickly she stumbled forward. He
caught her arm and, once she was steady, released her as
if she'd turned to molten lava and walked away.

Away from desire. Away from temptation. It had been
so much easier to keep his distance when he'd known he
would devastate her world again if he hurt her.

Except it wouldn't crush her. She'd be hurt, but she
would do what she had after the magazine article—rise
from the ashes and move on. It wasn't just about sex, either.
It would have been so much easier if it was just physical.
No, *she* interested him. Anna and her courageous leap from
the suffocating love of her family and being unemployed
to living in Paris, pursuing her dreams, walking a catwalk
and making changes instead of excuses when she realized
what she could do better in her own work.

Unlike him. As he stalked out the front door of his suite
and down the hall to the elevator, the past roared in with a
vengeance, the screech of rubber on asphalt mixing with
William's shout of fear before the world went dark.

He punched the button for the first floor, his hands trembling with suppressed self-rage and grief and guilt.

He didn't deserve happiness. No amount of atonement
would ever make him worthy of happiness, let alone being
with someone like Anna Vega.

CHAPTER ELEVEN

ANNA STARED AT her reflection in the full-length mirror. She'd pulled her hair into a loose bun at the base of her neck. A video chat with Kess had confirmed that her sundress, a creamy creation with pale green ivy tangling over the bodice and full skirt paired with a wide-brimmed straw hat, was a solid choice for "lunch on the terrace" in Positano. When she'd first spied this material, she'd thought of a gown inspired by the forest surrounding Sleeping Beauty's castle. The dress had morphed after Paris into a summery concoction with ties on the shoulders for a vintage vibe and an open back for a hint of sexiness. Not the kind of look that would have worked for Kess's show, but perfect for her first outing.

Pride had her raising her chin. Like the gold gown, this dress felt *right*. Hopefully, it would capture the right attention when she and Antonio went out for lunch.

Her mind strayed for the fiftieth time to the disaster of last night. When he'd pulled her tight against his body, irritation had fled, replaced by a desire so intense she'd nearly thrown caution to the wind and kissed him.

Embarrassment had been her first reaction, followed swiftly by confusion and a hint of anger. The man made no sense. In Rome, he'd been polite but aloof. That is, until the Via Margutta, when she'd caught glimpses of her old friend. Now…now he vacillated between an overly protective big brother and a cold, distant ass who kept secrets very close to his well-toned muscular chest. She'd told him she didn't know who he was anymore. Judging by his ever-changing demeanor, he didn't, either.

After he'd left, she'd curled up in one of the chairs with her book and tried over and over to read. But after an hour of gazing blankly at the same page, she'd finally gone into his luxurious suite, crawled beneath the silk sheets and fallen asleep…only to wake every hour to see if he'd returned. When she'd finally awoken to sun streaming in through the stunning floor-to-ceiling windows, it had been to a empty penthouse suite.

A knock on the door echoed off the walls and made her jump.

"Ready?"

Antonio's deep voice vibrated through the door. She inhaled deeply. She could do this.

She crossed the suite, her sandals noiseless on the plush Turkish rug. The door swung open silently, giving her a moment to gaze at Antonio standing in the hallway. Dressed in khaki slacks, a perfectly tailored black polo and a stainless-steel watch that probably cost more than her first car, he looked every inch the suave billionaire. Handsome, controlled, with a slight edge to his stance that told everyone who looked upon him that *he* was in charge.

Yet as her eyes drifted up to his face, to the slight curve up of his lips and the softness around his eyes as he looked down at his phone, her heart twisted. She still saw her friend hidden behind the walls he'd constructed over the years. What had happened to make him so buttoned up and reserved?

Don't go there. Business arrangement, not a happy reunion. Be strong.

With that reminder echoing in her head, she walked into the hall. Antonio glanced up.

"One of yours?"

"Yes."

The smile that spread over his face melted her insides. *So much for staying strong.*

"Those bastards don't know what they're missing."

The statement made her laugh. "What?"

He walked forward and, before she could steel herself, grabbed a hand and twirled her in a circle. The skirt flared out in a billowing cloud. As she spun around, she caught sight of Antonio's infectious grin, the crinkles at the corners of his eyes, glowing golden brown in the sunlight streaming in from the balcony. A moment that was exceptionally dangerous, chipping away at her defenses and letting wispy tendrils of emotions long buried through.

But, she told herself as she stopped spinning and the skirt settled against her legs with a delicious silky softness, a moment she would always remember. One of those that, on bad days, she would summon and relive over and over.

"It's an incredible dress."

"Thank you. It's one of my favorites," she added shyly.

The smile disappeared from his face as quickly as it had appeared, leaving her unsteady on her feet, as if she'd just been hit by a rogue wave on the beach. She'd thought he was sweeping last night's disaster under the rug. But apparently not. Regret flickered through her. She stood behind everything she'd said, except for comparing him to her uncle. As irritating as his protectiveness had been, she'd overreacted. There was a big difference between her uncle installing a tracking app on her phone and Antonio not wanting her to fall off a balcony.

"Let's go."

He walked to the door and opened it for her. A gentlemanly gesture, but he barely looked at her as she walked into the hallway. On their ride down in the elevator, he stood on the opposite side, eyes fixed on the numbers as they descended.

Well, this is going great. How were they supposed to

sell a fake relationship when he could barely handle being in the same elevator?

The number dinged to floor two. She readied herself to walk out into the lobby alone.

Until warm fingers threaded through her own. Her gasp bounced off the mirrored walls, her cheeks growing hot. A glance at the mirror showed no reaction from Antonio, just that same intense gaze on the numbers. Maybe he'd been so lost in his own thoughts he hadn't heard her. Although, how he wasn't affected by their palms pressed together was beyond her.

Because you're Anna. Little Anna Vega and he's never wanted you.

Harsh talk from her rational brain, but it threw a much needed dose of cold water on her out-of-control hormones. The elevator stopped, the doors swooshed open, and she walked into the lobby with a poise she didn't feel.

Antonio called out a greeting to a group of workers standing off to the side clustered around blueprints, hailing several by name. At least he hadn't lost his appreciation for his employees. He'd always treated the staff at the mansion like they were people versus minions there to do his bidding.

She smiled at the men and they smiled back, one even giving her a playful wink. Antonio's hand tightened around hers and he tugged her forward toward the double doors. The limo sat in all its gleaming luxurious glory right outside.

"Do you always take the limo?" she asked as a chauffeur walked around to open the door.

"Yes."

She frowned as he sat across from her. "Why?"

"I don't drive."

He bit out the words so tersely that she refrained from asking any more questions and instead focused on the passing scenery outside her window.

Ten minutes later, Antonio escorted her down a lane filled with boutiques and storefronts, each one overflowing with flowers, jewelry and other handmade goods. As they walked past a clothing stall, a flash of color caught her eye.

"Oh!"

Her feet moved of their own accord, drawn as if the material called her name in a language only she could hear. A bolt of deep, seductive, red silk partially unraveled over a table. The threads sparkled, the specks of silver set into the scarlet fabric glinting like far-off stars. She reached out and the material flowed over her hand like water.

"Buongiorno."

Anna looked up to see a tall man with a kind smile set into a weathered, craggy face. He nodded at the silk.

"Beautiful, no?"

"It's stunning," she breathed.

"Handwoven by myself and my wife." He pointed to the barely visible threading along the edge. "Handwoven silk blends in with the color compared to machine-woven." He took up the other end of the material and rubbed it between his wrinkled fingers. The soft crunch made Anna smile.

"Like snow underfoot."

"Exactly, *signorina*." His smile widened in pride. "One of the marks of true silk."

"How much?"

He named a price that made her inwardly wince. It was more than a fair price for handwoven Italian silk. Back in Florence, she'd most likely pay twice that at one of the luxury stores dotting the city. But with so much of her budget already consumed by her rent in Paris and her living expenses, she couldn't afford the splurge right now.

"Perhaps my next visit."

She looked up and realized Antonio had disappeared. Had she upset him? She'd broken off without a word. Rude, but not intentionally so. She glanced around the crowded lane.

There.

It was like watching a sea part as Antonio walked toward her, his eyes concealed by sunglasses. People stood to the side, watching him out of the corners of their eyes or, in the case of one bold woman, with open admiration.

He stopped in front of her, a small violet gift bag hanging from his fingers.

"I wondered where you were," she said, her voice coming out breathier than she'd intended.

Before she could blink, he leaned down and pressed a quick kiss to her lips. The light caress sent electric currents charging through her arms, her legs, everywhere. Her eyes fluttered shut. She was about to stand on her tiptoes to return the kiss when she felt him step back.

"For you, *mariposa.*"

Butterfly. He'd called her that the first time he'd taken her out into the wilderness beyond the walls of the Cabrera family estate. He'd laughed and called her *mariposa* because she "flitted from flower to flower." And she had, soaking up the first bit of joy she'd found since her parents had been taken from her as she'd rambled over the grassy slopes. Between the nights she'd awaken crying for her mom to the tears that had formed in Tío Diego's eyes the first few weeks anytime he'd seen her, tears that had made her agree to his laundry list of stringent conditions, Antonio's invitation to get out of the house had been a lifesaver she'd desperately needed.

It felt like butterflies were fluttering in her stomach as she accepted the gift bag and opened it. Inside, wrapped in lavender tissue paper, was a diamond tennis bracelet.

"Oh!"

Not cubic zirconia. Not paste gems. No, these were real diamonds, a row of them set in silver with a hidden clasp. Antonio lifted it from the tissue paper and wrapped the diamonds around her wrist, his fingertips skimming the underside of her arm. A place, she learned as she froze, that was incredibly sensitive as he secured the clasp.

She looked down at the bracelet and nearly gulped. How much had it cost? Ten thousand? Fifteen? More? She was probably wearing nearly a year's worth of rent for her Paris apartment on her arm.

"You didn't have to do that, you know."

"I know. But I wanted to."

The simple statement warmed her. Even though it wasn't the kind of bracelet she would normally wear, the thought had been very kind. She started to reply, to echo her thanks once more, but he continued.

"There was a photographer just behind us. Between yesterday and today, we should be giving them plenty to talk about."

The bracelet grew heavy around her wrist, no longer a stunning piece of jewelry but a manacle. Of course the gift had been for show. So had the kiss.

So much for staying removed. Less than twenty-four hours from making her commitment to maintain a professional attitude toward this arrangement and she was already entertaining thoughts that any action Antonio took even hinted at his harboring feelings for her.

Self-pity beckoned. But the strength she'd slowly been building ever since her job loss surged forward, rescuing her from that precarious cliff. After this whole arrangement was over, she'd give the bracelet back.

She raised her chin. She didn't need Antonio to find her attractive to be happy. Emboldened, she leaned her head against his shoulder. "If not, perhaps this will." She leaned up and kissed his bearded cheek. When he looked down at her, she smiled, her reflection mirrored in his glasses. "Can't have you doing all the work."

CHAPTER TWELVE

OVER THE NEXT few days, Antonio and Anna fell into a routine. They spent their mornings apart, Anna on the balcony and Antonio holed up in his office. Just before noon, Antonio would collect her and they'd go out to lunch at one of the many restaurants.

What he'd planned as a subtle way to be seen had turned into exquisite torture. Anna wasn't like the women he'd dated over the last few years. Instead of pushing salad around her plate with a fork or turning her nose up at a slightly charred quiche crust, she enjoyed her food. The way her eyes lit when the waiter had placed a plate of caprese salad in front of her, the little moan of pleasure when she'd savored a forkful of pasta pomodoro...

That moan tortured him. She wasn't immune to him. He caught the subtle glances, the flush in her cheeks. Yet her response seemed to be purely physical. She played the role of girlfriend when they were out and about. In private, though, she remained as aloof as he did, disappearing onto the balcony all morning and all evening once they returned from their afternoon activity. The first day, after he'd gifted her the bracelet and they'd enjoyed lunch on the terrace at an exclusive bistro, he'd been relieved that she had put so much distance between them.

But the second day, as they'd wandered through one of Positano's many art galleries and she'd grabbed his arm,

dragging him over to an oil painting of a beach, he'd felt...
happy. Happier than he had been in a long time. New emails
dinging his inbox every minute, contracts to review for Le
Porto, and he couldn't have cared less. He'd basked in Anna's enthusiastic joy over a painting that cost a fraction of
the bracelet he'd bought her, soaking up her sunshine like
a man who'd been jailed for ages in the darkest dungeon.
The third day, Anna had sweet-talked him into pizza and
red wine over the fancy hilltop restaurant he'd picked out.
Whether it was her luminous eyes as she bit into a slice
topped with cheese and fresh basil or her sigh of content-
ment as she'd sipped her wine, he'd felt his own tension
bleed out of his shoulders.

At night, the guilt that lurked all day beneath the blissful distractions Anna offered translated into nightmares
the likes of which he hadn't experienced since right after
the accident. He knew what his terrors were telling him;
that he didn't deserve any of this. That he was gleaning too
much joy from these sojourns with Anna.

God help him, he couldn't stop. Even the suffering of
waking up to the memory of William's gaping mouth, blood
trickling from his lips as he'd gasped like a fish and clawed
at Antonio's arm, was worth the pleasure of her company,
the moments of happiness he hadn't experienced in over
a decade.

The news had been humming, churning out steady pictures of his and Anna's adventures around Positano. His
tactic of basing their fake relationship out of his newest
hotel had also worked, with a significant uptick in both
media attention and reservation inquiries.

Except those indicators of success had fallen flat in the
face of the enjoyment he was getting out of being around
his old friend. His old friend who had the most stunning
legs, a thousand-watt smile and a zest for life's simplest
pleasures.

An intoxicating mix. One that was pulling him ever

deeper into the quagmire he'd tried to avoid ten years ago. Because the more time he spent in Anna's company, the more he wanted her. Case in point: when he'd spied her bare wrist as she'd walked out onto the balcony a couple of days ago, his chest had tightened. He liked seeing the bracelet on her wrist.

He'd paid more attention and realized that she only wore the bracelet when they went out. She clasped it on her wrist just before they walked out of the penthouse and removed it almost as soon as the door clicked shut. At first it had irritated him. Now it grated. A fifteen-thousand-dollar diamond bracelet.

Yes, he grudgingly admitted to himself, it wasn't the kind of gift Anna would normally have liked. He'd seen her drawn to the silk, the way she'd lovingly caressed it. The sight of her fingers trailing so seductively over the material had made him turn away in time and spied the jewelry store and the photographer almost simultaneously. It had seemed like a perfect opportunity. Yet every time he'd seen her take the bracelet off, her movements had been jerky, almost frantic.

He'd bought jewelry for previous lovers, even diamonds, so long as they didn't land on anyone's finger. It was expected. Even though Anna was nothing like his former paramours, they had at least enjoyed his gifts.

What was wrong with it? And, more annoyingly, why did it bother him so much?

He walked into the penthouse forty-five minutes early. A shower, a change of clothes and then he would whisk Anna off to Santa Maria Church. Given how she'd reacted to a simple painting, he could only imagine her face when she saw the white and gold interior of the twelfth-century chapel.

What the hell are you doing?

He stopped cold in the middle of the living room. When

had his plans become about Anna, about enjoying his time with her? When had his focus shifted?

Now was not the time to surrender his control.

He ran a hand through his hair. This was what happened when one rushed into a situation without proper analysis. When one made decisions based on emotions. The last time he'd done that, desperate to take a risk and do something for a thrill, he'd coerced William into doing something he hadn't wanted, something that had nearly gotten him killed.

He'd written to William after the accident, a letter full of apologies and offers to do whatever it took to give his former friend anything he desired. William had written back, told Antonio he didn't blame him for what had happened. But the references to how well physical therapy was going, that the doctors had been hopeful about his walking again, had been stakes in Antonio's heart, driving home the irrefutable fact that he'd hurt someone he cared about because of his own selfishness.

Pushing Anna away, not taking advantage of the incredible gift she'd offered him, had been one of the most self-less things he'd done.

If he didn't get this whirlwind of emotions for Anna under control, his rejection of her all those years ago would be a waste. Not to mention their plan, which they were now committed to with all of the press coverage, could blow up in both their faces.

A frown crossed his face. Between monitoring the press, overseeing the final phases of construction and enjoying his afternoons with Anna, he hadn't even asked about whether news of their supposed relationship had elicited any results for her designs.

Self-absorbed bastard.

Guilt, his most frequent companion, seeped into his skin. Reluctantly, he let his feet guide him to the balcony doors and stepped outside.

And stopped, his mouth dropping open.

The immediate surface looked just as it had, with two white lounge chairs arranged to look out over the balcony railing at the sea beyond, a matching table between to hold drinks, a book, whatever the sittees desired. For him, usually a laptop or business reports.

The balcony ran another thirty feet past the doors, with soaring columns and a netted ceiling covered in bougainvillea and ivy. Fans whirred silently, capturing the salty air drifting up off the waves and dispersing it in a gentle breeze over the artfully-arranged plush chairs and fire pit. At the far end, a wooden dining table had been arranged with ten chairs for the exceptionally rare occasion when Antonio would host private guests for dinner.

The table had been taken over by fabrics of all colors and styles. A thin rope had been strung between two columns, papers hanging by clothespins. In the midst of the mess, sitting on the stone floor with headphones over her ears, was Anna.

Oblivious to his presence, her hand flew over the paper, a pencil clutched in her hand. That thick, dark hair his fingers itched to touch had been pulled up into a ponytail. His gaze moved over her like he hadn't seen her in years, from her pert nose and defined cheekbones to her full lips and dark lashes hiding her eyes. His stare drifted down to the form-fitting black tank and lime-green running shorts.

Desire crashed into another emotion; a craving he couldn't quite describe. The bucolic scene before him stirred a longing in him, a longing not just to sweep the fabric off the table and lay Anna down beneath him, but to sit beside her on the floor, ask questions about her designs, watch her sparkle as she shared her passion with him.

Danger!

Retreating had never been a part of his DNA, not since he'd gone off to college. But if he didn't now, he risked one of two things: kissing the daylights out of Anna Vega or crossing the line into emotional territory that would be hell to crawl out of.

He took a step back, ready to turn. A gull soared between the columns, landed on the fire pit and uttered a loud, attention-seeking squawk. Anna looked up, smiling at the bird, before her gaze landed on him. Her mouth formed a little *O* as her eyes widened. The bird, damn him, glanced between the two with a rapid jerk of its head, turned and flew off.

Leaving Anna and Antonio alone on the balcony.

How long had Antonio been out there? Anna slowly removed her headphones, her heartbeat kicking into high gear. The pounding in her ears competed with the roar of the surf below.

"Um…hi."

"Hello."

Why did the man have to look so…calm? So in control? Eleven in the morning and he looked like he'd just walked off an Armani photo shoot in black pants that caressed his muscular thighs and a hunter-green polo fitted perfectly to his shoulders. His dark hair had been swept back from his face, probably to taunt her with those chiseled cheekbones and sinful brown eyes. Even his stubble looked sexy yet contained, shaved in a perfect line that drew attention to the defined cut of his jaw.

Except…her eyes drifted down and landed on his bare feet. Maybe it was the sight of bare skin. Maybe it was the glimpse of something vulnerable in the otherwise stalwart Antonio Cabrera. Whatever it was, it sparked something inside her.

Her head jerked back up to meet his neutral gaze.

"Were we going out early today?"

"No. I came up to shower and wandered out here." He nodded behind her. "I didn't realize you had set up office."

She winced. "Sorry. I should have asked." She waved

a hand toward the palatial suite. "I didn't feel comfortable taking over your space."

He cocked his head to one side. "Despite your newfound confidence, you say 'sorry' a lot. Did you always apologize this much?"

"When?"

"Before."

So much in that one word. Before they'd grown up. Before she'd gone and fallen in love, or at least developed a crush that had felt like love in her teenage mind. Before he'd broken her heart with cruel words she'd never expected to hear from the lips of the one person she'd thought understood her better than anyone.

"I did to others. My aunt and uncle especially."

"But not me."

"No," she agreed softly. "Not you."

With her aunt and uncle, she'd apologized whenever she had frightened them, which had been often. Eight minutes late getting home from school? Apology. Traipsed out of phone range in the vineyards and hadn't returned a text? Apology. Decided to move out of her childhood bedroom and go to Paris at the age of twenty-seven? Apology.

Kess had wanted to ride into battle for her, tell her aunt and uncle how much they'd scarred her with their incessant worrying. Anna had always stopped her. Not only did she love her aunt and uncle, but deep down she knew the fears that had driven their helicopter parenting style. She'd felt the same fears whenever they'd gone into Granada for a date night, had waited at the top of the stairs with her phone clutched in her hands, every *ping* sending fear spiraling through her veins. It hadn't been until she'd seen the headlights illuminating the driveway that she'd heaved a sigh of relief and crept off to bed.

Perhaps it had been the lifeline of distraction Antonio had first offered. How he'd been one of the few not to incessantly ask how she was doing. How he hadn't been afraid to tease her, to push her to do things on her own, to treat her like she was just another kid instead of an *orphan*.

So many reasons why they'd become friends. So many reasons why she'd fallen for him.

But that boy had disappeared. Whatever had happened that last week in Granada before he'd gone back to university had hardened him. Every time she slipped on that bracelet, the cool metal on her wrist served as a reminder that their relationship was an act.

Yet the last few days had been different. He'd seemed relaxed, happier. It had been all too easy to enjoy spending time with him instead of keeping her guard up.

"Is this just for fun?" He gestured to the drawings behind her and the swaths of fabric she'd picked up at a boutique.

"No." Shyness crept in. She tapped out a nervous rhythm with the pencil against the paper in her hand. "I actually got a call. Well, a couple."

There it was again, that damned genuine smile that blazed across his face and turned his eyes from opaque brown to sinful chocolate.

"That's great."

Add the warmth in his tone to those devastating eyes and she could feel her bones turning to mush as she ducked her face to hide the blush his praise brought on.

"Thanks."

His bare feet whispered across the stone as he walked over to her and crouched down. He reached out again, like he had in Rome, and tilted her chin up. In Rome, it had been electric, that touch of his skin on hers. Here, with questions swirling in her mind and emotions battling in her chest, she wanted nothing more than to lean into his touch and soak in his strength.

Weak.

She pulled back, ignoring the flash in his eyes. No

way was Antonio Cabrera hurt. She was seeing things she wanted to see.

"Why are the calls not good news?" His voice came out terse.

"They are."

"But?"

She sighed and sat back, pulling her legs into her chest.

"One was from a contest that had previously said they were full. Suddenly, they magically have an opening to consider my work. Two labels called, asking for a sample portfolio."

"Good labels?"

"Very good. Like never-in-a-million-years good. But," she continued as he opened his mouth to prompt her once more, "I submitted to them in May and they turned me down."

"Which means our plan is working."

She rested her forehead on her knees. "It does. It just…" She sucked in a breath. "What if it's only because of our fake relationship? What if this has nothing whatsoever to do with my talent?"

She was being torn in so many different directions. Ecstatic that her designs were finally getting a chance. Guilty that it most likely had little to do with her actual work and everything to do with her fake relationship with a famous billionaire.

And beneath it all, that pulse of awareness that jolted through her veins every time she and Antonio stepped out into the public eye. If she didn't have the reminder of the bracelet on her wrist, he could have convinced her that he felt something more than commitment to their charade.

Hands wrapped around her biceps.

Her head snapped up as Antonio hauled her to her feet and spun her around, keeping his hands cupped on her shoulders. Shock and the lightning that zapped from his hands across her skin kept her mute, allowing him to move her around like a rag doll.

"Do you see what I see?"

She blinked at the drawings in front of her. Some of them were good. Some of them were very good. All of them were *hers*. Instead of replicating, she'd opened the floodgates on her creativity and drawn what she'd felt instead of playing it safe. These designs had elements of royalty, the kind of touches that would make any woman feel like a princess. But the creations were all hers.

"Um…drawings?"

"Damned good ones."

His cursing teased a smile from her.

"Thank you. But how do you know these are good? What do you know about women's fashion?"

"I know enough."

Those three words dropped with icy cold precision into the pit of her stomach. Of course he knew. He dated supermodels and women with their own business empires. Fashion. Textile fabrication. Media.

"True." She wrenched that word out and started to pull away.

Antonio turned her around. "Why do you do this to yourself?"

"Do what?"

"Convince yourself you're not good enough? Talk yourself down?" He sounded angry.

She wanted to throw her hands up and scream. Yes, she was scared she wasn't good enough. But scared didn't translate to the end of the world. Not anymore. Just because she was scared didn't mean she would stop designing, stop trying. If she needed any evidence that he didn't see the new her, the woman who stumbled and fell but picked herself back up—figuratively and literally—then he would never see her.

"Go."

She managed to force the word out. She was done with people coddling her, ignoring the progress she'd made, the things she'd accomplished. All they saw was failure, meekness, innocence. Why could none of them see that even her failures were successes, stepping stones to helping her become not just a designer but a stronger woman, a better person?

Silence reigned. He'd let go of her shoulders but she knew he hadn't left, could still smell his woodsy cologne, feel the electric charge between their bodies.

At last, she looked up. Antonio stared at her, the blank expression back. Here she was, an emotional mess on the verge of letting tears of frustration flow, and he looked at her like she could have been a former friend on the verge of a meltdown or a stack of reports that required his attention. Both equally irritating, a nuisance in his otherwise structured life.

She started to walk past him. His arm shot out. She tried to duck under, but he lowered his arm and looped it around her waist, hauling her back against his chest. She turned, prepared to tell him to leave, to give her the day to get her head back in the game.

Except her hands landed on his chest, his muscles hard beneath her touch. His heart pulsed beneath her fingers, fast and furious. The warmth of his skin penetrated through his shirt. It wound through her veins, making her light-headed as she sucked in a breath. Her chest filled with the scent of *him*.

Dazed, she looked up. His eyes captured hers. They weren't just molten chocolate. No, they were a blazing mahogany brown. Her lips parted. He wanted her. Desired her. She wasn't just imagining it.

His gaze drifted to her mouth at the same time his hips pressed against hers. She gasped at the sensation of his hardness pressed against her thighs, arched into him as an ache built deep inside her.

"Antonio…"

A growl emanated from his chest. And then he leaned down and kissed her.

Danger!

Antonio had sailed clear past danger and was firmly in *Oh, hell* territory. But he couldn't have stopped if he'd wanted to.

Which he most definitely didn't want to. Anna fit perfectly in his arms, her slim body pressed against him as if she couldn't bear to leave even a sliver of daylight between them. Even though his lust demanded that he claim her, he kissed her slowly, caressing her lips with his own, cradling her head in one hand while he kept the other firmly pressed against her back.

If she pulled back, he'd let her go. But, dear God, he hoped she wouldn't. He would regret this later.

Later. Not now when she felt so good in his arms. So *right*.

And then she came alive. She moaned, throwing her arms around his neck. His fingers grasped at the ponytail band, pulling it out of her hair and tangling in the long locks that tumbled down her back.

Somewhere in the far recesses of his rational mind was the fact that he was kissing not only his former best friend, but his former *virginal* best friend.

It should have stopped him. But when he started to pull away, Anna simply pressed that incredible body against his. With a groan, he reached down, grabbed her thighs and hoisted her up in the air, spinning her around to set her on the table. She gasped into his mouth and he dove in, his tongue slipping in to taste her. The intimacy of the moment made him so hard he could barely stand it.

And Anna, his sweet, innocent Anna, kissed him right back. Her hands tugged at his shirt, pulled it free from the waistband of his pants. Her fingers grazed the tip of his erection straining past his belt. He reared back.

Anna stared at him, eyes wide and luminous.

"I… I…"

Before she could apologize, he swooped in again, crushing her body against his as he kissed her once more. Her legs spread as she inched her bottom closer to the edge of the table and pressed her core against his hardness.

"Oh, God, yes."

Her fevered words pushed him on, her hands creeping under his shirt and splaying across his rib cage. He reached down, ready to rip off his shirt, then hers, feel her bare breasts against his skin.

He wrenched his mouth from hers, started to trail searing kisses over her cheek, down her neck.

"Yes, Antonio!"

His name cut through the madness that had seized him. Hearing her say his name as she had a thousand times before sent a series of memories careening through his mind. Anna, in her black skirt and shirt, looking so lost in the palatial opulence of his parents' home. Anna, waiting for him by his locker after class. Anna, in her virginal white, telling him how much she loved him.

You are not worthy.

He yanked away from her so quickly he nearly stumbled.

"Anna…" He ran a hand through his hair, his breath coming in short gasps as he tried to get his raging lust under control. Hard to do when Anna sat right in front of him, legs splayed, breasts heaving as she sucked in deep breaths, lips swollen, hair tumbling past her shoulders in a sexy, rumpled mess.

It almost undid him. Almost. She wanted him. He wanted her. They were two consenting adults, no longer a young man raging with hormones and a teenager who didn't know any better.

But Anna deserved better than a quick lay. She deserved forever. And he deserved nothing she had to offer.

For the second time that week, and the third time in his life, Antonio walked away from Anna Vega.

CHAPTER THIRTEEN

Anna's arms sluiced through the warm waters of the Tyrrhenian Sea as she made her tenth lap across the cove. It had been ages since she'd indulged in a swim. With so much energy zipping through her veins, the sight of the long stone staircase winding down to the private beach she'd discovered as she'd explored the hotel had been too enticing to pass up.

Plus, it got her outside. Even though she hadn't seen Antonio at all since he'd walked away yesterday, she knew he was still inside. When she'd finally summoned up the courage to go downstairs and seek out something to eat, she'd smelled a wisp of his cologne in the elevator. Paul had arched a skeptical brow when she'd asked to go into town alone, but he'd done it. She'd waited by the empty flower beds, staring at the smooth earth, when she'd felt a hot flicker of awareness between her shoulder blades. But when she'd turned and raked her eyes over the windows of the front of the hotel, they'd been empty.

The afternoon had passed in a whirlwind. Relaxing beneath the red-striped umbrellas on Marina Grande Beach after a dip in the water. Sipping on a glass of Aperol Spritz on the patio of Franco's, an upscale bar overlooking the ocean. Savoring lemon sorbet from a street vendor.

None of it helped. The sea, the drink, the dessert. None

of it cooled the banked coals of lust Antonio had ignited with his incredible kiss.

It also didn't soothe the tension that had gripped her ever since she'd seen the sorrow in his eyes as he'd pulled away. The last few days, seeing how relaxed he'd been, echoes of who he used to be swirled in with the confident leader he'd become, had tugged at loose heartstrings. She saw how he interacted with Paul and the construction workers, the respect he gave those who worked for him. And the way he planned their sojourns, remembering little things she liked from long ago like no walnuts on her salad and a preference for as little ice as possible in her drinks, had made her feel known, an intimacy almost deeper than the soul-searing kiss they'd shared.

Why had he pulled away? What demons was he fleeing?

A rogue wave snuck up and smacked her in the face. She sucked in a gulp of salt water and coughed. The salt stung her throat as she came upright, trying to keep her head above water as her feet flailed for purchase.

An arm encircled her waist and pulled her into shallower waters. Her feet hit the sand and she bent over, coughing and trying to push her hair out of her eyes.

"You're okay, just breathe."

Antonio's voice broke through the pain of the salt water still stinging her throat. She scraped her wet hair back to see him staring at her, eyes wide, nostrils flared.

"What do you—" Her question was cut off by another round of coughing.

Before she could finish, Antonio scooped her up in his arms and carried her out of the sea to where she'd set her towel and beach bag. As her coughing abated, she pushed against his chest and tried to swing her legs out of his grasp. She might as well have been pushing against a mountain for all the good it did her.

With the coughing fit over and the pain receding, the sensation of being cradled in Antonio's strong embrace hit her with the force of a freight train. Paul had confirmed that the beach was private and would only be available to Le Porto's guests. The only way in and out was the stone staircase. So she'd pulled on an emerald bikini she'd picked up when shopping with Kess in Rome, the tie-string bottom and halter top showcasing way more skin than the one pieces she normally favored. Now, with so little on, she could feel every inch of his bare arms on her skin, his fingertips pressed firmly on her thigh.

The memory of how brazenly she'd pressed herself against him yesterday made her blush. What had come over her? She might be a virgin, but she'd certainly been kissed before. Never, though, had any of the boys she'd kissed, or been kissed by, in college ever come close to eliciting that kind of aching desire in her.

Antonio knelt next to her towel and set her down as if she were made of spun glass, his face turning from concerned to thunderous even though his movements remained tender.

"Are you all right?"

She nodded, keeping her eyes on the horizon. Why was he down here? Had he come to apologize? Or finish what they'd started on the balcony?

"Yes, I'm fine. I just swallowed a little water."

Finally, she turned to look at him.

And promptly wished she hadn't.

He'd worn khaki shorts and a black T-shirt for his trip down to see her. After going into the water to rescue her, his shirt was molded to his powerful frame, outlining every muscle beneath. She'd felt those muscles yesterday when she'd ripped his shirt out of his pants.

"Why were you swimming here alone? You should never swim by yourself."

The patronizing tone cut into her fantasy and dragged her back to earth. Nothing had changed. Judging by his voice, yesterday had been an unusual occurrence, a brief moment when Antonio had seen her as a woman, not as a friend or child to be taken care of.

Short-lived.

Pre-Paris, that knowledge would have made her duck her head, apologize and scuttle off. But after the taste she'd just had of what physical pleasure could offer, of what she'd been teased with before having it yanked away, she found herself irritated.

"I spoke with Paul before I came down here. He said the cove had been vetted as a safe swimming spot and to just stay within the confines of the rocks."

Antonio ran a hand through his wet hair. "Still, you should have told someone where you were."

"I did," she replied testily. "Paul. I just told you that."

"I meant me."

"Why would I do that? You didn't care where I was yesterday after you had your fun." The anger in her voice surprised even her, but she didn't back down. Not this time. Yesterday she'd been so consumed by the revelations kissing Antonio had revealed, it had masked the confusion and years of thinking she hadn't been good enough, hadn't been desirable enough. It hadn't just been that Antonio had told her he didn't feel the same way. He'd *hurt* her.

He started to speak but she held up her hand. Strength and anger combined to create a confidence that surged through her and propelled her to her feet.

"One, I told Paul. I confirmed it was safe to swim here. Contrary to what you, my uncle and almost everyone else seems to think, I can make intelligent decisions."

"I never said—"

"No, but you implied it. Multiple times. And second, do you have any idea how confusing all of this is? Ten years ago you told me I was just a girl with her head in the clouds and that you would never want someone like me." He winced hearing his own words spoken aloud, pain flashing across his face, but she didn't let up. No, it was time for him to finally see how much he'd hurt her. "I thought something was wrong with me, that all my fears were true. The person I was when I was with you was just an illusion and one that you'd seen through." A sob rose in her throat, but she swallowed past it. She would *not* cry in front of him. "Your rejection was confirmation that I was fanciful, naïve. You told me I wasn't mature enough, wasn't good enough—"

"I remember every word I spoke that day," he ground out as he stood, "and I never said you weren't good enough."

The sob rose higher as her eyes grew hot. "It was implied."

He leaned forward and grabbed her by the shoulders. "No! I was the one who wasn't good enough. I will never be good enough for you."

The words hung in the air between them.

Antonio's chest rose and fell as he stared into her eyes, his expression deadly serious. She stared back, speechless.

"Anna, when you…when you told me how you felt…"

The pain in his voice wiped away her anger. She started to reach out, to lay a hand on his shoulder to comfort him, but stopped before she touched him.

"I had noticed you." She leaned forward, barely discerning his words over the waves splashing onto the beach and the gulls cawing overhead. "I'd noticed you the week before you told me how you felt."

"Noticed?"

His shoulders rose then fell as his breath came out in a *whoosh*.

"Physically."

Did the earth actually shift under her? Maybe it was watching the waves move up and down that gave her the sensation of being caught at sea, tossed back and forth in a maelstrom.

"So when you said you had no interest in me…"

"You're just a child, Anna."

The look of disgust on Antonio's face froze her in place as dread built in the pit of her stomach.

"We've had fun the last few years, but your head is always in the clouds. For God's sake, you're a child!" he repeated. "We could never be a couple."

She stared at him. "But... Antonio, I—"

"Don't say it." He cut her off. "I heard you the first time. You think you love me, Anna, but you don't. You love a fantasy you've built on fairy tales and who you think I am."

"That's not true!"

He laughed. A cruel, harsh sound that tumbled from his lips as he looked away from her toward the sun setting over Granada. Her heart ached as the golden light illuminated his face. How could he look so handsome when he was breaking her dreams into a thousand pieces?

Then his gaze swung back to her, pinned her in place as his brown eyes hardened. "It's best if whatever relationship we had ends now."

No! What had she done? If she'd just kept her mouth shut, if she hadn't told him how she felt, she'd still have her friend.

"Let's just pretend this never happened. I won't bring it up again, I promise."

He shook his head once.

"It's too late for that. Goodbye, Anna."

Antonio sucked in a shuddering breath. "I said what I had to. To get you to let go."

"So you made a decision for me?"

He turned to look at her, regret hanging over him in a heavy cloud that enshrouded her in his misery. Why had she accepted his words that day? She'd known something was wrong. Antonio had never spoken to her like that before, had never treated her so cruelly. Yet she'd been so focused on herself, on her own pain and humiliation, that she'd let him walk away. If she'd been stronger then, more confident like she was now, she would have run after him, demanded answers.

Although as she stared at him, something else tugged at her. He met her gaze head-on. Was it the shifting of his feet, the slight twitch of his left eye, or the subtle clenching of his fingers that told her he wasn't being entirely truthful?

A tiny white scar above his left eyebrow caught her attention, triggered a memory. When he'd dismissed her so coldly, the scar had been a wound, ugly and red and barely visible beneath the tumble of dark hair that had fallen over his forehead.

Her hand came up, her fingers reaching out. Antonio jerked back.

"Don't."

He bit the word out, as harsh as that horrible day all those years ago. He turned to leave.

"You're really good at walking away, Cabrera."

He whirled around. The black T-shirt clung to his body, the rippling of muscles beneath the wet cloth reminding her of a panther. Sleek, fast, powerful.

"I don't deserve you, Anna." His voice, so gravelly, sent shockwaves of awareness rippling across her skin. She shivered. He swore and tugged her cover-up out of her bag, draping it over her shoulders and tugging it over her almost-nude body. "I'm not interested in marriage. Never have been, doubt I ever will be. It wasn't on my radar to begin with, and after what I've seen, I don't want it." A hoarse laugh escaped him. "My mother is under a delusion that she and my father were a love match, and I've never seen any evidence of that. You want what *your* parents had. Marriage and kids and the whole love-of-your-life bit. You told me so yourself."

She had. Numerous times. At first, they had been the ramblings of a teenage girl confiding in a friend. A longing for the kind of relationship her parents had had, one built on not just love but respect, admiration and friend-ship. What many would call a fairy tale.

Although, as far as she could remember, Prince Charm-ing had never kissed his princess the way Antonio had kissed her yesterday, with a possessive fire that had seared her from head to toe.

"I never meant to put that kind of pressure on you, An-tonio."

"I know. But what I felt for you…" His voice deepened. "It wasn't good. Not for someone like you. Not after what I did."

"What you did?" she repeated. "Antonio, talk to me."

The sorrow in his eyes nearly broke her. His hand came up and cupped her face.

She hadn't known true heartbreak before. In this mo-ment, realizing that Antonio felt something for her, that he'd felt something for her back then and she'd been too cowardly to pursue him, to find out what had made her best friend act so terribly and that he was still carrying the weight of that secret all these years later, shattered her heart into a million pieces.

"I wish I could. Just know, Anna, what you made me feel back then…" A shuddering breath escaped him. "What I feel now…"

She swayed forward, hypnotized by the longing in his words.

"What do you feel?"

He stared at her for the longest time, so long she won-dered if he'd heard her.

And then, finally.

"Hunger. Like I'm starving for you."

Antonio stepped out of an ice-cold shower and grabbed a towel, wrapping it around his hips. The water had done little to assuage his erection. Neither had his own touch, a few quick jerks meant to take the edge off.

Except when he'd touched himself, he'd imagined Anna's hands wrapped around him. When he'd found his release, he'd envisioned sliding into her body, hearing her gasp his name.

His fingers curled into fists as he stalked to the mirror. It had been a mistake to go searching for her, to apologize for the kiss. He never should have sought her out. He never should have confessed how he'd felt about her all those years ago. But when she'd stood up to him, her fire shadowing a deep-rooted hurt, and her gut-wrenching admission of how much his cruel words had affected the last ten years of her life, he hadn't been able to lie to her any longer.

Besides, it was better this way. Now she knew the truth, or at least most of it. He hadn't been able to bring himself to tell her about the accident. About William. About why he would always be alone.

He ran a comb through his hair, each stroke blunt and angry. Deep down, he was still the same reckless teenager who had nearly gotten his friend killed. Take last night. He'd given in to the slightest desire and had nearly taken Anna right then and there on the balcony table. Anna had proved time and again over the last week that she could take care of herself. That didn't mean she was impervious to the pain that would come from a man like him taking her virginity and then kicking her back into the real world. That he'd almost done just that was further evidence he wasn't, and never would be, the kind of man she deserved.

That was why, after he'd confessed how he'd actually felt all those years ago to Anna, he'd let his hand drop from her face before she could respond to his bold admission. He'd told her that if she no longer felt comfortable continuing their charade, he would arrange to have his helicopter fly her to Paris. She hadn't answered, had just nodded while staring out at the sea in that damned bikini that revealed the sensual swell of her breasts and legs he'd imagined wrapped around his waist last night.

Once more, he'd retreated. Each step up that long, winding staircase had killed him.

You've waited long enough. She wants you. What are you waiting for?

The need pulsed through him, insidious and hot. He pushed it away. If Anna decided to continue their charade through the wedding as they'd planned, he'd move into one of the guest suites. Paul could make up some excuse to the cleaning staff. Although it probably wouldn't be necessary. He'd revealed everything to her, and she'd barely been able to look at him when he'd left the beach.

Well, almost everything. When she'd asked him to talk to her, the story had risen and rested on the tip of his tongue. He'd wanted to tell her. Knowing that he would see only disgust in her eyes had stopped him.

God willing, the details of that night would never again see the light of day.

He stalked out of the bathroom, running through a mental checklist of what he would need to move into the suite down the hall should she stay. Computer, phone charger, toothbrush…

The scent of daisies hit him, stopped him in his tracks. He sucked in a shuddering breath then slowly, so slowly, raised his head to see Anna framed in the door leading out to the balcony, her slim form wrapped in a pale pink robe. Her hair tumbled down her back and over her shoulders in cascading waves of dark brown.

His mouth dried.

"Anna…what are you doing here?"

She stared at him for a long moment, as if trying to make up her mind about something. Then she stepped into the room.

"I want us to have sex."

His mind stuttered. His brain shouted *Danger!* even as his lust shouted back *Yes!*

"Perhaps you didn't hear me on the beach," he replied as coolly as he could manage.

She took another step. The sun hit the robe and illuminated her sensual figure through the thin material of her robe. His fingers curled on the doorway, a physical reminder to stay put.

"I won't be what you want, either."

Surprised, he asked, "How so?"

Her long lashes fluttered. "I do want it all. Eventually. Marriage, kids, love, flowers and romantic cards. You said yourself you'll never be that kind of man, and I'm not settling for less."

The words should have brought relief, not created an ache in his chest.

"That doesn't explain why you think we should have sex."

Was that his voice? The casual, almost bored, tone? How did he even achieve it when flames were licking over every inch of his skin?

His fingers dug deeper into the doorframe, so hard, he was surprised it didn't splinter beneath his grasp.

"You gave me a taste yesterday of something I'd never experienced before."

"A mistake that will not be repeated."

"What if I want you to repeat it?"

God, her voice. So breathless, so sweet and soft. How could he possibly give in to the temptation she was offering without hating himself for the rest of his life?

"You don't know what you're asking."

"But I do." Another step into the room. "I've kissed other men before."

Who? The possessive shout sounded from within, primal and jealous that any other man had laid a hand on her, much less his lips.

"And?"

This time his suave casualness had disappeared, the word coming out on a growl.

"And it was nothing like what I shared with you yesterday. I want more of that. You said yourself the world can be a bad place. What better way to be introduced to sex and the physical side of pleasure than with someone I know and trust?"

"You shouldn't trust me," he ground out. "I'm just going to break your heart."

"Only if I give it you," she countered. "I offered it to you once. I'm stronger now. Wiser. I won't make that mistake again."

Smart girl, even if that cut deep.

"But what I do want," she continued, "is to know more about sex."

He should say no, needed to say no.

Yet, his body argued, *she'll just find someone else to introduce her to sex. She knows where she stands with you. What if the man she finds breaks her heart or hurts her?*

Before his brain could come up with a logical counter, Anna reached up and parted the folds of the robe to reveal her body underneath.

Her nearly naked body.

CHAPTER FOURTEEN

ANNA TWEAKED HER shoulders and let the robe fall in a silken pool at her ankles. Amazing how she could stand in front of Antonio in just a bralette and thong without joining the robe on the floor. Outwardly, she tried to replicate what she'd seen when she'd spied the woman in the window in Rome. Confidence, poise, sensuality.

She hoped she was doing it right because inside she was a bundle of frayed nerves. Her heart slammed against her ribs. The bottom of her stomach had dropped and stayed somewhere down around her feet when Antonio had walked out of the bathroom, that towel casually wrapped around his waist, displaying his muscular abdomen, glistening wet from his shower.

Hearing what Antonio had had to say on the beach, realizing that he had lied to her all those years ago, that the desire he'd shown for her yesterday on the balcony had been real, had emboldened her. She had offered herself up once and failed to follow through when she'd known something had been wrong.

This time, she knew exactly how things stood. Antonio had made her feel things she'd never experienced with the few men she'd dated. If her career took off, there was no telling when she would find the time to meet someone, fall in love and get married. What better way to be introduced to the world of physical pleasure than by someone she knew? Someone she trusted? Even though he'd changed over the years, she found that she still trusted him. Even if he didn't trust her enough to share what had caused him to retreat into this closed-off persona.

And, if he rejected her, at least she could say she had tried this time.

The longer he stared at her, the more she steeled herself for his rejection. She'd handled it once and recovered. Armed with her newfound knowledge that he'd at least wanted her, it would hurt, but she would emerge from this.

He inhaled, the sound audible in the stillness that had settled over the room. His eyes moved from hers, sliding down her neck to her breasts, then further still over her stomach and down to the juncture of her thighs. The electricity in her veins hummed louder, sparking little fires throughout her body everywhere his gaze roamed.

Dear God, even if the man said no, at least she would forever have this moment burned into her memory.

"Terms."

She blinked. "What?"

"I proposed our fake relationship with few terms and little forethought," he bit out. "What are the terms for this arrangement?"

A quiver raced through her. Was this actually happening? Was he saying yes?

"Um…well…" What was she supposed to ask for? She'd never had sex.

"Just the once?"

"I was thinking more throughout the remainder of our fake relationship."

One corner of his mouth twitched. "What if you don't like it?"

She snorted, her hand flying up a second later to cover her mouth in mortification. "Sorry. I just, uh, don't see that being a likely scenario."

His lips curved up more.

The heat in her core grew hotter. She shifted, suddenly acutely aware of the dampness on her thighs. Antonio's eyes flickered down to her legs, lingered, then slowly crawled back up her body.

"Protection."

"Of course," she agreed hurriedly.

"Anything else?"

She bit down on her lower lip. "I don't know. I've never done this before. Am I supposed to ask for a certain number of orgasms or something?"

He stared at her then threw his head back and laughed.

"God, Anna, you're going to be the death of me."

Before she could process that statement, he moved forward, his steps slow but sure. *Panther-like*, she thought again, as sunlight flowed over his muscles. Her eyes swung to where the towel clung to his hips. She'd seen superhero movies where the men had Vs carved into their stomachs that went down toward their thighs, a not so subtle trail to what lay between their legs. She never thought anyone actually looked like that.

But Antonio did, and he was coming straight for her like he was going to taste every inch of her body and make her go up in flames.

What have I done?

Then he was there, a breath away, the heat from his body seeping into hers. Her nipples hardened beneath the weight of his gaze. She kept her hands fixed at her sides. She would not touch herself, would not try to assuage the ache building so deep inside it almost hurt.

She expected to see the same raging lust in his eyes that she'd seen yesterday. But when their gazes collided, she saw desire mixed with a tenderness that tugged at the loose threads of the past.

"Are you sure?"

A pause. Then she nodded.

He slid his arms around her waist. This time when she

gasped, she didn't bother to hide her reaction. She embraced the arch of her body into his and savored the feel of her breasts pressing up against his chest. He leaned down and brushed his lips across hers, a whisper that made her whimper. She wanted the fire and passion of yesterday, the burning desire to touch each other everywhere.

But Antonio had other ideas. Every time she tried to deepen the kiss, tease him by stroking her fingers over his chest, nip his bottom lip, he simply smiled against her mouth and continued to kiss her as if she was the most precious treasure in the world.

Finally, she relaxed and let him explore, her body melting against his. His fingers skimmed up and down her back, leaving trails of tingling heat in their wake. She slowly eased her hands up the back of his neck and into his hair. Who knew touching someone's hair could be so erotic? When she tangled her fingers in the silky thickness, his kiss firmed, his tongue darting out and tracing the seam of her lips with masterful precision.

His hands moved with aching slowness over her waist, skimmed up her sides. A moan escaped her as he cupped her breasts. Her head lolled back. He left her mouth, pressed his lips to her cheek, then her jaw, then down her neck. He kissed her pulse beating frantically in her throat, his fingers working under the band of her bralette. Then he was pulling the lace up, over, and suddenly she was standing in front of him in nothing but her lace thong.

Her confidence wavered. She'd never been this close to being naked in front of a man before. It made her feel vulnerable.

Antonio must have sensed her hesitation because he paused, her bralette in one hand, the other fisted by his side.

"All you have to do is say 'stop,'" he whispered, "and I'll stop."

His reassurance soothed some of her uncertainty. It had

nothing to do with him and everything to do with her own insecurities.

"I know." She reached up and laid her hand against his stubbled jaw. His gaze darkened and he turned, pressing a kiss to the middle of her palm that made her eyes drift shut. She'd never imagined the various parts of her body that could experience sensual pleasure. Each reveal elicited more joy, the physical delights mixing with her sense of adventure. If she'd known it could be like this, perhaps she would have sought out a partner sooner.

Although that wasn't true, she acknowledged as Antonio's hands returned to her bare breasts, cupping the globes in his hands. No one had ignited this need inside her. After Antonio's rejection, she hadn't trusted anyone else with her body. Ironic that the man who had broken her heart was also now touching her in ways she had only imagined.

He leaned down and captured a nipple in his mouth. She cried out, her hands returning to his hair as she pressed her breast more fully against him. His arms encircled her waist as he let out a primal growl that thrilled her to her toes. Each suck sent lightning arcing through her body. The hair on his jaw scraped across her breasts before his mouth latched onto her other nipple.

Before she could further explore his body, he scooped her up into his arms and carried her to the bed. He lowered her down as he had on the beach. Yet this time his lips fused to hers in another passionate kiss that made her toes curl and one hand grip the silky comforter while the other grabbed onto his shoulder. His muscles rippled beneath her touch, a steadiness she desperately needed as her emotions rose and fell like the waves on the beach. Excitement, elation, desire, need...beneath it all, running so deep she almost missed it in the headiness of being wanted, the longing for the man she'd once loved slowly creeping out of its hiding place.

No.

That feeling had no place here. She and Antonio had made a pact as mature adults. Just a little over a week of pure pleasure and then they would part ways.

Although, she acknowledged as he reached down and tugged at the towel, a week didn't seem like nearly long enough.

The towel fell to the floor. Antonio stood there in all his naked glory. Her breath caught in her chest. She'd gotten glimpses of his arms, his chest, his abdomen over the past week. His legs were thick, similarly muscled and dusted with dark hair. Between his legs, his erection jutted out.

"There's a question on your face." He spoke the words softly, as if he was afraid he might spook her.

"You just...um..." She bit her lower lip. "You look really big."

His chuckle hummed through her. *"Gracias, mariposa."*

Something flickered across his face when he said her nickname. Before she could decipher it, he climbed on the bed, caging her between his arms, and leaned down to kiss her once more. She arched up, trying to press her nearly naked body against him, but only found cool air. Every time she lifted her hips, he stayed just out of reach, smiling against her lips.

"For a virgin, you're awfully eager," he said as he nipped her jaw.

"Have all your other virgins been terrified of *that*?" she asked, pointing to his hardness.

He went down on his elbows, his chest grazing hers, and cupped her face in his hands. The tender look in his eyes spoke to that current of longing, pulled it closer to the surface. He leaned over and pressed another kiss to her lips. "I want to take this slow. If you're going to give me the honor of being your first, I want to make it memorable."

She blinked rapidly to keep the tears at bay. She wouldn't be making a good case for her ability to stay emotionally detached if she cried before they'd even had sex.

"Well...thank you."

He chuckled then sank to press his body flush against hers. The sensuality of feeling his naked skin, of being able to run her hands over his arms, his back, up his neck and into his hair to bring his face back to hers for a more intense kiss, thrilled her.

Slowly, he kissed his way along her neck, back over her breasts. He cupped them in his hands, brought them to his mouth and nipped and licked all over with excruciating thoroughness, before continuing over her belly.

When his fingers settled on the edge of her thong, he paused. She looked at him and caught her breath. His eyes burned, dark mahogany in flames.

"I want to taste you."

Thank goodness she was lying down, because otherwise her knees would have collapsed at his words. She nodded once. His fingers skimmed beneath the material, slowly rolled it down her hips and over her thighs as he continued to press kisses to the sensitive skin of her legs.

And then she was just as naked as he was. Shyness crept in but didn't have time to linger and spread as Antonio moved back up her body. His hands settled on her thighs, gently parted them. Anticipation kept her body strung taut as a bowstring. When he kissed her *there*, her hips lifted off the bed as she cried out.

"*Antonio!*"

How was it possible to feel such pleasure? His tongue drove her mad, spiraling her higher and higher. She should be embarrassed to have her most intimate places bared to him, but it felt too good, felt too right, for her to dwell on that when the ecstasy was building with such intensity she could barely catch her breath.

The pleasure burst and she cried out his name again, her hands fisting in his hair as her hips pumped against his mouth. Then, slowly, her body dipped back to the bed as she went limp, cocooned by Antonio's warmth on top of her and the silk of his bed beneath her. Her eyes drifted shut as a smile curved her lips. She'd deal with the emotions later, because they were most certainly there, stronger than before, circling in the wake of the most intense passion she'd ever experienced.

Later. Because right now she was going to be glad she took the risk. For the rest of her life, she would never regret asking Antonio to take her to bed. Not when he'd given her such an incredible gift.

"That was…"

"Just the beginning."

Her eyes flew open to see him tearing open a condom packet. He sheathed his hard length, his gaze never leaving hers. She started to sit up. Curiosity and a hint of wickedness made her reach out and wrap her fingers around him. His breath hissed out. Before she could explore further, he tumbled her back onto the comforter.

"Later." Another searing kiss that rekindled the flames in her body. "Right now, I want to be inside you."

She swallowed hard, nodded. His hardness touched the delicate folds where his mouth had just been, her flesh even more sensitive. She arched up against him and he groaned, pushing slightly inside her.

Huh. She'd always heard the first time hurt, but this didn't, it felt naughty and sensual and so—

"Oh!"

As he slid further in, a pressure built, followed by a stinging sensation. This time her cry was sharp as her hands grabbed onto his arms and she winced.

"I'm sorry, Anna." He paused, kissing her forehead. "Do you want me to stop?"

"No, just…" She sucked in a shuddering breath. "Hurts."

"I've heard there can be pain sometimes, yes."

"Okay. Okay." Another breath. "Just…slow."

His head came down, his lips brushing her temple as he whispered something in Spanish. The deep timbre of his voice wound around her, the lilting phrases of his native tongue relaxing her taut muscles and distracting her from the pain. Each movement of his body was accompanied by a kiss. By the time he'd slid fully inside her, he'd kissed every inch of her face, from the tip of her nose to the shell of her ear.

"How does this feel?"

She wiggled around a little, adjusting to the sensation. He grimaced.

"Did I hurt you?" she asked, her hand coming up to rest on his jaw.

"Not in the way you're thinking. I'm trying to hold back so I don't hurt you."

She wiggled again, savoring the flare in his eyes. Plus, the ache had started to fade, the pleasure returning in a slow but steady current that spread throughout her body. She reached down and let her hands rest on his hips.

"I want to feel more."

His eyes darkened to almost black. One more kiss. One deep, soul-searing, mind-numbing kiss.

Then he began to move, sliding in and out of her with growing intensity. Each thrust went deeper. Their bodies moved into a natural rhythm, her hips arching up as he pulsed inside her. She savored his muscles flexing beneath her hands, the heat of his body, the feel of him inside her. The sensation collided with the carnal knowledge of what they were doing, the intimacy of their bodies being joined, that she was giving him as much pleasure as he was her.

The pressure began to build. She spread her legs wider to feel him even deeper inside her.

"Anna…"

Hearing her name whispered lit a fuse inside her core. Her arms flew around him, her fingers digging into his back.

"Antonio…please… I'm…"

His thrusts quickened, deepened. She was on the verge of something incredible, so close, almost…

"Antonio!"

His name burst from her lips as her body came apart in a blinding rush. He captured her breath with a kiss. She moaned against him, her body shuddering, quaking, the pleasure so intense, she almost couldn't take it.

He drove into her one last time. A groan escaped him as he found his release. Slowly, he lowered his body back onto hers, propping himself up on his elbows as he kissed her lightly, his lips tracing over hers in a soft, sweet kiss.

"That…that was…"

He lifted his head and smiled down at her. Another true smile, one that nearly broke her heart after the intimacy they had just shared. What would it be like to share this kind of affection with him day after day?

Stop.

She focused on the little tendrils of satisfaction still drifting through her body, the hazy warmth permeating her consciousness.

"That was amazing," she finally said.

"I'm glad I could impress."

"I'm also glad we agreed to a week of this." She couldn't imagine only sampling this once.

His smile flickered, disappearing for a split second before reappearing as he smoothed sweat-dampened wisps of hair off her face.

"Have I created a monster?"

No, he hadn't created a monster. But she might have unleashed one. She had severely underestimated her ability to stay detached, to enjoy sex without letting her emotions get in the way.

"No. I guess I just like sex."

With a laugh and another peck to her cheek, he got up and disappeared into the bathroom. She lay on the bed, the cool air swooping in to press down on her heated skin and whisk away the fantasy she'd briefly indulged in. How had she ever thought she was truly over him? If things had continued the way they had before their kiss yesterday, she could have convinced herself that he was too different from the boy she'd fallen for, that he had no interest in her and they were better off severing this briefly rekindled relationship after Alejandro and Calandra's wedding.

But knowing that he had wanted her, that he had rejected her out of some misguided act of chivalry, sharing her body with him...

How was she supposed to just let that go?

Because he told you how things stand. This time around, at least, he'd been nothing but honest with her.

Mostly honest, she amended as she stood and grimaced at the ache between her legs. The scar...whatever had changed him from the boy he'd been at the beginning of summer to the man who'd broken her heart at the end was still a mystery.

The sound of water running drew her from the past. Antonio stepped out of the bathroom, still completely naked. With the sun shining in from the balcony, his skin looked like it was lit from within, a golden tan that, coupled with his black hair, made her think of a dark angel.

"Would you like to join me?"

He extended a hand, one eyebrow arched up at a rakish angle. Her body stirred.

She had a little over a week to enjoy what he was offering. A week, if she didn't muck it up with her naïve fantasies. Antonio had already shared so much with her that she hadn't known before. If he'd wanted to share what else had happened that summer, he would have already done so.

Time to be a big girl.

She raised her chin and smiled.

"I'd love to."

She accepted his hand, loved the way his fingers closed over hers possessively as he tugged her toward the shower.

Hot water cascaded from a waterfall shower that fogged the glass doors and created an intimate haven. He lathered her body with a woodsy-smelling soap, taking special care to wash the remnants of her first lovemaking off her thighs as he cradled her in his strong arms. This time, when he pulled on a condom and slid inside her, her body welcomed him as he lifted her up, wrapped her legs around his waist and pressed her against the wall.

Beneath the steaming water, he made love to her again, drawing out each thrust and teasing her until she dug her nails into his shoulders and begged for a release. He obliged by quickening his pace and reaching between their bodies, his fingers finding the sensitive bud above where their bodies were joined and stroking it until she came apart in his arms.

CHAPTER FIFTEEN

ANTONIO HIT END and cut off Alejandro's incessant questioning. His brother had called to confirm that Antonio and his "girlfriend" would be present at the rehearsal dinner the following day. A ruse, Antonio had discovered too late, for his brother to pester him with questions about Anna.

"So the tabloids were true," Alejandro had said with a laugh that had grated across Antonio's nerves.

"I don't kiss and tell. Unlike some people I know," he had shot back. His brothers didn't know about the ruse. God willing, they wouldn't find out. They had come through for him years ago with William's accident, making sure nothing had been leaked to the press and that their parents were kept in the dark. Adrian, already a moneymaking machine at that point, had covered all of William's care, from his time in the hospital to the lengthy physical therapy. When Antonio had made his own first six-figure deposit into his account, he had sent Adrian an amount he'd estimated would cover all of William's expenses. Adrian had tried to return it, but it was one of the few things Antonio had stood up to the eldest Cabrera sibling on.

Although, it wasn't like he and his brothers were close. Not only had their recent interest in matrimony and family driven them apart, but he'd always kept himself distant from them since the accident. He'd been sick with guilt and, eventually, ashamed that he'd fallen into the traditional baby brother role of needing his older siblings to bail him out. That he'd also put their hard-earned reputations at risk, as well having to rely on Adrian's money initially to do the right thing by William, had killed him.

Too bad, he reflected as he walked back into the restaurant. Because he could sure as hell use someone to talk to right about now. He stalked up the stairs, his heartbeat kicking into overdrive as he neared the top.

She was waiting for him up there. Their last night in Positano. Tomorrow was the rehearsal dinner. Saturday, the wedding. Sunday, the post-wedding breakfast.

And then it would be over. Anna would depart for Paris and begin to sew as if her life depended on it. Five more requests had come in over the last week, along with offers from several major brands and influencers. The more their photos appeared in magazines, Instagram feeds and entertainment talk shows, the more her inbox piled up. Her friend Kess had hopped on several conference calls, providing guidance on which designers and shows Anna should focus on.

Their charade had continued to prove successful for him, too. The more they'd wandered Positano, the more *Le Porto* had cropped up. His head of marketing had yakked on and on about their social media metrics, excitement vibrating through the phone on their last call.

Still, in the last couple of days, he'd noticed fewer photographers and mentions of their romance and more of Alejandro's upcoming wedding. If he and Anna staged it right, they could continue the pretense of their relationship continuing past the wedding. Flowers delivered to her apartment in Paris, an occasional "mention" to the press by a discreet friend who gushed about how much fun they were having.

It had all fallen into place despite his lack of planning.

He reached the top of the stairs and walked onto the rooftop terrace of the restaurant perched on the mountain-tops overlooking Positano, Capri and the Galli Isles. He'd reserved the entire terrace for privacy. At least, that's what he'd told Anna when he'd surprised her with the limo ride up the mountainside.

But in reality, he wanted her all to himself. A notion he was glad he'd paid attention to because when she'd walked out into the living area of the penthouse earlier this evening, possession had sunk its talons into his skin.

Mine.

The dress hung from her shoulders by silver-braided threads, the straps holding up a gossamer fabric the color of lilacs. The plunging neckline and thin strip of sheer material wrapped around her waist had given him a glimpse of bare skin before falling into a wide, fluffy skirt that stopped just below her knees. Flowers and ivy vines crawled over the bodice. A nod to her love of the outdoors, she'd shared with him.

Now she sat by the terrace railing, the evening light creating an enchanting glow that catapulted the entire scene from beautiful to stunning. The private table, set with a deep blue tablecloth, boasted plates of rice balls stuffed with tomato sauce, mozzarella and peas, and wineglasses filled with Barbaresco. A candle flickered romantically in the center next to a small vase of orange-colored blossoms. The view of the mountain, craggy outcroppings and cascading slopes tumbling into the ocean seemed almost too perfect to be real. The Italian cities he wished they had more time to explore twinkled below.

Yet the one thing that stood out to him in the midst of all that splendor was Anna. The sparkle in her eyes. The smile lingering on her lips. How she still looked so sweet despite the many lessons in debauchery he'd given her the past week.

Guilt crept up on him, fast and venomous. The magic dimmed a little. All week, he'd been ignoring his conscience. Mornings had still been reserved for work, but as noon had drawn near, he'd found himself walking quicker and quicker to the penthouse to collect Anna.

Before he'd made love to her, they'd made their way down to the lobby in an efficient manner. Now he hurried to be by her side, linger on the balcony as she showed him the sketches and samples she'd put together that day. He loved watching her eyes light up, looking at the pictures of what had inspired her that morning, and offering suggestions here and there when she asked. Or sharing his own ideas for where he wanted his business to go and she'd asked questions, showed enthusiasm for his aspirations. That was one thing that hadn't changed about her. She'd always been interested in him just for him, not for his name or wealth. He'd loved how she'd cared more for flowers picked on a mountainside than all the exotic blooms his money could buy.

Love.

His step faltered. That word had cropped up more and more throughout the past week. He couldn't pinpoint the moment he'd gone from living in the moment to thinking of the future. A future he had never before contemplated; at least, not one with a woman in it. But now when he thought of the future, he couldn't see one without Anna in it.

What would she say if he told her all? Over the past few days, she'd slowly drawn out details he hadn't shared with anyone. How he felt even more estranged from his brothers in recent months. Anna, bless her, hadn't coddled him or backed down. No, that newfound fire had surged forth once more and she'd challenged him to talk to them after Alejandro's honeymoon.

"You've put up the walls," she'd said. "So why not tear them down if it's making you unhappy?"

She'd accepted everything so far. If he told her about the accident, about the guilt he'd been carrying around for so long, would she stay? Could confession be the first step toward a life that meant something more? Toward healing not only himself but his relationships with his brothers? With Anna? Maybe even William?

Anna looked up, her smile falling when she saw his face.

"Is everything okay?"

"Everything's fine," he said, leaning down to kiss her. Another selfish indulgence, but one he'd embraced gladly. The first day they'd gone out after spending the previous afternoon and evening in bed together, Anna had curled into his side and wrapped an arm around his waist with an intimate ease that had both terrified and thrilled him. Aware that photographers could be hiding anywhere, he'd allowed it. As the day had progressed, he'd found himself responding in kind, kissing her cheek, reaching out for her hand.

It wasn't just sex with Anna. No, it was the intimacy, the familiarity, that made his time with her so enjoyable. He hadn't felt like himself in a long while, but she dragged it out of him, made him relax.

He sat across from her and picked up his wineglass, watching the candlelight play over the ruby-red liquid.

"Alejandro called to confirm tomorrow."

She grimaced. "I'm not looking forward to that."

"Why not? You'll get to see your aunt and uncle. My family's looking forward to seeing you, too."

"And that'll be nice. It's just…" She bit down on her lower lip. A habit, he'd noticed, when she was worried about something.

"Just what?" he asked, reaching across the table and capturing her hand in his. She slowly breathed out.

"I don't like lying to our families."

"I don't, either. But it won't hurt them in the long run."

One bare shoulder rose and fell in a shrug. "True. It's not like we're pretending to be engaged or something."

His eyes dropped to the diamond bracelet on her wrist. What would it be like to put another type of diamond on her hand?

"I'm also surprised at how easily my family accepted the

story of us dating," Anna continued, oblivious to his inner turmoil. "They were intrusive, almost obsessive, about who I dated in college. But they've barely talked to me the past two weeks."

He kept his expression neutral. The couple of times he'd been in touch with Diego, the butler had been surprisingly overjoyed at the thought of Anna and Antonio dating. Antonio hadn't been able to bring himself to tell Diego that it was all a lie.

"They knew you and I were close as children. I wouldn't read too much into it."

She squeezed his hand and gave him another heart-stopping smile. "You're probably right. No sense worrying about it right now when we have this view." A dimple flashed in her cheek.

He tried to refocus, to enjoy the rest of their evening. But their brief conversation about the wedding, the impending deadline on their fake relationship, clouded his earlier happiness. Even seeing Anna's eyes widen in delight at the dessert, lemon sorbet drizzled with red raspberry sauce and topped with fresh mint leaves, did little to assuage his bad mood. He was at a crossroads. He could tell Anna and risk her rejection.

Or she could accept him, ugly past and all. He didn't know which of the two frightened him more.

The ridedown the mountain increased his impending sense of doom. His driver took a curve a touch too fast, the move making Anna fall against him as his heart thundered in his chest. He'd slept next to Anna every night the last six nights. Each morning, he'd awoken nightmare-free. Another sign, he thought, that perhaps his time with Anna was healing the past.

But now, as the car moved back into its lane and continued on, adrenaline pumped through his veins as tires screeched in his mind and William cried out.

Anna, bless her, looked out the window, soaking in the

sights and thankfully missing the past burrowing its way back under his skin.

He helped her out of the car back at the hotel. She smiled at the freshly painted flowers and now working fountain, the water splashing down in a tinkling melody. She'd mentioned it to him the other day, about how she looked forward to seeing the final results. He'd paid triple for a local gardener to come in and plant an array of lush blooms, as well as a bonus to the construction workers to get the fountain working before Thursday evening.

Before they left. Because he'd wanted Anna to see it. Not because it was a practical business decision or because it was a necessity. No, he'd done something spur-of-the-moment just because he'd wanted to make her happy.

The elevator ground to a halt. Antonio swore and punched a button.

Paul's voice filled the small space, smooth and refined. "Yes, sir?"

"Paul, the elevator's stuck."

"One moment, sir." A crackle of static, followed by, "Sir, one of the construction crews stayed late. They shut down the elevator to work on something. It'll be just a minute."

He ground his teeth. He wasn't paying one of the top construction firms in Italy as much as he was to have them—

Anna's hands moved up over his chest, grabbed onto the lapels of his suit jacket and pulled him down for a kiss. His arms wrapped around her, a habit now when she kissed him. She tasted sweet, like lemons and raspberries.

She nibbled on his lower lip, eliciting a groan. The first two days, he'd been adamant that she allow him to teach her, to go slow and savor each moment. But once he'd allowed her to sink to her knees in the shower and take his length in her mouth, he'd been lost. Anna approached lovemaking with the same carefree joy and curious adventurousness she approached life with. It was intoxicating.

"Might as well make the most of our time," she whispered against his mouth with a smile.

She had no idea the battle raging inside him. But her words hit hard. They had one night left before they joined the rest of the family in Marseilles. One more night to enjoy her body before he had to make the most critical decision of his life. He might have a lifetime of this kind of pleasure with her...or this might be the last time.

The thought of another man touching her, kissing her, made his hands tighten on her waist and pull her body against his. She gasped, arched against him. His fingers tangled in her hair and, with a gentle tug, he tilted her head back, baring her neck to his lips. He trailed kisses along her throat to the beautifully tanned skin of her breasts swelling past that seductively plunging neckline.

One hand drifted up, the diamond bracelet winking under the lights of the elevator. With a tug, the bodice sagged, the straps sliding down her arms to reveal her bare breasts. His lust became a living thing, pulsing in his veins as he dipped his head and sucked a pebbled peak into his mouth. He kept one hand on her waist, the other drifting up to cup her other breast and tease the nipple with his thumb. Her fingers delved into his hair, frantic, as her breathing quickened, the sound urging him on. He glanced up to see her eyes closed, lashes dark against her skin, rosy lips parted as she panted. His gaze drifted to the mirrored walls behind her, the reflection of his seductive foreplay and her passionate response reflected a hundred times all around them.

"Open your eyes, Anna. Watch."

Her lashes swept up. Pink tinged her cheekbones as she smiled shyly at the mirrors. God, he loved that about her. How, even after everything he'd introduced her to, she could still be so innocent.

As he continued to lavish attention on her breasts, he caught her gaze in the mirror, held it. Her smile turned daring as her touch drifted away from his hair, down his back and then around front. He felt her fingers on his trousers, heard the hiss of his zipper and then groaned as she reached in and wrapped her fingers around him.

He calculated the likelihood of how long it would take Paul to reach the construction workers and get the elevator moving. Probably too soon for him to make love to her the way he wanted to, but not too soon for him to still make her come apart in his arms.

He reached down, fisted her skirts and lifted the frothy material. Her eyes glazed over as his fingers slipped inside the silk thong she'd donned for the evening.

So wet, so hot.

He rubbed her silken flesh, watched her face as he slipped a finger inside her molten heat. She writhed against him, moaning his name. Her hand tightened on his hardness, but before she could start the rhythm that had undone him two nights ago, he pulled her hand away, grabbed her arm and lifted it above her head. He paused in his sensual ministrations to her core and captured her other arm, pinning both above her head in his grasp.

He would remember her like this forever. Hair tumbling down over her shoulders, her naked breasts barely visible through the dark curtain, lips swollen and eyes alight with desire for him.

He leaned in, kissed her as he reached back under her skirts, slipped a finger inside and savored the clench of her muscles around him. He slid in and out, brushing his thumb over her most sensitive place, savoring the hitch in her breath, the scent of her passion curling around him and making him feel like a god for bringing her such pleasure.

"Antonio, please."

He wanted to drag out the moment, tease her, savor the feel of her as he gazed in the mirrors and saw every single angle of their bodies pressed together.

But he had no desire for Paul or any of the construction

workers to see Anna like this. Because then he'd have to kill them.

He quickened his pace, stroking his finger in and out as he lovingly massaged her. When she came, his name escaped her lips on a cry as she shuddered against him, her head dropping to his shoulder. He turned his head, pressed a quick kiss to her temple, then slid the straps of her dress up to cover her once more.

Not a moment too soon. With a grinding of gears, the elevator jerked back into motion. Paul's voice came back on.

"Is it working, sir?"

"Yes. Good night, Paul."

A breathy laugh sounded against his throat. "Are there cameras in here?"

"Not yet. Next week."

Dios mío. He hadn't even considered that they might be recorded.

Because you weren't thinking with your brain.

He glanced down at Anna as she straightened the straps of her dress, smoothed her hair and shot him a thousand-watt smile that rivaled the brightness of the mini chandelier overhead. Being with her, thinking about everything but what was safe, made him reckless.

His feelings for her had made him reckless once before. He felt differently now, more in control…but what if he hadn't really changed?

Enough. Time for self-contemplation later.

When the elevator doors opened, he scooped her up in his arms and carried her down the hall and across the threshold. She threw back her head and laughed. He laid her on the bed, climbed up next to her and covered her body with his, his fingers cupping the back of her head as he kissed her deeply. He started to pull the straps down once more. But before he could bare her breasts to his gaze, she shimmied out from under him and darted over to the doors leading out to the balcony.

"May I share a secret with you?"

That shyness killed him every time. With other women, he might have assumed it was an act, an attempt to be coy. But not his Anna.

"Given how much you've shared with me this week, I think I can handle one secret."

"The first time you kissed me…" Her hand fluttered toward the far end of the balcony. "When you put me up on the table…"

He rolled off the bed and stalked toward her, enjoying the quickening rise and fall of her chest.

"Vividly."

He reached her side but didn't touch her, heightening the anticipation.

"I imagined you laying me down on the table and making love to me."

It was the first time either of them had said the words "make love" out loud. He noted her blink, the quick disconnect as her mind scrambled to come up with an alternative term.

"I mean, have se—"

He cut her off, wrapping his arms around her, lifting her up and tossing her over his shoulder. Her laugh filled the night air, melodic and sweet.

"Antonio! What are you doing?"

"Fulfilling your wish, *mariposa*."

He flipped a switch on the wall. Lights Paul had insisted on being installed among the ivy lit up, creating an intimate glow. He made a mental note to give Paul a raise as he set Anna down and watched her look around the balcony with awe.

"This is beautiful." Her smile landed on him. "I'm really happy for you, Antonio. This place is going to be so successful."

Pride swelled in his chest. No one outside his family had

shown any interest in his hotels, other than to inquire about free rooms or how much money his properties raked in.

"Thank you, Anna."

Before she could reply, he slid his fingers under the straps of her dress, tugging the material down over her body. As the fabric peeled away, he pressed kisses to her heated skin, delighting in the sounds she made for him. By the time he'd finished, she was panting, her skin flushed with desire. He scooped up her naked body, laid her out on the table. She watched as he undressed, slowly, teasing her as he took his time unbuttoning his shirt, sliding off his slacks and rolling a condom onto his hard length.

He started to join her on the table, but she sat up and shook her head.

"Lay down."

He nearly came right then and there. He laid back on the table, watched with bated breath as she straddled his hips. She braced her hands against his shoulders. Then, with aching slowness, she lowered herself onto him, eyes closing as she moaned. As she found her tempo, he met her body with his own thrusts. When she found her release and cried out, he reached up, his hand tangling in her hair and bringing her head down for a kiss. He followed a moment later, his body shaking as his climax shuddered through him.

Anna collapsed on top of him. He stroked his hand up and down her back, savoring the feel of her body against his. He took mental note of everything: the silken caress of her hair against his face, the heated dampness of her skin, the freckles dotting her nose.

No matter how the weekend ended, he would remember this for the rest of his life.

CHAPTER SIXTEEN

THE SOFT STRAINS of a romantic song drifted across the deck of the ship. A dance floor had been cordoned off by lights strung up above the wood decking. Couples swayed together, dressed in a sea of vividly colored gowns and ebony suits. In the midst of the crowd, Alejandro and his bride, Calandra, had eyes only for each other.

Anna smiled down into her champagne glass. Who would have thought the boy she'd once spied filling the sleeves of the British ambassador's coat with shaving cream would end up married to someone as straitlaced and put together as Calandra?

Her gaze lifted, drifted over the crowd. Antonio had disappeared after the dinner. The few times she'd spied him, he'd been talking with men who looked very important, the kind who were still answering emails during the ceremony held in the grand ballroom below.

Apprehension pricked her skin. Ever since she'd woken up yesterday morning to an empty bed and a brief note saying Antonio would meet her in Marseille, she'd known. The fairy tale they'd created the last week had been over. Paul had conveyed that Antonio had had to take the helicopter and help his brother.

"Last-minute wedding details," he'd told her.

The twist of his lips beneath his magnificent moustache had told her he hadn't believed Antonio's excuse, either.

When she'd arrived at Alejandro's villa, it had been to find her aunt and uncle eagerly waiting for her. Instead of the worried frowns that normally carved wrinkles into their expressions, they'd been glowing with happiness. They'd gushed over her, the requests that had been pouring in for her design portfolio and, of course, her relationship. Aunt Lonita, especially, had peppered her with questions. She'd nearly swooned when Antonio had shown up to escort them all to dinner on the lawn where a long banquet table had been set for the Cabrera family and rehearsal guests.

He'd played the part well. Whenever people asked if Anna had been his secret girlfriend all along, he'd smiled coyly, saying what mattered was that she was with him now, as he pressed a kiss to her fingers.

Hollow. She'd sensed the distance behind the gestures, observed the tightness around his eyes. It hadn't surprised her that he hadn't visited her room last night, or that he'd kept his distance until the reception when he'd escorted her into dinner.

She took a long drink of champagne. It was what they'd agreed to. She'd been mentally preparing herself for it the closer and closer they'd gotten. But she would have rather he just disappear after their last night of lovemaking than continue with the pretense in front of their family and friends.

She looked up from her glass and stretched her lips into a smile as her uncle approached.

"Enjoying the reception?" he asked, his eyes twinkling beneath his bushy brows.

"I am."

Another lie. She'd always heard once one lie was uttered the others stacked up faster than they could be tracked.

Diego glanced around. "Where's your beau?"

"Antonio? Um…talking with someone about business, I think."

His eyes settled back on her. An ache formed in her

chest. Over the years, she'd gotten used to seeing his blue eyes, so like her mother's. But right now, when she desperately missed and wanted her mom to hug her, to tell her everything was going to be okay as she cried on her shoulder, it hurt to see the reminder of what she'd lost.

"Why do I think there's something you're not telling me?"

Her pulse skipped a beat. "What?"

"You were never good at lying, Anna."

"I…that is, we…"

Where was Antonio when she needed him? Much as she detested the suave, professional side of him, he would be able to talk their way out of this.

"You looked very happy in the photos your aunt and I saw." His head tilted to one side. "You don't look so happy now."

"I'm sorry about the photos, Tío." The one detail she could latch onto and discuss without spinning more falsehoods. "I should have given you and Aunt Lonita more of a heads-up. Everything just happened so fast."

Her uncle chuckled. "We were surprised, but not shocked. I'm more surprised it took the two of you so long to figure things out."

Panic started to claw at her throat. She knew she'd only be able to keep up the pretense so long.

"What do you mean?"

"You were so close when you were younger. He was the only one I trusted with you. I can't believe he didn't snatch you up sooner." Concern deepened the wrinkles in his face. "But something doesn't seem right. You disappear to Paris to focus on your design career. You run off to Rome with a friend from college. Then you appear in the tabloids with the youngest son of my employer."

She winced. "I'm sorry. I didn't mean to make you worry."

Diego's thick brows drew together. "I know."

"It's just… I know you and Tía Lonita worry about me."

He leaned against the railing of the ship. "We do." He sighed. "Too much, I'm afraid."

Her mouth dropped open. "What?"

Diego looked out over the black waters of the Gulf of Lion, his expression darkening. "When you came to Spain, you were so afraid. Every time Lonita and I went out, I remember coming home and seeing you at the top of the stairs, waiting for us."

Her hands tightened around her champagne glass. She hadn't realized her aunt and uncle had observed her.

"I was afraid, too." His words were spoken so softly, she almost didn't hear them. "But I think I used your fear as an excuse to act more like a dictator than your uncle. We put guidelines and boundaries into place. To make you feel safer." Diego's blue gaze landed on her. "But we made it worse." He reached out, his bearlike hand resting on her shoulder. "I never wanted you to fear another day in your life. But when I saw the photos of you in Rome, then with Antonio, the joy on your face compared to how you grew up around us…" He swallowed hard, his eyes glistening. "I realized how much I'd hurt you."

Tears stung her eyes, hot and fierce.

"I thought you didn't trust me," she finally whispered.

"As much as it pains me to say this, it had little to do with you and everything to do with how I reacted to losing my little sister. The more I took charge, the more in control I felt."

Her free hand gripped the railing of the ship and she stared out over the darkness of a night-shrouded Mediterranean Sea.

"I felt so lost after Mom and Dad died," she finally whispered. "Lost, and like I was drowning in fear." Tears spilled over. "I said goodbye that night, but I didn't kiss Mom. I was too busy watching a show." Her hand drifted up, touched her forehead. "But she kissed me. Right here. And then, twenty minutes later, she was just…gone."

Diego's hand settled over hers on the railing. "I was happy you and Antonio became friends. He was always a good boy, responsible. And he seemed to do the one thing I couldn't." When she glanced up at him, he smiled. "He made you happy."

Her lips quirked. "Everyone else treated me like glass. Antonio was the only one who didn't. When we walked out onto the mountain that first time..." Her voice trailed off as memory assailed her. The velvety softness of the lush green grass cradling her bare feet. The breeze carrying the faint scent of earth. A boy holding her hand and tugging her forward, pulling her out of the dark hole she'd tumbled into. "It was like I'd been holding my breath ever since I'd been told about their deaths and I could suddenly breathe again."

"We were very grateful for him." She glanced up to see Diego's eyes glinting in the moonlight, as if he, too, were fighting back tears. "He did what Lonita and I couldn't."

"So you...you didn't think I was too immature? Incapable?"

"No. Just the opposite, Anna. To lose your parents and travel across the world to live with relatives you'd only met a handful of times? I thought you were one of the most resilient and strong, young women I'd ever met. We just didn't want you to hurt anymore, and horribly enough, we did just that by trying to protect you."

She nearly dropped her champagne glass as she sagged against the railing. How had they not had this conversation in all these years?

"I'm sorry, Anna." Her uncle brushed a fatherly kiss against her cheek. "But look at how far you've come, despite everything Lonita and I did."

"With good intention—" she started to say, but Diego cut her off.

"Intentions, at least in this case, don't absolve us of the sins we committed."

"Perhaps. But after…" She'd started to say *after Antonio's rejection*, but she wasn't quite ready to share that humiliation just yet. "After graduation, those restrictions were safe, a cocoon from the real world. Even my job in Granada had been safe, a way to indulge in my love of fashion without risking rejection."

He chuckled. "We all do things like that, find ways to not confront the more challenging parts of ourselves. But you broke free, Anna. When you lost your job, I was ready to step in, take care of everything."

"I know," she said with a smile. Amazing how just a few minutes of conversation transformed her emotions about the moment she'd told her aunt and uncle "thank you but no," she was moving to Paris, and seen the twin looks of horror and listened with quiet anger to their warnings of all the bad things that could happen.

"I was scared. But despite my fear, I was proud, too." His eyes crinkled at the corners as he smiled. "Your mother would be, too."

Warmth bloomed in her chest She'd taken more risks in the past six months than she had in thirteen years. Never in her wildest dreams would she have imagined moving to Paris or walking in a professional fashion show in Rome, much less inviting her childhood love to be her first lover.

But she had. And each risk had resulted in something incredible. Her own apartment covered from floor to ceiling in *her* designs. Walking the runway and having her work seen by the public for the first time. A week of the most incredible physical pleasure she'd ever experienced, of loving and being loved by Antonio.

Because she did love him. She probably hadn't ever stopped loving him, not fully. But the last week had pulled those suppressed emotions back to the surface. Not just the sex, although, she acknowledged with a rueful smile, that had certainly helped.

No, it had been seeing the man Antonio had grown into

emerge from beneath the façade he presented to the rest of the world. The pride he took in his work. The way he remembered the names of the construction workers and interior designers scuttling around the hotel, holding them to his standard yet still complimenting their work and remembering that the foreman's daughter had just started college. How he'd asked questions about her work, shown interest, encouraged her to fully embrace what she loved to design. How he'd finally started to share the ghosts of his past, to trust her once more with his secrets. He still held something back, but she could be patient, wait and support him while he came to terms with whatever had altered his life so drastically. He was worth it.

The boy she'd fallen for had turned into a man she loved very deeply.

Resolve took hold of her. Perhaps it was time to take one more risk. If he rejected her again, the result would be the same as if she kept quiet; Antonio would be out of her life after tomorrow.

She set her glass down on a passing tray and wrapped her arms around Diego's tall frame.

"I love you, Tío."

Diego hugged her back.

Her eyes grew heavy with the weight of more tears that she thankfully blinked away. "Thank you." She stepped back. "If you'll excuse me, I need to go find Antonio."

Questions appeared in Diego's eyes, but he only nodded. She turned and almost ran into a woman standing right behind her.

"Oh, I'm sorry…" Her voice trailed off as her eyes widened. "You…you're…"

The woman smiled, red-painted lips curving up. A pixie haircut kept her silver hair short and slicked back from her face, except for a dusting of fringe that lay on her smooth forehead. Her expression was friendly, but the green eyes that assessed her from behind black circular frames were shrewd and alert. "Sylvie Smythe."

Legendary designer. Queen of fashion.

"It's an honor, Ms. Smythe," she managed to choke out.

Sylvie nodded her head with the regal aplomb of a queen. Her eyes darted to Diego, who still stood by the railing.

"May I have a moment of your time, Miss Vega?"

Anna nodded to Diego to let him know she was okay. Then Sylvie's words registered and her head snapped back around as Diego walked off.

"You know my name?"

"The Virgin Designer."

Her stomach dropped. Would she ever escape that horrid article?

Sylvie leaned in. "Leo White doesn't know anything about fashion, and even less about women."

"Oh. Well, he was—"

"Rude. And a bastard."

Anna choked on a laugh. "Yes."

"But he did do one thing right. He brought you to my attention."

Don't panic, don't panic. "You looked at my portfolio?"

"Yes. I'd like to think I would have looked at your portfolio regardless, but…" She shrugged. "The important thing is I did." Sylvie glanced down at Anna's dress. "One of yours?"

"Yes."

Sylvie walked around her in a circle, assessing the violet-hued, strapless gown. Anna stood frozen to the spot, afraid to even take a breath.

Sylvie stopped in front of her. Her eyes traveled over every inch of the garment. At one point, she reached out, captured a piece of skirt between her fingers and rubbed the fabric.

"Exceptional. The one you wore in the article—" She

made a face. "But this, the gold one in Rome, everything I've seen since...exceptional."

Dizzying elation spiraled through Anna as she fought to maintain a neutral expression.

"Thank you, ma'am."

"Sylvie, please. I didn't spend the last twenty years getting Botox to be called 'ma'am.'"

"Sylvie, then, I—"

"Have you entered into any agreements since you became famous?"

"Agreements?"

"Brands, department stores, boutiques."

"Oh. Um, no, I was going to make a decision next week." Sylvie regarded her for another long moment.

Anna resisted squirming, meeting the older woman's gaze.

"What would you say if I asked you to reject all those other requests and start your own line with me?"

The world rocked under her feet.

"What?"

Sylvie took a phone out of the folds of her gown and pulled up a picture. She held it out to Anna, who accepted it with trembling hands. It was a picture of her on her first day in Positano outside the silk merchant stall wearing her cream sundress as she gazed at the red fabric with loving eyes.

"This is beautiful." Sylvie's gravelly voice softened. "This is the kind of dress that could make any woman feel beautiful, as she should." She took the phone from Anna's trembling fingers and hit another button. A collage of photos sprung up, each one from a tabloid showing Anna in the clothing she'd worn in Positano. "I want you to make these dresses for Sylvie Smythe."

Any moment now she was going to wake up and pinch herself because she had to be dreaming.

"I would love to. It's just..."

Sylvie's eyes narrowed. "What?"

"I want to make them the right way. I know making ethical clothing affordable can be challenging but it's important to me to be involved in the whole process, including sourcing the fabric and labor."

Sylvie's face smoothed into an unreadable expression. *The Botox probably helps with that*, Anna thought frantically. How unorthodox for a woman to be told by one of the most famous designers in the world that she was going to give her a chance, only to have that little nobody set terms and conditions of her own?

And then Sylvie smiled, an even bigger smile that made her radiant in all her silver splendor.

"I think you and I are going to get along very well, Miss Vega."

CHAPTER SEVENTEEN

THE INANE BLABBER coming from David Hill, the slightly inebriated hotel mogul next to Antonio, rolled off him as he kept an eye on Anna, who was now conversing with a silver-haired woman. A smile tugged at his lips, despite his best efforts, as pride rushed through him. He didn't recognize the woman on sight, but he'd asked David who she was, and he knew the name. If Sylvie Smythe had taken notice of Anna's work, it was only a matter of time before she became a household name.

David resumed his diatribe. His hands flew out as he described the site of his next hotel and nearly smacked Isabella Cabrera in the chest.

"David!" Antonio said sharply.

"It was an accident, Tony," Isabella said with a gracious smile for David, who had the good sense to look abashed.

"Still, my apologies, Isabella." He rubbed his palms against his suit jacket. "I think I'll go find some coffee."

He scuttled off before Antonio could chastise him further for nearly hitting the mother of the groom.

"I've never seen David so animated," Isabella remarked as she glided forward and hugged Antonio. Amazing how, even at twenty-nine years old, seeing his mother calmed him.

"Three glasses of champagne on an empty stomach probably had something to do with it."

Isabella laughed. "I'm surprised you're talking to him and not spending time with your lovely new girlfriend."

He tensed. Reintroducing Anna to his family yesterday had gone well. But he'd sensed Isabella's curious gaze scrutinizing them during dinner. The relentless slew of events had kept him busy all day. The post-rehearsal dinner drinks with the groom's party had lasted far longer than he'd anticipated, and he'd opted to sleep in a guest room in case he woke Anna up. He'd entertained the idea of sliding into bed with her, waking her up with long, languid kisses…

Much as he loathed the idea, they needed to talk first.

"She's talking with Sylvie Smythe."

"Oh! Is Sylvie interested in her work?" At his nod, she clapped her hands together. "How wonderful! You must be so excited for her."

"I am."

He felt more than saw his mother's eyes move over his face, searching for answers.

"Something's wrong."

A statement, not a question. Of course, Isabella would pick up on whatever was bothering him. She'd always been tuned in to whatever he and Alejandro had been thinking.

Before he could answer, Javier Cabrera walked up. Antonio had never been so grateful to see his father in all his life.

"Father."

Javier reached out and clasped his son's shoulder.

Antonio blinked in surprise. It was the closest Javier had come to hugging him. Ever.

"Son. Congratulations on your upcoming hotel."

Had he landed in an alternate reality? One where his father paid attention to his life?

"Thank you, sir."

Javier glanced at his wife. Antonio noted the beads of sweat on his brow, the shifting of his weight from one foot to another. It took a moment to dissect the motions as signs of nervousness. He'd never seen Javier as anything but unflappable, save for the one argument he'd overheard between Alejandro and Javier when Javier had allowed his anger to rule and raised his voice.

"Hello, dear."

He kissed his wife on the cheek. Isabella flashed him a strained smile. "Darling."

They stood there, the three of them, in a long moment of awkward silence. Then Javier mumbled—*mumbled*—something about checking on the wedding cake, pressed another kiss to her cheek and disappeared into the crowd.

Antonio watched his father walk away then turned to his mother, one brow raised.

"What was that about?"

Isabella's smile was brittle. "Just some things your father and I are dealing with."

His mother had always had her head in the clouds every time she'd talked about her husband. Adrian and Alejandro had hinted at trouble the last time he'd seen them, but given Adrian's contentious history with their mother and Alejandro's ability to annoy their father just by walking into a room, he'd brushed it aside.

"Things?"

Isabella gazed at Alejandro and Calandra as Alejandro dipped her on the dance floor before bringing her back up to kiss her.

"I'm glad you and Anna have known each other so long." Her fingers curled so tightly around her wineglass, he was surprised it didn't shatter. "When you fall in love with a fairy tale and rush in without thinking, it's easier to get hurt."

Her words knifed through him, added a new worry. Had his last two weeks with Anna been real? Was what he felt for her real? If he asked her to actually be in a relationship, would they discover that, away from the glitz and glamor of Positano, he had created a fantasy built on the flimsy foundation of lust and old memories?

Or was he being a coward and throwing up roadblocks?

"Darling, I didn't mean to upset you." Isabella laid a hand on his cheek. "Your father and I will get through this. I'm so happy you and your brothers have found women who love you as much as they do."

His heart kicked into overdrive. "Love?"

Isabella smiled. "If she hasn't told you yet, she will soon. I saw the way she looked at you."

Words meant to assure, to bolster. But instead they dropped with lethal intensity, grabbing hold of his doubts and insecurities and inflating them until they were pressing in on him from all sides. Anna had kept her emotions in check, giving no hint that she'd cared for him other than as a friend or casual lover. Another reason the thought of talking with her scared the hell out of him. She'd survived, even thrived, despite the heartbreak he'd put her through. How would he handle such a rejection?

The selfishness of that thought hit him hard, swamped him in a tangled mire of guilt, fear and self-anger. He hadn't changed. Not really, not the way Anna had as she'd grown and blossomed. He'd taken her under his wing to fill the void left by Alejandro. He'd pressured his friend into joining him for a joy ride he hadn't wanted to go on so he could escape his own illicit desires. And he'd suggested this whole fake relationship to get the media off his back and make *him* feel better that he'd done something to help Anna.

Knowing he'd been right all along, that he didn't deserve the happiness Anna brought him, nearly knocked him off his feet.

Resolve straightened his spine. There would be no conversation with Anna, except to wish her well and thank her for helping him. And then he would set her free to find a man who deserved her. Even if it killed him.

He was about to excuse himself when a man walking along the deck caught his eye, cane in hand. His head was down, but Antonio knew him in an instant.

William.

William lifted his head. A jagged scar cut down his old friend's face. In one hand, he clutched a cane. Somehow, over the music, the conversation, the clink of glasses, Antonio could hear every fall of the cane on the deck, offset by the scraping of William's right foot that dragged slightly on the ground.

"Is that William?" Isabella asked, her voice excited. "Goodness, I wonder what happened. I haven't seen him in years. Do you two keep in… Antonio?"

He walked away, his mother's voice fading as he stalked toward the stern of the boat. He knew Adrian and Alejandro had both kept in touch with William over the years. It shouldn't be a surprise that he would be there. If William still felt the same way he had when he'd written that letter, he would probably be at least cordial, if not friendly, if they ran into each other.

But Antonio was feeling too raw to deal with another piece of his past right now.

He reached the stern. Thankfully, the deck chairs and recently added pool were empty. Lights brought the water to life, ripples spreading over the surface from the barely perceptible rocking of the great ship.

Alone, he sucked in a deep breath, his lungs filling with salty sea air. It was no wonder William walked with a cane. His right leg had been pinned, blood darkening his jeans to almost black as Antonio had pried him from the wreckage, the overwhelming scent of leaking oil spurring him on to free his friend. He'd managed to drag William, half conscious and moaning in pain, back up to the road.

He'd already made his decision. Seeing William like this was just confirmation he was doing the right thing.

"Antonio?"

He closed his eyes, savored the sweet melody of her voice, before turning around.

She stood at the far end of the pool. Dear God, she looked just like a princess, a gown of deep purple clinging to her body before flaring out at her knees. The hemline kissed the deck and gave the impression that she was gliding rather than walking as she drew near.

"Are you okay?"

"Fine," he bit out. "I'd like to be alone."

She froze, uncertainty crossing her face. "Okay. I just—"

"You don't need to be here, Anna." He inhaled, mentally steeling himself for the task at hand. "After the wedding breakfast tomorrow, I'll arrange for your flight back to Paris on our jet."

She stared at him. "I saw William."

His throat tightened. Not what he'd expected her to say. But perhaps it was better this way.

"And?"

She tilted her head, her gaze piercing through his armor. "That's it, isn't it?"

"What?" The harsh laugh that grated past his lips sounded cruel, as it was meant to. She had no way of knowing the source; the pain of his past combining with the anguish of losing sight of a future he'd never thought possible. "Find another reason if you want to, Anna, but our arrangement was through this weekend."

"Your mom mentioned William was in a car accident." He despised the pity he saw on her face. "Were you driving, Antonio? Is that what this is all about? You punishing yourself years later?"

"I'm not talking about this," he snapped. "We had our fun. Judging by your chat with Sylvie Smythe, the plan worked for you. It worked for me. End of story. Contract terminated."

"Is that all I am to you? A contract?"

The words came out almost curious, detached. Had she

uttered those same words ten years ago, tears would already be pooling in her eyes, threatening to spill over as her voice trembled.

But that also meant he was going to have work harder to push her away, keep her from fighting this time.

"Yes."

She took a step forward. "I still don't believe you."

"Do you know why I was in Rome? Because your uncle asked me to check on you. It had nothing to do with you."

He'd expected the news to have more of an impact, but she just blinked.

"We only spent the past two weeks together because I agreed to do a loyal employee a favor and because we could help each other out." His jaw tightened. He needed to say it. Needed to push her away for the last time.

He'd expected tears. Insults. Something other than the long, long stare she gave him.

"You may not love me, but I think you felt something more than just casual lust for me," she finally said, her voice echoing over the pool and filling the space. "You're pushing me away like you did ten years ago. But," she added, holding up a hand as he started to speak, "you clearly don't trust me enough to share what happened. And for that reason, I'm ending our arrangement tonight."

The unexpected words locked him in place. "That's not what we agreed to."

"No." She raised her chin. "The situation has changed. I fell in love with you again."

Each syllable reverberated throughout his entire being. The last time she'd uttered those words, it had filled him with guilt and self-loathing. Plenty of both still existed, but after the happiness he'd found with her these past two weeks, it also filled him with a longing so strong he nearly gave in.

"I love you, Antonio," she repeated. "But you would rather stay in the past and keep your walls up than trust me. When you say you don't love me, I believe you, because if you did, I think you'd trust me enough to know I care about you, sins and all." Her head tilted to the side, some of the fire leaving her expression to be replaced by sadness. "Or, if what I think is true and you do care for me and you're just trying to do the noble thing, then you're repeating what you did back then and making a choice for me. Either way, hanging on to the past is more important to you than looking toward the future."

The air rushed out of his lungs as she reached down, unhooked the bracelet and laid it on a small table next to one of the lounge chairs.

"You can keep it." His voice sounded strangled.

She shook her head. "No, thank you. Every time I would look at it, I'd think of why you bought it for me."

He frowned then closed his eyes as he remembered. He'd told her he'd bought the bracelet to play up their relationship for the cameras. Not because he'd wanted to, but because it looked good.

"I bought it for you, Anna."

Her smile this time was sad, fleeting. "We both know that's not true. But I appreciate it." She started to turn away.

His heart twisted, ordered him to stop her from leaving, but he managed to keep his feet rooted in place.

She paused. Glanced at him one last time with that blue-amber gaze. "I meant what I said that night at the restaurant. Thank you. For everything."

She turned.

In the blink of an eye, she was gone.

CHAPTER EIGHTEEN

ANNA WIPED ANOTHER pesky tear off her cheek as she propped her feet up on the metal railing of the balcony surrounding the rooftop. Someone had dragged an old metal chair up and left it there. She'd spent her first Sunday back, the morning she should have been at the wedding breakfast, painting it a yellow so bright it almost made her eyes hurt to look at in the direct sunlight.

But she'd needed something cheery. In the week since the wedding reception, she'd spent every morning and every evening on the roof, sipping a latte in the morning and a glass of wine at night as she evaluated her drawings of the day.

Thankfully, Sylvie Smythe had helped keep her mind off things. Her partnership with the legendary designer would be announced on Monday, followed by a whirlwind tour of Sylvie's existing European warehouses and then a trip across the sea to a new textile mill opening up next month just outside her old hometown.

Kess, who had dropped by to lend an ear and brought a bottle of wine, had pronounced the opening of the mill as fate. She'd also denounced Antonio as the "biggest ass on the planet" and offered to set Anna up with a male model from Sweden that she promised would fulfill every one of Anna's dreams.

A sigh escaped her. She couldn't regret having Antonio as her first lover. Unfortunately, she suspected that every relationship she would have from here on out would be overshadowed by loving and losing him. Again.

Except this time, she'd been mature enough to see past the cruel words. Antonio had been hurting. He hadn't told her why, but she had made her own deductions. Seeing William, knowing he had been injured in a car accident the same week Antonio had ended their friendship. The way Antonio had tensed up in the car ride on the way down the mountain from the restaurant, how he never drove, his nightmarish mumblings in the night. His attempted rejection had bounced off her this time. No, what had hurt the most was that she had shared everything with him about her life, her fears, her insecurities, allowed him to pry into her hopes and dreams and talk her up.

Yet he hadn't trusted her enough to do the same.

Her hands curled around her mug of coffee, savoring the warmed ceramic. Fall had started to slip in early as August had turned to September. A cool wind blew through the streets, carrying the occasional leaf up over the rooftops. She stood and walked to the railing. The horn of a scooter filled the narrow alleyway and brought a sad smile to her face. That was the one thing they hadn't done in Positano: ride a scooter up and down the hilly streets. She'd asked, but Antonio had made excuses or whisked her away to something else every time.

She'd thought at first he hadn't wanted to look silly. She could hear his voice in her head, deep and with a faintly horrified tone. "A billionaire on a scooter?"

Now she knew better. Antonio didn't trust himself. Not to drive, not to love. Not to be happy. Amazing how much growing up and becoming stronger had done for her. Back then, the part that had hurt the most had been him not loving her back. What hurt now was knowing Antonio would probably keep himself in that hellish prison he'd created for himself for a very long time, possibly forever.

A buzzing drew her attention away from the rooftops of Paris. She padded back down the circular stairs and rushed to her front door where a frazzled-looking delivery woman stood, a box under her arm.

"Bonjour." The woman shoved a clipboard at her, showed her where to sign and then pushed the box into Anna's arms before disappearing back down the narrow hallway. Anna glanced at the label and savored the little thrill that shot through her veins. The first true burst of happiness she'd felt since she'd woken up to an empty bed.

She brought the box inside and unwrapped it by the window. The standard cardboard shipping container contained a sturdier box, plain white with a small note on top in loopy cursive.

Congratulations on the upcoming line.

The wish from a shopkeeper she'd only met once made her smile. She closed her eyes, breathed in deeply, then opened them as she lifted the lid.

She had to rear back to keep tears from falling on the mounds of red silk inside. She reached inside, stroked the fabric. She'd accused Antonio of living in the past. Yet as she'd clicked through the photos of her and Antonio's time together, available online through a variety of media outlets, she'd seen images of herself touching the red silk that first full day in town. The silk she'd walked away from because she'd been unsure. After everything she'd accomplished, and still she'd hesitated.

No more.

Even if Antonio couldn't move forward, she would. For herself and in honor of the time they'd shared. And the possibility of what they could have been.

She reached into the box and pulled out the first bolt of fabric. She had some work to do.

Antonio stared down at the advanced copy of the November issue of the luxury fashion magazine. Had it really only been six weeks since he'd kicked her out of his life?

Anna had accomplished a lot in six weeks. Photos of her and Sylvie Smith had popped up everywhere. Despite his aversion to social media, he'd kept up with her daily posts on Instagram and what she was working on in her Paris flat. Usually, the camera was focused on her fabric, her sketches, her latest creation. But once in a while her hand appeared, or her feet crossed at the ankle as she sat on her rooftop holding up a square of fabric to the setting sun.

Ridiculous how much he savored those glimpses of her.

The media interest had initially flared when Sylvie Smythe had announced a partnership with up-and-coming designer Anna Vega. Each mention of Antonio had been met with a shy smile and a "No comment" from Anna and a snarky "Do you want to know about her work or not?" from Sylvie.

His brothers, mother and even his father had also been pestering him with texts and calls. But after the wedding breakfast, when he'd lied through his teeth that Anna had had to hurry back to Paris for an amazing opportunity, he'd disappeared to Positano to oversee the final phases before the grand opening Mornings were for reports. Afternoons for reviewing the work done that day.

And evenings…most evenings he spent holed up in his room, avoiding the balcony like the plague and sleeping on the couch. The couple of times he ventured into town, he avoided the places that reminded him of Anna. Hard to do when he saw her every time he passed someone eating lemon sorbet or sipping a glass of wine. Seeing couples zip by on scooters was the hardest. He knew she'd been crestfallen when he'd said no. It was absurd that even now he wouldn't get behind the wheel. How much damage could he do going ten miles an hour up and down teeny streets?

It hadn't been worth the risk to find out.

He was more than aware of the double standard he'd imposed, being so proud of Anna's journey to finding her own inner strength while he clung to the ruins of his own past. The nightmares kept him from picking up the phone, calling her or sending a quick text of congratulations, even if his heart fought him. They still plagued him, every night but now with a twist; no longer William's face but Anna's covered in blood and broken glass.

So different from the beautiful face gazing up at him. Anna's face, smiling at something off-camera as she sat on the floor of her flat surrounded by silk. *Her* silk, he'd realized when he'd seen the magazine on a stand outside a little shop in town and bought it before he'd been able to talk himself out of it. The title declared Anna Vega: Rising Star of Sustainable Fashion. The diamond bracelet had sparkled from where it sat on the corner of his desk, cold and hard. The opposite of Anna. He'd seen her looking at the silk, had thought of purchasing it for her. But it had unnerved him, the thought of doing something so personal, so he'd bought the most impersonal thing he could find.

...hanging on to the past is more important to you than looking toward the future.

His hands tightened on the magazine. Perhaps he would go down to the gym this evening, run on the treadmill until his body was so exhausted he couldn't think of blue-amber eyes and a smile that made him warm and possessive. His fingers settled on the pages. Did he dare open it? Further torture himself by reading her words, seeing more photos?

His phone buzzed. He glanced at the number and answered.

"Yes, Paul?"

"Sir, your guests are here."

"My what? Paul, we don't open for another two weeks."

"That's what I told them, sir, but—"

"*¡Mi hermano!* Call off your guard dog and get your stupid *culo* down here."

The muscles in his neck tightened as Alejandro's voice rang out.

"What are you doing here?"

A scuffling sound ensued, followed by an even deeper voice. "We're here to knock some sense into you."

Adrian. He leaned back in his chair and tossed the magazine onto his desk. It was only a matter of time before his older brothers came knocking.

"I don't know if I have any rooms available."

"Of course you do."

Antonio rolled his eyes. Adrian always had been a self-assured bastard. He'd assumed some of his brother's mannerisms; aloofness, professionalism, an air of confidence that made most people believe what he said. But now that he heard it tossed back at him, he had to wonder if he sounded that pompous.

"You wouldn't turn away your pregnant sisters-in-law, would you?"

His eyes fluttered shut. Dear God, had they brought the whole damned family?

"Antonio?"

His eyes flew open at the sound of Isabella's voice. Apparently, they had.

"Please may we come up?"

With a long-suffering sigh, he told Paul to bring them up. Minutes later, his brothers and mother crowded into his office. The room that had felt so large when he'd claimed it as his own shrunk as Adrian stalked to his desk, Alejandro tossed himself into one of the leather chairs, and Isabella walked around the room, her maternal curiosity making her stop and examine everything from the books on his shelves to the framed pictures.

"Where are Calandra and Everleigh?"

"Downstairs with Father," Alejandro said.

"Father's here, too?"

Could this day get any worse?

"What happened between you and Anna?" Adrian demanded, placing his hands on the desk and leaning forward. A power move meant to intimidate. But Antonio had learned from the best. He leaned back in his chair, his fingers forming a steeple as he met Adrian's dark stare.

"None of your concern."

"It is when my little brother is ruining his life. Again."

Anger surged through him and propelled him to his feet.

"Careful, *hermano*." His voice turned to ice, even as his gaze flitted to Isabella. He didn't want her knowing his shameful secret. He was the only man in this family who hadn't caused her pain. To do so now, after so many years and when she was going through her own hell with her husband...

"I know."

He froze then looked away. He couldn't look at her. Couldn't bear to see the disappointment, the hurt.

The rejection.

"How could you?" he managed to grit out. He had never once hit his brothers. But now his fingers itched to do just that.

"I didn't." Adrian nodded toward the door. "He did."

Antonio's head swung around, his pulse pounding so loud he couldn't believe it didn't echo off the walls of his office. A room that suddenly felt like a prison as William Tomàs appeared in the doorway.

The details he'd glimpsed at the wedding—the cane, the scar, the slight drag to his right foot—all sharpened with less than twenty feet between them. When William smiled, the scar stretched into a gruesome curve.

"Hello, Tony."

Say something.

"William."

William walked into the room. Shuffled, was more like

it, each step intentional, the click of the cane on the hard-wood floor deafening and damning.

"It's been a long time."

"*Sí.*"

William drew closer, his eyes searching Antonio's face. "You stupid bastard."

After the letter William had written him, the edges now worn, the ink faded from being unfolded, read and refolded so many times, he hadn't expected to hear such words from his former friend. "What?"

"Did you even read the letter I wrote you back?"

Antonio frowned, aware that four pairs of eyes were watching him intently.

"Yes. Doesn't change that I caused the car accident that left you disabled, William. You didn't want to go that night, and I pushed you." His hand jabbed toward the cane. "If I hadn't pushed you, you wouldn't need that thing."

William frowned. "I didn't want to go because I had just broken up with Abigail and was wallowing in self-pity. But I agreed, didn't I? And as I recall, I was egging you on, telling you to go faster."

A dim echo sounded in his head. William's voice. *Seriously? I came out for you to drive like an* abuela? *Punch it!*

William walked around the desk and put his hand on Antonio's shoulder. If he saw Antonio flinch, he didn't mention it.

"I've moved on, Tony." A grin split his face. "I'm in my final year of medical school in America. The accident set me on a path I'd never even thought of. This time next year, I'll be completing my residency in pediatrics."

Antonio swallowed hard. "I didn't know."

"I figured after you didn't respond to my last letter that you didn't have an interest in being friends anymore." The grin disappeared as William's jaw tightened. "I had no idea it was because you were still carrying so much guilt.

And if that's the reason you're no longer with Anna, then you're a damned fool."

A muscle ticced in Antonio's cheek. "The doctor told me you didn't remember what happened. But I do. I relive it over and over again. The pain I caused you, the time I stole from you. Do you know why I asked you to go with me that night?" he bit out. Suddenly, he didn't care. Let them know everything. Then they could all know what he'd known all along; that he was unworthy. "Because I was falling for Anna. My best friend, seventeen years old, still in school, and I wanted to go do something wild so I could stop thinking about her."

The words hung in the air, so silent, he could hear the varied breathing of everyone staring at him.

Alejandro broke the silence.

"Good God, man, that's why?"

"Yes," Antonio snapped. "Even if I didn't deserve to be happy after what I did, I'm too selfish for someone like Anna. She deserves the best. That's not me. Never will be."

"Antonio, there was only two years difference between you two," Adrian pointed out matter-of-factly. "Had you dated her the year before, you would have both still been in school."

When phrased like that, his attraction suddenly didn't seem nearly so illicit. Yet he'd felt so much older that summer, more worldly after his year away.

"Have you seen how I used to deal with bad situations?" Alejandro broke in.

"Chandelier in Vegas," Adrian muttered.

"Everyone brings that up." Alejandro's grin said he didn't mind. "Going fast on a mountain road is nothing." A grimace crossed his face. "I can't count the number of times I could have seriously hurt someone with the way I used to behave. You just had bad luck to have the first time you tried to rebel result in something dire."

"But I didn't do things like that, period. I was the good son."

"Oh, Antonio." Isabella's eyes welled with tears. "You are a good son, but that doesn't mean you had to be perfect."

His throat closed. "I never wanted to hurt you. I wanted to make you happy."

"And you do!" Isabella moved forward and cupped his face in his hands. "How did I not notice that you took on such responsibility? My happiness was my own to manage. That I refused to see the problems your father and I had, or not communicate with your brothers, was my burden to bear, not yours."

"Nor was it your responsibility to try to fill the gaps Alejandro and I left," Adrian said. A slight smile crossed his face. "Remember how you told me years ago you hated being in debt to us for helping you and William that night? I've just realized that he and I are in your debt for seeing what we couldn't and trying to fix the pain we caused our family."

"Plus," Alejandro added, "if you think you're too selfish for Anna, I'd say trying to be the perfect son for years to make our mother happy nixes that thought. Which means you need to call her, grovel, and hope she'll take you back."

As the words of his loved ones sank in, the ties that had kept him bound loosened, fell away. A lightness crept in, regret and shock and relief swirling together in a heady combination.

William wrapped an arm around Antonio's shoulders and pulled him into a bear hug. "Go be happy. You deserve it."

Antonio clapped him on the back, his throat constricting. When he stood back, it was to see William grinning from ear to ear. The scar no longer stood out. Just the glimpse of the boy Antonio had once known and the man he'd become.

Isabella moved to his side and enfolded him in an embrace. "My child." She leaned back and smiled. "Despite your ridiculous height, always my child. Not my husband, not my protector. It was not your job to assume so much responsibility, and I'm so sorry I didn't see it sooner."

"I'm sorry, too," Adrian chimed in. "*Madre* and I...we had a lot to work through. Still do." He came up and put an arm around her shoulders, pressing a kiss to her forehead that put another sparkling sheen of tears in her eyes. "But it's much better now."

"Father and I are even getting along," Alejandro added from the chair. "Telling him we're having his first grandchild helped matters."

Adrian rolled his eyes. "By a month."

"What about Father?" Antonio asked, his gaze going back to his mother. "At the wedding, you said things weren't going well."

"They weren't." Isabella sighed. "I was in a bad place for a long time. I maintained a rosy view of what your father and I had. I made excuses for him not being there, for him not being involved in your lives. He shared some things with me this summer, too, that hurt very deeply." She inhaled, her shoulders straightening. "But he's working on himself, just as I'm working on myself. We want to make our marriage work. It's not easy. It's very, very hard. But sometimes you have to fight harder than others."

Antonio let out a harsh breath. "Anna and I...relationship wasn't what you think it was."

"Drop the pretense, baby brother." Alejandro stood in one fluid motion and stalked closer. "Adrian overheard you fighting at the reception."

"What exactly did you hear?" Antonio asked with a glance at Adrian.

"Every word. The fake relationship was a nice touch. Although," Adrian added, "it looked damn real to me in those photos."

It had felt real, too.

"She won't want to be with me. Not after I pushed her away."

Isabella shook her head. "I can't believe that. Not with the way she looked at you."

"You don't understand, *Madre*. I've hurt her so much."

"That's a risk we all take when we care about someone."

All heads swung toward Alejandro.

"What?" He grinned. "I'm in love. And so are you, even if you deny it," he added to Antonio.

Adrian hit something on the screen of his phone then handed it to Antonio. His heart twisted. It was a tabloid article, the headline screaming Hotel Billionaire and Childhood Sweetheart Indulge in Ice Cream in Italy.

Sorbet, he mentally ground out. But then his eyes landed on the picture. Anna's eyes were partially shut, her mouth open in a laugh as sorbet dripped over her fingers. A photo most women would shudder to see; normalcy instead of poised elegance.

But Anna looked happy. Happy and beautiful and joyful, her dark hair pulled up into a ponytail, her mint-colored skirt and white blouse shown off to perfection against her tanned skin.

His gaze slid over. In the photo, he was smiling at Anna. Truly smiling, his lips curved up at the corners, his eyes crinkled as he watched her. It had been early in the second week, after he'd taken her to bed. One hand rested on her knee, fingers splayed across her skin that he remembered had felt like warm silk beneath his touch. She made him enjoy the little things in life, achieve a balance that had eluded him until she'd literally landed back in his life and offered him her heart once more.

"*Dios mío*, what have I done?"

"Get him the whiskey," Adrian ordered.

Alejandro pressed a glass into Antonio's hands.

"Don't worry. Alejandro and I have both been where you're at."

"Just a couple months' ago, actually," Alejandro added cheerfully. "And look at us now."

"I said things to her...horrible things." The whiskey burned a trail down his throat, but also banished some of the panic threatening to burst in.

"Yeah, I think you said even worse things than Adrian did when he broke things off with Everleigh."

"Not helping, Alejandro," Adrian ground out.

"None of you are helping!" Isabella clapped her hands. "Adrian and Alejandro, go to your wives. William, darling, Paul will set you up with your room. Once my youngest has gotten Anna to forgive him, I'm sure he'll want to catch up with you."

Twenty seconds later the room was cleared, the door closed. Antonio sank into the chair Alejandro had recently vacated, pressure building behind his forehead.

What have I done? What have I done? What have I done?

"Tony." He looked up to see his mother's compassionate face in front of him. "She loves you."

"Love isn't always enough."

"No. But it can be a start." She kissed his forehead before leaving him alone to his thoughts.

He needed to tell Anna how he truly felt, that much was obvious. But just telling her wouldn't be enough. No, he needed to prove that he was moving beyond the past. Setting his sights on the future and moving on.

A thought popped into his head. He'd failed miserably with the diamond bracelet. She'd already bought the silk. But there was another gift he could give her, something she truly wanted that would also show her he could move on.

He tossed back the rest of the whiskey, set the glass down and stood. Anna had been so brave, telling him how she'd felt all those years ago and then again at the wedding. She had no idea how incredible she was, how resilient and courageous.

Now it was his time to be strong for her. And, God willing, she still loved him.

CHAPTER NINETEEN

ANNA GLANCED DOWN at her phone again and frowned. Kess had said she would pick her up at four p.m. A chill had settled across Rome, the cold sinking into the stones and chasing tourists off the street as the sun started to set.

Fortunately, when Sylvie Smythe's fashion show at the Trevi Fountain took place in three days, the temperature would be more agreeable, a little warm for early November. But then again, Anna thought with a smile, Sylvie had probably ordered it that way.

It had all moved so fast. The magazine feature, written by a new writer. Sylvie had suggested the publisher drop Leo White. Last Anna heard, he was writing for some conspiracy theory tabloid in the US. Her designs had come together in record time. In three days, they would be featured on a see-through runway that would run across the bubbling water of the world's most famous fountain.

The first time Anna had laid eyes on the fountain two days ago, she'd barely bit back a sob. It had been over two months since she'd last seen Antonio. There had been no calls, no text messages, no emails. He'd said it was over, and he'd truly meant it.

She still didn't regret it. None of it. But, dear God, it hurt so much more than she could have ever prepared herself for.

Thank goodness for Sylvie and Kess. At Anna's suggestion, Sylvie had snatched up her friend as producer for the show. Not only had Kess put together a dynamite show, but she had managed to sneak a couple of hours away for an early dinner.

Anna glanced down. Kess had said they were going somewhere nice, and had suggested Anna wear one of her red-silk creations. She hadn't worn any of them. It had been too painful. But Kess had practically begged, pointing out that she would most likely be photographed while they were out and about, and pictures of her work would only help bolster the show.

So she'd pulled out this dress, a vintage-inspired creation with a full skirt, a square neckline and sleeves down to her elbows. Classy and sophisticated, topped off with a white pea coat and matching gloves.

A tiny beep-beep sounded. A scooter. She looked up, a smile starting to form. Before she left Rome, she would most definitely be renting one to see the sights.

A bright blue scooter rounded the corner. It took a moment for her eyes to drift up, to see the person at the helm.

When she did, her heart stopped.

Antonio.

He stopped the scooter in front of her, the tire skidding a little on the street. He winced then turned to her with a grin that restarted her heart and kicked it into overdrive.

"A little harder to drive these things than I thought." His eyes latched onto hers, burning with intensity. "I missed you, Anna."

Had he truly said those words out loud? She'd longed to hear them, had dreamed of him whispering that and other sweet phrases at night, only to wake up over and over to the realization that he was no longer a part of her life.

Except now he was here. In Rome. Again.

She swallowed hard, a million questions running through her mind. *Why?* was a popular one, followed by *How did you find me?* What popped out was, "I can't believe you fit on one of those things." If he didn't look so damned handsome, it would almost be comical.

He smiled a little then inhaled deeply and extended a hand. "I know I've done absolutely nothing to earn your trust. But I'd like to take you on a ride and explain."

"I'm waiting on Kess."

"Actually, you're not." He had the good grace to look slightly abashed. "I roped her into my plan. She's working tonight."

Anna looked skyward. Her friend meant well. But right now she'd love nothing more than to strangle Kess and her romantic tendencies.

"Ten minutes, Anna. Ten minutes and, if at the end, you never want to see me again, I promise to never contact you."

She'd found herself at so many crossroads lately. Making decisions and taking risks had proved to be mostly beneficial, but sometimes it was utterly exhausting. Part of her wanted to turn around, go back up to her hotel room, crawl beneath the covers and cry.

But if she didn't take this risk, she knew a part of her would always wonder.

Her fingers settled in his. Her breath hissed out between her teeth at the electricity that arced between them. He brought her hand up to his lips and pressed a kiss to her knuckles that made warmth pool between her thighs.

Perhaps this is a bad idea.

Before she could ruminate on that, he tugged her forward. She swung a leg over and sat on the little seat behind him. He handed her a helmet. As soon as she had it buckled on, he reached back for her hand once more.

"Put your arms around me."

Did he have to sound so seductive? She leaned forward, her arms slowly wrapping around his waist, doing her best to ignore how good his body felt, how familiar and comforting his scent was.

And then they were off, cruising along the streets of

Rome, cafés and shops flashing past as light spilled forth from their windows.

"The first time you told me you loved me," he said over his shoulder, his voice slightly raised so he could be heard, "it was three days after I got into a car accident."

Her arms tightened around him. She'd suspected as much, but to hear it spoken out loud made her heart ache for him. More questions arose, but she bit them back.

"William Tomàs was in the car. He was hurt very badly." Guilt and grief made his voice heavy and tightened the muscles in his back. She wanted to rub her hands over him, soothe the pain away as her heart broke for the young man who had nearly lost a friend. "We were up on the mountain, going to a party. I was driving too fast, lost control of the wheel and wrapped the car around the tree. I wasn't hurt, but William was. By some terrible twist of fate, the ambulances were all engaged for a big wreck in Granada and wouldn't have made it in time. I called Adrian, who by some miracle was at home. He and Alejandro drove up, took William and me to the hospital." His voice dropped so low, she could barely hear his next words as he turned onto a little side street. "You saw the cane. That's because of me."

Tears pooled in her eyes. "I'm sorry."

He kept one hand on the handlebars of the scooter, but another came down to rest on her hands clasped around his waist. A gentle squeeze and then he resumed.

"I was torn up about you. After the picnic, I wanted you. Physically. It's why I went to the party, to distract myself because I didn't know what to do. I was nineteen. I didn't think I wanted to get married or have kids. But I knew you did and, to enter into a relationship with my friend who did want those things when all I could think about was sex, seemed so cruel. And after William's accident, I felt…toxic. I'd always been the good one, doing the right thing. The one time I deviated from being the good son, and I nearly got my best friend killed."

She started to say something, to reassure him. He must have sensed it, because he glanced over his shoulder and held up a hand. "It's hard for me to talk about this. I need to get it all out, and then I'll listen to whatever you have to say."

She nodded. She had no idea where this conversation was going, how it would end. So she gave in to temptation and let her head drop against his back, her cheek rubbing against the cozy warmth of his blazer.

"After the accident, the physical desire I felt for you seemed even more wrong. Crude. You were so beautiful and pure and innocent, and I felt like a murderer."

The tears spilled forth and dampened the back of his coat. Her heart ached. Why hadn't he just told her? Even if he hadn't returned her romantic feelings, she would have been there for him. As a friend. Had he truly not trusted her?

As if he could read her mind, he said, "I withdrew from everyone after that. My mother, my brothers. I felt so guilty for what happened to William, humiliated that I had prided myself on being the good son only to go and do something so stupid that rivaled anything Adrian or Alejandro had done. And I started to live my life very rigidly after that. I never drove. No play. No fun. No exceptions."

The scooter slowed. She lifted her head just as the Trevi Fountain came into view. Antonio parked the scooter next to a building, helped her off and set their helmets on the back of the scooter. Even with the barrier of her gloves, the warmth from his hand seeped through. She followed as he tugged her toward the fountain, the surrounding plaza mostly deserted. The ramifications of what he'd done, operating a vehicle for the first time in ten years, hit her and fanned the flames of her hope.

"And then you landed in my lap, Anna." His hand came

up, faltered, then slowly settled on her cheek, cupping her face with an exquisite tenderness. "Still joyful, innocent. And yet so strong. The desire was still there. The friendship was still there. But something new was, too."

Her breath hitched at the emotion brimming in his mahogany eyes. She wanted to believe it, wanted so badly to think it was possible, but did she dare?

"Love, Anna." He leaned down, pausing to see if she would turn away. When she didn't, he pressed his forehead to hers, his breath coming out in a rush. "I fell in love with you. I fell in love and I was so consumed with the past, with seeing myself as unworthy of love and too selfish to deserve someone like you."

Her eyes drifted shut, tears clinging to her lashes. "I thought you didn't love me."

"Open your eyes."

She did, her lips trembling at what she saw on his face.

"I love you, Anna. So much. And I will spend the rest of my life making it up to you. If you'll let me."

Her mouth dropped open. "What?"

He reached into his pocket. Her heart started to beat faster. His fingers uncurled to reveal…

Three cents?

She stared at the coins in confusion. Coins?

Then the rhyme returned. Her head snapped up, hope tearing through her so quickly it nearly made her dizzy.

Three coins and you'll be married soon.

"Antonio…"

"I have prayed every night for the last two weeks that you still feel about me the way you did the night of Alejandro's wedding. Because if you do…" His other hand disappeared into his pocket and came out with a black-velvet box. "I hope this diamond will be one you'll wear knowing it is solely because I love you."

Had she thought she'd taken risks before? Because none of the risks she'd taken in the last ten months meant anything compared to what lay before her now. Antonio had hurt her not once but twice in spectacular fashion. Could she trust him again?

"I know I hurt you," he whispered, reading her mind once more. "I know loving me after what I've put you through is a risk. I can't promise I won't hurt you again, because love is not perfect. But I can promise I will spend the rest of my life doing whatever I can to make you as happy as you deserve to be, and striving to be the best man I can be." He swallowed hard. "You make me feel like the best version of myself, Anna. I can't picture my life without you and I want you to be mine, forever and always."

It was the most realistic declaration of love she'd ever heard, one that paled in comparison to any love story she'd watched or read. With a tremulous smile, she reached down and scooped the three coins out of his hand. She turned her back, tossed them over her shoulder and listened as they fell into the fountain. When she turned back to Antonio, it was to see a mix of love and desire and hope in his eyes.

"Is that a yes?"

She flung her arms around his neck, threw back her head and laughed as he scooped her up in his arms and swung her around in a circle.

Somewhere off to their right, a light flashed.

"Damned paparazzi," Antonio swore. "I'll kill—"

Anna cupped his face in her hands and kissed him, cutting off his remaining statement.

"Think of it this way," she said as she pulled back. "We'll always have a picture of your proposal."

His laugh rang out across the plaza. "Are you always so positive?"

"Better get used to it." Her face hurt from smiling so hard as he set her down and slid the diamond ring onto her finger, the oval-cut beauty offset by two gems, a blue sapphire and an amber-colored topaz. "Because I'm positively in love with you."

EPILOGUE

Three years later

ANTONIO CHASED HIS niece Ava through the waves, the two-year-old's squeal making him grin. Just a few steps ahead of her, his nephew Xavier scrambled up onto the warm sand.

"Xavier, why don't you give Tío Tony a break?" Calandra called. She was relaxing on one of the chaises-longue, her six-months-pregnant belly round and evident even in her black swimsuit.

"I don't mind," Antonio called up. Besides, he needed the practice. He glanced over at his wife as she chatted with Everleigh and Everleigh's father. His gaze drifted down to her stomach, concealed by the loose fabric of her sundress. Excitement zipped through him. They planned to make their announcement this evening at dinner when the whole family was gathered. Not just the Cabreras, but Calandra's little sister and her boyfriend from North Carolina, and Richard Bradford and his former housekeeper now girlfriend. William had joined them, too, along with Kess.

Although, Antonio reflected with a smile, those two hadn't been seen since dinner last night. He'd had his suspicions with the verbal sparring they had engaged in since they'd arrived for the annual family summer trip to Positano last week. Perhaps the family would be celebrating another wedding soon.

Adrian dashed into the waves and scooped Ava up into his arms. The little girl let out a squeal of delight before turning and wrapping her chubby arms around her father's neck.

"When are you going to have one of these?" Adrian asked with a boyish grin.

"Someday soon," Anna answered with a conspiratorial grin aimed Antonio's way as she walked into the warm waters of Le Porto's private beach. Antonio had set aside three hours for the family to enjoy the cove before reopening it to the guests of the hotel. Given that the hotel had become Positano's number-one choice for luxury vacations and had received award after award since its grand opening, he'd felt confident notifying his guests that the beach would be briefly closed for a private gathering.

Antonio pulled his wife close and kissed her.

"Eww!" Xavier squealed before dashing up the beach to his grandparents. Javier scooted over on his lounge and hauled the little boy up onto his lap. It still took some getting used to, seeing his formerly buttoned-up sire act like a teenager around his grandchildren. But Javier Cabrera had undergone a truly remarkable transformation, building relationships not just with his grandchildren but his sons as well.

"I want to tell them now," Antonio said, his hand sliding down to cup her belly. He knew it was too soon, but already he imagined her stomach round, the feeling of new life kicking beneath his fingers.

"No!" Anna said with a laugh as she batted his hand away. "Tonight."

"Did you hear from Sylvie?"

Anna nodded, her smile rivaling that of the sun shining overhead. "Another record-breaking quarter."

Antonio kissed her cheek. Anna insisted that the cult following her designs had developed was possible because of Sylvie. But in the conversations he'd had with the older woman, he knew that Anna had revitalized the legendary designer's brand. Her stunning designs, her passion for sustainable clothing and her genuine kindness had drawn in and retained thousands of new shoppers.

"Do you remember when you were first here and didn't know if you'd make it as a designer?"

Anna rolled her eyes. "Blah-blah-blah. Yes, for the hundredth time, you were right."

He tugged her closer, savoring the feel of her in his arms. "I was right about something else, too."

She looked up at him, smiled. "Oh, yeah?"

"Yeah. You're mine. Forever and always."

* * * *

COMING SOON!

We really hope you enjoyed reading this book.
If you're looking for more romance, be sure to
head to the shops when new books are
available on

Thursday 31st
March

To see which titles are coming soon, please visit
millsandboon.co.uk/nextmonth

MILLS & BOON®

Coming next month

REVEALING HER NINE-MONTH SECRET
Natalie Anderson

She needed him to turn. Would she see those disturbingly green eyes? Would she see a sensual mouth? If he stepped closer would she hear a voice that whispered wicked invitation and wilful temptation? All those months ago she'd been so seduced by him she'd abandoned all caution, all reticence for a single night of silken ecstasy only to then—

A sharp pain lanced, shocking her back to the present. Winded, she pressed her hand to her stomach. How the mind could wreak havoc on the body. The stabbing sensation was a visceral reminder of the desolate emptiness she'd been trying to ignore for so long.

She'd recovered from that heartbreak. She was living her best life here—free and adventurous, bathing in the warm, brilliant waters of the Pacific. Her confusion was because she was tired. But she couldn't resist stepping closer—even as another sharp pain stole her breath.

'That's interesting.' He addressed the man beside him. 'Why are—'

Shock deadened her senses, muting both him and the pain still squeezing her to the point where she couldn't breathe. That *voice*? That low tone that invited such confidence and tempted the listener to share their deepest secrets?

Massimo hadn't just spoken to her. He'd offered the sort of attention that simply stupefied her mind and left her able only to say *yes*. And she had. Like all the women who'd come before her. And doubtless all those after.

Now his brief laugh was deep and infectious. Despite her distance, it was as if he had his head intimately close to hers, his arm around her waist, his lips brushing her highly sensitised skin—

Pain tore through her muscles forcing her to the present again. She gasped as it seared from her insides and radiated out with increasingly harsh intensity. She stared, helpless to the power of it as that dark head turned in her direction. His green-eyed gaze arrowed on her.

Massimo.

'Carrie?' Sereana materialised, blocking him from her view. 'Are you okay?' Her boss looked as alarmed as she sounded.

Carrie crumpled as the cramp intensified. It was as if she'd been grabbed by a ginormous shark and he was trying to tear her in two. 'Maybe I ate something…'

Her vision tunnelled as she tumbled to the ground.

'Carrie?'

Not Sereana.

She opened her eyes and stared straight into his. 'Massimo?'

It couldn't really be him. She was hallucinating, surely? But she felt strong arms close about her. She felt herself lifted and pressed to his broad, hard chest. He was hot and she could hear the thud of his racing heart. Or maybe it was only her own.

If this were just a dream? Fine. She closed her eyes and kept them closed. She would sleep and this awful agony would stop. She really needed it to stop.

'*Carrie!*'

Continue reading
Revealing Her Nine-Month Secret
Natalie Anderson

Available next month
www.millsandboon.co.uk

MILLS & BOON

THE HEART OF ROMANCE

A ROMANCE FOR EVERY READER

MODERN

Prepare to be swept off your feet by sophisticated, sexy and seductive heroes, in some of the world's most glamourous and romantic locations, where power and passion collide.

HISTORICAL

Escape with historical heroes from time gone by. Whether your passion is for wicked Regency Rakes, muscled Vikings or rugged Highlanders, awake the romance of the past.

MEDICAL

Set your pulse racing with dedicated, delectable doctors in the high-pressure world of medicine, where emotions run high and passion, comfort and love are the best medicine.

True Love

Celebrate true love with tender stories of heartfelt romance, from the rush of falling in love to the joy a new baby can bring, and a focus on the emotional heart of a relationship.

Desire

Indulge in secrets and scandal, intense drama and plenty of sizzling hot action with powerful and passionate heroes who have it all: wealth, status, good looks…everything but the right woman.

HEROES

Experience all the excitement of a gripping thriller, with an intense romance at its heart. Resourceful, true-to-life women and strong, fearless men face danger and desire - a killer combination!

To see which titles are coming soon, please visit

millsandboon.co.uk/nextmonth

JOIN US ON SOCIAL MEDIA!

Stay up to date with our latest releases, author news and gossip, special offers and discounts, and all the behind-the-scenes action from Mills & Boon...

 millsandboon

 millsandboonuk

 millsandboon

It might just be true love...

MILLS & BOON

Desire

Indulge in secrets and scandal, intense drama and plenty of sizzling hot action with powerful and passionate heroes who have it all: wealth, status, good looks…everything but the right woman.

MILLS & BOON
MEDICAL
Pulse-Racing Passion

Set your pulse racing with dedicated, delectable doctors in the high-pressure world of medicine, where emotions run high and passion, comfort and love are the best medicine.